Rach,

victoria jones xx ♡

Jack,

"Pull the trigger."
dahli.

Nichi ofynne
x
♡

4

JAMES STOCK

VICTORIA L.

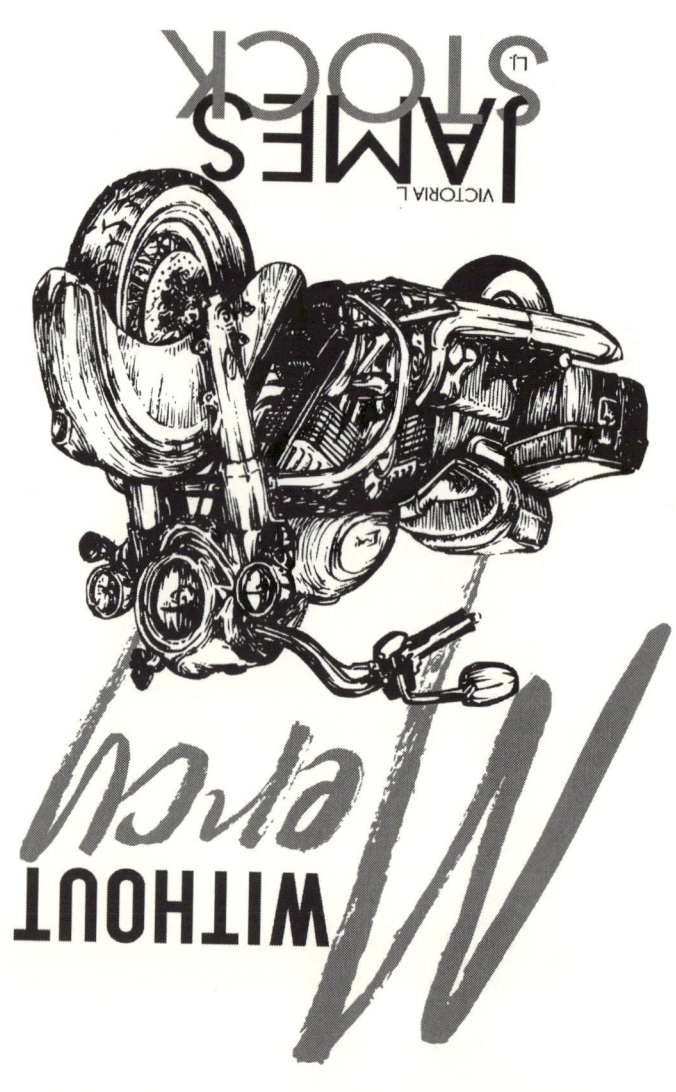

WITHOUT Mercy

A NOTE TO THE READER:

Without Mercy is book two in the Babylon series, all of which are written by both Victoria L. James and L.J. Stock. Book one, Without Consequence, is available on Amazon.

For more information on the authors' work together as well as their individual projects, please visit the following pages.

www.facebook.com/Babylonseries

www.facebook.com/VictoriaLJamesAuthor

www.facebook.com/LJStockAuthor

WITHOUT MERCY ©2015

Victoria L. James & L.J. Stock

All rights reserved. No part of this book may be reproduced in any form without written permission from the author, except that of small quotations used in critical reviews and promotions via blogs.

This is a work of fiction. The names, characters, places and incidents are products of the authors' imaginations only. Any resemblance to actual persons, living or deceased, events or any other incident is entirely coincidental.

Front cover design: L.J. Stock

Front Cover Image: ©Depositphoto.com

Edited by: Heather Ross

OTHER BOOKS IN THE SERIES

Without Consequence

Without Truth – Coming 2017

Acknowledgements

L.J. Stock:

There's so many people to thank I always feel like I'm rambling, but here I go. First and foremost, I would like to thank Victoria L. James for taking this journey with me. Babylon and the characters are a beautiful escape for me, and I can't ever thank you enough for being a part of that. I can't ever get enough of Babylon, Texas either. If it wouldn't have me committed I could quite happily recede into the recesses of my mind and reside there.

To my family, this is gonna take a minute, Dad, Ellen, Rachael, Emily, Kevin, Adam, Alicia, Jason, Dawn, Jacob, Kyle, Michael, Audrey, Cortney, Zed, and Willem. It doesn't matter where you are or how often we speak, you're a huge compass in my life and I love each and every one of you. To my family in Plymouth, thank you for your endless support. I can't put into words how much it means to me.

There's a crazy amount of people to thank in the post writing process, and I feel like I'm lucky to have the team we do. To Heather Ross, thank you for your edits and the hours you put into the manuscript. Katleen and her beautiful and thorough attention to detail, you amaze me with the things you find. A huge thank you to the ladies who beta read for us – Francesca Marlow, Charlie M. Matthews and Amy Trevathan. Your reactions were priceless. Thank you so much. To our biggest supporters, you know who you are – your endless promotions and sharing has been invaluable. Bare Naked Words... What you do for us and other authors is appreciated more than you know, but you ladies, Claire Allmendinger and Wendy Shatwell, go above and beyond and I love you!

Lastly, a huge thank you to the one person I wish I could share this with and can't. The woman who gave me every creative bone I have in my body and always believed and encouraged me: My mum. There's never a day where I don't think of you. I love you.

I can't forget you, the reader. You took a chance and picked up a book by two relatively unknown authors. Your support is appreciated, even if we can't thank you by name.

Victoria L. James:

It goes without saying that my first thank you goes to L.J. Stock for going through the whole book release process with me once again. Babylon is our happy place, even when it's pretty barbaric, and I couldn't ask for a better partner to navigate the unknown roads with. You're such a talented lady and one hell of a friend. Wilma, I love you very much. Thank you for all the smiles you've brought to my life.

There are so many people to thank behind the scenes, too. Heather Ross, Francesca Marlow, Claire Allmendinger, Wendy Shatwell, Amy Trevathan, Charlie M. Matthews and my little hidden treasure, Katleen – We couldn't do this without any of you. Thank you for spending all your free time on us, for being honest and for being supportive. But most of all, thank you for being our friends. I adore every single one of you. I forgive you all for saying you hated me and L.J. Stock during your read through of Without Mercy. *winks*

To my family – Mum, dad, sisters, brothers-in-law, nieces, nephews, aunties, uncles, cousins… I love each and every one of you and your support. To Granddad Jim and Grandma Bess, I wish you were still here. I miss you so very, very much. Thank you for all the invaluable things you taught me and thank you for listening... still. I live to make you proud.

As always, my biggest thanks will be served on a shiny, gold plate to my CPCCH unit. Carl, you are my rock. When I want to scream in frustration or if I'm looking a little frazzled, a hug from you is like magic. You're my Drew – just a little less Drew like. *laughs*

My step-babies, I'm so grateful to have you in my life. To my two beautiful boys, *you* are a constant reminder of what is *truly* important to me in this world. I love you all to the sunshine and back (because it's further than the moon) and I always will.

Last but certainly not least, I want to thank YOU.

Thank you for spending your hard earned money on two new indie authors.

We hope the story gives you all that you expected... and maybe that little extra cherry on top.

Welcome back to Babylon.

We've missed you.

A Note From Both Authors:

To the Babylon Beta Facebook group, who offered up their valuable time to help us during our reworking of both books… we cannot thank you enough for your encouragement and feedback.

Babylon is better because of the following people:

Mary Green, Charlie M. Matthews, Joanne Bulmer, Laura Smith, Karyn Lawless DeGiorgio, Tara Bryant, Kristie L. Koste, Lina Rutyna and Katie Louise Young.

They're officially our Hound Whores. ;)

DEDICATED TO

All the dreamers,

Whether it's writing, music, art or love –
Never give up.

Keep reaching for what you really want and
keep doing whatever it is that you truly love to do.
The world is our stage.

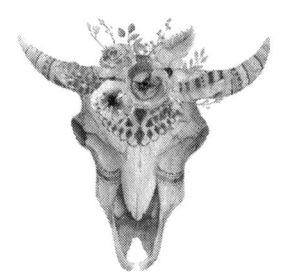

PROLOGUE
DREW

I knew the difference now.

I'd been to Hell and back with the devil riding wingman, and I'd dropped my soul in the depths of a bottomless pit where everyone I'd ever fought and killed had been laid to rest.

That was the thing with any kind of war. It broke you down piece by piece and made you analyze your whole being. You no longer felt human, just a machine made of parts—a machine that had the ability to be both evil and good and to see no difference in either act.

Kill or be killed.

In the midst of battle, emotions don't register, but when the dust settles and the bloodstains are tattooed upon your hands, what's left is a shell of a body and an endless confusion that flows so wildly under the river of your blood, all you can feel is how I had felt.

Lost.

Returning to the club after so long in prison was like returning from war. I'd seen things I shouldn't have. I'd been put through shit no man would ever expect to endure. I'd tasted my own blood more times than I'd tasted bread. I'd watched men die at the hands of sadistic bastards who deserved to take their last breath beneath my angry, pulsating fingers. I'd had to stand by and remain silent. I'd watched the innocent suffer and the guilty reign supreme. I'd become one of them, and I'd become numb.

Numb, bitter and cold. So fucking cold.

It was the way the pieces of my machine had functioned to survive.

My brothers didn't exist in that world.

I didn't exist in that world.

And when I finally walked free and tasted clean air in my lungs, I'd forgotten who the fuck I was.

Until *she* showed me.

When I thought Ayda was about to die, I knew. I knew without question who I was and my purpose in life.

That's why I was standing where I was, both fists balled-up and pressed against my forehead while my brothers gathered behind me. For thick, heavy men, they moved quietly when it was needed of them. They knew when to bring the riot, but they also knew when to act invisible.

The night was as black as the bottom of the ocean and the moon barely shone through the trees. No stars graced us that night. I doubted anyone wanted to bear witness to what we were about to do or what we had already done. The blood felt heavy on my hands, and even though we'd gotten the result we'd wanted, there was a part of my mind that was beginning to wander back to her. I couldn't let Ayda in too soon. I couldn't allow myself to see anything else but the end goal. Until all the Emps were buried beneath six feet of rotten earth and hard soil, I wouldn't rest. I had to keep my family safe. That would only happen once they were gone.

"Let me see your faces, you cowards," she cried shakily.

Not one of us moved. We stayed in place, staring her down like a sea of death, willing to do whatever we had to do to bring the Emps to their knees. The ski masks we wore kept us hidden, and the uncertainty of who her enemy was had the girl's eyes frantically searching all around her. As I stood over the body of her—now dead—Emperor boyfriend, with one foot rising to land on his chest, the only sound that could be heard besides her breathless whimpering was the sound of my boot crushing down on his bones.

"They'll find you," she cried again. "Cortez will find you and he will kill you, every single one of you. You won't get away with this. Even if you… if you kill me." She paused, stumbling over her own words as her thick mascara bled down her face and stray strands of hair stuck to the wet spots on her cheeks. "You'll regret this. H-he will finish you."

Nobody moved. Not even an inch. Not until the silence and our calm broke her so much, we were convinced she was certain of her impending death.

"Finish it," she eventually sobbed, turning away from us and closing her eyes in preparation.

This was the side of the job I hated—the side where the innocent paid the price for the guilty's actions. It was the part of being a monster that seeped into my conscience and made that small flicker of doubt flash through my mind.

Stepping over the dead Emp's body, my feet broke all the twigs beneath my sole, and each time my boot fell onto the ground, I purposely dragged out the crunching sound to make her wait. To me, she was one of them now, and the time for worrying about their tribe was a long distant memory of a better time before my brother, Pete, had died in the ring.

Bending down in front of her, her body sat tied to the

base of the thick tree trunk, I twisted my head from side to side and let my eyes shine down on hers. She couldn't see me. Who wanted to stare their fate in the eye and see nothing but evil and hell glaring back? Not this girl. She'd never expected to be on the receiving end of the brutality. It was only when I eventually spoke and my hands reached down to grab her knees that I think she finally began to understand.

"You're going to watch as I tear your world apart in front of you. Every limb, every tooth, every single hair on his head will fall at your feet. By the time we're finished, you'll be *begging* me to kill you. By the time this is through, you'll have forgotten how to breathe. Then, and only then, will you get to leave. You'll walk away with your worst nightmare forever etched on the backs of your eyelids." My fingers squeezed her tighter until a small cry of pain and fear escaped her cracked lips. I leaned closer, my teeth grinding as I spat out my final warning. "Then you'll go to Chester Cortez, and you'll tell him that the Navs are circling and if he so much as gets close to Babylon, he'll be starting a war he can't win. The Hounds have our backing. The next man to attack their family will end up being torn apart like this brother here. Make it known."

Her eyes opened slowly. Each lash fluttered heavily and rapidly as she tried to take in some breaths through the sobs of tears that were drowning her face. When her eyes locked with mine, I lifted one hand away from her knee and rolled up the sleeve of my black hoodie to show her my mark. The Navarro Rifles trademark gun was drawn heavily upon my skin, and the look in her eyes told me enough.

We'd won the battle that night.

We'd probably win the next few.

All we could do was hope that each victory helped us to

win the impending war I was creating. Otherwise, we were all about to die.

CHAPTER ONE
AYDA

It was odd, sitting in the big, main room of The Hut around a makeshift table with the pack, their women and, in some cases, children. I had a sublime sense of belonging. There weren't many times in life you got to feel like that. In my limited experience, there was only one that had counted in the past, and that was my family: Mom, Dad, and my kid brother, Tate. They were the people who had loved me unconditionally through all of my shortcomings and faults. When Mom and Dad were killed, I only had Tate, and he'd become my sole focus in life, something I wasn't entirely sure had been all that healthy, if I was being honest.

Now I had this extended family surrounding me. It had taken a while for some of them to accept me, and even longer for others to fully trust me, but weeks of hard work had paid off. I'd taken the time to get to know as many of them as I could, and sitting at the head of our Thanksgiving table, next to Drew, I was happy to realize I knew every one of the pack by name, including their significant others and families. They had come to love me as much as I adored them, and although it had been a baptism of fire, we—Tate and I—were now a part of them. We were a part of their family and the brethren who protected one another above all else.

My life had changed drastically since the fire. I'd gone from existing to living, and I was enjoying every second of it. I cried from laughing too hard, I shouted to be heard over the family, and I worried only about the safety of those men that had come to mean the world to me.

Then there was Drew and I. We weren't perfect. We had too much passion to live in complete harmony. We bickered. We fought and then we made up. He made me laugh, and I loved him with every inch of my mind, body, and soul. Even if he still hadn't said the words aloud, I knew he loved me. Whether it was his actions or the surprised looks of his brothers, he'd set a precedent with our relationship. It was as new to him as it was to me. We were learning with one another, and taking one day at a time, which only served to bring us closer together.

There were things I still did against his better judgment, like working at the diner. The insurance from the house fire meant Tate and I could pay off the land and still have enough to send him to college while living comfortably. I, technically, didn't have to work, but I still picked up shifts when I wanted to. There were two reasons for this, the first being I missed Rusty, Janette and the gang. They had been a large part of my life for years and I loved them. Just because I didn't need to be there, didn't mean that I didn't want to be. The second was getting out of The Hut. I loved them all, and I loved the club, but I needed time away and Rusty's diner was my salvation.

It wasn't often I needed an escape, though, and it would have taken a pack of wild horses to drag me away on Thanksgiving. We invited everyone in the pack to join us, along with their families, and everyone showed up. It was bedlam to cook for that many people, and sitting there watching everyone enjoying the meal was more satisfying than I ever could have imagined, even when Tate was pushing his luck. He and Kenny were trying their hardest to be surreptitious. The hands under the table meant one of two things, and the first was a little farfetched even for their budding bromance. It was a credit to him that he almost got away with it, too. They'd just underestimated my attention span when it came to my kid brother. I actually managed to get the next shot of Tequila out of his hands before he could knock it back.

"Hey!" Incredulousness dripped from Tate's tone as he watched me take the drink and down it, his eyes widening as the sound of Kenny's laughter grew.

"Do you remember what happened the last time you got wasted?" I asked, sliding the glass onto the table and wiping my mouth with the back of my hand. I wasn't a complete killjoy. He'd already gotten away with two shots that I'd pretended not to see.

"It all worked out," he said, flinging his arms about, barely missing Kenny's face. "Look where we are now."

"T, you gotta know when to pick your fights, bro." Kenny laughed, raising his own glass to me and knocking it back. "Your lovely sister still gets to tell your ass what to do."

"Fuck off, K-dog."

"Jesus, Tate, language."

"Yeah, Tate, language." Kenny laughed again, elbowing Moose who was sitting on the other side of him.

"Don't you start, K. I hold you personally responsible for his foul mouth."

"Says the only woman I know who can curse my ass under the table."

"You're spending more time with him than I am these days," I said, picking up my fork and waving it at him. "All in the name of football, right?"

"That and girls."

"Plural?"

Tate's elbow was firmly planted in Kenny's ribs before he could fire back his response. Kenny wasn't all that great at holding his tongue. He said what he was thinking, and he would deal with the consequences. It was only because Tate was a minor under my ever-vigilant eye that he had to edit himself. Even then, he never put that much thought into it. He didn't think he was doing anything wrong. That meant that Tate was feeding him a line of bullshit.

"I think you and I need to have a chat, T."

"Come on, A. He's a teenage boy. He's practicing safe se—"

"Do not finish that sentence, *Kenneth*."

I heard the murmur of laughter from the men on the other side of Kenny as he growled at me. I was abusing the fact that I knew his full name and we both knew it. It really wasn't his fault. He was living the way he had since he'd become a part of the club, and it was on Tate that he was going against my wishes. I was just trying to convince Kenny to see where I was coming from. It was also my issue that sex and Tate in the same sentence made me shrivel up and hope the world opened up to swallow me whole. Okay, so it wasn't quite as bad as all that, but they didn't need that information.

"I'm going to pretend I didn't hear that," I said, shoving mashed potato in my mouth, my other hand landing on Drew's thigh. He was in conversation with Harry and Jedd on the other side of him, even though I was pretty sure he was also listening in on our little chat. The arm that sat along the back of my chair had fallen between the wood and my spine and was currently making soothing circles just above my ass. For the most part, it was working. Things had been tense for weeks, and the only time Drew seemed to relax was when he and I were alone in our room, where he didn't have to be anything other than himself. Today had been the first time the ease had been universal, when everyone could see what I saw every day. This, more than anything else, helped my calm return, and I relaxed back into his touch, smiling at the two faces turned in my direction with their eyes narrowed. "Eat your green bean casserole, assholes."

Drew's hand soon slid to my waist before he leaned closer into me, pulling my body to his but keeping his face away from mine as he whispered, "You do realize that the more you berate those two, the worse they will behave, don't you?" I didn't have to turn to see his face. I could hear the smile in his voice when he spoke, and I knew that he found my misplaced maternal instincts funnier than anyone else at the table did.

As Tate and Kenny suddenly found their plates very interesting, I turned my head the smallest amount to affectionately rub my cheek on his shoulder. "Oh, I know, but one day they're going to push me to the point where I retaliate. I went to college. I know some tricks their pea brains haven't even considered yet."

"I don't doubt that for one second, Hanagan. You're full of surprises." Planting a small kiss on the top of my head, Drew pulled away again, sitting upright in his seat and breaking contact. I hated it instantly. Resting his arms on the table, he turned to flash me one of his signature smirks, followed by a wink before he picked up his fork and began to eat.

I let my cheek linger on his shoulder for a moment before returning to my own food and looking around the table. At the other end, leaning into a woman I'd started to get to know now that I was aware of her existence, were Deeks and his "girl," Autumn. He hated me being in the vicinity of her most of the time, mainly because she was more than happy to share stories about their past. They had a unique take on partnerships. They'd been together for the last twenty years, but they had an open relationship. She knew Deeks slept with other women; in fact she encouraged it. When I asked how she dealt with it, she said, "*Variety is the spice of life, honey. Deeks was never a one-woman kinda man. If I wanted him in my life, I had to make compromises. Turns out it wasn't all that bad as long as it was a two-way street.*" She'd winked at me, and leaned forward, her finger pushing my chin up so my mouth closed. As long as she was the one Deeks went home to, the one he loved, she said the rest was just noise. I think it was that moment where I fell in love with her myself. Deeks, though hating the sudden camaraderie, seemed to find some satisfaction in the fast-growing bond I was developing with her. I may never have her take on life. I may never have the open-mindedness to share Drew and be okay with it, but that didn't mean I didn't admire her.

My hand, still on Drew's thigh, squeezed gently. There were times I wondered whether I would have to make a judgment call like that in my life. As much as I knew I didn't want that, I loved Drew in a way I never thought was possible. Would he want that? Could I put aside my need to have him to myself just to keep him in my life? I wasn't sure, and I hoped I would never have to make that decision.

CHAPTER TWO
DREW

Thanksgiving had arrived, and for the first time in a long time, I had a lot to be thankful for.

Two weeks had passed since the night in the forest, four weeks since my life had flashed before my eyes and I'd seen Ayda's home turn into a blazing beacon of orange and black. Time was flying by, yet dragging its ass. I had a reason to live when I was locked up in the room with my woman, the blinds on the rest of the world closed and nothing but her quiet whispers in my ear.

That also meant I had a reason to die—a sacrifice I was willing to make today if it meant keeping her and the rest of the men around me breathing. I held no fear of that moment happening so long as they were safe. All I felt was strength. The only thing I knew I would feel would be regret. Regret that I didn't meet her sooner, regret that our lives couldn't have been better together, and regret that I hadn't been able to save what I now knew she couldn't live without anymore: the man she loved without restriction, even when he struggled to love himself.

As I looked around the table and Ayda's grip on me tightened, I gave her another curious, sideways glance. She was the most beautiful woman that existed. Not just for the way she looked, but for the stuff that went on inside of her, too. That heart of hers was big enough and strong enough to take on the whole fucking world, but even she had moments of weakness. She had moments where her mask slipped as much as mine did and right then was one of them.

Following her gaze, I glanced over at Deeks and Autumn before turning back to study that look on Ayda's face. She was lost in a cloud of her own curiosity, and, given who she was currently staring at, it wasn't hard for me to guess what she might be thinking. I wasn't going to press her about it. I was slowly learning that there was shit I should know and shit I most definitely shouldn't. Picking my battles with her was becoming an art form. There was no way I was going to ruin Thanksgiving by daring to stamp her with my *do-not-even-think-of-asking-me-to-fucking-share-you* stick. It would turn into one of those fights where I end up apologizing for shit I didn't even know I'd done wrong.

I hated those fights.

Those, I had no clue how to win.

I was just about to lean over and bring her back to the land of the living by whispering what I was going to do to her later, when Slater leaned over my shoulder to speak quietly in my ear, making sure I was the only one who could hear him.

"Is this a no business day or can we discuss something?"

There was an edge to his voice, one I'd heard a thousand times before, growing up with him. It made my spine stiffen. With everything going on in our lives, living like we were breathing on borrowed time was a new part of our everyday routine—one that I tried like hell to hide from Ayda and Tate.

Keeping my face forward, I jabbed my fork onto my plate, not bothering to look at what food I was scooping up as

I casually shoved it in my mouth and spoke through tight lips.

"It's Thanksgiving, Slate."

"No shit," he replied, shuffling his feet closer as his hands found the back of my chair.

"And Ayda has gone to a lot of fucking trouble to make sure we *all* enjoy it." I turned subtly to the side, my eyes straining to lock with his as I flashed a look that told him enough.

"Message received."

"Unless it's urgent, I'm not interested."

Ayda's hand roamed farther up my thigh, and I knew that her attention was now on my brother and me. The downside of spending so much time with this woman was that it was getting harder for me to cover up the stuff I didn't want anyone else to see.

Whether she knew the tenor of the conversation or not, she smiled at the people around her and leaned in, her lips barely moving as she reached over me for the salt.

"Do what you have to do. You can make it up to me later." There was a hint of humor in her voice, but under it was a level of understanding.

Keeping my eyes trained on Slater, I didn't have to say or do anything other than raise my brows in question.

He shot Ayda an apologetic glance before he tapped the ends of my chair with his hands and slowly shook his head. "It can wait."

"Thank you," I said through a flat smile. All I wanted was one day. One day to try and at least pretend that we were capable of living in some kind of normalcy, for her and her brother, not for me.

Harry and Jedd both made it clear that they'd seen our

exchange and, as reliable as ever, Harry pushed his chair back and went to follow Slater without even a second thought. If there was anything I needed to know, Harry would make damn sure I was made aware of it, whether it was Thanksgiving or fucking Christmas. I trusted his judgement more than my own.

Rubbing my lips together, I cleared my throat and spun around in my seat to face Ayda. Not giving her a chance to respond, I grabbed a hold of her cheeks and pulled her closer, pressing my lips to hers with enough force to show her how much she meant to me, but not enough to scare her. I knew how nervous she got when it came to club shit.

"What was that for?" she whispered, lifting her hands to cover mine, the tips of her fingers dusting over my skin. "Not that I'm complaining, of course."

"Can't I just find my girl irresistible enough to want to kiss her whenever I feel like it?"

"When you put it like that, of course you can." Her face lit up with her own smile, one hand pulling away from my face to push her brother's aside as he leaned in making kissing noises.

A fleeting thought of Pete flashed through my mind. Tate's mimicking reminded me of something he would have done to me, but I quickly shoved it aside, focusing all that I had on Ayda.

"Tell me something," I said softly, pausing as I pulled her focus back to me. "How does this compare to all your other Thanksgivings?"

"Well," she said, bringing her hand back to my cheek and stroking gently. Her attention flickered from my eyes to my lips and back again, her gaze filled with a mixture of happiness and sadness. "This one is extra special because of you and every one of our extended family. It makes me happy to have so many people here. I'm thankful for every one of you. It's just a sad holiday for me, too. This was my mom's favorite of the year, the one she always had us all together for. In comparison, though, you win hands down. Only because I know what's going to come later."

"The pie?" I teased.

"Of course the pie. I made it." The blue of her eyes intensified before softening again. "I have one hidden in the mini fridge in your room. I want to pig out, watch movies and eat pie. Then later we can work it off… together."

"Watch movies and drop crumbs in your own room," I hit back, smiling at her as my hands fell to the tops of her thighs and rested there. "If you're laying down on my bed, you better be ready to be naked and played with from head to toe, dusk 'til dawn. From ready and willing to completely broken and destroyed."

"You're such a romantic and you drive a hard bargain, but I'm game if you are. Working off calories while eating them. It's revolutionary."

"And I'm all about a revolution," I groaned, leaning forward to gift her with another small kiss, which earned yet another insult from her little brother. Before Ayda had time to react to him, I lifted one hand to the table, grabbed the first thing my fingers could find and launched it in his direction.

From the cries of pain that filled the air, I guessed spoons really fucking hurt when they connected.

"I think it's a sign. Tate just volunteered to do the dishes." Ayda gasped, her head turning to peer at her brother.

"I think I heard Kenny offer to help, too." My face followed hers, my attention landing on Kenny, who looked as though I'd just asked him to rip out the heart of a pig with his bare hands and dress it up in whipped cream. "Isn't that right, brows?"

Kenny's arm snapped out to the side, connecting with Tate's bicep as he gritted his teeth together and spat out, "You and me can't be friends anymore, fucker."

"You do realize it's a commercial dishwasher? It's really not that difficult, but I can put it out of order if you're that intent on hand-washing them," Ayda said, her face impressively straight.

Harry re-entering the room caught my attention, even though I didn't want to look away from Ayda in case I missed that smile that I knew was due to arrive at any moment.

Casting a quick glance his way, I didn't drop the happiness from my face as I watched him walk back across the club. The moment he closed his eyes and shook his head, I had the all clear. Whatever it was that was on Slater's mind would have to wait. If Harry didn't think it was urgent, neither did I.

Shuffling my chair closer to Ayda, my knees parted to pull hers in between mine. As much as I loved the banter between her and Tate, I was suddenly in the mood for being selfish again. My brothers had had enough of her time for today. I was ready to show her how thankful I was for having her in my life.

"Can we escape these fucking monkeys and skip the pie?" I growled, tilting my head to one side and softly massaging her legs beneath my hands.

"I thought you'd never ask," she whispered, her teeth sinking into her bottom lip before they stretched out into her smile.

Reaching for her hand, I clasped it in both of mine, my

lazy half smile trained on her as I stood up and began to guide her away, ignoring the sounds of the men who began to whoop and howl around the table. Now that I was certain we were in the clear for one more day, I was going to make sure Ayda Hanagan knew how much I loved her. I was going to let my hands say the things that my mouth had yet to figure out how to set free.

CHAPTER THREE
AYDA

One thing about living in The Hut, you learned not to be bashful. Not because I paraded around naked. I was very careful not to flash any thigh when I made a mad dash to grab clothes from the room if someone happened to be in there talking to Drew. I just saw more than I ever thought I would in my lifetime, and I'd come to accept that shit happens and worrying about it would only cause more problems than it would solve. So the fact that my clothes were already hitting the floor before we so much as made it through the office door was neither here nor there.

Drew Tucker had some mystical force over me, one I was powerless against. There was sex, and then there was sex with Drew. The door had barely slipped into its frame when I was in his arms, my thighs around his waist, being pushed against a wall. It was my legs and back keeping me upright as his hands pushed my breasts together, and he wrapped his lips around the closest one to him. His tongue flicked at the nipple as he roughly pulled the material of my bra out of his way.

We'd only made it so far, and I thanked God he kept the blinds to his office closed these days. I was pretty sure we weren't going to make it much farther. His hunger and the complete urgency as my abdomen tightened in anticipation was always like standing at the edge of a diving board, daring yourself to take the leap. You knew you would enjoy it. You knew you would be gratified and satisfied, but you also just wanted to stand there and take it all in.

This was my standing—feeling the roughness of his stubble against my skin, the flex of his muscles under my hands, and the way everything disappeared as we worked in unison to find that rapture that the basic, physical task of coming together gave us.

My shoulders pushed against the wall as his teeth grazed the raised, sensitive flesh. The electrical current had a direct line to my clit, which forced my hips to rock against his, the denim rough against my bare thighs. I was starting to understand his appreciation when I wore dresses or skirts. Granted, it was only on special occasions, but his look when I dressed that morning baffled me right up to the point when I was pressed up against the wall, and again when his hand found its way between us, making quick work of the thin underwear I'd been wearing. I tried to raise my head to gaze at the small piece of material that probably looked pathetic and completely useless in his hands now that it had been destroyed.

His mouth moved away, the dampness left by his tongue hit by the cool air, making the tightness of my skin almost painful and forcing my hands into his hair. My nails grazed his scalp in an attempt to bring him close again, to keep the sensation going and drag it out for as long as I could, but he was having none of it. Instead, his lips came together and blew a cool stream of air against my nipple, teasing a moan from me as I released his dark hair and slapped his shoulder playfully. Even in sex he had to have complete control. It had to be in his power to bring me to the edge, and either push me over or pull me away again. This time he wasn't ready to let me get even close to the edge, and the small smile on his lips as his arms moved around to my back to support my ass told me we were actually going to make it to the bedroom for once.

We moved quickly, him carrying me while I began to undress him, starting with his most prized possession, which I dropped safely onto the chair in the corner of the room as we passed it. With the cut gone, there was no need for me to be quite so calculated in my movements. My hands pushed under the white of his T-shirt to unbuckle his belt, which turned out to be a little premature as his jeans fell down around his ankles. When he tried to take another step forward, they hindered his movement, tripping him up. Thankfully, the bed wasn't that far away. I found myself unceremoniously dumped on top of the mattress, his hands landing on either side of me, keeping as much of his weight from my body as he could manage while the two of us blew out a shaky laugh.

I wasted no time in finishing my job. My hands slid up the warm expanse of his back, coasting over the flexing muscles as I pushed the material up and over his head, forcing him to rock onto his knees and pull the damn thing all the way off before dropping it off the side of the bed. He hovered over me, naked. There was no sight I enjoyed as much as looking at him this stripped down, his dick standing proud, showing me just how aroused he was.

He almost seemed as mesmerized by my body as I was with his. The backs of his hands moved down and over my hips with such precision, I held my breath as his touch fell to my thighs, his hands stopping only when he reached my knees. Drew paused briefly, long enough for his eyes to meet mine as his hands moved to the insides of my knees and slowly pushed my legs apart. All the humor that had been there only seconds before was sucked right out of me as he dragged his fingers back up the inside of my thighs and over my folds in a feather-light touch.

I'm not sure at what point I started breathing again—whether it was the slide of his fingers grazing my clit or the way he pushed two of them inside of me. I inhaled as my hips rose, rolling and accepting him deeper while my head dropped back into the mattress beneath me. As much as I wanted to look at him, I knew I couldn't. I could feel his eyes on me, reading every breath and flutter of my eyelashes, each rise and fall of my chest as I dragged in air. More than anything, I knew the moment he made eye contact his focus would drop to where his fingers were thrusting in and out of me, drawing my eyes to the same thing until wild horses couldn't hold back my orgasm.

This time I was holding out. My eyes were scrunched closed tightly as I let myself get lost in his touch. I felt the stretch and curl of my toes as they gripped the sheets, and I knew the moment he felt the challenge. His fingers twisted inside of me, skilfully finding that spot he'd claimed as his own every time we'd been together.

Drew never said much during sex. Even though I could almost always feel the certainty of his emotions through his actions, he preferred to let his fingers, his tongue or his cock do the talking for him. There were quiet moments of appreciation, though. I never missed the way he inhaled sharply when his fingers parted me, and I never missed the flex of his chest when he hovered above me or the way his eyes closed whenever we made love—and make no mistake, whether or not he liked to call it fucking, Drew Tucker and I made love. Whenever he did choose to say a few quiet words to me, I held them in my chest and soaked them up as though they alone had the power to make me climax. Before dropping his tongue against my clit, his fingers pulled out, working inside my creases before he dropped an almost inaudible whisper against the extremely sensitive parts of my skin.

"You're the most beautiful woman I've ever laid my eyes on."

He didn't give me a chance to respond. When I finally let my eyes flutter open and lifted my head to look at him, his head dropped and his lips parted just enough to suck against my clit as he pushed three fingers inside of me, causing my back to arch violently as my hands pushed into his hair and a cry fell from my lips. He wasn't going to let my defiance go. His free hand moved under my thigh and weaved over my hip, his palm flat against my stomach, holding me in place as my legs trembled around him. It was going to be my first orgasm of the night, but it sure as hell wouldn't be my last.

I was limited in my movements when I was faced with his strength, and it only served to create more tension in my body until I was forced to hold my breath in an attempt to control the impending storm. I had no power around this incredible man. With a twist of my body, my climax rocked and wound my spine, my nails scratching at his scalp as my legs turned to jelly, my body clenching around his slowing digits.

Drew flattened his tongue against me one last time, the wet heat making me squirm in his unrelenting grip. My feet rose from the sheets and landed on his calves, his head finally lifting as my toes curled against him. There's something to be said for the hunger in a man's eyes when his predatory side comes to the forefront, and as our eyes met, I knew without a doubt that he was going to take what he wanted, and I was going to enjoy every last second of it.

It didn't mean I was going to make it easy for him.

Sliding my feet back onto the bed, I pushed up, defying the bar of his arm over my stomach. Digging my elbows in, I squirmed out from under him with a small laugh, telling him the game was afoot, even though I was pretty sure I wasn't going to make it very far when my legs felt absolutely boneless.

It was times like this that made me certain he loved me, because the Drew Tucker I met at Rusty's all those weeks ago—he wouldn't have given into anything or anyone. He would have been the man to pin me down, bruise my arms, make my thighs his toys and show me who was boss. But this man in front of me was different. Despite the darkness that lingered there, there was a lightness, too. He wanted to let me win, or at the very least let me think I had the victory.

Falling back, he raised both hands in the air in surrender.

"You can run, Hanagan, but you can't hide. In fact, I retract that statement. You can't even run." One hand of his fell to my right ankle, gripping it tightly before lifting it in the air as he raised a brow and smirked down on me. "I think I just broke you."

"There's something to be said for a humble man," I said with a playful smirk. Leaning forward, I tapped his chin with one finger. When there wasn't so much as an inch between our lips, I blew a stream of cold air over them, gathered my legs under me and attempted to spring from the bed.

Drew's growl filled the air, but to my surprise, he let me go. When my feet found solid ground and I turned around in a breathless mess to see him, his eyes screamed of danger and his body of fire. I'd just started a game with a man who didn't know how to quit until he won, and there wasn't anything that could have turned me on more than that look he flashed me from his blue-green eyes. The green shone more when his thoughts turned dark, and as I backed up against the closet in his room, my hands finding the wood and spreading across the coldness of it, I knew that I was in trouble. The exact kind of trouble I'd been deprived of before I met him, and come to crave since the first time his lips met mine out on that football field.

Dropping his fists into the mattress in front of him, Drew crawled to the edge of the bed, his intentions narrowing in on my thoughts. "Is this how you want it to go down, Hanagan?"

I had a thousand answers to that question and only one of them came to fruition on my lips. As we stared one another down, I sucked in as much breath as I could. "I'll take anything you want to give me, Tucker."

"Then come here, darlin'. Ain't no point running from something you ain't ever gonna escape," he whispered as he dipped his head and crooked a single finger at me.

How it was possible for my body to respond to him with the intensity it did after the orgasm I'd just had was beyond me, but it wasn't just my abdomen aching anymore. It was my entire being. I could feel the tingles in my fingertips and toes, and I knew the more I made him work for it, the more unrelenting he would be, and whether he knew it or not, I think he needed it. We made love every night. He was an amazing lover, and he knew how to give and take, and that night was a taking night. I just happened to be in the mood to give. Shaking my head, I stepped back toward the dresser and set my hands on the edge, lifting myself with my arms and swinging my ass onto the surface, slowly crossing my legs as I shook my head from side to side.

There was a moment's pause, a silence that seemed so thick neither one of us knew what the other was going to do with it. He showed me no game. He gave me no signs of his emotions. All I saw was the color of his eyes popping back at me and the obvious arousal he felt... until he moved.

When he did, it felt like the whole hut shuddered as he swung to the floor, landing with a thud. Maybe I gave him too much weight in that moment, but with each step he took, I seemed like nothing more than food for the animal that was stalking towards me.

Drew's face met mine before anything else. His hands didn't go near my skin, and his erection was only a touch away from me when his nose met mine. His body was like its own island. It towered above me, making me feel small, even though I knew I held a certain kind of power, too.

"You know," he whispered in that special voice that he reserved for me. "Before I met you, I was a man who took what he wanted, when he wanted it. I was the guy who made women beg." He paused, drawing out that silence again as my breaths came heavier and louder against him. "I could make you beg, Ayda. I could make you fucking scream my name in agony until you cried enough for me to do what I know you want me to do to you, but I'll be damned if I don't admit what we both know right now. You're the first woman I've ever wanted to chase, and I'm not going to hide behind my mask to try to prove otherwise. So you'd better..." His hands grabbed my legs, quickly parting them aggressively before he took the final step closer and grinned that sexy grin of his. "Tell me now if you want me to stop."

He was right there in front of me, but my hips rolled forward, looking for any kind of friction as our eyes met. My breathing was labored, but it had nothing to do with the orgasm or running around the room like a fool. This was raw, unfettered passion for the man that stood before me.

"Never stop," I whispered in response, my ankle wrapping around his calf and pulling him toward me. "I'm yours, only yours. Don't ever stop."

With his fingers digging into my hip, he pulled me to the edge of the dresser, the other hand holding his cock as he slammed into me with enough power to shift the wood beneath me and the breath from within me. He paused only for a moment when our hips were flush together. I could see the grinding in his jaw as he let me adjust, his forehead meeting mine as he tried to find the words he'd been attempting to say since I'd said them to him. That he tried at all was enough for me. He had no idea how many times he showed me his true feelings with the little things he did. When we made love in the middle of the night, one of us waking up just needing the human contact and moving slowly together. Then there were times like this, the breath before he left bruises and gave me the hardest orgasms I'd ever had. I'd known it would be hard for him. I'd known he'd struggle to say it, but I never had to wonder if he felt it. I already knew.

My release of breath must have been a signal of some sort. His body swung back in one smooth movement as he pulled away, his eyes drawn to where we were joined. I would normally follow his gaze, but his hand reached behind me, twisting my hair around his grip as our bodies found a harder but stable rhythm.

All I could see was his face, the parting of his lips as he released a breath with force, the stubborn line of his jaw as he pounded against me, his grip on my hair arching my back until he was hitting hard and deep. He had no idea I was watching him. He couldn't have known. He was so intent on watching himself fuck me that I took my time to trace every line of his face until his eyes rose to meet mine and we locked on.

The corner of his mouth curled up in a knowing smile, and before I could prepare myself, his free hand was between our bodies, his index finger pressing down on my clit with force so I didn't have time to suck in another sawed breath. My arms reached out for anything to hold onto as my body took over, bowing from the dresser so I was giving myself to him.

Drew grunted in satisfaction, not for any other reason than that he'd managed to satisfy me first. My walls tightened around him in small waves until he had no choice but to slow his movements and wait me out.

I went limp in his arms, but he wasn't through with me yet. His hands gripped my ribs and pulled me from the dresser before guiding me around and over until my hands were on the surface, and his chest was pressed to my back, pushing me forward. When the scruff of his chin brushed over my shoulder, my body moved automatically, accepting him inside me and revelling in the wash of heat from his breath.

"Ayda…"

Lifting a weak hand, I reached over my shoulder and cupped his cheek, my ass wiggling against him. "I know."

It didn't take long for him to follow me over the edge. My body worked with his, my toes curling in the shag of the carpet, pushing me up and deeper as I slammed back against him with as much force as he was pushing into me. When he came, he came hard, my body bent so far over the dresser that my cheek was pressed against the wall, the paint damp from my panted breaths.

I was pretty sure there wasn't a soul other than the two of us who would understand our relationship, but that's what made it special. We spoke a language of our own, and as long as we were fluent in it, we'd be okay. As I lay with my fingers curled against the wall, I realized that it was exactly what Deeks and Autumn had. They had a language of their own, too.

My thoughts were soon cut off as Drew's heavy yet satisfied breaths blew into my ear, and I heard the one confirmation I didn't need, but loved more than he could and would ever realize.

"I really do, Ayda. Fuck, I really do."

CHAPTER FOUR
DREW

The final smash of Ramirez's fist landing square across Pete's jaw had been designed to do nothing except finish the whole thing for good. I didn't have to wait for a verdict. I knew he was gone three hits ago. The dread had been pooling in my stomach until the sickness had rendered me immovable. Everything happened in slow motion. Pete's head flew back one final time, the spray of blood washing out to the side of the ring, raining down over my face and clothes as Jedd used every bit of his weight to hold me in place, just like he'd been ordered to do.

Pete's eyes rolled to the ceiling, all the life draining away from every feature he held until his body finally gave itself over to gravity, and he fell, limp and lifeless.

There was no convulsing. He didn't shift. He didn't push out his arms to stop himself from falling, and when his body made contact with the floor, every Hound in the room froze.

Jedd couldn't stop me as I threw him away like he was nothing more than a fly for me to swat before I charged toward the ring. Flashes of leather and darkness passed me by as I grabbed the ropes and jumped over them in one swift leap. The moment my feet landed, the ring shook and Pete's body bounced from the weight of it, yet he never groaned or called me the thoughtless dick he normally would have.

I didn't breathe until I'd scooped him up in my arms and was cradling his lifeless head against my chest. Blood poured out of his ears. The gashes to his cheeks were so deep he was an abstract work of purples, reds and browns. His bare chest felt like glue. Cold glue against searing skin. Glue that was once warm but was already turning to ice from all the lifeless crimson that was escaping him. Each eye was swollen as I sucked in the harshest breaths I could force myself to take and begged him to stay alive. The razor blades in my lungs were nothing compared to the knives in my heart. I felt his chest move and for a single fucking moment, I saw a glimmer of hope that he would make it out of this alive. But then it was gone, and that's when I knew that the man who had brought me up, the man who had loved me more than all my brothers put together, and the man who had been a father figure had just taken his last breath in my arms.

My knees sank into the floor, my legs parting as I adjusted and pulled him harder against me, squeezing him so tight I could practically hear his bones screaming in my grip. The strength he'd always possessed vanished, and all that lay in my arms was a broken shell of the greatest Hound I'd ever fucking known.

Pete was dead.

The world around me shifted until my mouth eventually fell open, my eyes scrunched together in agony, and I roared out in anger. I'd killed men before that moment—many, many men—but there were no words for the destruction I was about to cause Ramirez for what he had just done to my brother.

The laws of our lawless community were broken.

The calls to end the fight were ignored.

More blood would have to be shed, and I was desperate to spill the first drop.

Men charged around me but I couldn't see them. My eyes fell to the mass of broken muscle in my hands as my fingers clawed at his skin and the silent tears of agony fell straight from my eyes, down onto his wounds. I gasped for air. Every nail I possessed dug into his flesh as I rocked us to hide the violent shaking that was taking over my body.

"No," I began to whisper, my tight lips barely able to move as I watched and waited for him to move, as I watched and *begged* for him to be okay.

My skin turned cold and a shiver of disbelief rolled down my spine like death himself was taunting me with the fingertips that had just dragged Pete away and tossed him into a pile of the deceased.

My head rolled back as I pulled his body farther up to mine and screamed out my brother's name in despair one final time.

The arrival of someone new, and the sudden touch upon my shoulder felt misplaced. There wasn't anyone who would have approached me as carefully as that person was doing. Harry would have wrapped me up in his arms the way I was holding Pete. Jedd would have gripped me to the point of causing pain, passing on his sorrow because a man like him couldn't handle feeling so helpless or lost. Slater would have taken Pete from me. The others would have stayed away. The Emps would have run. The strays and the spectators would have fled the fucking country.

This touch stayed there like an angel on my shoulder.

Then the voice followed, but I was too lost to hear it thanks to the grief that was currently tearing a knife through my dark soul, moving at an extra slow pace to make sure the pain hit every nerve-ending I held inside me.

"Drew…"

I growled, the tears staining my cheeks and the fire burning harder in my throat.

"Drew, it's me. I'm here."

Pete's body turned into dead weight, and I clawed at him with even more desperation as I began to shake my head from side to side. Whoever it was beside me needed to leave before I hurt them the way I'd unintentionally hurt my brother. Everyone who got close got hurt.

She whispered soothing words in my ear, her warm breath causing my brows to crease as I tried to warn her to escape without having to say the words. Didn't she know I was grieving? Couldn't she see there was no consoling me after what I'd just lost?

Her hand moved to my neck, her fingers placing feather light touches against my skin until her nail grazed my jaw. I gasped for breath again, my mouth wet from the tears I couldn't hold onto, and I instantly felt guilty for wanting her to do it just one more time. I tried to pull Pete closer, reassure him that I was focused on him and nothing else, but when I moved my arms, he was gone.

She spoke again, her words unclear as my hands reached up to clutch my heart. I wanted to rip my chest open and squeeze it tight, to end my own life right there and then because this kind of pain was already threatening to choke me to death.

"Drew."

"No," I whispered back, shaking my head slowly. "No."

I began white knuckling the bed sheets that had somehow

worked their way beneath me. The woman's touches kept on coming. It felt like her hands were everywhere until I was forced to open my eyes again, struggling to get enough oxygen into my lungs.

The cold hit my body first. Every part of my skin felt wet, and the tension in my limbs sent shockwaves through every muscle I possessed until her face came into view above me. Her legs scissored mine as she pressed her chest to me as gently as she possibly could.

"Come back to me, Drew," she said quietly, her lips barely moving as one hand lifted to trace the worry lines away from my forehead.

"Ayda," I croaked out desperately.

She never broke eye contact with me. Her baby blues were glassy and her breathing was heavy, but her touches kept coming, gentle and reassuring. "There you are."

It took time for me to realize what had happened, but the moment I did, I dropped my head hard against the pillow beneath me. "Fuck," I gasped.

Ayda laid still, only her fingers dusting over my skin. She seemed to understand that I just needed time to catch my breath before she spoke to me, but the gentle stroking of her fingers and the breeze of her exhale over my skin were all designed to remind me she was there when I needed her.

This was what she did.

My eyes closed and my hands unclenched from their death grips. I needed to touch her, but I couldn't do much in that moment other than find my center again. Rolling my head lazily to the side, I looked up into her eyes.

"I'm sor—"

The words got caught in my throat as soon as I heard

the clawing and scratching sound that came from outside my bedroom window. Whether exhausted or not, my body shot upright, my arms circling around Ayda as I pulled her to me, as though she were another Pete that someone was about to rip from my grip.

Both of Ayda's hands brushed through my hair before her eyes flickered to the window and back with a stuttered breath, "I-it's just Tank, the yard dog. We're safe here."

I moved my mouth to argue with her, but nothing came out at all when the sound soon disappeared, and I realized she was right. My paranoia was at an all-time high, and with her tiny frame in my arms, I should have felt like the strong one—only I didn't. I felt like a fucking baby. Closing my eyes one last time, I dropped my forehead to hers and blew out all the air in my lungs, refusing to look at her when I finally found my voice again.

"I'm sorry."

"You have nothing to be sorry about, Drew. Nothing at all. I just..." She stopped as I opened my eyes and she blinked up at me, a small reassuring smile there before she rocked forward and kissed me lightly on the lips.

"You just wish I wasn't so fucked up and complicated." I paused, my chest expanding more than it should have been. "I wish for that, too. Things... They will get better."

"No!" Ayda pushed up on her arms. "I wouldn't ever change you, Drew. I love the man you are, faults and all. I just wish you knew you could talk to me about... about Pete and everything that happened. I know it was one of the worst days of your life, but if you keep it all balled up inside like this..."

She paused, unsure how to go on, but her eyes held mine.

"There's nothing to say that will ever bring him back,

Ayda. I fucking hate that you've just seen me that way."

"Drew, the more you push it away, the longer your subconscious manifests it as dreams or nightmares. I'm not psychoanalyzing you. It's just what our bodies do. It's how we're wired. The less you deal with it, talk about it, the more it plays on your mind."

She pulled one of her elbows from my chest and replaced it with her hand, the other turning to hold the side of my neck.

There were so many things I could have done to make the conversation move in a different direction. I had so many ways to silence her without having to say a word, but the way she was looking at me held me in some kind of trance.

"I miss him," was all I could manage.

"Tell me about how it was before he died. The good memories."

Letting her go completely, I shuffled back, resting my head on the pillow and holding my arm out for her to come lie down. She fell into place, and I kept my eyes trained upwards as I tried to find a way or a place to begin when it came to talking about Pete.

"He was good to me when everyone else kept me at a distance. He was the first man to treat me like an equal, not a project or the guy who would one day be handing them their own asses on a plate." I laughed weakly, but I didn't find anything funny. "You already know I was created for all the wrong reasons. My father wanted a son who could make the dreams he never managed to achieve come true. An heir. Pete hated it. He hated that I wasn't allowed to be the kid I should have been allowed to be, so he took me under his wing. He taught me everything I know: fighting, business stuff, women, even how to be the biggest asshole on the planet." I smirked and ran my fingers through her hair.

"He saw the real you—the one that hides away from the rest of the world."

"I guess so. I didn't know anything about the real world until he showed me it for what it was. He pushed me to think, to make decisions for myself. He knew when to let me run ahead and when to pull me back in line. I'd have been dead a long time before him if he hadn't shown me how to survive, which is why him dying because of what I got him into is something I know I will never be able to forgive myself for. I can't see beyond that. He was in that ring that night because of me—because of deals I made and promises I couldn't keep. I thought I had it all figured out..." My voice trailed off as my nostrils flared, and I pulled in another long breath. "I got us into so much debt from the boxing shit. It started out as an outlet for bad guys to go against bad guys. Keep the violence off the streets and put it where it belonged. Bring a little extra cash into the club if we could keep it underground. But bets started getting placed. Debt grew for some and others got rich from it. It became addictive. It turns out more men get high off blood than we realized, but things went sour so quickly. Before I knew it, I was fixing fights, forcing my brothers to do shit like drug running for other clubs, asking them to always go that step too far so we could get back in control. I fought most days to try and keep our heads above water. I thought I was a man playing a man's game."

The bitter taste of reality on my tongue made my body tense again before I turned my head away.

"Drew," she said gently, her fingers light on my chin, trying to coax my eyes back to her. "We all make mistakes. We all do things we aren't proud of, and sometimes we do things that change the courses of our lives forever. The way you talk about Pete tells me that he loved you, but that he was as much of a leader as you were. He was a father figure for you. It wasn't your fault."

I held her gaze for what felt like such a long time before I finally let the sadness out. "The Emps wanted revenge for the fact that I tried to double cross them. I cost their clubs money by fixing fights, all to satisfy the likes of the Navs, the Gray Skulls, and the Descended, among others. I've hated Cortez since I took my very first breath in this club. I wanted him to lose. I played with fire and I got burned. My whole family did, too. Only the Emps knew where to hit me hardest. They knew I'd try to take the fall I deserved. So they offered our club a fight to the death with one man left standing."

My hand rose to her hair, my fingers carefully tucking it behind her ear as she waited for me to continue. "Ramirez had this evil, smug smile on his face when he called Pete's name. He knew. They all knew what they were doing to me. I tried to stop it, I told them it wasn't going to happen, but Pete... he volunteered without question. He jumped in that ring without a single glance backwards. Jedd could have killed an Emp. Slater, too. Kenny was just a kid. Harry would have died after two rounds, no doubt about it, but Pete, he wanted to pay my debt for me. He wanted to try to win, even though, deep down, we both knew he had no chance against Ramirez. It was a suicide fight, Ayda. Jedd was forced to hold me in place and make me watch the whole fucking thing. They held a gun to Jedd the whole way through."

"Still not your fault, Drew. You were willing to pay for your mistakes, but that was taken away from you. You obviously tried to stop it from going where it went, and they wouldn't let you. The only people to blame here are the assholes that put you between a rock and a hard place. Pete wanted to protect you. He got in that ring and there wasn't a damn thing you could have done to stop him." She ran her hands along my jaw and kept them there. "He wanted you to live, to go on, probably because he knew that you would never let yourself get in that position again, and you haven't."

"Sometimes I think I could tell you I shot ten men just for fun, and you'd still tell me it wasn't my fault," I whispered to her.

"I emphatically deny that," she said with a small smile, dropping her hands to my shoulders. "This world you live in doesn't have the same rules as the one out there. I just know you're a good man in a fucked-up situation, doing the best that you can to survive."

Exhaling slowly, my hands found the small of her back and began to trace their way up and down her spine. I wasn't sure how to explain the shit that went on in my head to anyone, but I loved that she was so hell-bent on making me try to figure stuff out.

"I learned one lesson from it, though—one lesson that lets me know exactly what I need to do from this point on," I said softly.

"And what's that?" she asked, searching my eyes.

"I need to protect what's mine, no matter what it takes. And you are mine, Ayda Hanagan. All mine. I won't lose you to anyone."

CHAPTER FIVE
AYDA

Black Friday.

It was the one day I willingly hid away from the rest of the world. The thought of having to be out in the crowds was enough to make me want to screw my feet to the floor. I'd heard some of the Hound Whores moving around the place not long after Drew had drifted back to sleep, and I didn't pity them their fool's errand. They were heading to Corsicana to hit the sales and the crazy people that went with them. I stayed right where I was, my fingers brushing over the warm skin of Drew's back as he finally fell into a deep sleep.

He'd been through so much in his life, and I didn't even know the half of it. There were small pieces that he would feed me when he thought I needed to hear it, but other than that, he was shut up like Fort Knox most of the time. I wasn't the type of person who needed to know everything, just as he didn't seem to have the inclination to know about every bad decision and hairstyle I'd ever had in my lifetime. We drip fed one another, and for the most part, it worked.

That was the most Drew had spoken about Pete since I'd met him. I knew he blamed himself for his death. I knew he wore it like a funeral wreath around his heart until there were times it almost suffocated him. The life that Drew and the others led wouldn't be something I ever fully understood, but the more time passed, the more I realized I didn't need to. As I'd said to him only hours earlier, they lived by a different set of rules. They were born from honor and a code of brotherhood that ran deeper than most bloodlines I'd seen. Yes, they were an MC, a ruthless, relentless entity that was unreasonable at times, but even so, above all of that, they were a family first and foremost. They did what they had to do to protect themselves and one another, which was exactly why Drew had ended up in prison, although he spoke even less of that part of his life than he did about Pete.

Those thoughts were the ones that plagued me as I lay there in the bed next to Drew, running my hand over his warm skin in calming circles. Every subtle ridge in his flesh that my fingers danced over was a scar, another story from his past I wasn't privy to. They were all a part of him, though, so I accepted them with love and moved onto the next. Unfortunately, there were still some thoughts that hounded me as I crawled from the bed at the first sign of the sun kissing the horizon. It was those very thoughts that sent me out of the room and down the hall to Tate's room, where I stood in the doorway watching him sleep before I finally pushed off the frame and headed toward his bed.

It had been a while since he and I had hung out, and even longer since we went to visit our parents in the cemetery. In fact, I hadn't been to my parents' grave since Drew Tucker walked into my life, and I didn't deem that as a bad thing. It meant I wasn't dwelling on their death or what I'd lost. It meant I was living, and I knew that they would understand.

Not on Black Friday, though.

That was a tradition, and that's what had been nagging at the back of my mind as Drew's words smashed around in my head.

Crawling onto the edge of Tate's bed, I leaned over his hulking form and prodded at his dimples. He was smiling in his sleep, and that meant one of two things. I was pretty sure they would both scar me for a month.

"Hey, kid."

"Not now," he whimpered, pushing my hand away and tugging the blankets back up and over his shoulder. He rolled toward me, his face pushing into his pillow.

"Tate, wake up."

"Ayda?"

"No, it's Pocahontas. Yes, it's me. Wake up!"

"Why? It's too early, and it's a vacation day. Why would you do this to me?" He pulled the pillow out from under his head, his face planting into the mattress below it. The groan was audible as he pulled the pillow down over his head, covering his ears.

"Drama queen, it's Saturday tomorrow. I'm going to see Mom and Dad and I want you to come with me."

"Now?" he asked, dumping the pillow off the side of his bed and propping himself up on his elbows to look at me. "It's barely dawn, A. Why can't we go later?"

Looking down at my hands, my fingers began to tangle over my thighs. There was a chance he would reject the idea, just like I knew Drew would be pissed if he had any knowledge of what I was planning on doing. I understood the risk. I understood that he wouldn't appreciate what I was about to do, but I needed it.

"You want to go without a chaperone," Tate said, his tone

accusing. He'd grown so used to Kenny tailing him that it was more like hanging out with a friend—which they were—than having some leather-clad bodyguard following him everywhere he went.

For the most part, it didn't bother me having someone follow me. I liked spending time with Deeks, even when he was being grumpy and throwing his wisdom around. More often than not, he had some wild tale to tell about his days in the army and the glory days of the Hounds when they had traveled around the country almost three times over, looking for recruits and coordinating with the other charters.

Deeks loved the pack. He breathed it and lived it to the point I wasn't sure he would know how to survive outside of it. He lived by their rules and honored them. He'd seen people come and go, and he knew when to keep his mouth shut. I wasn't always sure that Drew and the others knew how lucky they were to have his loyalty. He was an asset, a living chronicle, a memoir dedicated only to the Hounds of Babylon.

Even with all of that, there were times I just needed to be alone. I needed to move around knowing there wasn't a set of eyes watching my every move. Those measures were in place to keep me safe. I wasn't naïve; I knew there was a set of cross hairs on my back, and not just from the Emps. After making it clear where my loyalties were cemented, the honorable Chief Sutton had declared Tate and me the enemy. He was gunning for us. Tate already had a ticket for littering when he'd thrown his gum wrapper at the trash can on Main Street and missed, and I'd been pulled over twice. The first was for being over the line at the red light and obstructing the pedestrian crossing, and the second for driving over the double white lines when exiting the highway to get to Rusty's.

Both were things he would have normally overlooked in the past, but our association with the Hounds was a line drawn in the sand, one that was conveniently encouraged by the chief's white trash wife and evil spawn. They just failed to realize we were made of tougher stuff than that.

"Do you want an audience when you're talking to Mom and Dad?"

"Not really, but it ain't like they're gonna hang over our shoulders."

"T, I need to see them."

Tate flopped onto his back on the mattress, almost bouncing me right off. His hand clutched at the blankets covering him before he sighed heavily.

"Fine. You think you could make me some breakfast while I get dressed?"

"I think I could manage that. Do you want a toaster pastry or toast and grape jelly?"

"Toast, please."

"Orange or milk?"

"Milk, chocolate if we have it."

"You got it, kid. I'll be in the kitchen. Please try to be quiet."

I pushed up off the mattress and ruffled his hair, the indignant huff as he swatted my hand away making me laugh. It was another example of forgetting how young he really was. I seemed to have been making that mistake more often, leaning on him when I should have been the one he could depend on. With life finally settling down a bit, I needed to bring back some kind of routine for him.

I was halfway down the hall when I decided to turn around and make sure he had towels. I should have known better really. I should have just kept walking. Nevertheless, I didn't, and the moment I opened the door, I realized my mistake. Tate stood frozen. By some divine intervention his boxers were on and his sweats were halfway up his legs. On the other side of the bed, a HW whose name was Libby, if memory served, was struggling into her bra, her arms twisted behind her back, her denim skirt hanging on her hips and a hickey in a place I didn't want to think about my brother's mouth being.

I covered my eyes with both hands, turned to face the door and then back around to double check I wasn't seeing things.

It was a spur-of-the-moment reaction, but the disappointment I felt was more than I could take. My hands raised, palms toward them as I shook my head. "You know what? Don't worry about it."

"A!"

I shook my head and backed away. I'd never before felt as big of a failure than I did in that moment. I'd fought so hard to keep the whores from his bed. He was fifteen, his sixteenth birthday not even this side of Christmas. I couldn't do anything about a girl his age. He was going to do what he was going to do; he was a teenager. A woman almost the same age as me, however, was a line I hadn't wanted him to cross, and I felt as though I'd let him down, that I'd let our folks down.

I needed to speak to them even more than I had earlier. I needed to get all the twisted and jumbled thoughts out of my head. I needed to dump the guilt that was suddenly eating me alive. I just had to go it alone.

Before Tate could sort himself out, I was slamming his door and marching down the hall with intent, swinging by the kitchen only to grab my bag and keys before dashing across the minefield of half-naked bodies and out into the cold fall morning air.

CHAPTER SIX
DREW

She wasn't there when I woke up. It wasn't unusual. We had our separate rooms, after all, but that didn't mean those were my favorite mornings. No, my favorites were the ones where she allowed herself to feel like she could live here without having to pay her way. The mornings when, instead of getting up and putting food in the stomachs of men who were big enough and smart enough to do it for themselves, she would allow herself to lay next to me without feeling guilty. No matter what Ayda tried to tell me, I knew more than anyone how she felt about living under this roof for nothing. It's why she did what she did. It's what made her different to all the whores out there. She didn't want to be another taker.

It took me a while to wake up. The thoughts of the conversation we'd had through the night and the black smoke of that dream were still lingering around the edges of my mind, even when I showered and slowly dressed myself as though it was my body that was aching, not my chest. I stayed in my bedroom as long as I could, doing what I never did and straightening out the comforter in case Ayda chose to spend the night in my place again. It was only when I stood back from the bed and stared down at the neatness of it all that I crossed my arms over my chest and scowled.

Huh.

Was I becoming one of *those* guys?

Well, shit.

I couldn't help smirking to myself at the thought. All those nights I'd spent alone, staring at cold, bare walls inside the joint. All those women that I'd fucked for the sake of fucking, trying to feel something other than the self-gratification it would eventually give me, and never once did I think I'd be the guy who straightened out his bedding and picked his socks off the floor for a chick.

Fuck. My socks!

Giving the room a quick glance over, picking shit up and shoving it all on the chair in the corner, I eventually walked through the bathroom and back into my office, wearing a slightly too smug look on my face. There was no denying that talking to Ayda last night had taken some weight off the nightmare that had haunted me. Maybe she was right about the grief eating me up and making everything darker when I kept it all hidden away. I didn't know. I was trying things that I would never have dreamt of before she came along, but the further I opened up to her, the more I began to like the idea of who I could become if only she chose to stick around.

Running my thumb over my bottom lip and walking to my desk, I pulled the first black account's book in front of me and flipped it open, tucking one hand into the back pocket of my jeans as I started to read the rows upon rows of figures that stared up at me. Credit to Harry, the pawn shop was doing better than everything else was these days. There was money in gold. There was money in things people didn't realize—even people's misery, which is where the repo side of work came into it. The guys had done well since I'd been away. They'd done better by being on the right side of the law. They'd achieved what I'd thought I could have with the boxing rings.

As it did most days, my thoughts began to drift back to the businesses I'd sent underground, and before I knew it, I was sliding into my chair, grabbing a pen and trying to ignore that twist that instantly churned my stomach up. A lot had changed since the night of the fire at Ayda's old house. A lot of truths had had to be shared, and my speech at the safe house seemed to open up a wave of small secrets that had been kept from me since my release. One being that the second I took the fall for the underground dealings, the club sold off every single asset that was connected to anything that would remind me of Pete's death.

The old building we fought in was cleared out and auctioned off to try to repay some debt. Who to, I had no fucking idea. The moment Jedd had pulled me to one side and explained that there was no going back to that old life, I'd lifted my hand to his shoulder, squeezed him tight and closed my eyes in acceptance. They'd been right to make the call. No matter how many dreams I knew Pete had had before his death, it was time to face the facts and acknowledge that it was the root of those dreams that had led us to fighting. There was no way to make it completely legitimately in our world. When you lived on the outskirts of society, you had no choice but to accept that. There was no way we would get the licensing we needed. I'd held my hands up to both Jedd and Harry and told them I trusted their call. Whatever they'd needed to do to survive and keep the club alive, they'd done. There was no need for me to know any more about it.

It was time for new beginnings now. For them, anyway. All I could do was hope that I survived long enough to catch a glimpse of my family in more comfortable, carefree times.

Staring down at some of the account's papers in front of me, my pen hovered over the page while one hand rested on the top of my head, the tips of my finger's grazing over my scalp as I tried to concentrate on anything other than the amount of blood we'd shed since the night they tried to kill Ayda and Tate.

Whether skin to skin or hand to weapons, I was now responsible for six dead Emps. So far, the Navarro Rifles hadn't gotten wind of anyone trying to imitate them, or at least not that we'd heard, and the likes of Chester Cortez had apparently gone so deep underground, not even the rats knew where they were living anymore. The boys and I had done a few rides out of Babylon since we sent the girl back from the forest with nothing more than a few raspy breaths of air in her lungs, the clothes on her back, and a lifetime of scars printed on the backs of her eyelids, but we'd seen nothing and nobody on our travels. The Emps' club and bar were now locked up, abandoned as though they didn't exist. But we all knew that they were out there forging alliances as we spoke, trying desperately to figure out why the Navs would side with us over them after everything that had gone down with Pete all those years ago.

All my hopes were pinned on one thing I was certain to be true. Deep down, Cortez was a coward, and he was about as likely to contact the Navs directly as I was to fly to the motherfucking moon, tomorrow, at dawn. The Rifles' charters spanned across the whole of North and South America, as well as Canada, with a few smaller charters spattered across the four corners of the world. To start a war with them would be dire.

To imitate them and wear their sign upon your non-Rifle-approved skin would be suicide.

I was just hoping that my balls would prove bigger than Cortez's and his stupidity would eventually dig his own grave. He would seek revenge for his dead brothers. He would seek revenge for the girl. He would eventually find a way to poke the bellies of the beasts who were the Navs and if all went to plan, he would eventually die.

My hounds and I just had to survive one day at a time and hope against all hope that whichever god was looking down on us was feeling generous and amused by our plan. I figured we had to at least get bonus points for bravery. Or idiocy.

The rows of numbers on the paper stared back at me, looking more confusing than ever. I felt like they were moving, one jumping over the other, switching places whenever I blinked so that when my frown grew deeper and deeper with confusion, those fuckers got some kind of laugh out of it.

Dropping the pen on the page, I pinched the bridge of my nose and pressed my eyes shut tight together. The noise as we tore that Emp apart started ringing in my ears louder than ever. The sweat of my brothers seemed to fall at my feet under the desk to try to drown me in shame. My morning high was quickly turning into a slump as I listened to it all as though it was playing out right in front of me—the girl's whimpers, the dark night, the endless sky and the dirt mixed with blood on our hands.

I could smell it.

I could fucking taste it.

I was thinking too much.

My head snapped up quickly at the tap on the office door before it was pushed open and in walked Slater.

"Drew?" he said quietly, his heavy boots falling hard against the carpet.

"Yes, bro?" I croaked, glancing back down and clearing my throat quickly.

"You okay?"

"Champion."

"I'm not buying it."

"Fuck off."

"Now I'm really not buying it. What's happened? Lover's tiff with the old lady?" Before I knew it, he was sitting in the chair opposite me, the sound of his cut filling the air as it creaked when he slid down into place and crossed one ankle over his knee.

"Don't let her hear you calling her old, or she'll have your balls in tonight's stew." I smirked, quickly rubbing over my eyebrow before looking up at him.

"I'd say I'm not scared of her, but I think secretly, most of the guys in here daren't even piss in the wrong direction these days. Except Tate."

My laughter came freely as I dropped both my elbows to the desk in front of me. "I kinda love the way she keeps y'all in line. Saves me a job."

"You've fucking changed." He grinned.

"Don't say it…"

"Pussy whipped—that's what you've become."

I narrowed my eyes at the bastard, even though my smirk grew as though my head hadn't just been filled with a mixture of blood and soil. "Careful," I warned him quietly.

"The great Drew Tucker, broken by a woman. What happened to Cape Cock?"

I leaned forward, joining my hands together on top of the books in front of me. "If you don't quit your trash talk, I will slap my dick down your throat and make you apologize against my balls, fucker."

"Promises, promises." Slater grinned as he began to stroke the length of his wayward beard.

"Are you here for anything else, or just to flirt with me?"

His rough laughter broke free, and even though I knew I wanted him gone, that sound was exactly what I'd needed to hear to cut through the dark thoughts that lurked in the back of my mind like a never-ending horror movie.

"Actually, I am. Yeah."

Turning my palms so they were face up, I gestured for him to go on.

Slater's eyes found the sole of his boot while his free hand reached out to pick at the worn edges of the rubber. "Few things. I've checked around, still no sign of Cortez. From what I can gather, even their wives and kids don't know where they are. There's rumors that there was a mass ride out the night of the fire, which we already knew of, but then the second wave of riders took off three days after the girl went back. Or, at least when we assume she went back. I'm still not certain we can be sure she went anywhere near them. She was pretty messed up when we dropped her."

"She went back."

"She did?"

"Yep."

"How can you be sure?"

"Call it a hunch," I answered, running my tongue over my

bottom lip to try to gain some movement.

"Okay," he mumbled. "Then as far as that front goes, we're still waiting. No news is good news, right?"

"Sure." I smiled tightly, not wanting to tell him that no news in the MC world was the worst fucking thing that could happen. Plans of destruction were never made in the hustle and bustle of a crowded bar, and we both knew it. "It works for me."

He moved forward, rolling his shoulders in his cut before sniffing up and half grinning like he was just about to tell a rude joke. "We got another little problem, too."

"What kinda problem?" I frowned, my body instantly tensing under the desk.

"A kid kinda problem."

"What?" My eyes searched his face as I continued to stare him down. "Tate? Or, shit… You…" My mind immediately went to Ayda, and just the thought of kid and her in the same sentence had my balls shriveling up to the size of two peanuts and the nausea roaring to life in my stomach.

"Jesus, calm down, Drew." He laughed, clearly amused by my not so hidden look of horror. "I didn't mean that kind of kid, and if I knew before you, I'd imagine that was a bigger fucking problem than anything else you got at your feet right now. Tate's fine, although I think you're gonna have trouble with him soon. I know Ayda is set on his schooling, but I dunno. He's all over Kenny, and he's asking question after question after question about this life. And he's looking real antsy right now, stomping around and asking if anyone saw Ayda le—"

"Just get to the fucking point, Slater," I snapped, cutting him off as my shoulders sagged with relief.

"We got some copycat kids riding around."

"Copycat kids?"

"That's what I just said." He nodded slowly before landing both his feet back on the floor and leaning forward again. "We don't know where they're coming from, but they're not just in our town. They're everywhere, moving from place to place. They've been on the news, according to Deeks and Harry. Jedd has spoken to a couple of the cops he's got on the payroll these days, and they've said there have been a few incidents of minor theft, gang related petty crimes, that sort of thing."

"In Babylon?"

"Just once. The old man at the barber store got held at gunpoint by some boy that he thought was fifteen, sixteen at best. Unloaded gun dumped by the door, group of assholes running away and high fiving the shit out of each other down the road."

"Fuck," I whispered, shaking my head and looking back down at the pawn shop figures. "Just what we need, kindergarten clean up."

"Want me to take care of it?"

Looking back up at him, I gave him another flat smile before raising my hands in the air again. "We're not the baby police. Let's just keep our eyes and ears to the ground. If they have any kind of markings on them, we need to know what it is and who it belongs to. Tell everyone out in the club, too. Even the women. They could be a target for the wannabes. Ain't nothing like getting your cock sucked by an older woman to make you feel like a man." I leaned back in my chair and let my hands fall to my stomach. "Just make everyone aware. Sounds like something anyone of us could squash if we needed to."

"Got it." He nodded again, motioning to stand up before I called out.

"Is that what you wanted to tell me about yesterday?"

"Yeah. Harry told me it was no big deal and it could wait until today. Sorry about that."

"Can't blame you for being jumpy these days." I smiled flatly, glancing towards the door before the conversation we'd just been having began to replay over in my mind, the single point I'd somehow missed hitting me square in the jaw like it had the force of a bear behind its swing. "Hold up. Did you say Tate was looking for Ayda this morning?"

Slater perched back on the edge of the seat and raised both his brows. "Yeah."

My frown was instant. "She's not in the club?"

He didn't have to answer. His face told me it all. I was up and out of my chair within seconds, and I didn't miss the way it slammed against the wall, or the way Slater told me to hold up and calm down before I marched out of my office and into the bar, leaving my growl of annoyance to echo around the whole fucking club for everyone to hear.

CHAPTER SEVEN
AYDA

There was something calming about the cemetery. It wasn't that stereotypical place you saw in the movies, which was a small spatter of headstones in an open field, or even the New Orleans type of style with mausoleums dotted around and marble tombs, holding caskets above the water table. This was beautiful. It was like a forest meadow, hidden among the trees that had been claimed by visitors and the wind chimes that they hung there. In the summer, the air was stifling. The humidity hung around you like an unwelcome friend while you sat sweating over the people you missed most. In the winter, it stayed comfortable, out of the chill of the breeze that tended to bring the temperature down another couple of degrees.

I reveled in the solitude of it as I cleared their headstones and did a little maintenance of my own. The pennant Tate had dropped off after last season's game was looking a bit weatherworn and faded, but I put it back where he'd left it, along with my mom's collection of trinkets.

"There, that's better," I said, finally sitting down between them and crossing my legs. I leaned back, resting my weight on my hands as my eyes moved over their engraved names. "What the hell am I supposed to do about Tate, Momma? He's a good kid, but right now, I swear to God he's ruled by his hormones."

I sat listening to the wind and imagined her response. Her voice was so clear in my head. I wanted to close my eyes and pretend I was back on our couch with my head on her lap. *Hormones are leading him, pumpkin. Boys are rabid when they're adolescents. They think about one thing and one thing only. Why do you think Daddy was so intent on you being back by ten at night?*

I must have looked crazy sitting there alone, smiling at the mental image I had. My dad would have looked over his paper at me, one eyebrow raised in a knowing smile. He always knew me better than I knew myself. When I'd come in from my first intimate experience with Jacob, he'd been sitting at the kitchen table, a bourbon in hand and a small hint of sadness. It was probably designed to make me feel guilty, but I just remembered the way I'd interpreted it. He paid attention. He knew who I was.

"I wonder if I made a selfish decision where Tate was concerned. I couldn't be happier. I love Drew, and I love The Hut and the boys, but I feel like Tate is losing himself in it. He still goes to practice, but I think that's only because Kenny rags on him if he doesn't. His grades are still okay, but I can see the slow deterioration into not so great, and I know it's because he's distracted. I found him in bed with one of the girls this morning. She's one of the few sweet ones, but she's still older than him, and I'm not ready for that last part of childishness to be stolen from him."

Sitting up and dusting off my hands, I dragged them through my hair and made myself smaller by drawing my knees to my chest. I had so many questions to ask them.

I needed their wisdom, but all I had were my memories. I couldn't trust myself to give honest speeches. I loved where my life had taken me, and if I was truthful, I was being selfish when it came to Tate. Sure, he was happy where he was, but that didn't mean it was the right environment for him.

So what did I do? Set ground rules? Hope that all of those men would choose to honor them for me? I couldn't expect them to do that. The club was a place where they could be themselves, where they were free of house rules and regulations. I couldn't suddenly implement some purely for my own selfish need to feel like I was being proactive. Even so, I couldn't leave, either. I couldn't walk out of there and expect one of those guys to have to sit and guard our door, just so I could give Tate some kind of routine. Drew would never understand why I had to leave, and I didn't want him to have to understand. I just wanted to be with him.

"How do I do what's best for Tate and think about my own happiness? Or do I put his above mine?"

You do both, came the voice of my dad in my head. *Just because you think it's not a good environment, it doesn't mean that's true. You said yourself these guys are decent men. What's to say they won't help shape your brother into a good man?*

Maybe that was just wishful thinking; perhaps it was the truth. I wasn't a parent, and I was proving to be a shitty understudy for the ones we'd lost. I still had no idea how to handle a boy or know what was good for him.

I'd just hung my arms over my legs and started to lean forward to talk some more when an almighty crack came from across the silent cemetery. I thought I'd been alone up until that point, and it wasn't until I sat up and strained to look over the headstones that I saw a group of three kids laughing, while a fourth was using all of his strength to kick at a headstone in an attempt to break it.

"Speaking of misspent youth…" I grumbled, pulling my purse toward me and rocking to my feet. "I'm going to go and take care of that and figure out how the hell to talk to Tate. I love you both, and I promise I'll be back again soon. Oh, and I promise I'll bring Tate, too. Even if I have to dress him myself, and hog-tie him… Which I may do anyway."

I leaned down, kissing my fingers and pressing them to each name before looking back toward the kids who had grown louder as one of the others had joined in the goal of destroying property that didn't belong to them.

Whatever I'd been expecting, I got a sense of just how wrong I'd been as I made my way across the cemetery. From my place at my parents' graves, it had looked like the four of the kids had been wearing simple black hoodies. But the closer I got, the more I recognized the image staring back at me from one of the fake leather vests. The cartoonish skull had fangs, and the dog's teeth were dripping blood, but the similarities were too close, dangerously resembling the Hounds patch. This wasn't good for either group. These boys were putting themselves in the line of fire and incurring the Hounds' wrath, while the behavior of the boys would reflect on the pack's already sullied reputation. Whatever game the kids were playing, it involved fire, and they were going to get burned.

The ringleader wiped some sweat away with the arm of his hoodie as he paused to catch his breath. The granite hadn't shifted since the initial crack that had alerted me to their presence in the first place. Not one of them had noticed me, but as he pulled his foot back to try once more, my eyes were drawn to the name engraved on it, and the words were out before I could so much as think about changing my mind.

"Do that again and you've signed your death warrant, kid."

Four sets of eyes turned my way, the sneer of the one with his leg suspended in the air making an insidious shiver run down my spine.

I was outnumbered.

They may have been kids, freshmen in high school if I was judging right, but they could still be dangerous. Teenage boys were like dogs; put more than two together and you had a pack mentality, and that wasn't always a comforting thought. I wasn't safe. The look in their eyes as they assessed me told me everything I needed to know.

"Put your mouth to better use and wrap it around my dick, bitch."

Whatever line of thought was in my mind, whatever fear or caution I'd been harboring, it all seemed to go away with the little punk's deep, gravelly voice. My incredulity at his audacity was suddenly the only thing that mattered.

"I'd have to find it first, asshole." All his little friends made amused noises as they hid their faces. Point to me. "What the fuck do you think you're doing?"

"It ain't none of your business. So go back to whatever the fuck you were doing and keep your nose out of it."

He kicked the headstone again, forcing the grass around the base to move. The real patch that was engraved under the word's *Brother For Life* became visible.

"Stop it. Just stop it. That's disrespectful and disgusting. It's also a good way to get a target nail-gunned to your backs. The fact that you were stupid enough to wake up this morning and put on fake patches was bad, but to desecrate one of the Hounds' graves is suicide."

"We *are* the Hounds."

"The fuck you are, kid, and if you valued your balls, you'd take those terrible fakes off and forget you ever had them."

"Who the fuck do you think you're talking to?"

"You, asshole, but I have this overwhelming sense that you have no idea who I am, which would be completely understandable if you hadn't said you were Hounds."

"I don't got time for you, lady. Step off and fuck off."

"Oh, I will. I'm sure Drew Tucker would be very interested to know that you're here," I said, pulling out my cell phone to call one of the guys, hoping Drew would be with them. "What were your names?"

"Elbows," his friend said, suddenly wide-eyed and sheet white.

"Shut up, Mikey. She's bluffing."

"I'm really not," I said, flipping the phone onto speaker as a growl came down the line.

"Where the fuck have you been, Ayda?"

"I'm at the cemetery, Drew. You may need to get down here. We have a situation."

As much as I knew I would pay for it later, I hung the phone up on him and stared at the kid who looked like he was about to hurl. I didn't like throwing my relationship with Drew around. I didn't like using it to put weight behind my threats, but this was pack business as much as it was mine, and it was the only way I could stop the little fucks from ruining Pete's headstone.

I'd barely drawn breath when the four of them took off

like their heels were on fire. The one they called Elbows stopped as the others jumped the fence and turned his head to look back at me. With two fingers and his thumb raised, he cocked an imaginary gun and shot it in my direction, his smirk evident as he shook his head and bounced over to follow his friends. My original instinct was right. They were dangerous, but I'd won the battle this time.

Turning back to the grave, I felt an overwhelming sadness stab me in the chest. It wasn't the prettiest grave, or the neatest, but it was certainly the most loved. The face of it had been left clean, but over the years, the sides and the back had been decorated. Names, badges and messages were engraved all over it. All signs of love from his brothers and friends. To say he was missed was a ridiculous understatement.

Falling to my knees at the side of him, I placed my hand in the middle of the long grass and left it there. My eyes closed as I thought about everything Drew and I had spoken about the night before. This was the man responsible for the guy I loved. Pete was the reason Drew was still alive, even if there was a piece of him buried under my palm with his idol.

"Hey, Peter 'Frazier' Mitchell, friend, brother and legacy Hound. We finally get to meet. I'm Ayda, and I think I may have just inadvertently forced Drew to come and pay you a visit."

CHAPTER EIGHT
DREW

If there was one place I'd been determined to avoid since my release, it was where Pete's body had been laid to rest.

The tires beneath me kicked up more dust than usual as they tore up the pathway before I parked and spun around to find her. If it hadn't been for the urgency and quiet warning her voice had held, there was no way I would have agreed to be there. The last time I'd stepped foot in the place had been for his funeral. That was the day I made the decision to make a deal that would darken the following five years of my life.

The air around me seemed to shift as I searched for her, and it was only when I finally allowed myself to look in the direction that held more haunted memories that I saw Ayda next to his grave. The relief of seeing that she was okay was soon eclipsed by something else entirely.

"Fuck," I whispered roughly to no one but myself. My hand found the back of my neck, scrubbing at it as I tried to find the strength to go and stare down at his name etched in stone. Keeping my head down, I slowly started to make my way over, figuring out a way to stay calm and not go crazy at her for pulling such a stunt with me.

She'd coerced me here because of the nightmare last

night.

She was trying to fix the unfixable.

It had to stop before she even began.

With my eyes fixed firmly on the gravel path beneath my feet, I slowed to a stop in front of where I knew she was sitting, pushing both hands into the pockets of my jeans as I shook my head from side to side and felt the muscles in my jaw twitching.

"Was this really necessary?" I asked quietly. "Wasn't last night enough for you?"

"No, it's not that, Drew." I heard the rustle in the tall grass as she stepped closer and blew the breath from her lungs. "There really is a problem."

"What kind of problem?"

"I was here visiting my folks, and I heard a crack. I thought I was alone so it scared the shit outta me. There were four kids kicking at Pete's headstone trying to break it, and..." She trailed off with another sigh. She seemed unsure of what she was about to say next.

My head shot up without thought, my eyes finding hers as I stayed frozen in place. "And?"

"They were wearing fake cuts with an awful, yet close enough version of the Hound's patch on the back. From far away, it was pretty convincing. From close up, if you didn't know what you were looking for, it could be mistaken as genuine. The little fuckhead actually told me he was a Hound, too."

Closing the distance between us, my hands reached up to her shoulders, holding her still as I scanned her for any obvious signs of damage. Her clothes were pristine and her face only showed the kind of sadness that I felt inside, but other than that, she seemed fine.

"Did they touch you? Try to hurt you?"

"They were insolent, but that's about it. Vile little creatures." Her eyes met mine, trying to search for something more. "They've got a bad attitude and they could be dangerous, Drew. It was stupid of me to approach, but that's why I called you."

"They don't know the fucking meaning of dangerous."

"No, but they could do some serious damage in your name. People who don't know the difference are going to make assumptions. Then… Well, there's Pete's headstone. They cracked it, Drew. I'm so sorry. I was too late to stop them."

One of the things I loved about Ayda more than anything was the way she stood up for what she felt was right, but when it came to club crap, I wasn't going to let any of it land at her feet, and anyone who tried to put it there… They were as good as dead before they even realized it.

Pressing a finger to her lips, I dipped my head, raised my brows and waited for her to fight me off. When she didn't, I dropped my forehead to hers and pulled in a breath. "It's just a headstone. I'll get it fixed. No more apologies from you, unless you're willing to admit that leaving this morning was a fucking stupid idea." I paused, smirking at how she could calm me when, just moments before, I'd been raging. "As for those kids…"

She shook her head against mine, a ghost of a smile on her lips. "I know. Pack business, right?"

"I'm not cutting you out of it for any other reason than your own safety and sanity."

"You're so thoughtful," she said, grinning. Pulling

back, her hands pushed against my stomach as she turned her head to look in the direction I'd been avoiding. "But it's not just a headstone, Drew. The carvings on the back, the inscriptions…"

"Outlets of grief from brothers who previously only knew how to draw stickmen and write their own name. I'm sure Pete appreciates them, but this isn't even where he is to me."

"I get that. It's just that it's turned into a shrine of sorts. Can I see what it would take to get it fixed before you replace it? I realize it seems silly, but I would like to do this for y'all, if you'd let me?"

It was harder than I thought it would be not to look in the direction of where my brother lay. For a moment, I felt my head twitch to the side before I stood up straight and forced my eyes to stay trained on Ayda. "Can we talk about this later?"

She seemed to contemplate for a moment, her head twisting back in my direction to meet my eyes. Lifting one hand, she cupped my cheek and nodded. "Absolutely. How about we get out of here and go grab a coffee at the diner?"

"That was easier than I thought it would be," I said through a half smile, running my fingers in between hers before I wrapped an arm around her shoulder and turned us both away from the grave to walk back in the opposite direction. "And the diner sounds like a good idea. I think I'm going to need a few witnesses around when I ask my next favor of you."

"Witnesses?" She gave off one loud fake *ha* before grinning up at me, her fingers squeezing mine. "This should be interesting. Your favors have an unsavory way of turning into commands, or worse, rules."

As the distance grew between Pete and me, I allowed myself to relax against her, laughing and rolling my eyes as my hand ran up and down the top of her arm. "Have you always been dramatic, or is this a recent development?"

"Are you calling me a drama queen? 'Cause you ain't seen nothing yet."

"Believe me, sweetheart, neither have you."

"You're a drama *queen,* too? Oh, this I have to see." She laughed and leaned her head back on the shoulder closest to her, turning her head in search of a kiss.

Stopping just short of the bike, I turned and carefully placed my hands on Ayda's cheeks. Now that she was in my grip again, I allowed myself a few seconds to appreciate her, letting my eyes go on a small exploration of her face before lowering my lips to hers. The soft, barely there moan that escaped her did the same thing it always did to me. Besides the obvious, it made me count my lucky fucks for the fact that she was still around and willing to stick by me.

I drew the moment out, making her feel the weight of my emotions while I could, because I had a feeling that once she heard what I was about to ask of her, I wouldn't be getting kissed like that again any time soon.

CHAPTER NINE
AYDA

The drive to Rusty's was quiet. I didn't have my radio on because I wanted to think, which left only the sound of the car, the road under the tires, and the roar of Drew's bike following me. There were kisses, and then there were kisses like the one he'd just given me. It was full of unspoken words, and I was curious about what he thought was going to piss me off so much.

The moment I pulled into the parking lot, the familiarity of the place filtered in and shifted the nagging doubt that had followed me from the cemetery. Rusty's had always been a home away from home. There were days I felt like I could handle anything the world threw at me, simply because I was within its walls with my second adopted family. The old proverb, "Home is where the heart is" was pretty indicative of my life these days. The Hut and Rusty's were the two places in the world where I wasn't thinking about what was next or dwelling on the charred remains of our previous family home.

With the cold wind blowing off the interstate, I rushed to the door and inside, my ass holding the thing open for Drew as I let off a little shiver at the sudden change in temperature. The smell of bacon and fresh coffee twisted around my senses and made my stomach howl, just as Drew's hand flattened on it.

"You've awoken the beast," I whispered, venturing farther inside to my favorite booth in the place—the one Deeks always hid in when he was following me around. It was also the one Drew and I ended up in so we could avoid the stares. Living in a small town sucked most of the time, but when people were making assumptions, it was even worse. I'd heard it all. I was pregnant, doing drugs, and gang initiated by sleeping with every Hound in the pack—in some cases including all the other charters that had rolled in. I'd heard every idle piece of gossip and all the bullshit stories they could conceive. I'd heard everything but the truth, which was simple even in its purest form. I loved Drew Tucker, and his bunch of misfits was like a pack of brothers, all ready to draw blood in the name of my honor.

Pulling off my coat and sliding along the vinyl covering, I dragged my legs up under me and grinned across the table at Drew, who was running his hands through his hair and arranging his cut without so much as a glance around the place. I envied him his ability to shut out the rest of the world, to look without seeing. I wasn't naïve enough to think he wasn't constantly on high alert, but sometimes I liked to believe that the rest of it—the gossip and judgment of Babylonians—was just white noise to him.

"Okay, Mr. Tucker, once you and I have coffee, you need to start talking. The intrigue is killing me."

His signature smirk was ever present as he ran a thumb down one side of his beard and assessed me. Drew's hands fell to the surface in front of him before he linked them together.

"Let's hope Janette isn't too fast on her feet today then, huh?"

"Janette's always quick on her feet. Sam, on the other

hand…" I said with a grin, my eyes hitting the kitchen door to see Sam's face light up. She was working more since I'd cut back on my hours, and though she didn't mind it, or the money, she looked exhausted most of the time. She didn't bother coming over immediately. She headed straight to the coffee pot, giving me time to look back at Drew. "Coffee's on its way. If you give her a complicated food order, you might just get the time in."

"Dammit." He groaned playfully. "I was hoping for Janette. She doesn't hide her love for me like the rest of them do. Together, we could have made a beautiful distraction from the shit I really need to hit you with." Drew's eyebrows rose, his arms and hands sliding forward on the table before he ran his tongue over his lip and bit down. "Before we get into anything, you need to answer me one question."

"Drew, you're killing me here. Talk already."

"Patience."

"Drew."

"Do you trust me?" he asked firmly, ignoring my not so silent pleas.

"With mine, and more importantly, my brother's life. You know that." I reached over and nudged his hands with mine on the Formica of the table.

"Good answer… because it's Tate's life that I'm going to be needing to borrow from you for something."

The air stuck in my lungs the moment my brother's name fell from his lips. The tips of my fingers were so cold. I barely noticed Sam sliding the cup of coffee onto the table, or the brief conversation she had with Drew. He ordered us both food, his face turning back to mine the moment she was out of earshot.

"Talk fast. I trust you. You know I do, but *life* and *borrow* don't sound very promising."

Shuffling in his seat, he rolled his shoulders once before leaning forward and dipping his head to get as close as he could. "I wouldn't do or ask anything from either of you if I thought that anything was going to happen, so just hear me out. Club business is club business. Don't think for one moment that I don't want to keep you away from that, because I do, but there are things going down with these kids, and if there's one thing I've learned in my life, it's that you have to go to the level of those you're trying to defeat if you want to figure out what the fuck is going on."

He paused, his lips parting to say something before he quickly decided against it, choosing instead to clear his throat and take a different route.

"It wouldn't be anything dangerous, and me and the boys would be right beside him the whole time, but I want Tate to approach these kids. Try to find out what the hell is happening and who they are. This could work in your favor, too, Ayda. This isn't just me sending him on some mission. This could be our chance, *your* chance, to scare him off this life we both know you don't want him leading. Tate talks the talk, but when it comes to walking the walk…"

There were a million disasters popping in my head, and a million and one scenarios that ended badly. The truth was, I had a choice to make, because Drew was right. The direction Tate was taking was away from the one he'd always talked about. He was intrigued by, not just the life that the Hounds led, but by the brotherhood, the acceptance, and the sense of belonging. I knew all of this because I felt it, too. I may not have had a dick, but these men were family to me. The longer I was there, the closer Drew and I became, the more I was a part of it all. I didn't want to take that away from Tate, mainly because the word *no* only seemed to bring out his determination.

Picking up packets of sweetener, I went through the motions, shaking and ripping each one individually to give me time to think without looking at Drew.

I had to face the inevitability. I brought Tate into this life. I made the choice for the two of us, and he thrived on it. He wanted it, and no matter how much I said no or tried to scare him, he would continue to want it.

What Drew was offering was an opportunity. Not to scare him away from the pack life—I'd have been a hypocrite if I did. No, this was to give the kid a few more years of childhood, a chance to think about whether it's what he wanted from life or not. A chance to see what being a part of the MC meant.

The only question was... how the hell was I going to make it through this *mission?*

"Walk me through this, and don't leave out details. I need it all. How long would he need to do this? How much danger is involved? How are your boys going to be there for him when these kids realize what they're doing? How do you plan on getting him out of there if he starts to like it?"

He didn't blink as he answered, staying as calm as he always did when he was challenged by not just me, but anyone who ever questioned him. Unclasping his hands, he turned both palms upright and shrugged casually. "We'd put him out on the streets with a tail on him at all times. He'd need to be planted on a route where we knew these kids were hanging. Initially, we'd need him to pretend to be casing the town for drugs or something, so he'd have a reason to approach them that wouldn't make them suspect anything other than he was some pumped-up kid looking for some juice to make his veins sing. I'm thinking it will be a one-time thing, but that all depends what information he brings back to us. If those imitators tell him to fuck off and don't communicate, if he doesn't get a good enough look at them or find out a few details we need, then we might have to send him in again. Kenny is handy with wiring guys up, so we would be able to hear everything that was going down and set up some kind of code word—have him sneeze or cough or whatever Tate feels comfortable with—and once it's done, we'd be in there in less than thirty seconds." Drew's eyes searched mine and I almost choked when I saw a small smile creeping on his face. "And if the whole thing doesn't scare him and he starts to like it, I'll fire a shot from a distance and put a bullet through his ass, then tell him it was an Emp. That ought to scare him enough to go back to school."

"Drew, this isn't funny. I know that this life is enchanting to him as much as it is to you, and that's always going to be his choice to make, but I need him to be a kid for a while, to finish high school and go to college if that's what he wants. The moment he turns eighteen, it's out of my hands, but for now, if you think this will help for even a few months, I will consider it. Just promise me he'll be safe."

Reaching out for his coffee, he pulled it in front of him, curling one hand around it before leaning back in his seat and draping his other arm across the back. His fingers drummed along the cup in a slow rhythm, but he never once took his eyes away from mine.

"On my life, he will be safe."

Rubbing one eyebrow with the tips of my fingers, I looked up at him, our eyes meeting and holding. "Then you have my permission to ask Tate. I can't make the decision for him."

There was a moment's silence while Drew tried to hide the twinkle of victory flashing from his eyes. If I didn't know him so well, I'd have missed it, but I was learning all of his faces the same way he was learning mine. His body leaned forward ever so slightly towards me. "Ayda?"

Dropping my elbows on the table and resting my chin on my clasped hands, I watched him carefully, reading the subtle movements in his jaw. "Yes?"

"Sometimes, to get the things we want from life, we have to go to the places we hate the most. I'm doing this for his future as well as for the club. Don't doubt your trust in me."

"I know. I believe that, and I do trust you, Drew, but now I have a favor to ask you." I paused and dropped my hands again, tracing the fake wood grain on the surface of the table. "I want to talk to you about your whores."

The gasp from above had my head snapping up. Sam looked completely uncomfortable as she held two plates in her shaking hands. I normally would have laughed it off, and maybe upon reflection I should have, but in that split second I just nodded at her, spurring her into action.

Placing the plates in front of us, she left as fast as she could without running.

Drew's face lit up before he turned back to give me a questioning glance. "*My* whores?"

I started laughing, my hands covering my face as I groaned in defeat. "One in particular, actually. The one I found in Tate's bed this morning."

His lips pressed together as he tried to control his obvious amusement. "Go on."

"It's not funny," I said, dragging my hands down and dropping them to the table. "She's too old for him, and he needs to do the high school thing. He can't take a HW to homecoming or prom."

"Okay." He swallowed slowly, lifting his coffee to his mouth, obviously to buy himself some time before he dropped it back down to the table and cleared his throat. "What exactly are you wanting me to do about it?"

"Tell them to..." I lowered my voice in an attempt to hide what I was about to say next. "Back off or at least make him work for it. He can't go through life thinking he can get his dick sucked just because he asked for it. The real world isn't like that."

"It was for me," he huffed out, laughing quietly before seeing the look I was giving him and straightening his face. "Sorry. I'll speak to him. I mean them. I'll speak to them."

"Thank you." I sat back in my chair and looked at my plate of food with a level of disgust. The hunger I'd had less than thirty minutes earlier had left due to the topic of conversation. Unfortunately, I knew my body, and it would only give me hell if I didn't at least pick at it.

Swiping up my fork, I shoved the scrambled eggs around my plate for a while before dropping it and looking across the table at Drew again. *It was for me* was echoing through the channels of my brain, making it impossible to concentrate. I suddenly wasn't sure of anything. Was I denying Tate some rite of passage women didn't know about?

"Am I wrong, Drew? Do I need to let him just make his own mistakes?"

He didn't look at me when he answered, instead choosing

to concentrate on the food in front of him, his appetite obviously as big as ever. "When it comes to your kid brother, go with your gut. It's the only thing that will ever make the two of you happy. Over thinking is what will make you lose your appetite." Shoving his fork full of whatever into his mouth, Drew looked up at me through hooded eyes as he began chewing slowly, and it was in his silent communication that I thought I heard his loudest message. I'd never doubted my choices with Tate before... Why should I now?

He was right, of course. I'd been left alone to learn from the things I'd done, and it was, in a way, a rite of passage for Tate. I just had to leave him to it like I always had with Sloane. He was going to do what he was going to do, and I'd rather be a part of it than be locked out.

That didn't mean I couldn't mess with Drew a little.

"Oh well, if he knocks her up, I guess we'll be the ones saddled with the little thing..."

CHAPTER TEN
DREW

"So what do you think?" I asked them all from my seat at the head of the table. Glancing around from left to right, my eyes eventually fell on Jedd as I waited for him to speak.

"I think," he said slowly, inhaling before reclining back in his chair. "I think if Ayda is happy enough with what you're asking of Tate then it could work." Jedd began to nod, his head turning to the right of him as he glanced at Slater.

"Am I the only one that wants to rip these little fuckers' heads off?" Slater asked quietly.

A few grumbles erupted deep from the bellies of the other men.

"Spoken like the true sergeant at arms," I muttered under my breath.

"Nope. I'm with you, Slater," Kenny agreed from my right where he sat next to Harry, one hand on the table while his arm hung limply over the back of his chair. "They disrespected us in the worst possible way. We should make them pay."

"More importantly, they disrespected Pete." Slater's brows rose as my attention slowly turned to him. "And I've got to be honest, Drew. I'm a little surprised by how well you're taking this."

I clasped both hands together and just shrugged. There wasn't much I could say about any of it, mainly because my mind was so weighed down with the thoughts of the real threats that were out there, waiting for us to slip, ready to pounce from the shadows.

"They'll get what they deserve at some point," I muttered, not meaning to smirk at the men who were sitting around my table. This meeting was almost comical. Where once we'd been talking about which one of us would do the drug runs across the border, now we were discussing who was going to play dress up and deal with a bunch of kids.

Harry's chair creaked beside me, and without him having to say anything at all, he commanded everyone's attention, just like that. Even mine.

"I think what Drew is trying to say is this: The more attention we give these boys—and make no mistake, these little pissants are just *boys*—the more they will think they are winning. Let a fighter get a few punches in and suddenly he thinks he's a champ, right? We've got bigger fish to fry, but that doesn't mean we should ignore them. At the end of the day, we're all here every single day, for three reasons. One—because we love the shit out of each other, and we're a family. Two—because we need the freedom of riding like we need the air in our lungs. And three…" He paused to pour all his attention onto me, a small smile playing on his lips as if he was already feeling smug about being able to explain our motives better than me. "Because we love Babylon. And if there's anyone out there that's going to try to damage this place, we'll do our best to protect it, whether it's against the law or not. Ain't that right, Tucker?"

"Don't even try to pretend you ain't here for the free pussy, Harry," I said, raising a brow.

The whole table began to tremble, each man slapping his hand down on the top as their rough laughter got stuck in their throats. Harry's elbows hit the surface before he dropped his head and ran both hands over his bald head, back and forth, back and forth. "It's like dealing with infants, every damn day," he muttered from beneath his arms.

Leaning over to slap him on the shoulder, I straightened up in my chair, pulling my cut down against my chest while I tried to get back to business. "But what he's saying is right. I'm not going to treat these little fuckers like they're dangerous because then they'll start to believe it. There's nothing more explosive than a kid with too much ego and no fear in his heart."

I didn't miss the cough from beside me or the way Jedd raised his balled up fist to his mouth and uttered a not so quiet, "Sounds like someone we once knew," at Slater's shoulder. My arm shot out to the side, my finger jabbing in his face. "Fuck. You."

"When? Name the time and the place and I'm there, stud." Jedd's laughter was so deep, raw and infectious, it wasn't long before the whole place was up in arms. This meeting had gone downhill so fast I didn't see much point in carrying it on. Running a hand down over my mouth to try to contain my own grin, I shook my head and reached for the gavel beside me, slamming it against the wood before throwing my arms in the air and falling back into my seat.

"Get the fuck out of here, all of y'all. I'll take your jokes as a yes vote, and we can move the hell along."

Jedd and Slater jumped up out of their seats first, but Jedd was out of the doorway before Slater—his hand holding onto the door as he looked over his shoulder and gave me one last glance. It was a look that told me this wasn't over in his eyes and while he might be playing his part in this circus we'd created, he'd be pulling me aside to talk about this later.

Harry's chair scratched across the floor as the weight of his body pushed it back. For once, he seemed happy enough with a decision I'd made, and the firm but careful slap to the top of my arm as he walked by told me so. I wouldn't admit it to anyone, but I kinda liked those moments from him. It made me feel like I might not be quite the fuck up I'd always imagined myself to be.

I was already thinking of ways to spend the night with Ayda without focusing too much on the worry that she was trying to hide from me. My thoughts were traveling down several paths until I heard a small cough escape from Kenny beside me. Peering up at him and then glancing at the door, I let my head roll slowly to look back at him and just waited.

Kenny shuffled in his seat a few times, his neck stretching from side to side before he brought his hands to rest on the table in front of him. Eyes down were never a good response from him. He was one of the cockier members of our club. He was the joker, the clown, the idiot, so much so that he struggled to do the whole serious shit, which is why he looked as awkward as he did then.

His mouth moved as though to speak a few times, but nothing came out.

"What's up, brother?" I asked quietly.

"I'm not used to this feeling that I've got right now, Drew. I-I've gotta be honest with you about that."

He looked more on edge than I remembered seeing him

since I got out of prison. He looked like the boy who I'd left behind back then, not the man who'd stood before me wearing nothing but confidence since I'd been released.

Scowling further, one hand rested on the arm of my chair, my body leaning away from it as my chin came to rest on the fist of the other hand. "What feeling's that?"

"This…" He batted the leather on his chest just once. "This unease I've got going on. I've never argued with you or questioned anything you've ever done. You know that, right? You remember all those times I've given you my yes vote, even when everyone else said no?"

"I remember, K-Dog."

"Good." He nodded firmly. "Good. Then you should know that I wouldn't argue with you unless it felt right to."

Flaring my nostrils, I held a big breath of air in my chest before releasing it slowly, my voice strained when I forced words out. "Spit it out, Ken. Honesty is always appreciated around this table, and that's something you should know by now. There's nothing you can't talk to me about."

Kenny's head snapped up in my direction, his expression deadpan as he spoke. "Don't get Tate involved in this. Kids or not, amateurs or pros, I've come to know him, and something tells me that once he's in, he's all in."

My eyes narrowed in his direction as my chin slipped, pushing my fist to my mouth. "Tell me why."

"Because I know him, Drew. He follows me around like he's a damn puppy and I'm the only one that can lead him out into the yard to take a piss. Don't get me wrong, I like having him here. He's become a brother to me, without having to wear the cut. But…"

"But…?"

Kenny's hands slapped down on the table weakly, his shoulders sagging. "He's just a boy—a boy who hasn't been allowed to be a child. I know he thinks he's got the world at his feet, and I know he looks at you as some kind of hero."

I couldn't help the raise of both brows, but I didn't speak, instead clearing my throat and silently asking him to go on.

"He sees what you are, flaws and all, and he asks a lot of questions about what you were like at his age. I think anything you do now to encourage him into this lifestyle could mark the beginning of the end. If he thinks he's been useful to the club, he's gonna want more of that. He's gonna soak up that high and feel ten feet tall."

"Like you did?" I breathed against my hand.

He nodded once, his eyes dropping back down to the table in front of him. "Yeah. Like I did."

"Do you regret the choices you made?"

"We all have our moments," he whispered.

"I guess we do." I sighed softly. "Kenny?"

"Yeah?"

"Thanks for being honest with me."

Rubbing his lips together, he pressed his hands down and began to stand. There wasn't much left to be said. He had concerns, and they were noted. He was no different than Ayda. He was no different than any of them out there. All I had to do was show them that no harm would come to him that wasn't intended. The only scare Tate Hanagan was going to get was going to be from me.

Because if anyone thought for one minute that I was going to allow the woman I loved to lose her only blood relative because of *my* club, they were all more fucked up in the head than I realized. I'd made the Hanagans a promise all those weeks ago at the safe house, and it was a promise I had zero intention of ever breaking to either one of them, no matter what that meant for me.

CHAPTER ELEVEN
AYDA

The earphones were pumping music into my ears, the beat forcing my feet to move as I separated the whites from the colors. I had the laundry down to a fine art in this place. I'd made it clear that I didn't care who owned what. I did colors on Fridays and whites on Sundays. You missed the day, you were on your own.

The truth was I'd been hiding in the huge laundry room. I still wasn't ready to talk to Tate. Even though the place was mainly free of the other women due to it being Black Friday and I should have been soaking up the time without them, I couldn't face my kid brother just yet.

You'd have thought after months of living with him and Sloane heading back to our home after school most days, I would have been better equipped to deal with that particular situation. However, there was something to be said for 'seeing is believing'. I'd never had to deal with the reality of what Tate and Sloane were doing, because I'd been too wrapped up in what bill was due next or whether I'd washed my sheets in the last month. That ignorance was bliss, and there wasn't an image scorched into the back of my eyelids that I couldn't get rid of.

Reaching into the container to grab a little laundry bubble,

I chased air around the damn thing before pulling it from the shelf only to find it empty. I'd barely turned half way around when I saw movement from the corner of my eye and threw the box at the figure with a yelp of surprise. The very feminine grumble of pain was the only thing I heard over my music, and it forced me to pull out the earphones and drop my hands to my sides.

"Was that really necessary?" Libby asked, pulling her hand from her head and checking for blood.

"Hey, you're the one sneaking up on me here," I said, even though the guilt was eating me alive.

"Right. I guess I am," she mumbled, pulling the bottom corner of her lip and chewing on it as she swung her arms and clapped them together as she started to pace. I watched with interest, my chest rising and falling as we stared at one another and waited for the next words to come. The question was, who from? I thought I had nothing to say to this woman.

"Tate doesn't know I'm here."

I blew my bangs from my face and headed toward the small closet where I stored and hung up anything that needed hanging. I almost wished it was bigger so I could step inside and hide, but there was barely enough room for me to push to my toes and grab the new detergent from the top shelf. "And why are you here, Libby?"

"Because I feel like I should explain."

"About sleeping with a fifteen-year-old boy? Please, do explain it to me, because I'm having a really hard time understanding what the hell you get from the relationship. I can see the appeal for my brother. You're cute. He gets bragging rights—"

"Oh, fuck you, Ayda. You don't know shit."

I spun on my heel and stared her down, but she wasn't looking at me. She was rocked back on her heels, her toes banging together while her hands gripped one of the shelves behind her. She looked as though she was in pain the way she held her lips. There were some days I really hated being as empathetic as I was, because I shouldn't have felt guilty about what I said or for the way she seemed to cringe at the thought of her own response of cussing me out.

"I'm s-sorry. That was out of line, and I didn't mean it. You have every right to be upset, but I need you to know that I like him. Tate, that is. I'm only eighteen, and the girls invited me in to help around the place."

"Wait. You're eighteen?"

"Yeah, but I ain't slept with any of the guys or nothing. I just served drinks so the girls didn't have to. The others said it was like an initiation or something, but it was more like free labor."

"Now that I believe," I said, ripping at the cellophane on the packaging. I continued to work, dropping the bubble at the bottom of the washing machine before starting to pile the clothes on top. I was struggling to find something to say. It was almost as bad as talking to Tate. "Why'd you stick around?"

"I didn't have anywhere else to go. My mom kicked me out, and I was staying with one of the other girls. If I backed out, I had nowhere else to go. So I stayed and did what I had to. The guys were really sweet. Then you showed up, and—"

"Everyone participated in hating me?"

"Something like that."

"What about you and Tate?" I asked, slamming the door and pressing buttons to start the wash. I gave the girl a

105

contemplative look and slipped onto the washer, folding my legs under me. "When did that start and how?"

"When?" She looked up at the ceiling with a small, wistful smile before catching herself and looking back down at me. "A couple days after the fire. He was pretty low and had taken a bottle of bourbon from behind the bar. I found him in the kitchen at two in the morning, hunting for munchies, and we started talking. Next thing I know he's kissing me. Tate's a force of nature, Ayda. I've never known anybody like him. I swore I wasn't going to see him again, but he grabbed me one night and pulled me in his room, and I couldn't say no. You don't see what I see. He's so mature and respectful. He loves to talk about anything, and he knows all this stuff from reading books. He's passionate about everything, including me, and I guess..."

"You're asking me not to stop him from seeing you."

Libby's shoulders slumped, her hands swinging around in front of her as something in her nails was somehow suddenly very interesting.

My brother the heartbreaker... Jesus, I was in trouble with that one. If it wasn't Libby, it would be someone else, someone who wouldn't give a shit how I felt about him screwing them, someone who just wanted to use him as a prize and would think nothing of breaking his heart.

Rolling my eyes, I patted the top of the dryer next to me in a request for her to join me. For a second she looked unsure, but moved anyway, sliding up onto the metal surface and swinging her legs against the front as she leaned back and turned her head to look at me in question.

"I'm taking a stab in the dark here and saying that Tate is just outside. He can't hear us. We both know that, but he's there to step in if needed. Am I right?"

"I told him it was a stupid idea. You're protective, not clinically insane."

"Gee, thanks!" I huffed with a quiet laugh. " And get used to stupid ideas. He has a lot of them."

I picked at nothing on my leg and looked at the girl who seemed to be holding her breath. She obviously liked Tate or she wouldn't have been the one in the room with me. He would have been here yelling and screaming like the child he was. With Tate about to turn sixteen in just under two months, I felt as though eighteen wasn't such a big leap. He was smart, and he was passionate. He wore his heart on his sleeve and still believed he had the world at his fingertips. Maybe he did, which was why this idea of Drew's seemed more and more like a good plan of action.

I wasn't asking Tate to give up a future that he wanted. I understood the draw of the club and even, to an extent, the draw of Libby, but I needed him to see what else was out in the world. I felt obligated to show him the decisions he still had in front of him, not make them for him. Who the hell was I to take away something that he wanted now?

"Tate!" I shouted, throwing a small wink at Libby. She seemed confused. Her eyes were narrowed and focused in my direction as she tried to read me. I wished her the best of luck with that. Tate had been trying to read me for years and he still couldn't figure me out. I was a perfect blend of our parents.

When the door finally opened, I schooled my face into a serious look and raised my eyebrows at him in question. He shuffled deeper inside and pushed his hands into his pockets, a sheepish smile aimed at Libby. Needing to grab his attention, I coughed once.

"What?"

Worked every time. "You know what."

"I really don't, A."

"Yeah. You really do, *T*. Why were you lying to me?"

"I wasn't lying."

"Like hell you weren't," I said, slipping down off the washer and approaching him. I looked up at him and smirked, shaking my head slowly as I finally let my smile show. "You sent a girl to talk to me."

"I know. I figured it would be less awkward and there was a chance you'd listen to her. Because let's face it, you sure as hell wouldn't have listened to me."

"Bullshit."

"Liar. You know you would have talked over me and not listened to a damn word I said."

"That's not fair."

"Like you're an ambassador of fair? Come on, A."

I pushed my lips together in frustration and nodded in agreement. I thought he was being a tad dramatic, but I could see the point he was trying to make. Libby softened the blow and opened up the lines of communication. She'd helped me see sense where Tate would have only incited me to see red. There was no way in hell I was getting that guardian of the year award.

"Just lock your door in the future, and stop fucking stealing bourbon, jackass."

"That's it?"

"You want more?" I asked, folding my arms and narrowing my eyes at him. "I have plenty more where—"

He kissed me on the top of my head quickly, almost shy about the affectionate gesture before he held his hand out to

Libby and backed away slowly. The eyes he shared with Dad were twinkling back at me, full of his usual mischief.

"That's what I thought, turd. Don't go too far, though, T. Drew wants to see you."

"Oh, come on, Ayda."

"Not about this, you brat. Stop whining and go make yourself useful."

Tate nodded as Libby hopped down from the dryer, her eyes flickering between the two of us. She wasn't as stupid as she looked. As much as she knew Drew was probably staying out of their business, she could read the uncertainty in my eyes, the doubt, the fear. I just hoped Tate had the sense to say no where I couldn't.

CHAPTER TWELVE
DREW

It felt like the right time to try to get all this dealt with. I was in no mood to be pacing back and forth over a gang of imitators—ones I was certain I could squash in a minute if I got close enough. I made my way through the club, my swagger a little heavy as I brought my hand up to the bridge of my nose and gave it a pinch. There was a constant, aching tiredness running through me most days—a tiredness which I put down to the fact that I seemed incapable of actually sleeping when I climbed into bed with Ayda every night.

I was becoming a fucking vampire, but I'd be damned if I planned on quitting that shit anytime soon. Thoughts of me pressed against her and inside her were what kept me going. They were also what made me walk around this place with a shit-eating grin most of the time.

Dropping my arm until it swung lazily by my side, I shoved the other hand in my pocket and rounded the corner to go find my woman, but as I did, I was instantly slammed into by a wall of muscle that wasn't far off from matching my own. Stepping back on one foot and pulling my chin back, I leaned away to see Tate muttering an instant apology under his breath.

"Fuck, man, I'm sorry."

I was about to tell him not to sweat it when something—or should I say someone—caught my attention from behind him. I peered around him to take a good look. As soon as I saw the chick whose name I didn't know, I fell back into place and flashed Tate a smirk.

"Do you have a death wish, young blood?"

"What?"

I pointed at the figure hiding behind him.

Tate frowned and pulled the girl closer behind him. "Uh. No. No death wish. Listen, if this is about Libby—"

"Who?"

"Libby," he repeated flatly, nodding behind him at the girl who had just pushed her thumb nail into her mouth and was now staring at the floor.

My laughter tore free, my shoulders bouncing as I spoke. "I don't give a fuck who you're nailing, Tate, but your sister might have a huge problem with it. I can't have Ayda unhappy here, bro. No matter how much I like you."

His eyes shot up to mine as his body sagged. "She's fine. I've just spoken with her. It's all cleared up."

"Ayda's alright with…?" I swished my fingers back and forth, signaling at the two of them with a raised brow.

"Well, I still have my testicles in place, and I can't hear any smashing of plates from the kitchen, so…"

I grinned at him. Despite not exactly wanting to play daddy at just twenty-fucking-nine, I couldn't help but like the kid and get that sense of pride when he did or said something that amused me. "Sounds like you got out of jail for free."

"We'll keep it out of sight, Drew."

"Ain't nothing to do with me. Just don't piss your sister

off any more than you need to. I have to sleep with her at night and let me tell you, I *need* to keep *my* balls in place."

"I can handle that." Tate raised his free hand to scratch the side of his head while Libby kept her eyes to the floor and tried to hide her blush. I'd never noticed her much before, or how young she looked. There was an innocence to her. Seeing those pale green doe eyes that hid behind the curtains of her long brown hair had me wondering how I'd never noticed her before, or at least asked who the fuck had allowed such a girl to hang around in such a fucked up place.

"So, Ayda said you were looking for me."

I gave him a quick nod, cocking my head in the direction of the bar for him to come and take a seat. "I need to have a chat with you about something."

"Okay," he said, seeming a little unsure as he pulled Libby closer to him, forcing them both to take a step forward.

My hand flew up immediately, pressing into his chest as I began to shake my head and say just two words to test him, "Club business."

Tate didn't move for a moment, but his eyes scanned my face with such concentration I felt like I was some kind of fucking lab rat. It was only when he saw I was serious that the same determined eyes from that night at the safe house flashed again. His shoulders straightened, and his chest expanded slowly. The boy who wanted to be a man. The kid who wanted to grow up a little too soon. He was back.

"Club business. Right."

He spun around, grabbing Libby by both shoulders before whispering something in her ear. I had no idea what he was charming her with, but by the look on Libby's face, it was obvious she wasn't too happy with it.

"Be careful," she mouthed at him.

That was my cue to leave. Walking over to the bar, I pulled out a stool and landed my ass on it. I could practically see the adrenaline pumping through his veins and shining out of his wild and determined eyes when he approached.

Tate had more hunger than I'd seen in all the men that passed through these doors. The last fifteen-year-old to want a challenge as much as he did was me, and there was no way I was going to let Ayda suffer the same fate that my family had.

Exhaling slowly, I leaned one arm on the counter, kicked out the stool next to me and told him to take a seat.

"You love this club, Tate?"

"I do, Drew. I really do."

"Then I have a favor to ask of you. A big favor. One that might get you hurt."

There should have been some fear in his eyes. There should have been a shift in the color to his cheeks. There should have at least been a little bit of surprise, but all that shone back was a great big, goofy grin, and I saw a fifteen-year-old version of myself staring back at me. Tate was desperate to be an animal, with no care in the world for the consequences.

Christ. Ayda was fucked.

She stumbled when she saw us both sitting at the bar, my hand on her brother's shoulder as I was giving him my 'I'm trusting you not to fuck this up' look. When I turned to face her fully, there was so much said in our silence, neither one of us having to speak the words as the reality of Tate accepting my proposal sank into her soul.

It was only when Tate twisted his head and saw her standing there that she sprung into action. "Hey, guys, what did I miss?"

Hopping off my stool and running my thumbs around the waistband of my jeans, I fixed on a grin and sighed. "Tate and I were just catching up. Ain't that right, bro?" My hand landed on his shoulder again before I gave it a squeeze and let him go.

She gave me a small smile and closed the distance between us, leaning in to give me a lingering kiss. Tate's snort was hard to miss, and as Ayda pulled away, she nailed him with her smirk. "Careful, kid. Payback's a bitch. Just think about that when you're making out with Libby in front of the club and everyone in it. You don't get to complain anymore."

She slung both of her arms around my neck and pushed her chest against mine with a more genuine smile. It was my second favorite smile of hers.

Curling one arm around her waist, I pulled her as close as I could, forcing my eyes back to her brother as my own smirk grew bigger. "I think this is your cue to get out of here before you see something you won't be able to erase from your mind, T." My wink was lazy, all my attention soon falling to Ayda as my hands moved to grip her hips while my ass perched on the edge of the stool again. "Wanna make him squirm?"

"Always," she whispered with a grin, her teeth worrying her lip mischievously.

"How high can you get your leg?"

"I'm not sure. It's not a theory I've tested before. You want to try now?"

"Over the pool table?" Tilting my head to one side to stare up at her, I waited it out, and I think it took roughly four seconds before I heard Tate cussing behind her.

He was already making a beeline for his room by the time Ayda turned her head to look at him, her head falling back on her shoulders before she laughed. It was short lived, as I'd expected it to be. By the time she was facing me again, her smile was a curl at the corners, and her hands found my shoulders, rubbing gently as she met my eyes.

"Are you completely certain about this?"

I parted my legs, pulling her in between them. "I'm absolutely sure about this. I won't let you down."

"That's not what I'm worried about, Drew."

"But it's what I'm telling you right here, right now. I'll keep him safe. He won't get hurt. Nobody will get hurt. It's just a bunch of messed up teenagers, Ayda. We've got this."

CHAPTER THIRTEEN
Ayda

I still wasn't confident about Tate's involvement in this plan of Drew's, but I had been appeased. Before we fell asleep, he walked me through every detail, completely upfront about anything that could possibly go wrong and the risks to Tate if something should go balls up, which he assured me it wouldn't.

I'd spent so much time mulling it over, I wasn't able to get much sleep for the second night in a row. My good mood was dwindling and my patience was wearing thin. The tiny fissures in my normally cheerful demeanor became huge cracks when I found all the coffee gone. Some asshole had taken the last cup and left the burner on to caramelize the dribbles because they were too lazy to make another pot. It was something that brought about some of my more colorful, less than flattering vocabulary.

"Okay, slugger, you and I need a day trip."

I turned around to face Deeks. One of his thumbs was hooked through a belt loop on his jeans, and the other hand was holding a beer glass full of orange juice. The small smile that was hidden behind his beard told me he'd heard my slew of expletives.

"Don't you mess with my emotions now, Deeks…"

"I'm serious, sugar. You need some air, and I know just the place for you to get some. Go get something warmer on and meet me at my bike."

He didn't have to ask me twice. As much as I loved living in The Hut, there were days I just needed some extra space to gather my thoughts together, and that wasn't always possible, not even in the little haven Drew built for me. There was always noise going on somewhere. Half of the men in the place were nocturnal, after all. Pair all of that with lack of sleep and the worry playing at the back of my mind at this business with Tate, and even I could admit I was a mess.

Dressed in layers with a smile on my lips from the goodbye I'd just shared with Drew, I bounced down the steps of the porch and headed to where Deeks was studying his bike, his thumb firmly rubbing the point of his chin before smoothing the hair again. He didn't bother looking up when I approached. He simply picked up a spare helmet and tossed it in my direction before pulling on the facemask to protect himself from the brisk wind. The printed skeletal jaw was a little creepy, but it was one of those things you got used to. Swinging his leg over the bike, he fired it up and tipped his head in the direction of the seat behind him. Out of all the bikes in the pack, Deeks' was probably my second favorite. He had a *Heritage Softtail*, which also came with a backrest for the passenger. As much as I loved riding on Drew's brand new blacked out *Sportster Iron*, it was nice to know I wasn't about to be flung from the back if I had an itch on my nose. It also meant I could sit back and not crowd Deeks while he rode. There was something intimate about being pushed up against someone like that. The first and only time I'd ridden with Kenny it had been more than apparent that it was no longer an option.

The growl of the bike coming to life was one of those sounds I was always going to love. The vibrations of all that power sitting beneath you gave you a rush of adrenaline and a promise, and it was easy to see why these guys loved their machines as much as they did.

Texas in November was chilly. It got colder the farther north you went. Deeks and I had only been riding for an hour, but my thighs and cheeks were numb by the time he turned off onto a narrow country lane. Most of it was dirt, forcing Deeks to navigate the terrain slowly as he avoided potholes and puddles. When we emerged from the wall of trees and dust, I sucked in a breath of surprise. We might as well have been in another world. Sitting in the middle of a plot of land was a beautiful and well-kept double wide that had been well loved and expanded over the years. There was a wraparound porch with hanging plants draping over the edges like waterfalls, and the yard was mesmerizing. The fairy garden that ran along the edge of the forest backing onto the property was elaborate and stunning.

I tapped Deeks on the shoulder with numb hands as he pulled up next to a beat-up Jeep. "Where are we?"

Deeks was still in the process of removing his gloves and mask when the sound of the screen door's creaky hinges caught my attention, and I saw Autumn hopping down the porch steps with a bright smile on her lips—one that was now matching mine.

"Well ain't this a pleasant surprise?" she said, sweeping me into a hug before I could swing my leg over to get off the motorcycle.

"Damn, woman, be careful of the bike," Deeks huffed,

gripping the handlebars to keep it upright.

"Oh, hush, baby. Selene could survive an apocalypse."

"Selene?" I asked, still caught up in the hug, my body at a weird angle. I turned my head to look at Deeks, who was more amused than pissed off.

"That's his bike, darlin'. He won't admit he gave her a name to anyone else, but you're family so you get all the good gossip."

"Why Selene?"

"She was a goddess, said to be the embodiment of the moon."

"Makes sense."

"That's what I said." Autumn looped her arm through mine and swung back to link her other through Deeks'. "Y'all come on inside. I have some fresh brewed iced tea, some coffee, and I've made cornbread."

"Baby, I told you we weren't gonna be here long," Deeks said, kissing the top of her head and reaching forward to open the door for us both.

"Are you telling me you can't escape that clubhouse of yours for the day?"

"The *Hut*," Deeks said with emphasis, kissing her temple and heading toward the kitchen, "ain't the problem. This one's old man said not too long."

The moment he was around the corner, I looked to Autumn and raised my eyebrows. Maybe it was one of those things I'd never thought much about, but she'd seemingly hit a nerve calling The Hut something else.

"What was that all about?"

"All what, honey?"

"The Hut stuff."

"Oh, that. It's all about traditions, baby girl. The boys who started up this charter built it from the ground up. The Hut started out as just that, four walls and a lot of liquor, and a porch to put their feet up. As their club grew, so did The Hut, but the name became significant, part of the history, and it stuck."

"Because that's what it will always be to those of us who were there in the beginning," Deeks said, stepping around the corner. "At the end of the day, whether it's sentimentality or not, The Hut is The Hut, and that's the end of it. Now feed me, woman."

Autumn rolled her eyes, but her affectionate smile was as genuine as they came. She loved Deeks, all his strange little habits and all. It was something I was beginning to understand. Knowing Drew and where he came from gave me a deeper comprehension and a higher tolerance for the things I didn't understand.

As it turned out, Autumn made some amazing cornbread, but that wasn't the reason Deeks had driven me out there. Nor was it to get more stories from his woman. It turned out that they owned a large parcel of land, as well as horses, cows, dirt bikes, and some four wheelers. It was like a playground of grown-up toys, all hidden in a barn in the forest behind their house. Deeks didn't like leaving Autumn alone with things people would find useful, not that he had much to worry about. The moment I walked into the house, my eyes were drawn to the rack of guns in the corner of the dining room.

Deeks saddled us a couple of horses and led me out of the barn and into the forest. He looked as comfortable on them as he did his bike. The only difference seemed to be that he traded in his helmet for a Stetson, which suited him almost as much. He pointed out boundaries and routes and let me lead, trailing behind to give the impression I was alone. Deeks was as intuitive as he was smart, and I didn't put up a fight.

Whether I'd known it or not, it was exactly what I needed. It was a different kind of breeze in my face and power between my thighs. The palomino with dark feet and ears seemed at ease as she led the way into the trees. Her head was bobbing up and down as she stepped surely on a path she'd probably taken a hundred times in her life. I felt every breath she took, her ribs pushing against my thighs as her ears swiveled and flicked.

I don't know when all the tension left me, or when I was deemed approachable, but Deeks trotted up beside me on his horse, aptly named Harley, and slowed down to keep pace.

"Feeling better?"

"Much, thanks, Deeks." I smiled at him and looked out over a large pasture that emerged beyond the trees. "How often do you come up here?"

"More than you think, sugar. I have two homes—one with Autumn, one with my brothers. It's okay to step away sometimes, sweetheart. It don't mean you're not loyal or that you ain't happy. It just shows you're human. I wanted to bring you here because you need that escape, too, and Autumn and I always have a room for you up here if you need it."

"I couldn't impose like that."

"Don't be ridiculous. You think I would invite you if I didn't mean it? This is my best kept secret."

"I can see why," I said, grinning over at him. "Thank you."

"It's not an easy life, Ayda. Ask Autumn about that. But if you love Drew, you're in it for the long haul. You're gonna need to clear your head sometimes, and this always works for me. If you see my bike out front when you pull up, though…"

I raised my hand and shook my head. "You don't even have to say it."

"Thank fuck for that. It was getting awkward."

We rode together in silence for a while. The horses were familiar with each other, and it was obvious in the way they veered into one another and instigated little nips and bumps of shoulders. I thought a lot about what he'd said, about the club, the life I was choosing for myself, and some of the history that he'd mentioned in the kitchen with Autumn.

There were certain topics that Drew didn't hit on. I don't even think he was aware that he avoided them most of the time. I was just steered away and left reeling like I'd been derailed without much effort. That didn't mean I didn't have questions, and poor Deeks was about to be my cornucopia of knowledge.

"Deeks?"

"Yeah."

"What's the deal with The Hut?"

"Oh, not you as well," he groaned with a smile playing on his lips.

"No, I just mean why not call it the cabin or the shack?"

"Blame Eric, kid. His mother was British and fell in love with a ranch hand. Eric spent so much time with her, he had names for shit we'd never use, words that stuck with all of us. The Hut was one of those words. He was the man in charge of the build so we all fell under his wing. I didn't think much of it really. I left after we finished building the place. I was still a bit of a nomad in those days. Settling wasn't something that spiked my curiosity. Not until I met Autumn."

"By Eric, you mean…?"

Deeks shifted in his saddle, the leather creaking under him as he rubbed Harley's neck with the flat of his palm. He was uncomfortable going on, that was obvious, but I could see the resolution in his eyes. He wasn't going to leave me hanging.

"Tucker. Eric Tucker."

"Drew's father?"

Deeks nodded, but I knew that was all I was going to get. His loyalty was solid as a rock, and any questions I had would have to be directed elsewhere. I knew he felt as though he'd said too much already, and I wanted to let him off the hook.

"Well, that explains a lot."

Deeks looked over at me, but my only response was a wink, which earned me an indignant huff of disgust.

I started laughing as I gathered the reins in my hand. My body leaned forward to run my hand over the horse's shoulder as it looked longingly out over the grass. The need to run was twitching under her muscles and had her rocking from one foot to the other.

"Deeks?"

"Yeah?"

"Race you!"

With a tap of my heel, all the air left the horse's lungs and the jerk of her taking off shifted me in the saddle, forcing a yip of excitement from me. Deeks gave a verbal command, and the huff of his horse was the only indication he was game as the thunder of hoofs drowned out the thoughts I wasn't able to escape.

Clarity was a beautiful thing. With the small piece of freedom I'd managed to find thanks to Deeks, everything else fell into perspective. Did I trust Tate not to fuck this up? No. I didn't. He was fifteen, cocky, and full of attitude. The one thing I did know was that I trusted Drew to watch out for him. I trusted the pack to stop the mess from going too far, and I believed him when he said they wouldn't let anything happen to Tate. As the peace began to settle, the nagging receded, but it wouldn't leave completely. Maybe it never would.

CHAPTER FOURTEEN
DREW

Two days had passed since my conversations with Ayda and Tate. The whole club had been made aware of the plans that were going to take place at any moment. It could take a day, a week or maybe even a month, but when the little boys wanted to play, we were ready to play.

When Jedd came charging into the bar, his hand holding onto the doorframe as he huffed out a breath and gave me a nod, I knew his tip off had spotted the youths. It was time to go.

Ayda's body, which had previously been wrapped around me from behind, deflated quickly. I didn't miss the hitch in her throat, and I definitely didn't miss the way she suddenly seemed to forget about everything and everyone in the room except her brother. She fell away from me slowly, her eyes following Tate as he came to life in front of everyone.

Throwing his big gray hoodie up over his head, he dug his hands into the front pockets and flashed his girl, Libby, a wink, with a brand-new swagger to the way he walked suddenly appearing from nowhere. He didn't look at Ayda. I wouldn't have, either, if I'd been him.

Turning around, I grabbed both her cheeks, brushing my

thumbs over the apples of them before I kissed her softly. She didn't kiss me back. Her mouth stayed numb like the rest of her, as though she couldn't really see anything anymore. Pulling away, I trailed a finger over her bottom lip before I leaned in closer and whispered, "On my life."

Then I was gone, Deeks taking my place as Ayda's comforter while me, Jedd, Slater, Kenny and Tate hopped into the yard, over to the van.

Slater took the driver's seat, the rest of us on the two benches that ran along each wall in the back. Tate didn't look nervous. In fact, he looked like a kid the night before Christmas, and when Kenny got out the kit he needed and began to separate all the wires and mics for the job, the twenty questions started. *What's this do? Where does that go? Oh, man, I can't believe it. I'm so fucking pumped!*

I gave him a quick glare, playing the role of the parent in Ayda's absence and silently chastising him for his language. Not that I gave a shit—I just knew she was doing her best to knock it out of him where and when she could, so I wasn't going to encourage him.

When the van crawled along in the darkness, pulling up alongside some thick trees, Kenny and Tate got around to testing the equipment out.

Jedd sat opposite, his jaw tense as he clasped his hands between his parted knees and glanced up at me. All I could do was smirk back at him and shrug. The kid wanted a baptism of fire, and we were going to give him one, for the second time around.

"All set?" Slater called back, clearing his throat before switching the engine off completely and knocking out the lights.

"Just about," Kenny croaked, his lip between his teeth in concentration as he pulled Tate's hood up over his head and patted him down to make sure no wires could be seen bulging through the material of his clothes.

"Come on, let's get this done already." Tate bounced his knees up and down, flexing the muscles in his arms as he expanded his chest and tried to show each and every one of us just how manly he was. Jedd's eyes met mine again, and I saw it there—recognition of the similarities between how I had been at the kid's age, and how Tate was then.

Shuffling to the doors, I grabbed the handle and paused, pressing one hand to Tate's chest and speaking quietly. "You remember what we said, don't you? Jedd will be a few steps behind you. He's not wearing his cut, so he won't get recognized that way, but he'll be there if you need him. Just do what Kenny told you and keep communication open. Clear your throat, sniff loudly, then clear your throat again. That's the key for us to get on your ass quick. That's all it takes. This isn't about you taking anyone down single-handedly. This is about you finding out what the fuck they think they're doing in our town, then we can find a calm, not so bloody way of convincing them to stop." I paused, thinking about what Ayda told me that little scumbag had done and said to her. "And the one your sister said was called Elbow, get close to him. If what she said is true, he's gonna be the one doing all the talking. He'll have the most to say."

Tate nodded along and then we waited it out until Slater leaned back in his seat and spoke up. "Group of youths up ahead, just like our tip off said. Looks like eight of them. No, wait." The van went quiet, waiting for him to finish. "Seven. One's a girl."

"Even better." I grinned sardonically at the kid. "Do-or-die time, brother. Do-or-die time."

"Let me loose. I'm ready."

Without saying anything else, I flung one door open, hopping out before I guided him down. Reaching inside for the bottle of water we'd brought along, I poured some into my palm before rubbing it over his forehead, across his cheeks and around his neck. Kenny had told me the places to avoid the wires, so when I tipped water down Tate's back to replicate sweat, I was as careful as I could be before tapping him on the shoulder and telling him he was good to go.

Jedd climbed out of the van slowly, his head shaking as we both watched Tate start jogging on the spot, his head rotating as though he was warming up for another Friday night game. His knees came up high in quick spurts before he slapped both his thighs and let out a small growl.

"Fucking hell, quit bouncing around. You'll dislodge the fucking things," Kenny growled quietly from the back of the van. I knew tonight was tough for him, too. He'd grown close to Tate. He was as worried as Ayda.

"Sorry, man," Tate answered in a rush of breath.

"Go on, young blood. Get going," Jedd commanded. Tate took off around the side of the van, his jog slow and controlled, his body feigning fatigue as he tried to look like he'd been on his run for hours. Jedd waited a good thirty seconds before he stepped out after him, wearing a long, dark trench coat and some creepy as hell hat on his head that made him look like a resident sexual harasser, rather than a Hound. Not that some folk around Babylon would see much difference between the two.

I climbed back into the van and made my way into the

passenger seat beside Slater, leaving Kenny where he could concentrate on all the technical shit.

"Are you still set on not letting me kill them for what they did to Pete's grave?" Slater muttered quietly, his eyes facing forward as his arms crossed his chest.

"All in good time, Slate. All in good time."

It didn't take long for Tate to approach them, and from behind, he really did look like a towering form of a man. All I could do now was watch, wait, listen and above all else, hope.

Kenny fiddled around in the back before he leaned over and shoved an ear bud in my ear and one in Slater's. "You guys listen in. If I hear them talking smack to the kid I won't be able to stop myself from getting out of here and showing them what it really means to be a fucking Hound."

"Is this the loudest it will g—" I was asking when a rustling of material against the mic rang into my ears, mixed with a heavy wheezing breath. "Got it," I said, leaning back in my seat and narrowing my eyes on the events up the road.

"Hey," Tate shouted out breathlessly. "Hey, hold up!"

No answer came. There was no sound of anything other than his clothes rubbing against him and his feet slowing to a more even pace. The group of youths were walking away, Tate following them and holding out an arm as he came up to one of the kids at the back and grabbed him by the shoulder.

The silence took over again, and I watched from afar as the whole gang turned around slowly, looking at Tate like he had three heads, or at the very least, a thing for group beat downs. The kid he had hold of shrugged him off, turning to face him fully before Tate pushed both his hands into the front pocket of his hoodie and bowed his head.

Just like I'd told him to.

Perfect.

"The fuck are you?" one of them challenged, his voice barely broken, but his manly bravado on show for all to see.

"Doesn't matter who I am," Tate answered, making his breaths ragged. "I just need something."

"A towel?" the girl squeaked from somewhere, giggling wildly as Slater and I rolled our eyes at each other.

"No," breathed Tate.

"Look, we don't give a shit what you need, dick. We ain't no running club. You don't just come up to us like we're fucking nothing. You hear me? Don't you know who we are?" the same guy challenged again.

"I do. I see it. You're—"

"What. We're what?" he said, pushing Tate's shoulder roughly.

"Stop," came a command from one of the other guys. This one was older. His voice sounded like it had gotten stuck on broken glass when escaping, but even from in the van, you could practically feel the respect from the others who surrounded him. That's when I knew whoever we were watching step up to Tate, he was the piece of work that thought he was in command of my town. My lazy smile instantly broke free.

"Elbow, get back, I can handle this," the first boy responded.

"No, Mikey. I got this one."

"Listen, I ain't looking for trouble. I can see who y'all are," Tate answered quickly, and for a split second, I couldn't tell if the wobble in his voice was just good acting or his first real show of fear. "I'm not into messing with that kind of shit."

"No?" Elbow drew out, pulling up to a stand in front of

him. "Then what kind of shit are you into messing with?"

"Drugs," Tate responded flatly, and even from afar, I could see the rise of his body as he bounced on the balls of his feet. "I need a hit of something and—"

Elbow laughed, throwing his head back as his body turned around in a circle, allowing him to put on the best show he could for his supposed crew before he stepped up into Tate's face again. "Drugs? Ain't ya a little bit clean cut to be snorting and injecting shit?" Elbow reached out to pinch at the material of Tate's hoodie and I heard Slater hold his breath as we both realized that was where one of the wires fell back.

I sat upright, leaning over my knees as I waited to see what happened, preparing myself to have that kid's ass for breakfast if I needed to. I really didn't want that to happen. Our reputation in this town was already screwed without adding child cruelty to our list of fuck ups.

"I used to be," Tate sighed back, "But I've got a big game on Friday night, and I'm hiding a shoulder injury. If I don't get something, I'm fucked. The whole town is fucked! One tackle and we're talking broken bones. I heard that…" He swallowed down, sucking in a big breath before pushing it back out. "I heard that you Hounds were protective of your town, that you liked to make sure things ran the way they should and that people should be kept happy. I need to win this game to keep folks in good spirits. I need to stay on the team. I thought you could hook me up with something, anything. I don't care what it is, just something that will take the pain away and let me play."

"That's what you heard about the Hounds of Babylon?" The humor and sarcasm in Elbow's voice was evident. "I think someone's been lying to you at bedtime, brother."

"What?" Tate asked.

"I said, dumbass, that whoever gave you that little piece of information is wrong. We help no one. This is our town and we, along with the MC that we belong to, own everything about all of y'all. You're ours to play with as we see fit. You're ours to fuck over, to ruin, to use as our little gophers. You get what I'm saying, twitchy?" Elbow reached up to jab Tate on the shoulder again, causing him to falter back just a step before he righted himself and puffed his chest out.

"No. No, I don't, and I don't want a history lesson. I just want some drugs, so if you can point me to where I need to go, I'd really appreciate it." Tate's voice had taken on a new kind of firmness, and in any other circumstance, the boy in front of him would be on his ass in three seconds flat.

However, he was being patient—something else I'd told him to be.

Good man.

"Move the fuck along," Mikey practically yawned from beside his buddy. "We haven't got anything to brighten up your day, so keep on jogging."

"I know you're lying to me," Tate muttered. "You're the Hounds. I've heard all the stories. The Hounds deal in drugs, or they used to or some shit, I don't know. I just... need... a hit."

"You need a hit?" Elbow asked, taking a step closer until there was nowhere else for him to go.

Shit.

I was about to get ready to jump out when a figure to the right of the group caught my eye, and Jedd started to cross the road. His hands were deep in his pockets, his head down and his beard in a hair tie as he tried to look like any old regular passerby. For a moment, it worked, all heads turning to him before focusing back on Tate.

Tate's swallow could be heard in the microphone before he answered Elbow. "Yeah, I need a hit."

"You asked for it." Elbow swung his arm back, his fist obviously aiming directly at Tate's face, until the night skies filled with flashing lights of blue and red from around the corner, and the sirens that hadn't been there before suddenly cried out in the air.

As if right on cue, the police car tore down the street, aiming straight for the kids we'd just had exactly where we wanted them, and I knew our mission was done and fucked before it had ever really begun. My shoulders sagged in defeat, my eyes on the gang of youths as they all turned their heads quickly and took off in different directions—all except the one who Tate had managed to grab hold of by his fake cut and hold in place.

Elbow.

Damn!

"What the fuck is he doing?" I cried at Slater.

"I. Have. No. Idea," Slater whispered.

"Dammit!" My hands flew down on the dashboard in front of me, my foot swinging and kicking at anything that was resting in the footwell. "*DAMMIT!*"

"Shh," Slater snapped back, holding a hand up to me so he could listen. If Tate hadn't been standing there with some punk kid in his grip and a cop car parking right beside him, I would have smacked my brother up the side of his head and told him that if he shushed me one more time, I'd be reminding his face what my fist felt like. None of that seemed important as I looked forward again and watched as Howard

Sutton got out of his car.

Elbow tried to fight his way out of Tate's grip, tugging, twisting and eventually shrugging out of his cut before taking off as quickly as he could like he had death on his tail.

"Tate Hanagan," Sutton said slowly. My eyes scanned the road for any sign of Jedd, and when I spotted him standing in Sutton's peripheral vision, I knew what he was thinking of doing. If he chose to take out the chief, we were all screwed.

Tate cleared his throat once, sniffed, then waited. Not that we could have gone to him anyway. We were statues, fixed in place because he'd decided it was a good idea to grab a hold of that little Elbow prick.

Standing before the chief, he dropped the cut in his hands behind him, the blinding lights of the police car flashing all around and providing enough of a distraction for Sutton to have not seen what he'd thrown to the ground.

"Evening, Chief," he answered politely, stepping up to him before he walked around, forcing Sutton to follow him in a half circle until Sutton's back was now turned on the leather on the ground, and that's when I slowly began to sit up, and the realization of what Tate was doing hit me a minute or two too late.

Sutton shook his head, slamming both his feet down, shoulder-width apart, before he hooked his thumbs into his belt and rocked back and forth on his heels. "Quite the little troublemaker these days, ain't ya, boy?"

"No, sir. I'm just minding my own business, out on a run."

"That's not what it looked like to me. That was quite a scene you were about to make, right there. I should arrest you for disturbing the peace."

"I..."

"I should have known you were connected to everything that's been going on around here lately."

"You've got it all wrong."

"Is this what you've become now, Hanagan? Looking up to your step daddy for guidance? Fighting in the street late at night? You're more of a waster than I ever even thought."

Fucking *step daddy*.

"Chief, I'd really appreciate it if you didn't talk about me that way. I haven't done anything wrong. I've done nothing that you can arrest me for. I'd just like to go home."

Sutton laughed roughly. "Despite what you and your biker friends think, y'all can't do what you like in my town. You do what I tell you. And right now, you're going to get in the back of my car so we can have a little civilized chat. You got that?"

Tate reached up to scratch his chest hard, immediately causing the ruffling of the material to make way too much noise for either of us to be able to hear anything. My face creased up as I pulled it away quickly, hovering it over my ear as I waited for him to take his hand from it, but he never did. He didn't once stop scratching at his damn chest.

"He's fading us out," Slater warned, sitting upright again and positioning his hand over the key in the ignition. "He's going dark, Drew."

"Which means he's about to do something really fucking stupid," I growled back, both hands moving to the door handle as I got ready to jump out.

Just like that, it all happened quickly again. One minute Tate was toe-to-toe with the chief of police, the next, Sutton had taken a punch to the jaw and Tate was running.

He was running in the opposite direction of us, shouting

down into the mic on his chest. "Get the cut. Get the fucking cut! There's something on there you need to see."

Then his wires were ripped off and thrown to the ground, the air filling with shrieking sirens again as Sutton mowed Tate into a corner and all the plans and promises I'd made to Ayda suddenly went to shit.

My head hit the dashboard hard as my shaking hands gripped hold of it and I roared as loudly as I could.

"*FUCKING* kids!"

CHAPTER FIFTEEN
AYDA

It was the longest night of my life. From the moment Tate was ushered out the door, I found myself pacing while everyone else went about their business as usual. Only Deeks seemed to understand my agitation, and he was sitting on a stool at the bar, nursing a beer as he watched me walk from one side of the room to the other.

No matter how many times I looked at the clock, the hands didn't seem to be moving. They barely inched to the next number on every pass, until it felt as though it was going backward.

"Why haven't we heard anything yet?" I demanded, stopping and spinning to face Deeks. He froze, his beer halfway up to his mouth, his eyes fixed on me like I was a wild animal about to pounce. He wasn't that far off the mark. The uncertainty that bounced around inside of me was almost too much for one person to deal with. I was beginning to understand why people put their fists through walls. The energy that was building up inside of me had nowhere to go.

"Just sit down and drink a beer. You're not helping matters."

"Drinking a beer isn't going to help anything, Deeks. Should I call them? Kenny always has his phone on him, right? Maybe I could call him and he could give me an update or something?"

"No."

"Why?"

"You don't know what the hell's going on, Ayda. Just give them time to get it done."

"But—" The syllable had barely finished when my phone started singing to me from my back pocket. Hopping forward and twisting awkwardly, I slipped my hand inside and dragged it free, sliding the bar over the bottom of the screen as quickly as I could before finally getting a good enough grip on it to hold it to my ear.

"This is Ayda."

"Ah, Miss Hanagan, I knew it was only a matter of time until I was calling you in this capacity."

My heart stopped in my throat as I froze on the spot. I would know Sutton's voice anywhere. His forced twang made him sound like a Wyatt Earp wannabe. It was the one thing that drove me crazy about him, even when we got along.

"Sorry, Chief, I'm already taken," I said, unable to stop the snide comeback. The condescending tone he used was like dangling a New York strip in front of a starved lion. He was pushing my buttons, and I was responding in turn, even though I knew it would only bring more trouble.

"Glad to see you still have your sense of humor," he said with a smug tone. He started to talk again, but the words were lost as the door to The Hut opened and Drew came bursting in with Slater and Jedd on his heels. "...So we hauled your delinquent brother to jail."

Kenny followed them in next, all the eyes on me as the door slammed home behind them.

"Can you repeat that, Chief?"

"Tate assaulted a police officer. He's in real trouble, and as his guardian—"

"I'll be right there."

I'm not sure how I managed to hang up the phone, but the weight of it brought it down to my side as I met Drew's eyes across the room. All the promises and reassurances I'd been fed since I'd seen the little assholes in the cemetery came floating to the forefront of my mind.

I broke eye contact first, mine moving to my phone in my hand and up to Deeks, who looked as though he was stuck between a rock and a hard place. Two sets of loyalties and he had no idea which side he needed to come down on. I wasn't going to force him to go against his brothers in the middle of The Hut, so I did the only thing I could. I walked away toward the room that I shared with Drew. I needed to get my hoodie, shoes and bag so I could bail my fifteen-year-old brother out of jail.

I should have known he wouldn't just leave me alone to collect my thoughts and not do anything I'd come to regret. It was Drew, after all. He didn't know anything about timing or sensitivity when it came to him wanting his own way.

Following me until I started picking up my shoes, he blocked the doorway completely, his intense stare practically burning holes into my back until he found the nerve to speak.

"Ayda, talk to me."

"Not now, Drew." I tripped over a pair of work boots and cussed up a storm as I stumbled into the dresser and stubbed my toe. Even the shocking pain that started in my bone and radiated outwards wasn't enough to distract me from my emotions. My free hand pushed my hair back from my face before I knocked all the clean laundry aside to pull the first warm thing I could find from it.

"Now is as good a time as any."

"Not really. I have to go and bail my kid brother out of jail while that smug bastard, Sutton, lectures me and threatens to call CPS. So, no, now is not as good a time as any." I pulled the sweater over my head and yanked it right off again as the club patch winked at the world from my chest. I dug deeper and found something a little more neutral and tried to ignore the man who was staring daggers at me.

He took a step forward, stopping and obviously sensing the big do-not-approach barrier I'd put around myself, but he was unable to stop the soft, frustrated sigh that left his lips. "You know I have no idea how to handle this, or you, or... any of it, right now. I know you're blaming me, but we need to talk about this."

"You promised me, Drew," I said, turning to face him as I pulled my leg up behind me and slipped on one of my sneakers. "You had so much to say in the way of reassurance. Now, when I need you, you're speechless. Thank you for that pearl of wisdom."

His sudden burst of sarcastic laughter caught me off guard. "I never once claimed to hold any pearls of wisdom, Ayda. What I did promise you was that he wouldn't get hurt. He didn't get hurt. Jedd was right there. We were all right there, ready and waiting. We didn't know Tate was going to switch up the plans, smack the chief of police, and run."

It was my turn to offer a humorless laugh. Pulling on my other shoe and spinning around in a circle, I found myself running out of steam, and both of my hands raised to my face, the heels of them pushing into my eyes as I tried to gather my thoughts. "You don't get it, do you? This is hurting him, Drew. This will go on his record. This has the ability to take the offers of a scholarship off the table. The kid can play ball. He has a natural talent, and he has the world in his hands."

I held my hands out in front of me for a moment before dropping them to my sides and shaking my head. I was wrong. This wasn't Drew's fault. It had never been. It was all on me. I'd agreed when I'd known better.

"I have to go."

"I'll make sure this doesn't affect his future. I'm not going to let this go on any record of his, despite what you think. There are ways around all that shit. Just let me come with you, and we can talk about this on the way there. Don't shut me out now."

"Sutton would just love that," I said, pushing my hands on my hips. "Please, tell me what happened? Why was Sutton even there?"

"I wish I knew. Pure chance? A tip-off? He's tailing us more than we ever figured? He got there at the wrong time. Jedd was about to dive in and pull Tate away from those kids. I was ready. Everything was going okay. Then fucking Sutton just appeared from nowhere, and whether you choose to see this right now or not, your little brother had a stroke of genius. He stood his ground to help the club out. He went beyond what I asked him to do, what I believed he would do. Was I naïve as fuck to think he would listen to me and not act like a cowboy? No shit. Did I have any damn clue that he was going to try and knock Sutton out to distract him away from the rest of us, so we could pick up one of those kid's cuts that he threw to the ground? No way in hell. If I could have gotten to him, I would have, but me jumping in between Tate and the chief would have just turned a bonfire into a fucking inferno, and we both know it."

"What the hell do those shitty, rip-off cuts have to do with anything? And why the hell would Tate hit Sutton to distract from them? Jesus, if you say to prove they're not real, I'm going to lose my shit, Drew."

"Lose your shit with who? Me? Because I didn't ask Tate to get any damn leather off of anyone's back for me. That was his choice to make," he answered with a little more force, the agitation in his voice becoming more and more evident as he ignored my question completely.

"Right. That tells me all I need to know then." I grabbed my bag and headed to the door, stopping when I felt him follow me. "Just don't, Drew. Let me go and do this. Let me cool off and talk to Tate. If you're with me, it's only going to turn into a bigger fight, and I can't do that with you right now. Go tell the rest of the boys what you found out and just leave me be."

His hand reached up to grab the top of my arm, spinning me halfway around to look at him, leaving me with no option but to stare up at the obvious hurt and anger he was wearing on his face. "Is that what you really want?" he whispered, the muscles in his jaw twitching as he waited.

Is that what I wanted? No. It wasn't. But the battle I was about to face with Sutton couldn't be won with him at my side. Sutton loathed him and now me, and if I continued to argue with him, I would make a fool of myself. What I wanted was to go back four hours and call the whole thing off. I didn't have that option, though. All I had was how I felt then and there and the destruction it was whipping up inside of me. When I had Tate out of jail, I was pretty sure there was a chance I could be a little more objective. I just needed to get out of The Hut. I needed to breathe.

"I need to get my brother. Please respect that."

Drew released me instantly, his hands dropping down by his sides before he gave me a short, sharp nod, and I saw the shadows that used to live there return once again.

I pulled the door out of my way, unable to look back at him and see that darkness resonating, but I faltered as I started to swing around the doorframe and stopped to look back inside. "I do love you, Drew. I just need to do this alone. I need time."

Drew thrust his hands in his pockets, the disappointment radiating from him as he rolled his shoulders inward and looked down. Then it was me who was stuck between that rock and hard place. I wanted to stay and talk to him. I wanted to understand, but I needed to go to Tate, and I needed some time to myself before I lost it completely and got myself landed in jail beside him.

CHAPTER SIXTEEN
DREW

The confusion was almost as insufferable as the disappointment. I'd fucked up with the one thing I knew she could never lose, and Tate was in a place that none of us had ever expected him to be. I should have handled them the way I once would have. I should have stormed in there, nailed the little shits to a tree and put the fear of God up their asses, but I was trying to do the right fucking thing for once. My second shot at life had to go right. I wanted everything to happen the right way. I was trying to change what I stood for. Thought before reaction. Words before violence. A new kind of power.

But Ayda had walked away from me.

Moving on instinct, I marched forward to follow her, but her parting words of *I need time* rang in my ears painfully, forcing me to stop as soon as she left. Time away from me was the one thing I didn't want her to have.

Just a few weeks before, I'd have made her stop. I'd have grabbed her and pinned her down, thrown her over my shoulder or marched her to where I wanted her to be. Only I found that impossible now. I respected her too much for that.

I fucking loved her too much for that.

I stood in the doorway for far too long, my eyes fixed

on the floor as all the negative thoughts in my head began to conjure up that ball of rage in the pit of my stomach. Every muscle along my jaw twitched, every vein in my arms throbbed as I pumped my fists in my pockets over and over again.

Even the sound of heavy boots working their way towards me couldn't force me to lift my head.

"Slater just filled me in on what happened," Harry muttered, coming to an abrupt stop in front of me as he blew out a heavy breath and let the silence linger. "Wasn't your fault, son."

My nostrils flared, hoping a small nod of feigned acceptance would appease him.

"Drew."

"I know, Harry. I know."

"Just the wrong place at the wrong time, brother. It's happened to us all. We can't control everything and everyone around here."

Slowly looking up, I rolled my jaw back and forth and waited to find something to say from the dusty corners in the back of my mind. The flames of rage were licking at the skin on my legs, up my arms, across my chest, and the most hidden, deepest parts of my being wanted to smash something to pieces, just to regain control.

Harry nodded behind him, his eyes fixed on mine as he turned sideways. "Let's go get you a drink and wait this out."

"I need to get out."

"And go where?" he asked, the last word getting stuck in the back of his throat, forcing his hand to smack down on his chest as he began to cough.

"Anywhere."

"Running isn't going to help here, Drew. First and foremost, that girl of yours is a mother. She might not have given birth to that boy of hers, but believe me, she is a mother. Anything she's said to you in here isn't what she means. That's her instincts kicking in, her need to protect her cub. They're all the same."

I exhaled slowly, bringing my hands up to my face and scrubbing roughly. "I don't give a shit what she said to me. They're just words. I fuck those things up every single day. It was the look she wore, Harry—the promises I broke and the disappointment in her eyes. I can't ignore those. I'm…"

"You're what?"

"I'm not used to that, and I'm not sure I can do this to her. My life ain't ever gonna change. She's too fucking good for all of us, and you, me, the club, the entire population of Babylon all know it."

"Stop," he commanded, but I ignored him, pushing past his shoulder carefully and making my way over to the desk. Walking around to the bookcase and pulling a stack of keys out, I flipped through them until I found the one I wanted. "Don't go down this road, brother. Ayda is lost without you, even when you're only a room away from her. She needs you right now."

"Does she?" I scoffed, not meaning to sound as much of a dick as I did. Throwing my arms out to the side, I gestured around the room and shook my head. "Then why am I here, while she's chosen to go through Hell without me?"

Harry's smirk grew. "Because she's scared that the two of you will say or do something you'll regret, and the thought of losing you is almost as scary as the thought of her brother going to prison. I'm guessing she can't have those two nightmares running side by side tonight and have any hope of surviving."

My hand ran down over my mouth slowly before I rubbed my lips together and marched forward towards my only exit, my keys in hand. "I'm no good at this."

"Do you love her?" he asked, spinning on his feet and forcing me to stop as my boots hit the threshold of my room.

Straightening my shoulders, I kept my back to him and answered without any hesitation. "Yes."

"And does she know?"

I scowled hard, my head turning over one side to glance his way. "It seems to me you and everyone else in this club know Ayda better than I do, so why don't you tell me."

Harry's head dipped before he walked closer towards me, looked up, and landed a hand on the back of my leather cut. "Have you *told* her, son? Have you said the words?"

"I've said enough."

"I'll take that as a no."

Staring into his eyes, the rumblings of anger began to scream out at me from inside. I wanted to tell him to fuck off. I wanted to slam him up against a wall and tell him to mind his own goddamn business. I wanted to wipe that smug, know-it-all grin off the fat, bald bastard's face. But I couldn't, because I loved him too much, too.

That was the thing with love.

It made you weak where you were once strong.

It made decisions that used to be easy, hard.

It made you care.

Pressing my lips into a thin, hard line, I shrugged him off carefully and turned to leave. There wasn't anything left to say. When I walked back into the bar, Kenny was standing behind it, capping three bottles before sliding two of them along to Jedd and Slater. He didn't look up at me once. Not once. His verbal vomiting in the back of the van had told me he was firmly fixed in Camp Ayda. Jedd gave me a nod of respect before bringing his bottle to his lips and tipping it up at an awkward angle, and Slater —well, Slater did what he always does. He followed me out into the yard.

"This isn't on you, Tucker."

"Save it, Slater. I don't need the talk down. I'm not going to do anything stupid."

"Stupid comes far too naturally to you for me to believe that."

"Believe what you like," I said calmly, lifting my hand up in the air and flashing him the middle finger before giving him his orders. "Get back inside. Man the phones and tell everyone to do whatever the fuck Ayda asks of y'all when she calls."

"You know the only thing she'll ask for is you, brother."

I smirked to myself, thinking about how I would have thought that was true before I saw the look she was wearing when she left. "Then tell her I'm honoring her wishes and giving her the time she needs."

My boots crunched the stones on the gravel path, my finger spinning the loop of the key around and around as I walked past the bikes and over to the garages. Pressing the red button on the side of the first one, the screen began to roll up slowly, cranking and causing an almighty noise as it rose to let me in. Slater didn't follow me any farther, but I heard the expletives he called me before he turned and headed back into The Hut as he'd been told to.

The perks of being king.

When the wheels I needed came into sight, I was also

grateful for being part owner of a repo business, which had towed in a *Ram* a few days before. Slipping into the driver's seat, I pulled that thing out of the garage slowly, the low, throaty growl of the engine crying out across the yard. Slater didn't come back out like he once would have. None of them bothered to stand in front of the truck and beg me not to go out alone. They were learning about the new me as much as I was.

As I turned the wheel to the left and headed onto the road that led straight into Babylon, I leaned back in the leather of the chair and rested a limp hand on top of the steering wheel for guidance. Glancing out from left to right, I took in the homes I passed along the way. I saw the white picket fences, the sprawling green lawns of well-kept gardens, the family *Volvos* in the driveways and the lights that shone from bedrooms where people's children slept. For a few minutes, I allowed myself to imagine what a normal life must feel like. One where things were simple, and the biggest fuck up you could make was buying the wrong cereal for breakfast. No death, no violence, no tearing bodies apart and burning their remains.

I tried to imagine myself living like that, surviving the mundane existence that the majority of the world seemed to do.

It lasted all of three minutes before I was shuffling up in my seat and smirking, the thought alone turning my blood cold and forcing my head to shake in protest. My fingers curled around the top of the wheel as I felt that fire erupt in my stomach again, and I knew that I was doing the right thing.

Pressing down on the accelerator, I leaned back and blew out all the air in my lungs, knowing exactly where I was going and what I needed to do.

Whether Ayda approved of my actions or not.

CHAPTER SEVENTEEN
AYDA

I knew long before I went inside the station that Sutton was going to take great satisfaction in making me look like a fool, and he didn't disappoint. The smile he wore as I stepped inside was enough to set my teeth on edge, but the sanctimonious condescension that he started with had me in defensive mode from the get go. Stepping from his office with his arms folded across his chest, he watched as I was escorted through the heavy doors and into the sea of workstations.

"Ayda Hanagan."

"Howard Sutton," I spat back with no less acid on my tone than he'd afforded me. Whatever acquaintance had been there before I met Drew was long gone. This was a man who was filled with hatred, and now that I was associated with Drew and the Hounds, I was tarred with the same brush. It didn't matter who I'd been before that. It never would again.

"Step into my office. I have some paperwork for you to fill out."

"Can't I do that out here?" I asked, looking around at the more neutral territory of the open floor where the half dozen other officers were milling around doing nothing.

"No, I think you and I need a talk."

Of course we did. My day wasn't complete without yet another lecture from the great Howard Sutton, chief of the Babylon Police Department. It seemed he had some wise ass statement every time we crossed paths those days.

I followed him into his office, shoulders slumped and dragging my feet. I dumped my purse on an empty chair before sliding into the one next to it, my body dropping low as I looked over the endless questions that were staring back at me. I was going to be there all night at this rate.

Sutton closed the door and meandered back to his desk before slipping into his chair and steepling his hands in front of him. Neither of us said a thing to one another. The longer we went without speech, the more uncomfortable things became. Eventually, I pulled the pen from the top of the clipboard, just to stave off the discomfort that had started to eat up all of the oxygen.

"You fucked up, Ayda. You're a failure. You failed yourself, your brother and your parents. How could you have been so *stupid*?"

"Is that your professional or personal opinion, Chief?"

"Don't get cocky with me. I've known you almost your whole life."

I sat forward, slipping the board onto the edge of his desk. The pen immediately rolled toward the picture of Sloane, Maisey and the twins that sat on the surface. My eyes took them all in before narrowing and aiming directly at him. He hadn't known me at all. He saw me around while I was growing up. We'd shared polite conversation, but he had no idea *who* I was or what I stood for.

"What was my major?"

"Excuse me?"

"What was my major, Chief? You claim to know me, but you couldn't. You know nothing about me other than that Tate is my brother, my parents were murdered on your watch, and I dated Jacob in high school. Whatever else you think you know, I assure you, you're completely fucking wrong."

"I know you've made the worst mistake of your life falling in with the likes of Drew Tucker and his band of fuckups."

"Another assumption. You don't know one of those men personally, especially not Drew."

"Maisey—"

"Was a club whore who got pissed off when she realized the only thing Drew ever remembered about her was her mouth around his dick."

"Listen here—"

"No, I'm not going to listen, Howard. Your prejudice against Drew and the club clouds your judgment. You and I have never been friends, but we got along okay. The only reason that's not the case now is because of what you *think* you know, what you *want* to believe. Drew isn't a bad guy, Chief. Neither are the others. Your wife was once associated with them and that fucks with your head more than any of their stupid mistakes. You've made this rivalry personal, and I'm not going to let you, or anyone else for that matter, make me or Tate a pawn in it."

"Tate *assaulted* an officer."

"No, Howard, he assaulted *you*. I'm just curious about what you said to make him react that way. You and I both know he has to be provoked in order to react like that. So what was it? An insult about him? Me? His friends? Maybe something Sloane said or did?"

"I'm not at liberty—"

"The hell you're not. He's still a minor, Howard—a minor with good grades, who's a star on the football team and is known by his teachers as a respectful young man that works hard. So tell me again how you're not at liberty to discuss what was said. My guess is you knew what you were doing, and you got exactly what you wanted."

"Sit down, Ayda."

"No!" I shouted, half standing and slapping my hand on the desk. "I will not have a bigoted, discriminating, son-of-a-bitch dictate to me who I should and shouldn't love because he's a small-minded, insecure asshole. Now have someone go and get my brother so we can go home."

"Sit your skinny ass in that chair and listen to me, *Ayda Hanagan*. I've done nothing but look out for you since your parents were killed. I tried to save you this trouble you got yourself into but your mind was poisoned against me and what was right."

The maniacal laughter that suddenly filled the room belonged to me. I hadn't sat down. I hadn't been cowed by his roar of position and entitlement. It had only straightened my back and raised my chin so I was staring at him with venom.

"The only mind around here that's been poisoned is yours. Mainly because your whore of a wife is still drooling over my boyfriend and that just makes you crazy. Whatever vendetta you have against Drew and the Hounds is your business. It's between you and them. I can sit and argue the finer points until the sun comes up, but you don't want to hear it. So, before I call city council, the state troopers, the rangers and whoever else I can get to listen about your corrupt little department, I would get my brother and save yourself the shame of being hauled through every court in the state for your shitty decision making."

"I've got nothing to hide, you stupid little girl."

"My brother dated your *daughter*, you dick."

"You've got nothing." He was calling my bluff. His back was as straight as mine, his eyes flashing a warning at me. He obviously had no idea how much his daughter overheard, or how often she'd confided in me when she was worrying about whether or not she should tell her father what she knew.

It was my turn to call his bluff, so I did the only thing I could do and pulled out my phone, dialing the direct extension to Drew's office, hoping he wasn't there.

"What the hell are you doing?"

"Calling Judge Atwood. He's a customer down at the diner. He was very complimentary about my coffee. We got to talking about Tate and football the last time he was in—"

"Hang up the goddamn phone, Ayda. You have no idea what the hell you're doing."

"Don't I?"

"Jesus. I'll let Tate go with a warning, but it's the only time I'm going to let this happen. You think about trying to blackmail me again—"

"I'm not—"

"This is called blackmail."

I called it using what I had while I could. I was running the risk of getting myself thrown into a cell with Tate, and nothing would be able to help me if that happened. A nag of doubt made a shiver roll cruelly down my spine as I faced off against him.

I was about to dig my way out of the hole I'd created when Sutton gave me a look that had me swallowing my words. He picked up his phone and dialed a number, his eyes scalping me where I stood. "Bring Tate Hanagan to my office… Yes, I'm aware of that, but it was a misunderstanding so I'm letting him off with a warning. No, he wasn't part of the group. Asking them to buy beer for him, that's right. Just get it done."

Sutton hung up the phone and put his hands on his belt, the right one on his gun as his index finger ran the length of it rather than curling around the trigger. There wasn't much more to be said between us, but he pulled up his pants before dropping his hands again and leaning on his desk.

"This is the only time I will ever be this generous, Ayda. I'm going to be watching the two of you like a hawk. You so much as put a foot out of line and you're mine. Am I clear?"

"Crystal."

"Wait out there," he said, pointing to the hard plastic chairs on the other side of the nest of desks. "I'm sick of looking at you."

I didn't waste any more time. I didn't say thank you, and I sure as hell didn't linger. I was out of the door and slamming it behind me before he could so much as take another breath. By some miracle, I managed to get Tate out of there without a warning on his record, but that didn't mean I was calm and in control. My feet tapped out a rhythm on the dingy linoleum of the waiting room until some asshole in a uniform shoved Tate through the door with a nod in my direction. Tate looked cautious and a little nervous, but otherwise unharmed as he pushed his hands in his pockets. If I hadn't known better, I would have said he was contemplating asking them to take him back to the cell.

I turned away from him and pushed through the door to

the outer waiting room, stopping as Tate collected what little he'd had on him before he followed me like a reprimanded puppy. We didn't say a word until we were standing on either side of my car, my shaking hands fumbling with the keys.

"A?"

"Just get in the motherfucking car, Tate, and if you value your life, keep your mouth shut."

Now that he was free and in my hands, I was pissed off. The fear had left the moment we'd stepped out into the cool evening. The breeze had washed away the last of the confusion and panic and all that was left in their place was anger and regret. Anger at Tate for making such a reckless move and getting himself arrested. Anger at Sutton for using that mistake to play me into his hands. He'd been trying to get to the pack through me.

Then there was anger at myself for talking to Drew the way I had. At the time, I thought I was justified. I thought I was right to blame him for something out of his power. He'd made me a promise and several reassurances, and he'd used my undeniable faith in him to make sure I saw and believed it, things I realized I still had—faith and trust.

Tate smacking Sutton had been the decision of one person—Tate himself—and there was nothing Drew and the others could have done to stop it.

I was the one in the wrong to agree to it in the first place, but Tate was the one to push it over the edge and into the territory of disaster. That meant I'd been the one to place the blame where it didn't belong.

I'd hurt Drew, all in the name of fear. What did that make me?

A big, fat hypocrite.

"Tate, give me my phone."

"Can we talk first?"

"No. Give me the phone."

Of all the times to become a petulant teenager, Tate chose that one. He pulled my purse from the footwell by his feet and wedged it between him and the door so it was out of my reach. There was no playful smugness in his face when he looked at me; there was no challenge, just apologies and as much regret as I was harboring inside of myself.

"Tate."

"No."

"Tate!" I reached over, and he smacked my hand away.

I should have left it at that, but I needed to talk to Drew. Taking a chance, I pushed myself across the center console, realizing a second too late that the car swerved in the same direction I had.

CHAPTER EIGHTEEN
DREW

I felt every word she directed at Tate, even though I couldn't hear anything as I stayed low in my seat and watched them through the tinted windows of the truck. Her feet were stamping all over the place, her mouth moving fast and those little frown lines of hers appearing on her forehead. Even angry, she still made me smirk. I found her hot as hell when she couldn't control her emotions.

The disappointment I felt was quickly replaced with a need to grab her by the shoulders and make her listen to my apologies. I might not have been able to give her the white picket fence lifestyle, but that didn't mean I wouldn't make sure she had everything she'd ever want that money couldn't buy.

As she sped off in her car, the back wheels spun uncharacteristically and I knew Tate was getting the ass ripping of his life. If only I could tell her what we'd found on that cut, maybe then she'd realize just how good the kid had done out there.

But all of that could and would be dealt with later. I was more interested in seeing her face when I pulled up beside her, showing her I could be just as defiant as she was capable of being. I rolled out of my spot in the shadows, following her down the small lanes of traffic until a car pulled away in front of the truck, leaving me directly behind her.

Then everything happened quickly. The brake lights flashed a couple of times as if they'd been caught by accident, the outline of her body reaching over to where Tate sat. Somewhere over the next few seconds, I stopped breathing.

Her car swerved across the road, hitting the grass banking on the right, unstopping as the back end of her Corolla vanished over the edge.

"Fuck, no. Please, no." My spine stiffened as I yanked the wheel to the right, skidding to a halt at the top and jumping out as fast as I could.

All I could think about was getting to her. All I could do was hold all the breath in my lungs and move on autopilot, barely even registering the sound of the bikes that rode past me as I slammed my hand on the hood of the truck and ran full sprint to where she was.

The grass banking wasn't steep, by some stroke of fucking luck, but the cold weather and rain of the week had sent the mud to the surface, causing me to slide down like Bambi on fucking ice as soon as my foot made contact. The thick soil clung to my leg, but I didn't slow, jumping up from the bottom as soon as my feet landed on more even terrain again. The car had stopped completely, the tail lights on full as the car seemed to sit there, waiting until one of us remembered how to breathe again.

The edges of my cut swung under my arms as I ran to her, sliding to a stop at her side before even thinking to check on Tate. I grabbed the handle, yanking the one thing standing between us away as I shouted her name through a heavy, strangled breath.

"*Ayda!*"

Leaning in, I reached out to her shoulders in a panic as her hands remained clung to the wheel, her head bowed low and her eyes closed, every breath she took in, deep and slow. The groan of pain and disorientation seemed a long time coming. Her hands dropped from the wheel and raised to her head where a trickle of blood slowly started to descend from a fast forming bruise.

"Fuck. Tate?"

Pushing myself farther in, I leaned over to Tate and carefully gripped his shoulder.

"Tate, buddy, talk to us."

His head rolled lazily from side to side, but the twitching of his arms as he flexed his fingers back and forth told me enough. He was fine, but shaken up to fuck. Groaning as I reached farther over, not wanting to press my body weight on Ayda in case she was hurting anywhere else, I hooked my hand under Tate's chin and carefully began to raise his head. The small hiss and moan of pain as his hand flew up to the back of his neck had me pausing.

"That hurt?"

"Just a bit," he winced out, managing to lift his eyes up to mine as he moved at a much slower pace. "Whiplash or something. No big deal. Ayda? You okay?"

"I don't know. I'll tell you when everything stops hurting." She groaned, her hand moving to where the seat belt was cutting into her shoulder. I wasn't sure what was happening as she slowly started to tremble, and then, without warning, she burst into tears, her head burying in her hands as "sorry" came out in a frequency only dogs could decipher.

Moving without much thought, I unclipped her seatbelt

and pushed it away from her, somehow wedging myself in the footwell as I grabbed her face in my hands and held her. I'd never held a crying woman that way before, but I knew that all I wanted to do was kill every one of those tears that dared to fall down her face. I wanted to destroy anything that was causing her pain.

"Tell me what's hurting," I whispered, my eyes briefly leaving her covered face to glance down at her body before rising to the bump on her temple. Her shitty old car had no airbags, so I could only imagine the force she hit the steering wheel with when she somehow slammed to a stop. "Is it just your head, darlin'?"

"My head, my heart, my pride... I'm so sorry, Drew. I was a bitch." She reached out with her right hand, and without much prompting, Tate's fingers wrapped around hers and squeezed. "I'm sorry, Tate. I didn't mean—"

The sob that had been building stole her voice.

"Come on, A. I'm fine," Tate grumbled quietly, looking between his sister and me, asking me for help.

Pulling her other hand away from her face, I lowered it into her lap and dipped my head to catch her eyes.

"The kid's fine. He's had worse injuries than this out on the field. Ain't that right. Tate?"

He mumbled something beside me that sounded vaguely like reassurances, but he was in as much shock as she was. Reaching up, I brushed a small trail of blood out of the way before it dropped over her brow, sighing heavily as my skin prickled.

"You didn't hit anything. You stopped the car. You're safe now. The heart and pride can take a back seat for a while. We need to get you home so we can take a look at your head.

We'll deal with all the other crap another day."

"This is my fault, all my fault. I just… I'm an idiot."

She swiped the tears from her cheeks with her trembling hand and sucked in a steadying breath. As she released it in a long stream, her cheeks pinked and her eyes closed, the sudden burst of emotion catching up with her. In need of drawing attention away from her emotional outpour, she held her hand between us, her eyes fluttering open as she studied it.

"I can't stop shaking."

Trapping her hands between both of mine, I stilled her, keeping my eyes on hers as I pressed my palms together and held her firmly. "There. All stopped," I whispered through a sad smile. "I've got you now."

Ayda stared at our hands for the longest time. Her breaths seemed to return closer to normal with every cycle of inhales and exhales. When she finally looked up and met my eyes, all I could see was everything she wanted to say, but couldn't with Tate in the car. Instead, her fingers curled around mine.

"I want to go home."

"That I can do," I breathed back. "I'm just going to need a phone from one of you to call the guys so we can get this thing towed away. Plus, Harry is better with tending to the wounded than I am, believe it or not." I smirked, lowering my mouth to her fingers and brushing my lips over them.

"Right. My phone," she said, tearing her eyes away from mine and looking over at Tate, who pulled her purse from between his body and the door sheepishly.

I didn't wait around to ask what that look meant. Slipping out of the car, I pulled her bag out with me and reached inside for her cell. Scrolling through like the big thumbed, useless idiot I was, I found the number saved under 'Home' and despite the situation, felt my lips curling into a smile.

Kenny answered, but it was fleeting. He slammed the phone down in anger, still pissed at me for the Tate shit, and told me they'd all be here within fifteen minutes. That was enough time for me to have a walk around to the other side of the car and check the damage. It wasn't anything that a good wash down, a brake test, and maybe some new tires couldn't fix, but I wasn't going to tell Ayda that. From now on, she'd be riding in a car that at least had some airbags.

I helped Tate out, watching as he cracked his neck when he stood up straight, the new, baby-like wrinkles on his scrunched up face showing he was in more pain than he wanted us to see.

"You think you can make it up there, brother?" I asked, pointing back to the mudslide I'd come down. Not too far to the left was a gravel path, one that would be much easier for two wounded Hanagans to climb. Well, one at least. Ayda wasn't going to do anything but rest in my arms, no matter how much she fought me on it.

"Sure." Tate nodded. "I'm good."

The kid was earning more and more points for bravery as the day wore on.

"You grab her bag. I'm gonna go get your sister."

"Got it," he croaked out before clearing his throat.

"We'll talk about everything later, Tate." My hand tapped his shoulder gently before I ran around to the other side of the car and pulled Ayda up in to my arms. As predicted, she told me she was strong enough, and she told me she could walk, but my silence as my arms curled under her body told her this wasn't up for debate. With her hands clasped around my neck, I felt her breathe in against the leather of my cut before dropping her head to my chest and giving up her fight.

By the time we made it back to the roadside, the men were pulling up in convoy. We were now a twisted road army consisting of one tow truck, two bikes, a repossessed *Ram* truck and a crashed out *Corolla*. We couldn't have looked more like a *Mickey Mouse* motorcycle club if we tried.

Sliding Ayda into the front seat of the repo car, I let Harry through as he gave her the full check and tried to talk her around. No part of me wanted to take my eyes from her, but it was only when she repeated that she wanted to go home that I knew I had no choice. She needed looking after the way she'd done for me so many times before.

Walking back around the hood, I paused when I saw Slater coming towards me, his feet slipping and sliding as he climbed back up the slope with the end of a rope in one hand.

"Didn't you see the pathway over there?" I smirked, pointing over his head and watching as he squinted down in the dark before cursing quietly to himself.

"I like a challenge." He eventually grinned.

I was just about to reply when I saw his eyes drift over my shoulder and heard the thunderous roar of engines rolling down the street we were parked on. It was now the early hours of the morning and no one should be on the streets of Babylon except for us and the cops, and seeing as we were all accounted for, the fact that three bikes were heading our way had my spine straightening and my eyes narrowing as I turned to watch them fly past us.

Only then did the noise seem familiar, and I remembered the bikes that had tore past me on my way to rescue Ayda and Tate.

As I watched their backs disappear into the distance, I

heard Slater step up closer behind me.

"Unmarked," he said quietly.

"No leathers," I added.

My teeth ground together, the muscles in my jaw flexing back and forth as I squinted down even more and flared my nostrils. What we'd just seen didn't make sense, but then again, what did make sense these days? All I could do was listen to that sixth sense of mine that made the hairs on the back of my neck stand to attention.

"Vacation riders just passing through?"

I didn't answer right away, instead turning around and taking a glance at Ayda who was resting her wounds with her head back. "Probably," I lied to Slater, not telling him that I'd seen them before, as I tapped him on the shoulder and began to walk away. "Let's get my girl and her brother home."

CHAPTER NINETEEN
AYDA

We didn't speak much from the moment he pulled me from the car all the way back to The Hut. We barely said more than a full sentence to one another, but it wasn't that stilted, uncomfortable silence I'd expected after the way I behaved when Tate was arrested. Whether he knew it or not, Drew's protectiveness spoke more than he ever could have.

I had been replaying those shock-fueled moments when he first opened the door, over and over in my head, and I saw real fear there. He was worried about losing me, and no matter what had happened only hours earlier, my stupidity behind the wheel had made some clarity appear. I'd handled the situation with Drew badly, and I'd managed to handle Sutton far better than I ever intended to.

As he set me on the bed, more carefully than I probably deserved, I patted the space beside me, hoping he would take the invitation and join me.

He didn't hesitate in climbing on board, slipping out of his cut before he dropped down in place beside me and crossed his legs at the ankle.

"You sure you don't want me to get you anything? You're still pretty pale, Ayda."

"Just you," I said quietly, moving closer to him. My eyes flickered down to my hands and back to him as I wondered whether I would be welcome on his lap. I didn't think I'd ever needed contact with someone as much as I did in that moment. It was all guilt and love balled into one inexplicable and uncontainable emotion.

Ignoring the nagging of doubt in my head, I pushed to my knees and straddled his thighs, my hands cupping his neck and reveling in the warmth of his flesh against mine.

"I'm so sorry, Drew. There's no excuse for what I said and did before I left here and if I could take it back, I would."

Tilting his head to one side, he let out a small but weighty breath of air, a twitch to one side of his mouth eventually curling into a tired half smile. Dropping his hands to my thighs, he just stared into my eyes for what felt like forever.

"I thought I was the one who was meant to be apologizing? You didn't do anything wrong. You did what you thought was best for Tate. At some point, I'm gonna have to realize that you're not just mine and mine alone."

I found my lips answering his subtle smile with one of my own. I don't know why it was so hard to find a middle ground. I'd gone from zero to a hundred in the blink of an eye, and I was starting to realize I wasn't the only one. As much passion as there was between us, there were times when that walked a fine line with anger. One step and you could find yourself on the wrong side. I'd stepped over, my confusion turning understanding into blame, and it had taken Sutton's attitude to remind me of something.

"It wasn't your fault, Drew. You didn't do anything wrong, either. You stuck to your word and delivered. It occurred to me, while I was standing there yelling at Sutton, that it was a bullshit charge. He provoked Tate. Even if my kid brother was creating a diversion, I can't see him swinging like that without a good reason. Sutton's been on his case since he and Sloane broke up and we moved in here. It's personal."

"I couldn't give a fuck about Sutton. He'll get what's coming to him when the time is right." Drew paused. "But that's twice now. Twice I've had to contemplate the thought of you being taken away from me. First the fire, then seeing your car disappear over the edge…"

"Wait!" I sat up and narrowed my eyes at him. It was more playful than angry. I should have known he'd follow me. No matter how many times I said no or how angry I was at him, he wasn't going to let me put myself in harm's way. Just because I was an idiot and drove off without thought, it didn't mean I couldn't tease him. "You followed me?"

"Noooo," he lied, his lips forming into a perfect 'O' shape as his brows rose high.

"You're so full of shit," I said with a laugh, one hand dropping to his chest so I could push against it and get a good look at him. I stared at his mouth for a while before rising to meet his gaze. "But I'm glad you did. I hate fighting with you, Drew. I just wish…"

I let my head fall forward, staring at the zipper on his hoodie as I tried to find a way to word what was playing on my mind. We both had a propensity to react before thinking, and I had a terrible habit of speaking before thinking, too. The last thing I wanted was to say something the wrong way and start another fight before we'd truly recovered from the first.

"What do you wish?"

"I wish you wouldn't shut me out. I know you're trying to protect me from club business, that you're trying to keep the pack business and me separate, but I feel like I'm missing out on a part of who you are. I don't want to know everything, but those kids… I know there's something more there. Those bikes on the road tonight… I saw the look you and Slater exchanged."

Lifting his hand to my cheek, he brushed my hair back as he spoke. "I'm not trying to keep anything separate. You're too involved for me to do that. But, Ayda, I can't tell you what I don't know myself. Sometimes, I feel like… like you expect me to write you a list of what I learned that day. I can't do that, not in this life. Things change from minute to minute. It's unpredictable. As much as I'd love to share the burden sometimes, this is who I am. The club, my men—they're my job as much as the diner's yours. There're gonna be days where I need time to figure stuff out. There're gonna be days where I know I need to let you figure stuff out, too."

"Okay." I laid my hand flat on his chest and took another deep breath. "Can you explain what happened to Tate tonight? Why he felt the need to distract the police?"

"You sure you want to hear what I have to say about Tate? The truth?"

"He's my brother, Drew. I need to know the truth about it. I know I'm overbearing at times, but I want what's best for him in the long run. I can be objective. At least, I hope I can."

I held his gaze, trying my best to reassure him as I offered a nod of encouragement. There was a chance I wasn't going to like what I heard, but I had to be prepared. I had to think about the bigger picture.

"The truth is that he did better than we could have hoped." His finger rose to press against my mouth, cutting me off before I even thought about attempting to share my thoughts. "I know him hitting the chief of police wasn't part of the plan, but he showed no fear and he brought home the info we needed. I don't want to admit this any more than you want to hear it, but he was a natural out there. It's gonna be harder for us to pull him back than I thought. When he made the decision to grab that little shit, I thought he'd lost his damn mind. I could have killed him myself. But he saw the cut, Ayda. He saw what the fake HOB patch was hiding."

"What exactly was it hiding?"

Drew's face seemed to brighten all at once, even if his eyes still looked as tired as I felt. "Some old patch that represents a group of kids from way back in the nineties. They were doing the same things these boys are doing. Saw themselves as big shots, went around stealing cars, starting fires, throwing bricks through innocent folks' windows. Real set of assholes who were craving their parents' attention or some shit. I don't know. Four of them ended up with life sentences after setting fire to the gas station on the other side of Babylon. They hurt people, ruined lives to create egos." He sucked in a breath, his sarcasm dripping from him as he spoke through the release. "Called themselves *The Widow Makers*."

"So this is some group of kids copying another stupid group of kids? Why would they be dumb enough to wear your patches, though? Why now?"

"Wish we knew. They could be family of the old gang, seeking some kind of retaliation on the town, even though Babylon didn't even try to defend itself at the time. From the stories I've heard, it all happened fast. But my guess is that they're wearing our patches to get instant recognition. They want everyone scared and they want them scared fast—and who does everyone in Babylon already fear more than anything or anyone else?"

"The Hounds," I whispered, wriggling on his lap. "They have to know that you and the guys aren't going to take it lightly? Why incur your wrath? Why risk getting caught, even if they do want to instil fear in people?"

"Maybe they didn't expect us to give a shit." His hands moved around to the base of my spine, his chest expanding and the muscles flexing beneath his hoodie. "If we're taking part in a confessional, before seeing how they squared up to Tate tonight, I wasn't sure how seriously I was gonna take them at all. I didn't want to give a shit. Now that I know what they stand for and who they're connected to, they won't be around much longer. I know you don't want to hear it, but it's thanks to your brother that we know what we know now, and that can only be a good thing for everyone in Babylon."

The pride was shining from Drew's eyes. Tate had done them a service. He'd been asked to do something and he'd exceeded expectations. The kid never did anything by halves so I should have been prepared for it. From the moment he brought the Hounds into our lives, I had seen his focus shift slowly day by day. The running was the only thing he indulged in. He cut back on almost half of his practice time to do weights in the Hounds' gym with Kenny and some of the others, and the Bulldog pride he'd been so certain of was slowly diminishing, replaced by running errands for the pack. He still loved football. I saw it on the field behind the yard where he threw the ball to some of the guys. I just wasn't certain it was his endgame anymore.

"I need you to be honest with me, Drew. Tate's not going to leave, is he? He's not going to want the scholarship or the pro career in football. He's going to buy himself that

Street 500 he keeps researching and he's never going to leave Babylon unless it's a ride out to another charter."

His blue-green eyes shone back at me. "If I can stop that from happening, I will. I don't want this life for him any more than I want you to have to endure it. And since when has he been researching bikes?" Drew's smirk was weak, and I knew he was putting on a show to distract me. Some things didn't need to be said for them to be heard.

"Since he rode with me into Corsicana. There's a dealership there. He begged me to stop and I did, not thinking anything of it until I saw him climb on the damn thing. It suited him, Drew, and the smile he was wearing…" I dropped my head, leaning forward to rest it on his chest as my hands gripped just under his ribs. "You can't stop this any more than I can. I love that you would try for me, but he's made up his mind, and the kid is just like my dad in that respect. You could say no until you were blue in the face, but he'd only keep at it and resent me for taking it away from him. I have a feeling this will be his last season."

I felt the heat of his words against me when he pressed his lips to my hair, while his hands ran up and down my spine in soothing lines. "Darlin', sometimes you've just got to stop thinking so much and see where the road takes you. And sometimes you've got to believe in the power of bribery. He's fifteen. Tate will do whatever you ask of him if we just dangle the right toy a few feet away from his grabby little hands."

I let out a half laugh and turned my head to press my cheek against the warmth of his chest. "You think I'm stubborn? The kid is ten times worse, but he has charisma and charm. He's going to be sixteen in just over a month, and in two years, he will be old enough to do whatever the fuck he wants."

"The benefit of being part of this fucked up family is that you're never of an age to be old enough to do whatever the fuck you want. Tate is no exception to that rule. We'll figure it out," he said, his hand making its way through the ends of my hair before I felt it slide down to my ass. "And you have your own charisma and charm. I like to call this charm," he said through an obvious grin, giving my ass a squeeze, before he pulled his hand around and slid it between our bodies, groping my breast. "While these are called charisma."

My teeth sank into my bottom lip as I watched his fingers flex, his thumb brushing over my nipple that was beginning to become very obviously hard from the interaction with him.

"You named my ass and boobs? I'm honored. This is a first for me, Mr. Tucker," I said a little breathlessly as my hands slowly slid from under his ribs to the buckle of his belt. My body was already responding, the tightening in my stomach reflecting where I was pushed against his thighs.

"I have more in my head, but I'll never tell." Taking me by surprise, Drew's hand found its way to mine, pressing down carefully to stop me from doing anything with his belt, his other hand rising to my chin and forcing me to look up. "Not until you tell me what happened with Sutton, since we're laying all our cards on the table."

Dipping my head and slipping his thumb into my mouth, I sucked gently, my teeth grazing the edges as I pulled back, eventually releasing it with a soft kiss. "I'd be glad to explain, but later. I'm horny and he's just going to make that go away." Pushing up to my knees, I shuffled closer to him, my eyes still locked on his. "It'll make a good bedtime story."

"Ayda," he groaned. "Your head is still bleeding, for

fuck's sa—Ooh. Oh, shit. Okay."

CHAPTER TWENTY
DREW

"I'm not sure I understand," Slater said from the old sofa in my office. His ankle was resting over his knee as he ran his hand through the back of his hair and frowned at me.

"That's because you're a dumb fuck," I said through a grin, my feet resting on the floor, moving my chair from side to side as I bought myself some time.

"Either that or someone slipped some strong shit in my coffee this morning, 'cause I swear I just heard you tell us all that you want to work with Sutton."

I gave him a sharp nod, my smile turning sarcastic as I widened my eyes.

Jedd leaned forward next to Slater, his hands clasping together in between his parted legs. "Gotta admit, brother, I never thought I'd hear those words come out of your mouth, either."

"I like it," Harry piped up from across the desk, his cough cutting his last word off before he brought his hand to his chest and smacked it. It didn't stop him from grinning like I'd just told him Liz Hurley was on her way to blow him, though. He'd always had a thing for her.

Planting my feet on the floor, I turned to him and frowned.

"When was the last time you saw doc?"

"About what?" he choked out, growling as he cleared his throat.

"You know what, dickhead."

Harry rolled his eyes before resting back in his seat. "It's just the smokes. Don't you have a woman to save your nagging for now?"

"Quit that shit, Rogers."

"I will." He smirked. "When I die."

I shook my head but held his gaze. That fat son of a bitch had no clue what he meant to me or this club, but I wasn't about to go ahead and sing him his very own love song just to stroke his ego. "If you won't listen to me, maybe you'll listen to Ayda," I threatened.

"You wouldn't?" he gasped.

"Sure about that?"

"That's foul play and you know it."

I shrugged and looked back at Jedd, Slater, Kenny and Deeks. I didn't miss the fact that Kenny was the only one with his head down and the only one showing no hint of amusement.

"Kenny," I called out, raising my chin.

"What?"

"What's with the wounded puppy dog look?"

Half lifting his head my way, he struggled to hide his scowl. "What?"

"You haven't said a word about this since you walked through the door. Anyone would think you didn't want to be here."

The whole room fell silent as we waited for him to answer. Kenny's tongue poked the inside of his cheek before he grabbed the edges of his cut, rolled his shoulders and straightened up on the arm of the sofa. "Sorry."

Four sets of eyes suddenly fell my way. I didn't have to see them all to feel Slater, Jedd, Deeks and Harry's confused faces. My focus was all on K-Dog. "You don't have anything to say about the plan to work with Sutton?"

Kenny shrugged, his hand rising up to rub his temple before he looked around the room. "Does Ayda know about this plan?"

"No."

"Don't you think she should?"

"Don't you think Ayda's my goddamn business?"

"Okay." He sighed, dropping his eyes back to the floor again. "I'm good with whatever the rest of you decide. I'll fall in line."

I opened my mouth to reply when Jedd caught my attention from the corner of my eye, the slow, subtle shake of his head telling me to leave it. Suddenly irritated, I pulled myself closer to the desk, facing forward and picking up the pen laid out on the surface, quickly drumming it on the top to pour my agitation out in some kind of new *Bic*-rhythm.

"Listen, I know this is a surprise to you all, and believe me, I hate Sutton more than anyone else in the state of Texas, but if we go around handling a bunch of snot-nosed brats, things are going to look bad on the club. With everything we've got going on with the Emps, imitating the Navs and already feeling like we've got more targets on our asses than a whore in a prison cell, we don't need child-abuse adding to the fucking list. That's something we can never come back from. If we point Sutton in the right direction, anonymously contact his superiors and tell them that we've given him substantial evidence as to what's going on in Babylon, he won't have any choice but to act, regardless of whether we were the ones to hand him the info in the first place. We back Sutton into a corner, he can't argue the fact that we helped out. He gets a pat on the back from his chiefs, we might get a bit of a reprieve from him, and he can forget I've fucked his wife for a while..." I trailed off, eyes scanning the room as my hands turned palm up and my pen pointed to the ceiling. "We look good in the day, we save our blood and dirt for the night. We're a motorcycle club trying to do the right thing for once. That's how they'll see it. That's the image we've got to put out there. These kids ain't our problem. The more we distance ourselves from them, the more the people of the town will believe that, although they might be wearing the Hounds' patch, they have nothing to do with our brotherhood."

"Babylon is our problem," Harry reminded me quietly.

"And this is the best solution for Babylon," I answered.

"I'm with Drew," Jedd piped up.

A rough exhale came from Slater, his foot twitching as it rested across his leg. "Can't believe I'm fucking saying this, but I agree. This is for the Five-O. Let them do the policing for once."

"Okay." Harry began to nod his head, his nostrils flaring as he inhaled sharply. "Let's go to Sutton."

"Just one question," Deeks spoke up. Letting my eyes drift over to where he was standing, leaning against the wall with his arms across his chest, I raised my chin to give him the go ahead to speak. "In theory it works, but which one of us will approach Sutton? It can't be you, Tucker. You won't even get through the station doors."

"I know where he lives." I smirked.

"He'll never listen to you. It needs to be someone he would give the time of day to. After everything, that ain't gonna be you, brother. No offense."

"None taken."

"Ayda?" Jedd offered, not daring to look at me as my head practically spun to throw daggers his way.

"Are you fucking stupid?"

"Just an idea." He shrugged.

"Not Ayda," I hissed back at him. "She stays out of our shit from now on. Besides—"

Deeks interrupted, finishing my sentence for me. "After the ass ripping she gave him last night, Ayda is about as high up on the popularity list as our president is, Jedd."

"I'll do it," Kenny pushed out, his voice louder than it had been all day as he jumped to his feet, ran his thumbs around the insides of his belt and stared holes into the floor. "I'll do it."

"What?" Slater asked, as confused as the rest of us.

"I said I'll do it," Kenny hit back, lifting his head and turning it to the side to look back at Slater. "I'm good for more than guard dog and babysitting duties, you know."

Slater burst out laughing, throwing his head back as the strong, rough bellow erupted from deep within his stomach. Soon Jedd was following suit, his hand running over the thick, black hair around his mouth as he tried to hold in what was trying to get out, but his shoulders were bouncing too much to hide shit. Harry was grinning as he shook his head, but my eyes soon found their way to Deeks—the one man who was seeing what I was seeing and didn't find anything remotely funny.

"Jesus," Slater huffed out, dropping his head to his chest

as he tried to contain his laughter. "Whatever's got your dick trapped in a vise, let us know so we can help free you up a bit, K. You're funny as fuck this morning."

"Screw you," Kenny said through gritted teeth. "In fact, screw all y'all. I don't need this shit today." And with that, he took off, marching across the room before pulling the door open and slamming it shut behind him. Before I had a chance to join in with any of the banter in the room, I pushed up from my chair and marched myself out to find him. This was going to fucking end and it was going to end there and then.

Pulling the door closed behind me, I left my brothers and charged through the bar with my head held high and anger strewn all across my face until I eventually caught up with him outside on the porch.

Gripping the top of his arm, I spun him around, my fingers digging into the flesh under his T-shirt sleeve as I stepped closer.

"What the fuck was that?" I spat out.

Kenny tried to shrug me off, but I was unrelenting and soon losing grip on my relatively good mood. "Get off me."

"Not until you tell me what the hell has gotten into you."

"Does it even matter?" he said through a tired sigh. His shoulders sagged, his face turning away as he looked out at the yard.

"Clearly. Otherwise I wouldn't be here, handling you like a child and about to put you on the motherfucking naughty step, would I?"

"Right," he huffed out, his eyes rising back up to mine and narrowing. "'Cause I *am* the child of the group that no one listens to unless they want something, yeah? I'm just the dumb little kid with weird eyebrows and an irrelevant opinion."

I searched his face for some sign that he was joking, but all I saw staring back at me was a man I'd never seen before. I felt a shitty stabbing in my chest that he could think any of that was true. So much so that I couldn't think of anything profound to say at all. "What?"

"You heard me," he snapped, pulling himself free as soon as my grip loosened. Taking a step back, he straightened up his cut and shook his head.

"You are my *brother*."

"Am I?"

"Your opinion is always relevant. Always. Don't you dare suggest otherwise."

"Or what? You're gonna cut me off from my never-ending list of chores?"

"Chores?" I frowned hard, leaning closer and lowering my face to his. "I don't ask any more of you than I do the rest of them."

"Yeah, well that ain't how it feels. You respect the others, Drew. Even Deeks has somehow gained more respect since Ayda came along. Let's face it, she's the only one any of them listen to anymore, especially you. May as well stick the pres badge on her chest and be done with it."

"Careful," I growled. "Be very fucking careful."

"I'm past caring about being careful. It's gotten me nowhere before and it's not gonna get me anywhere anytime soon. You go back inside and let me know when you figure out what my next order is. I'm sure it will be filled with lots of dos and don'ts. Do this, Kenny. Fix that, Kenny. Be here, Kenny. Look after the kid, Kenny. But don't you go too close to Ayda, Kenny."

The moment her name passed his lips a second time, my

spine stiffened and my eyes narrowed. The ends of my fingers tingled with a need to knock him flat on his ass, right then and there.

"So that's what this is about," I muttered, the anger expressing itself by the convulsive twitching in my jaw.

"What?"

"You heard me."

"I don't know what you mean," he whispered, with no conviction in his words at all.

"Like fuck you don't." I took a step back, distancing myself from the reality of what was staring me in the face.

"Drew."

"Don't, Kenny." My growl was quiet, but the threat mixed with the irony of what I'd just said to him was obvious. "Don't lie to either of us. I'm a man with a dick and perfect vision. I know what she is, I know how lucky I am, and I know she doesn't belong here with me. She could do better, she deserves better, but that doesn't mean I would ever give her up without a fight—and by fight, I mean until the man who tried to take her away from me wasn't left with a single breath in his lungs. I'm the most selfish bastard to walk this earth. Everyone in Babylon knows that. But just because I've learned how to hold a girl in my arms without bending her over a table, don't you dare make the mistake of seeing me as weak. She is *mine*. Fucking mine. Do you understand me? Mine. Make of that what you will. I won't be having this conversation again."

My eyes lingered on him for a few seconds longer, but when I finally chose to turn away, I was left with an image of my brother imprinted on my eyelids. An image of a man who saw me as both someone he loved and someone he despised, and no matter how much I tried to ignore that as I wandered back through the bar, I couldn't.

There were certain types of problems that couldn't be solved with any kind of strategy.

I had a feeling Kenny was going to be one of them.

CHAPTER TWENTY-ONE
AYDA

I wasn't sure why I agreed to a new car. I blamed Drew and make-up sex. I was normally so lost in my own head and the numbness in my limbs that I didn't even realize what I was agreeing to until I saw that look of victory shining from his eyes. Apparently I needed airbags and a frame that wouldn't bend when I sneezed on it. The truth was I was expecting to end up with a tank, although I wasn't quite sure they had airbags. I made a mental note to look into that.

Against my better judgment, my poor *Corolla's* fate had been decided. It was older than me, and finally being sent out to pasture. Beyond that motorway to retirement, I wasn't sure I wanted to know. That thing had taken me to college, brought me home and taken me to and from three shitty jobs with great gas mileage. It had done everything I'd asked of it and more. Even then there was nothing really wrong with it. I just saw that *don't argue* look when I finally realized what I'd said yes to and left it at that. I justified it to myself as keeping Tate safe and giving my over protective meathead some peace of mind.

I was so lost in my thoughts as I passed through the main room, I almost walked straight into the man of my dreams, all while envisioning myself in the *Camaro* I'd seen them tow in last week.

"Hey, you," I said, reaching out and fisting the front of his shirt, just above his belt. "I thought you had a meeting with the boys this morning?"

It was only when our eyes met that I saw the look he was wearing. Drew's nostrils were flared, his chest heaving as he looked down on me and I was instantly reminded of the time I tried to leave the clubhouse, before we got together. The anger in his face was apparent, but just when I was about to ask what happened, his hand flew up to my face, gripping tightly as his lips crashed down against mine.

He caught me by surprise, and before I'd so much as thought about it I was on my toes, my body pressing against his as a quiet whimper left my mouth, only to be swallowed by him. There was no intimacy in the kiss he was giving me, no tenderness or adoration. It was possession, one hundred percent marking his territory in the only way he knew how.

Not that I was complaining.

By the time he pulled back, I was breathless and boneless. My body was upright only because he was keeping me there in his grip, and by the small glint in his eye he'd achieved his directive, although I wasn't entirely sure who it was for.

"Damn. I should run into you more often."

"Or never leave my side," he said quietly, his eyes falling to my mouth as his tongue ran over his bottom lip.

"That's tempting, but I fear you'd get bored with me. It's my absence that keeps the mystery." I finally rocked down flat on my feet, but stayed grinning up at him like the love-struck fool I really was. "I was just going to drool over the *Camaro*, unless you have a *Trans Am* out there. Wanna come?"

His jaw set tight, even though he was now smiling. "No to both those options. I want you in an inflatable car that doesn't go above fifty." His laugh was much softer than his desperate grip on my waist as he dropped another kiss to my lips and spoke against them. "As much as I'd love to make sure you don't burn my money on something you'll get yourself killed in, I have some things I need to take care of."

"Hey! They both have airbags and solid frames. They're American-made muscle cars. If I'm upgrading, I wanna look cool, not like a soccer mom," I said, partly in humor, partly serious. I put my hands on his shoulders and rubbed gently. "Not nagging, but do these things need your attention now? Is it something I can help with?"

"You can help by not buying yourself a muscle car, darlin'." Pulling back and forcing us both to stand taller, he didn't let me go as his eyes flashed to the door of his office then back at me. "Apart from that, it's all good. I'm just speaking with the guys about clearing up the mess with these kids. Then I have some accounts crap to go over, which will bore the hell outta you and make you horny while I try to work and look all studious. It's probably best you climb this mountain without me. Don't expect to go too far, though. My guys will have their eyes on you the whole time." His grin faltered and his grip tightened, those small frown lines of his making a quick appearance before disappearing again. "Stay close to Deeks for me, okay?"

"I'm only going out into the yard, Drew," I said quietly, my hands running down to his biceps as I tried to read the undecipherable look he was giving me. Lifting one hand, I tugged on his growing beard. "I may just punish you and pick out a *Harley*, or would that be a blessing?"

"Hmm. Interesting," he whispered before sliding his other hand down to the top of my ass. "That could be a blessing and a major distraction. Best get that charm and charisma out of here before I show you just how good you'd look on one of those things."

My laugh was genuine as I pushed my ass back into his touch, my eyebrows rising as I bit the tip of my tongue.

"Somehow I think our visions differ considerably." I pulled one hand to my temple and narrowed my eyes. "Wait. I'm getting a psychic vision. You're seeing me *bent* over a *Harley*, breasts down ass up? Is that about right, Mr. Tucker?"

"Fuck. It's uncomfortable how well you know what goes on in my mind." He stepped back, breaking contact completely, throwing both his hands in the air as that signature smirk of his spread up into one cheek. "Take your voodoo elsewhere, woman. I won't be a part of it."

"Aww, c'mon," I said, purposefully jutting my hip out and curling my hair around one finger. "You like my brand of voodoo. It's just a shame you have to work. We could have tried out the *Harley* thing."

I gave him a wink and side-stepped his frame, sauntering slowly toward the door and swinging my hips. When I was past him enough that he'd have to actually chase me, I turned my head to glance over my shoulder at him, a small laugh coming as I dropped my hands to my side. "Maybe later?"

Walking backwards, he raised a finger and pointed it in my direction. "Your charm is mine, Ayda. All mine."

"So are Char and Isma," I responded, turning and giving him a little jiggle. I mouthed *I love you* at him before spinning on my heel and skipping toward the door in an exponentially better mood than I had been.

I thought our interaction was over until I heard him shout out across the bar, "I'm sending Deeks out right now to watch over my assets."

"Why could I possibly need protection in the yard?" I sang, my body turning while my eyes stayed on him.

"Sometimes there's wolves among the sheep, sweetheart."

"Don't worry, baby. I'm a carnivore." I snorted, shaking my ass at him before pushing through the door and out into the beautiful fall day.

I breathed in the soil-scented air with renewed vigor, the day's outlook now brighter than it had been. I barely made it two steps toward the picnic table when I saw Kenny leaning against the rails, looking out over the closed gate that led to the highway.

"Kenny? What are you doing out here? I thought y'all had club business?" I skipped toward him, turning my back to the rails, my hands gripping the edge as I pulled my ass up onto it. Once again, I realized that my distraction had blinded me to his body language and the joint in his hand. "Everything okay?"

"Fucking peachy."

"Really?"

"Yep. What you doing?"

"Why, I'm picking out a *brand new car*," I said in a game show presenter's voice, my arm sweeping across the yard. I was trying to cheer him up a little. There was something bothering him. Kenny was generally a laid back kind of guy. I didn't think I'd seen him like that since I'd met him. "There anything I can do to help?"

Kenny let out all the breath in his lungs and threw the butt of his joint into a chimenea I bought to keep them warm while they sat out there and smoked. Rolling his shoulders, he turned to the side, resting his hip against the railing as a ghost of a smile appeared.

"You've already done it." He sniffed and raised his chin in the direction of the yard. "What kind of car you looking for?"

"That's actually up for debate. I want something sporty, but I think Drew wants me in a tank."

"Well, in that case, you should probably do whatever Drew tells you to."

"Do you know me at all, Kenny?"

He smiled, huffing out a laugh before he rubbed his hand across his mouth. "Maybe you can compromise? We had a brand new *Tahoe* come in. Total upgrade package, including sound system, tow package, and four wheel drive."

"Sounds right up your alley." I laughed, pushing his shoulder. "I want some American made umph."

"Umph?"

"A car that growls."

"There ain't many Vipers in Babylon, A."

"I'm not that delusional, *K*."

"Okay, then what are you thinking?"

I kicked my legs against the rail and grinned at him sheepishly. "Shortlisted? *Camaro*, *Mustang* or *Trans Am*."

"All three of them are in the *fuck no* column," Deeks said, letting go of the door he'd just come through.

"Then I'll keep the *Corolla*. If I'm getting something new, it's gonna be something I want."

"Drew said you would be difficult," Deeks said, heading toward the porch steps, his hands in his pockets. "Let's just go do this. That way you might be able to add something to that shortlist of yours he'll be willing to compromise over."

"You got any *Ferraris*?" I asked, grinning at Kenny before hopping off the railing and jogging after him. "How about *Lambos*? *Aston Martins*? *Batmobiles*?"

"It's gonna be a long day." Deeks chuckled, pushing an elbow out for me to hook my arm through. I took it and slowed to his speed, the maze of cars suddenly looking more daunting than it had only ten minutes earlier.

"Where's your sense of adventure, Deeks?"

He threw his head back and let out a good hearty laugh, forcing my smile to almost quadruple. If I was going to be made to do this with anyone, I was glad it was him. Deeks knew me. He was immune to my bitching and antics, and that meant I had a good conscience with me for the afternoon.

CHAPTER TWENTY-TWO
DREW

I couldn't concentrate confined inside the walls of the office. The echoes of all the arguments I'd had within the last twenty-four hours were rattling off all the corners of my brain, until all I was left with was a white noise sound and the repetition of scrubbing my hands up and down my face. In so many ways, life pre-prison had been easier. There'd been no conscience. There'd been no need to consider anyone else's feelings. Once I'd been handed the chair, I was the man in charge. I'd been the boss, the decision maker. The merciless fucker who took what he wanted, when he wanted and always had a back up plan.

Now... Now I felt like Mary fucking Poppins, except my bag only had so many tricks inside it.

I both loved and loathed it, mainly because I had something else to love now besides the club, and I was aware that that, too, was making me a selfish bastard in a whole new set of ways.

I was getting close to brain overload, and as much as I loved spending time with Ayda in our room, I knew what I needed before Slater even suggested it to me.

I needed a ride out.

After Jedd, Harry and Deeks left us, he took one look at

me and told me to call him when I was ready. It was only as the numbers on the books started to jump over one another again that I realized exactly what he'd meant.

Grabbing my helmet from the edge of my desk, I spun it around on the ball of my finger as I walked casually through the bar and out to the yard. Even though it was cold, the sun was shining for another day, and as my eyes flashed out to the sea of people walking across the gravel, there was only one person I was ever going to allow myself to focus in on. Her little ass was sashaying around the place like she owned it, which in a way, she absolutely fucking did. She owned me, so whatever I had was hers.

I was still trying to adjust to that.

Her excitement as she worked her way around the new wheels we had on court was adorable. Deeks was only two steps behind her wherever she went, his slow nod and genuine smile following her as her hands flailed around while she told him whatever story she had to tell. For reasons I'd probably never understand, the two of them loved one another without having to even say it. It made me feel relaxed. It made me feel happy knowing she was happy—and wasn't that a fucking foreign feeling if ever there was one?

When her eyes caught mine, I nodded to the side, giving her the silent communication that I had some shit to sort as I lifted my helmet up to her with one hand, then held up two fingers with the other. Two hours at the most. I'd be two hours. Then I planned on cashing in on my time with her charm. Ayda's lips curled into a smile as she bounced on her toes and continued to spin around as though she didn't have time for me. Another thing I was growing to love about her—the way she pretended those two hours apart wouldn't be the worst of her day.

Slater pulled up beside me before I even fired up my bike, his feet landing on the ground as he adjusted the strap under his chin and shouted over the throaty roar of his engine.

"Ready?"

"I'm always ready."

"You got some place specific in mind?"

Sniffing away the cold, I leaned over, gripping the handles and flexing my wrists as I stared at him and yelled back, "Actually, yeah, I do."

"Strip joint?"

My smirk grew into a smile as I started up my bike and slapped the kickstand back. "Nope. Nice try, though."

"What?" He laughed.

"You know what!" I shouted back, shaking my head and pulling out in front of him as I yelled over my shoulder. "Just trust me and take my lead."

I didn't miss the *'cause that's worked out so well for us before* look he threw me, but it only made me drop my head back between my shoulders and laugh. Fuck knows why I was even laughing at all. Nothing felt funny about that day. The tension in my stomach was growing with every passing second. There was an unsettled feeling emerging from deep within, something that was warning me that I was trying to juggle too many fiery balls of destruction all at once.

That was the problem with the new me, the one who had crawled his way out of prison with old scars on his back and new ideals in his mind. Nothing ever felt in sync. It was always a case of heart versus mind. Angels versus demons. Each day there was a new victor. I just never knew which one would come out on top from one moment to the next.

As soon as we pulled out onto the open road and I managed to let my body give in to the vibrations beneath me, I allowed myself to melt into the motion of the ride. When tire met asphalt, everything that seemed such a big deal suddenly took a back seat. All that was left were the sensations that ran through my body, the grip of the bars, the squeeze of my thighs, and the thunderous roar that started from the tips of my boots, shaking me all the way up to my helmet.

I was being cleansed. It was the next best thing to sex. Before Ayda, it had probably been better. It was hard to remember what came before her, which made it even harder to imagine a life without her at all.

Kenny flashed briefly through my mind, forcing my hand to pull down on the throttle as I tore through Babylon with no mind for anyone else.

Slater stayed the perfect distance behind me the whole way through, until we opened up to a wider road and he pulled up beside me. I cast him a quick glance, my smirk evident as he gave me the middle finger he'd just been sucking on. I loved that fucker like he was blood.

What I loved even more was seeing him pissed at the fact that I was leading him out to the unknown, and he couldn't whine in my goddamn ear about it.

The minutes flew by out there.

But as we rode out of Babylon and made the turns we rarely took, I felt the air around me grow tense and I knew that, even though he hadn't said it, Slater could sense what was going down.

We were going to Gun Barrel City.

The home of the Emperors.

He didn't say a word, not until we started to make our

way down their strip—the very place that changed all our lives just a few weeks ago—and I slowed to a crawl.

The bar they'd always resided in looked deserted when we pulled into their land, the dust from the unused and settled stones kicking up all around us until we were both parked side by side. In the daylight, the building looked even more ancient than I remembered it. Each wooden panel was worn and weary, the giant cracks in the material shining out as the sun showed all its faults like they were fucking trophies.

It was overused and under loved. Their absence gave it a sense of peace, like when someone dies and you bury them in the ground. They're finally allowed to rest. No more struggles. No more putting up with shit they hated. They just close their eyes on the world and finally exhale, letting all their faults shine.

That's what their place was doing.

It was shining, even though it was creepy as fuck.

"Looks clear," Slater coughed up beside me, his boots skidding out along the top of the loose stones as he repositioned himself on the bike.

"Hmm," was all I could reply with. My eyes were fixed and narrowed on the clubhouse in front of us.

"Mind telling me why we're here?"

I shrugged, my mouth turning down as I worked my helmet free before hooking it over the handles of the bike. "Let's just say I'm working on instinct here."

Slater groaned, his hands rubbing over the tops of his thighs as he spoke through a heavy sigh. "That's what I was worried you would say."

"Don't get scared on me now, brother." I laughed weakly, turning to face him as I swung my leg off to the right and made my way around to the front of my *Harley*. "You've never wussed out on me before."

"Yeah, and don't you live to fucking exploit that shit, Tucker," he huffed out, hopping up and around until he was standing beside me again, his face angled up towards the Emps' old base. "There's a good chance this place is rigged, in more ways than one. Just because we're in daylight doesn't mean things can't go boom."

"Boom?"

"Yeah, boom fucking boom."

"I like boom." I grinned, gripping his shoulder and squeezing it tight. "But there'll be no bang bang today. Pretty sure I beat the last breath out of their explosives guy."

"Hernandez?"

"Apparently so."

"Well, fuck."

"Besides," I said quietly, following his gaze up to the place. "I've got no desire to go inside. I'm here to check out the tire tracks that lead to their old storage unit back there."

"Tire tracks?"

I nodded slowly, my attention falling back to him as I waited for him to catch up. It took longer than it should have. Maybe one of the whores had sucked the last drop of fucking sense out of his dick the night before.

"Tire tracks..." he whispered. "This has to do with those bikes we saw drive past the other night."

"Let's give the man a prize," I said through a smile. Moving around him quickly as I jumped over to the side of the pathway, I kept my footprints away from anything that could mess this up.

"I don't know, Drew. The place looks pretty untouched

to me. There's not a fucking thing around here. Not even the tracks of their bikes. This place hasn't been touched for weeks."

"Dust marks travel into places dust shouldn't go," I muttered over to him, keeping my eyes on the cabin up ahead as my feet hit the dry grass at the edge of the woodland that framed this place.

Slater's voice fell someway behind me, and I could hear him mumbling something that sounded a lot like me thinking like the old Drew he'd once known, but I pushed it to the back of my mind and kept advancing forward. As much as the old Drew Tucker was still alive and well, he was the poster child for my youth, and the man now in charge was the one that was really holding the reins.

My legs crossed over one another as I moved forward, the twigs under my feet creaking and groaning as the soles of my heavy boots proved too much for them to handle. A loud crashing sound followed by the scurrying of feet quickly had the two of us freezing in place, hands reaching to the backs of our belts for our guns.

"Fuck!" Slater blew out as we both watched a coyote run out from behind the back of the building, two empty crates crashing and rolling over the ground as it sped away like it knew the devil's children had arrived.

"Coyote," I blew out in a breath.

"I hate those bastards."

"Rather them than an Emp."

"I wouldn't feel so bad about shooting an Emp."

Closing my eyes, I couldn't help but smile and shake my head. The tension was mounting, making my chest tighter and that ball of something in my stomach even more prominent. I rolled my shoulders in my cut, readjusting the leather around me and using it as some kind of security blanket as I opened them up again and continued to stalk closer.

When we eventually made it to the double doors and I saw there were only two locks holding the storage unit closed, I reached back around into the waistband of my jeans and pulled out my *Glock*, giving Slater a quick wink before I took aim and fired them off. The sound of shots filled the air, my shoulders flinching back and the muscles in my arms tensing to stay firm and enjoy the messed up vibrations that rang through my bones.

Sparks flew off the metal until I knew we were in, and I pushed up off my feet, flinging both doors open with an almighty shove as the old wood groaned against the ground.

I should have known their resistance meant something was wrong. I should have faltered when I saw just how easy it was to break in, but I didn't. Before I could fully register what I was seeing and the fact that two lines of wire ran from the handles on the door, into something in the middle of the garage, the triggers had snapped and the shots were fired.

Slater's shout filled the air as much as the blast did. The only thing I could do was try to duck out of the way before anything hit, but it was too late. The bullet whizzed past my ear, catching the edge and sending a jolt of fire down one side of my face as the deafening noise made me temporarily numb to everything.

"Drew!" Slater called out, skidding over to me once he'd pushed the doors out of the way.

Both hands flew up to cup my ear, my mouth set in a tight line and my face creased with pain as I hissed and cursed at the world that was suddenly ringing really damn loudly.

"Fuck!"

"Shit, brother. Shit!"

"Fuck, fuck, fuck."

"Talk to me. You okay? "

"Yeah," I croaked.

"Let me see it."

"The fuck was that?"

Slater pulled my hands away first, and I felt the small trickle of blood pour onto the creases of my lobe before dripping down onto my neck.

"You don't want to know," he muttered, brushing his thumb over the blood to wash it away. "How bad does it feel?"

Tipping my head to the side, I shook it slightly, watching as little droplets of red hit the dust covered ground. "Not too bad," I lied. "Just skimmed the top."

"You lucky bastard."

"Yeah, I've always wanted a chunk of my fucking ear taken out."

Turning back to look inside at what I'd already seen a glimpse of, I inhaled slowly, my nostrils flaring as the realization that I'd walked straight into a fucking trap started to sink in. When we both stood in the doorway of the place that once held the life and soul of our rival's beating heart, my lip curled up in anger and my hand flexed around my weapon.

Because as sure as I was the scum of the earth, there sat a single bike on a platform, two guns strapped to the handles, wired all the way to the front door.

Only it wasn't the bike I'd been expecting to see. Sitting smugly, taunting me with the epic fuck up I'd just made, was a pink fucking bicycle that a pre-schooler would have used, and on the white basket, with the bell sitting beside it, was a giant chalkboard displaying the words *Smile for the camera* written upon it.

We'd been expected. We were being watched.

It took thirty seconds for me to fire every bullet I had into the air and kill the surrounding cameras, but it was too little, too late. The damage had been done.

CHAPTER TWENTY-THREE
Ayda

Spending an afternoon with Deeks was always a nice way to pass the time, even if he did have an opinion on every single box with wheels that I picked out.

Drew would never allow that.

That's a foreign piece of shit, Ayda. What are you thinking?

Then my favorite: *Ayda, you get on that thing and Drew will kill me, not you.*

That was because I'd swung my leg over a crotch rocket—something that was just abhorrent to these men. Not to mention it also fell into the category of foreign piece of shit. It didn't leave me many options, so I gave up and promised Deeks I would torture Drew with the very short, shortlist.

The very same list I'd started with.

We were headed back to The Hut when the day got exponentially better. Tate was voluntarily out in the muddy grass off to the side of the yard with some of the other guys, throwing a ball around. They were all covered in mud, streaks of it caking their faces as the sweat cut lines through it. As always, the boys did nothing half way. Blood and slow forming bruises were already appearing on arms, legs and faces as they pushed one another around while Tate stood in the middle of his little huddle looking like he was in his element now that his two worlds had collided.

"Who's winning?" I asked, slipping onto one of the benches next to Libby as Deeks headed straight for the cooler with the beer.

"Who do you think?"

"That's our boy," I said, accepting the beer Deeks threw at me before he dropped down next to Harry on the porch steps.

"He's really good. That smile he's got on right now is just—" She cut herself off, grinned and looked down at her hands, her cheeks pink as she peeked back at my brother who was pointing his players to where he needed them to be. I got that she had a big thing for the kid, but hearing that from his older lover was a little bizarre.

"You've never been to one of his games?" I asked, steering the direction of our conversation into safer territory.

"Well, no."

"They still have a couple of games in the season, and if they get into state, even more. You should come with me next time." I cracked open my beer and drained half of it before kicking my feet out and crossing my ankles.

"I think I might. I also think you should know that he was a mess last night, Ayda," she said quietly, leaning forward to rest her elbows on her knees, her head turned in my direction and away from the men in the yard. "He sat up half the night talking about y'all's lives since your parents died. He worries about you. He worries that he's putting a strain on your relationship with Drew and that he's the reason you were so miserable before… Well, before you met Drew."

"Then he's a bigger idiot than he looks."

"Ayda!"

"Libby," I huffed, draining the beer I was holding and setting it by my feet.

I watched the play Tate had set up, the snap of the ball, the thunder of the feet and the perfect execution of Tate's throw. It was beautiful. It always was, no matter what position he was playing. I pulled my legs under me and brushed my bangs from my face before sucking in a deep breath and looking back to Libby, who was staring at me with a horrified expression.

"I'd never even thought about kids when my parents died. I was having too much fun being the selfish college student my parents always encouraged me to be. Man, they were good at loving us. They had their dreams, but they never pushed them on me. They just wanted Tate and I to do what made us happy, so I did. When they were killed, and I realized that I would be Tate's only role model in life, I freaked the fuck out. I wasn't worthy of that. I would never be our mom."

"But you did it anyway."

"I did. I've always loved Tate. Yes, he's my brother, but he was always a sweet kid with a big heart and dreams that reached further than the stars. I don't think we've ever been typical siblings and that's not just the age difference. We used to go camping and we'd drive to college games or to concerts in Dallas. When I was faced with my parents' will, it just seemed like a natural decision to make."

"What about your dreams?"

"They didn't matter so much anymore. His happiness made me happy; his dreams became my dreams. I never made the conscious decision to feel that way, either. When he got on the team in junior high and I saw that smile... I just knew."

"So, you're saying that he's an idiot because you weren't miserable?"

"Oh no, I was miserable alright." I laughed, leaning my elbows back on the table. "But Tate was the silver lining. He was the thing that made it all bearable. He was what made me happy. He's also the reason Drew and I crossed paths."

"Now that I remember."

"I think the entire pack does. What a night to try and rip off the Hounds."

Libby started laughing, her eyes moving back to the yard and finding Tate sprinting toward the makeshift end zone with Kenny and Moose at his heels. He made it over with time to spare, but it didn't stop Kenny from plowing into him. I was on my feet in a second, my hands cupped around my mouth to project my voice.

"That's a foul, asshole! Get off the field."

Kenny pushed up from the ground and looked in my direction, his hands slapping his chest as a challenge before he shrugged.

"Rules are rules, butthead. Move it or lose it."

"Pipe down in the cheap seats," Harry shouted, waving his beer at me. "I got a wager on this game, sweetheart."

"You bet against my brother, Harry?" I gasped in feigned horror.

"Better odds."

"How do I get in on that?" Deeks asked, his tone just as teasing as Harry's was. I loved seeing the club like that, unified and relaxed. A lot of them were still on high alert of course. That was only natural, but days like this were rare and I enjoyed them.

"Oh, y'all are going down."

"How you gonna manage that?"

I shrugged, pulling off my sweater, just leaving a T-shirt underneath. Handing it to Libby, I put my index finger and thumb to my lips and whistled as loud as I could. Tate's head popped up from his huddle and found me on the sideline, his eyes lighting up. It had been a while since I'd been on the field with him.

"You sure?" he shouted.

"What are you implying, Tater?" Tater was the name I'd used for him when he was born. I knew it wasn't right, but I used to tell Mom it was because he looked like a little tater tot all wrapped up in his swaddle blanket.

"You can be on Kenny's team."

"What? Why? I wanna be on the winning team," I shouted back, knowing what I was about to start.

"Hey!" Kenny's eyebrow shot up and his tone was full of incredulity. "You saying we're not winners, Hanagan?"

"That's exactly what I'm saying," I shot back, bouncing on my toes to taunt him further. "I could beat you alone with a hand behind my back. You're the worst player I ever saw, K-Dog."

"Come here and say that." Kenny laughed, spreading his arms wide. "I dare you."

Every man in the yard started to laugh, the whoops and hollers egging me on until I pushed off my toes and sprinted toward Kenny, stopping only when I was about four-feet away. There was a method to my madness. The mud was pooled by my feet. In an act of innocence, I clasped my hands behind my back and angled my body forward in a lean.

"You are the *worst* player I *ever* saw, Kenny."

The moment he moved to grab me, my foot kicked out,

spraying a line of mud right up his front and into his hair. He froze, I think in disbelief, as he tried to calculate just how much of a fool he'd been to fall into my trap. It wasn't like you could really tell all that much. They were all covered in mud anyway. My attack was just a little more deliberate.

"You got a little something…" I said, trailing off and pointing to my eyebrow.

"I'm gonna give you a head start."

"You think I'm scared of you?"

"One."

I was gone, my feet slipping and sliding in the mud as I headed straight for Deeks and Harry. Harry was laughing, but Deeks looked unsure, his humor evident only in a small smile as I dodged and cut a path in the opposite direction behind Tate's team.

Kenny didn't buy into my little game. He was like a train on rails, and he kept coming, his laugh maniacal as he finally caught me and took us both down and into the mud. He twisted to make sure he was on the bottom, ensuring my landing was softer, but he had one hand holding my arms as the other grabbed handfuls of wet mud to rub in my hair.

"Bastard. You're such a bastard." I half squealed and laughed. I finally struggled loose and rolled to my knees, my hand scooping up mud as I slid inelegantly to my feet. "Payback is a bitch."

I lobbed the mud ball at him and took off, sliding on my feet as I tried to sprint to safety but found myself defying gravity as he hoisted me over his shoulder with a shout of victory.

I was laughing so hard at my attempt to get free from his grasp that I didn't hear the bikes pull into the yard. I didn't know how long they'd been there when I finally caught sight of them, but I knew something wasn't quite right as Drew swung his leg over the bike and dropped his helmet onto the seat.

CHAPTER TWENTY-FOUR
DREW

The yard fell quiet as my eyes narrowed in on Ayda and Kenny. The moment my feet hit the ground, my shoulders rolled in my cut and my face tensed. I wasn't prepared to play by today's rules anymore.

Every part of my body was charging with a new kind of energy, the flames of anger growing and growing until they were curling around every piece of muscle, skin and fabric that was on me. Slater's quiet groan was the only thing I registered as I began to walk forward.

I couldn't fucking see anyone but the two of them, her and him rolling around on the ground, his hands touching places that didn't belong to him—touching someone he had no right to touch. There was no urgency to me reaching him. I knew that once this beast inside me was unleashed, things would get fucked up, so I took my time, trying to collect my thoughts as my chest heaved in and out and the muscles in my jaw flexed back and forth.

Everyone remained silent, their eyes wide as I gave each one of them a quick glance of fury from beneath hooded eyes. When they landed on Ayda, I saw her full smile fall slowly and the small scowl form on her face as she pushed the hair and mud away from her cheeks.

Her hands, which only moments earlier had been playfully punching Kenny's kidneys, reached up to tap his arm and gain his attention, but her eyes never left mine. They were still narrowed in confusion.

I groaned quietly, and as soon as Kenny saw me, he guided her down and avoided looking my way. His body tensed immediately, one foot shuffling on the ground as he tried to turn away, bringing the back of his hand to run under his nose.

The fucker knew.

He knew.

"Having fun?" I growled.

Ayda looked at me in confusion, her hands pushing her muddy hair from her face before planting her hands on her hips. "We were playing football."

"I was talking to him," I said through gritted teeth.

Seeming unsure, whether of Kenny's silence or my dismissal, she twisted her head to look at Kenny in question. "Okay."

He twisted back around, his head rolling as he closed his eyes as if to try and figure a way out of the shit he was obviously drowning in. When he opened them again, he gave me a resigned shake of the head and shrugged. "Not what it looks like, Drew."

"That so?"

He didn't answer.

"I asked you a question."

He still didn't answer.

"Tell me what it fucking looks like, Kenny."

Throwing his hand out to the side, he swallowed when his palm landed back down against his thigh. "Defiance, I guess."

"You guess?" I hit back, low and threatening as my eyebrows rose and I took a step closer. "Oh, I see it now. This is the part where you make me look like the possessive dick. This is the fucking part where you act innocent so I look like the bad guy, right?"

"Drew," Harry called out from somewhere around us, but I wasn't moving an inch. The blood was still dripping down one side of my face and all the adrenaline I'd been storing up for days seemed to have found a nice target in the form of Kenny's face.

"It was just football," Kenny finally spat out, turning around fully as he straightened up his shoulders.

"From where I was standing, it looked a lot like you were playing football with my girl's ass."

Ayda's eyes went wild as she stepped forward in an attempt to get my attention. "Wait just a goddamn minute. What the fuck is going on right now?"

She looked between Kenny and me, her confusion boiling over into anger.

My head snapped to her and I gave her the one look I didn't really feel inside. Disgust. My eyes raked down over her mud covered body as my sneer grew, only for me to turn back to Kenny and huff out a laugh.

"You tell her, K-Dog."

"Nothing," he said through an arrogant but shaky voice. "Nothing at all. Drew's obviously got the wrong idea."

There were many things that made me spitting fucking angry in life, but people talking about me like I wasn't even there was one of the main ones. If that's how he wanted to play it, that's how it was going to go down. My right hand curled even tighter, all my veins pumping in my arms as I tried to figure out a way to break his fucking jaw without losing Ayda in the process.

Pulling back slowly, I glared at him and lifted my hands to the edges of my cut. I had no idea of anyone else's position, but as I slid it off my arms, I tossed it to Slater behind me before nodding to the side of us. My shoulders were rolling, my neck stretching from side to side before I lifted my finger in the air and pointed it right at Kenny.

"I've had enough of this bullshit. You and me... training room. Now."

"Tucker, stop," Harry shouted roughly, a loud cough filling the air as the rest of the crew around us began to whisper and mutter.

"Drew..." Ayda said, her eyes on Harry as he approached. "Don't do this. You're bleeding and pissed off. Let me just take care of your ear. Then *talk* to Kenny."

My eyes raked over her face before I shook my head and whispered sarcastically. "Go. Away. Ayda. Your Oprah bullshit can't save this situation."

"What the fu—" Her words seemed to get stuck in her throat as she looked beyond me. Whatever caught her attention had her closing her eyes and breathing in deep breaths. When they finally flickered open, she looked between Kenny and me. "Don't do this. Please."

The fact that she was so concerned over the skull fucking I was about to serve Kenny only made my anger flare to life even more. I'd had enough of people telling me what to do and what not to do, and as I looked back up at my brother and stared into his eyes, I knew he wanted this as much as I did.

"No gloves," I breathed out, ignoring her completely before turning around and marching off towards the unit of the warehouse.

"I'm not going to watch you do this, Drew," she shouted after me. "This is ridiculous. When you feel mature enough to have a conversation, you know where to find me. This macho bullshit is…"Ayda trailed off, releasing a growled sigh of frustration at being silenced by whoever was closest to her.

I wanted to shout back that this macho bullshit was life in the club, but I knew 'if you don't like it, you know where the fucking gate is' would probably come back to haunt me later. Right then, all I could think about was Kenny's smug face as he realized my girl was pissed at me, not him.

Pushing through the door, I made my way into the middle of the room, the sound of my pack's heavy boots against the hard floor the only noise to fill the air. Not one person spoke until Harry came charging in, pushing through the men as he wheezed to a stop in front of me.

"Son, this won't solve anything."

I peered up at him through my heavy brows, my nostrils flaring as I shook out my arms and bounced from side to side on the balls of my feet.

"I know all you're seeing is red," he rambled on. "But Kenny can't beat you."

My eyes closed slowly as a small smirk played on my lips. I still didn't talk.

"You'll kill him."

"I know."

"This ain't right."

"I want to kill him. What y'all can't get your heads around is that he wants to kill me even more."

"Kenny?"

"You'll see," I said calmly, nodding to the side for him to

get the fuck out of the way as I watched Kenny walk in. None of my brothers said or did anything to either one of us, and it was only when Kenny shrugged out of his cut and ran his hands over the top of his hair that I saw the fight there in his eyes.

The natural laws of a good fight meant that the men in the room had formed a circle around us before we could even see it happening. My feet were planted firmly on the floor, my shoulders back as I stared down at my opponent and watched him work out and warm up the muscles in his arms.

Slater moved into the circle, one hand sweeping across his forehead as he held out both hands for us to head over to him. I glared at him like he was fucking stupid. This wasn't a boxing match. There was to be no referee. This was a street fight. Kenny wanted at me and I was gonna give him exactly what he wished for. Then I was going to break him.

"No need. This won't take long," I said flatly, shaking my head at Slater.

"That's what worries me." He sighed, shrugging his shoulders and moving back into the line.

The air was thick with tension, but all I was focused on was the man in front of me. Whether this was for me or for Ayda, I wasn't sure, but as I stood there completely still and watched him bounce to life in front of me, it was clear he'd been waiting longer for this than I ever realized.

Time seemed to stand still. I was unmoving and unblinking as I glared at him, both hands down by my sides, waiting for him to make his move. It didn't take much longer, and when Kenny launched himself forward, pushing up on the balls of his feet as he swung his right fist across my jaw, it was on.

The pain erupted in my face, and before I could even think about what he was doing next, Kenny's left arm swung until his knuckles connected on the other side, sending my neck snapping back in the direction it had just come from.

The kid was a real firecracker off the bat, smashing his jabs into my chest as he waited for me to attack. But I stood firm, tensing the abs in my stomach and accepting his blows one after the other, after the other. Every finger curled back and forth into the palms of my hands as I took his aggression, twitching, grunting, ready to take more and more.

After a good combination of hits to the center of my stomach, I stumbled back three steps, coughing out the aftershocks of the hits he'd driven into my flesh. Under different circumstances, I'd have been impressed.

My smirk took over one side of my face as I looked up at him and raised a brow. "Nicely done."

"Screw you."

"You finished?"

"No," he choked out. The look I was wearing was causing the exact effect I wanted it to. Within seconds, I had my arms up, my head bobbing from side to side as I fended off his next outburst. He hit right, then left, then right again, relentlessly trying to knock me on my ass as he worked harder than he ever had before. His face turned purple as he forgot to breathe, and as much as I wanted to remind him that I'd taken bigger beatings before breakfast while in prison, I knew he needed to think he was winning.

He needed to think he was better than me and more deserving of her.

I could grant him that for just a minute.

Pulling back, he danced on his toes, rolling his head from

side to side as his nostrils flared and he struggled to pull in enough air through his gritted teeth.

My chest heaved as I struggled to catch enough oxygen of my own, and as he took a second to collect himself, I bent over and pushed my fists into my knees, glancing up at the men all around me that were looking at me as though I'd lost my goddamn mind.

Slater was the only one who closed his eyes and let his chin drop to his chest.

Straightening my back to stand taller, I puffed out my chest and let my head fall to the side. Kenny had gotten more hits to my face and body than any man on the outside had in years. He could count himself a hero already, but something about the look in his eyes told me he wasn't quite there yet.

"Not bad," I breathed out.

His face set to murderous. "I don't need your motherfucking approval."

"You need to work on your sly kidney punches though, brother. Bit sloppy."

"Do not patronize me."

"I'm not here to patronize you. I'm here to let you get a few things off your chest."

"Fuck you, Drew," he wheezed.

My lips curled at both edges as I stepped closer. The throbbing in my face, my ear, my stomach and my chest was pretty intense, but it was my drug. Despite how much I tried to convince myself that this wasn't who I was, I couldn't deny it. I was all about the macho bullshit, as Ayda called it. Nothing was ever going to change that. Not even domestic life.

"Admit you hate me," I said quietly, dipping my head down to his level as the two of us struggled to speak through our heavy breaths.

"I hate you."

"Because I've got what you want, right?"

He didn't answer. Kenny's eyes searched mine frantically. I would have felt sorry for him had the anger not been drowning all that shit out.

Standing up taller, I waited him out. It took all of three seconds for his own frustrations to boil over and for him to snap. He swung for me, my left arm rising in the air to block him one final time before I threw all my power and weight into my right fist and hit him square across the jaw.

Kenny stumbled back instantly, his face creasing up as he tried to find his feet and his fight, but I didn't give him chance. Taking two steps forward, steps that felt like they shook the earth, I rolled my shoulders forward and hit him again. Right. Left. Right.

Then he was down. Falling to the side, his eyes rolled backwards as his head bounced off the floor and his body crumpled in on itself.

I stood over him, my fists down by my sides as I watched his arms come up to defend the yet to be broken bones of his face. Whatever he'd just suffered, he knew there was more to come. Someone beside me took a step into the circle, but quickly thought better of it before stepping back.

The silence lingered in the air again until I made my final move.

Leaning over him, I gripped the material of his T-shirt and yanked him forward. When I was close enough that I could practically eat the fucker, I stared into his scrunched up eyes and spoke.

"I'm not going to end you."

Kenny blinked slowly, his mouth falling open as he stared at me helplessly.

"I didn't want to have to fight you."

His face fell into confusion, the swellings on the side of his jaw already turning an angry shade of red.

"This was all on you," I said a little quieter.

A trickle of blood fell into my mouth and my tongue ran up to clear it away, not missing the cut in my top lip that he'd gifted me with. Kenny's attention fell to all the marks on my face and when his shoulders sagged in my grip, it was clear it was all over. He didn't have to say another word.

Pulling him to his feet, I stood him up on shaky legs, keeping a hold of his T-shirt until I knew for damn certain that he wasn't going to pass out on me. Collecting the blood in his mouth, he coughed and spat it on the floor beside us, the pain in his face obvious as he tried to roll out his jaw. When he eventually looked up through heavy eyes, I stepped away and went to the side of the circle to collect his cut. Travis handed it over without question, giving me a nod of respect as I turned back and walked over to my opponent.

Standing behind him, I slid it up both his arms while he just stood there looking dumbstruck, flinching when I slapped two hands on his shoulders before walking back to stand in front of him again. My eyes wandered to our patch on his leather and I let my thumb trace over it.

"Whether you hate me or not, don't *ever* give me a reason to hit a brother or question his loyalty again."

Then I walked out through a sea of bodies who all parted for me without anyone uttering a single fucking word.

CHAPTER TWENTY-FIVE
AYDA

Men! All of them were arrogant, ignorant, cocky bastards. What made it worse was the fact that the one I was in love with was currently treating me like a possession. I wasn't sure what had pissed Drew off so much. It wasn't the first time we'd all had some fun out on the field throwing the ball around. It had been a while for me, sure, but it wasn't unusual. I could have understood his reaction had Kenny and I been alone, but the whole fucking club had been out there with us.

I was pacing the room I'd been given—my sanctuary away from the MC, Drew, and the politics of the club. It was the only place in the building I could call mine, and it was exactly what I needed. If I looked at a cut, I was going to lose my shit. I was drowning in testosterone, and it was making me crazy.

"Ayda?" Deeks' gentle voice followed his soft knock. There was no judgment, no reprimand in his tone. Just concern. Everyone in the pack had followed Drew and Kenny, and here he was at my door, worrying about me and how I felt about it all. He was probably the only man in the world I was willing to talk to in that moment.

Diverting from my path, I circled around to the door and

unlocked it before heading to the plush bed and the million throw pillows that were scattered around. I dropped onto them, my hands landing on my forehead as I refused to look at the cut Deeks was wearing.

"Come on, darlin', ain't you supposed to be flattered or something?" Deeks asked playfully, forcing me to drag my hands down my face so I could see him.

"I'm insulted, Deeks." I pulled one of the cushions to my chest and wrapped my arms around it. The longer I thought about it, the more pissed off I became. All of Drew's wrath had been aimed at Kenny, but he'd dismissed me like a child, like my opinions meant absolutely nothing to him.

Deeks wandered deeper into the room and pulled the chair from the vanity to the middle of the room before straddling it and folding his arms along the back. His eyes locked on mine. It was then I felt annoyed at him for being so calm and logical. I needed to go to the diner so I could bitch about men and their pathetic pissing contests, so I wouldn't feel like the unreasonable one around there.

"You gotta realize, Ayda, a bunch of hard-headed assholes in one place and they're gonna have a fight about things on occasion."

"I'm not a *thing*, Deeks." I bounced to the edge of the bed and leaned forward, my hands pushing up my face and back into my hair. "You're missing the point anyway."

"Am I?"

"Yes, you are. Whatever Drew thinks is happening, whatever reason he's convinced himself to be jealous, he's forgotten one, tiny little detail."

"And that is?"

"Me."

Deeks lifted a hand and gripped his chin, pulling it down to the point and tugging to the ends of his beard before releasing it and his breath. "I ain't following, darlin'."

"We're supposed to be in a relationship. He's out there accusing Kenny, but where is his trust in me? If he thinks for a second I could ever do that to him, what's the point? He obviously doesn't know me, and he sure as hell doesn't trust me, so what do we have?"

"Kid, men sometimes have a need to prove a point to the men around them. Some choose to do it with displays of affection, hand holdin' and crap, and others challenge someone who would dare to consider so much as looking at their woman. It's not about possession, Ayda. It's about holding onto the one thing that he needs, that he can't live without. Drew challenging Kenny, he's saying Kenny needs to get a grip on his crush because Drew thinks you're worth fighting for."

"I hate you." I huffed in a half laugh, half sob. I should have known that his logic would appeal to mine. He always managed to play the devil's advocate. I knew if he'd been talking to Drew, he'd probably be describing my reaction with as much intuition as he was with me about Drew. When the man said he saw everything, he wasn't boasting, he was just being honest.

"No, you don't. You hate that I'm making it impossible for you to stay mad."

"But I really don't want to be pissed off, Deeks."

"Then don't be."

I made crazy hands at him and fell back against the mattress, my eyes searching the ceiling for some wisdom that would fit more along the lines of my irrational anger, but there was nothing. Deeks didn't say anything more. He knew he didn't have to. He'd given me food for thought and he was letting me digest it, while offering me silent companionship at the same time.

When a wave of voices reached us from the main room, I knew it was only a matter of time before the liquor flowed and my window of opportunity to have a conversation with Drew was diminished. I needed to talk to him before he got drunk. If I didn't, I would just let it fester until I blamed him for the lack of sweetener in the mornings. Deeks saw the decision in my eyes the moment I sat up. He stood, headed to the door and held it open for me until I bounced off the edge of the mattress and headed toward the main room, ignoring the trail of dirt as I turned around to grab Drew's cut where I'd dropped it after taking it from Slater.

"Thanks, Deeks."

"Anytime, kid. I guarantee any argument you can come up with, I've probably had at some point in my life.

"My encyclopedia of domestics," I said, patting his chest as I passed him. "What would I do without you?"

"You'd put your foot in your mouth more than you already do." He chuckled, heading toward the bathrooms with a wave over his shoulder. "Now go take care of this shit before you both think too goddamn much."

"We can't all be as wise as you," I mumbled playfully, heading toward the main room, hugging the supple leather to my chest.

I found Drew with Harry at the bar. He was nursing a whiskey while Harry tried to stop the bleeding on his ear with rubbing alcohol and cotton balls. I hadn't noticed quite how bad it was while we were standing outside, but being this close up, I could see it was more than a simple scratch.

"Hey, Harry," I said, sliding up slowly and draping Drew's cut over his lap. "You mind if I take over?"

Harry looked to Drew rather than me, his unwavering loyalty there to back Drew up on whatever the hell he needed. With a small nod, Harry dropped the cotton he was holding and shot me a surreptitious wink before heading toward Jedd and Slater at the other end of the bar.

I picked up a clean cotton ball, dipped it in peroxide and worked in silence for a while, watching as the liquid fizzed and bubbled around the edges of the wound, eating what little bacteria had already formed there. I was trying to think of what to say, how to start the conversation.

He twitched as I got to the fleshier part of his wound and wiped it gently. I'm not sure anyone else would have noticed, but I'd spent hours exploring that jaw of his and I knew how to read the subtle jerks. He took a mouthful of his Scotch and leaned forward to rest his elbows on the bar, forcing me to move with him.

"I'm sorry. It's really raw here," I said quietly, dropping the bloodied cotton to the surface and picking up a clean one. "What happened?"

"I got shot," he said robotically, the raspy sound of his voice annoying him as he cleared his throat and stared into the bottom of his tumbler.

"What? Drew!" My hand reached to cup the other side of his face, the panic in my gut becoming a painful knot of anxiety. "What the hell happened? Who shot you? Where?"

Dragging his bottom lip through his teeth, he looked up at me briefly before he glanced back down into his glass. "I took Slater out to Gun Barrel City. We went to the Emps' base and I walked straight into a trap. I'm fine. It's just a graze."

"No. You don't get to play this off as nothing, Drew. You could have been killed." I pressed the cotton against his ear a little harder than I'd intended and cringed as he hissed quietly. At least his bad mood had a bit more of an explanation.

"I think that's what they were hoping for."

There was nothing I could say to that. I knew the danger of his lifestyle when I fell in love with him. I knew that every time he got on his bike and went out there, it could be the last. Unfortunately, a slap of reality like the one I was faced with made the possibilities come crashing down around me like a ton of bricks. What could I possibly say to his cynicism without sounding like some nagging old wife?

"I'm sorry you were hurt, Drew, but all I ask is you be safe out there. I know you have to do what you have to do and all that shit, but I can't lose you. I need…" I trailed off, unable to follow the train of thought for a second longer. I could only handle so much before I started to break, and I'd convinced us all I was strong enough to do this. I had to stay true to my word. "I'll get bandaids."

"You know…" he started quietly, as though he hadn't heard a single word I'd just said. "Sometimes I don't think you understand that this lifestyle isn't exactly about choices. It's a nice concept, but talking and being safe aren't always the ways I get to keep this club and my family alive."

He glanced up at me, his wrist rolling the liquid around in the glass he was still loosely hanging on to.

"I never said it was, Drew. I would never ask you to put anyone in the club at risk. I'd never ask you to put your life above theirs." I had no idea where I was even going with that line of thought. Nothing I said would be right. I just had to say one more thing and hope that he actually heard it. "But don't ask me to stop caring. I love you too much to do that. The sooner you figure that out, the better."

He huffed out a small laugh, shaking his head before he raised a brow. "That's the difference between the two of us. I would never ask you to change a single thing about yourself. You wouldn't be who I…" For a moment, I thought he was going to say the words I knew he really felt, but when a small frown took over his face, I saw his disappointment match what I felt inside. "You wouldn't be you then, and it's you I want, not some stupid whore who just agrees to anything and everything I say. Not someone who would ask how high when I tell them to jump. I just wish you saw what you asked of me sometimes, too."

"I have never once asked you to change anything about who you are. I don't know how you could possibly think I would." I leaned in to make sure no one around us could hear me. "I've never asked anything but for you to love me, and it's the one thing you can't fully give me and I even love *that* about you. It's a part of your strength. But this is just cruel. Point the fingers of blame all you want, but you're the man I love, and every contrary little piece of politics that comes with you I've accepted."

I leaned back and threw what I was holding to the counter, my eyes scanning the group closest to us as I began to tremble with the emotions that had no outlet. I needed an escape, and as I looked down at myself, I found the one I needed.

"I'm going to take a shower."

His mouth moved to speak, but he decided against it, his shoulders falling forward as he drained the last of his drink and slammed the tumbler down onto the counter. "Okay."

I started out of the room, desperate to run but keeping my pace slow. I normally would have headed to our room, but I didn't want to see him. He'd not only insulted me with his unspoken accusations, but now he was accusing me of the one thing I'd made an effort not to do. I loved him for who and what he was, scars and skeletons included. *That* was the man I'd fallen in love with and shared my bed with—the man I'd accepted in every way a woman could.

Unfortunately, when you gave someone that much of yourself, you gave them the tools they needed to hurt you. Drew had used that love against me, and I used all my anger to slam the door closed, twisting the deadlock before I slid down to the floor, burying my face in my knees as I struggled to find my breath.

CHAPTER TWENTY-SIX
DREW

"Should I put up the *beware of dog* sign?"

I wasn't sure how long I'd been sitting there, staring into the bottom of my glass after she walked away, but the second I heard Harry's voice, I knew I was exhausted, mainly because that old joke of his would have brought a smile to my lips, once upon a time. Now all it did was float through the jumbled up web of thoughts in my mind, only to get lost among all the other shit.

I tried anyway. For him. My face was lifeless and I pushed the air out of my nose and attempted to make it sound like some kind of laugh.

Harry's sigh blew into the hair on the good side of my head, his hand resting down on my shoulder. "It's just a bad day, son. It ain't a bad life."

The irony of that statement should have been enough to snap me out of it, too, but still I stayed, as still a statue.

"Shit," he grumbled, before he left my side altogether and went to stand on the opposite side of the bar. The top of the bottle clinked against the edge of the tumbler in my grip, but not even the sight of that golden liquid made me look up. When it was half full, he stopped and let the bottle fall to the counter while I took a slow and steady sip of the good stuff and allowed the heat to burn me alive.

"Tucker."

"Yep." I gasped, smacking my lips together and wincing when the alcohol hit the cut on my lip.

"Look at me."

"Nope."

"Look at me, son."

"I'm a little bust up at the moment, Harry."

"Inside or out?"

Just like that he had my attention. My eyes rose slowly, taking him in as I tried to think of something to say. The stuff going on in my head hurt more than any of my external injuries, and the fact that someone else could see it stung like a bitch.

"I think you already know," I answered quietly.

"Still. It would be nice to hear you admit it for once." Resting both hands on the counter, he put all his weight on them and tilted his head to the side. As funny looking as I found him, his was the one face that usually felt safe to me, even when we were disagreeing. I never feared him walking away and never coming back, no matter what I said or did. His loyalty knew no limits. Neither did his love.

"Why?"

"Because then it gives me hope that all this shit you're putting yourself through isn't just in vain. I think I understand what's going on in that head of yours, but these days, you keep surprising me and making me second guess myself just that little bit more than I used to."

"I'm sorry."

"No need," he said through a sad smile, raising one hand to stop my apology before dropping it back down. "I like to be kept on my toes."

"Good job around this place." Lifting the whiskey to my mouth again, I took another big gulp and sighed heavily. "I'll be glad when today is over."

"Yeah, you look a bit more abstract than you did this morning."

I laughed genuinely that time. "I feel it, too."

"Inside or out?" he asked again.

"Both."

Leaning forward, he dropped down to rest his forearms on the bar, clasping his hands together in front of the two of us. "She looked pretty upset when she walked away just now."

"I know."

"Why haven't you gone after her?"

"Truthfully?"

"It would help."

I looked back down into the glass, closing my eyes as I took another drink, throwing my head back fully to drain it before slamming it back on the surface again. "Because I'm scared of what I will say to her if I do."

"She loves you, kid."

"So everyone keeps telling me."

"You don't believe us? Or her?"

"I believe all of y'all. Especially her. That doesn't mean that any of this is right for any of us. Especially her."

"Your old man always used to talk in riddles. Always confused the living shit out of me. I'm a straight shooter, Drew. You know that more than anyone. I don't have any filter and I've never been good at puzzles. I'm here for you, though. I'm willing to listen. You've just gotta give it to me in black and white."

"White. I love her. Black. She can't survive this world."

The slow nod of his head as he leaned even closer had me freezing in place.

"So this is you pushing a good thing away?"

"I think it might have to be the start of it," I croaked, clearing my throat quickly and frowning even harder, even though it hurt every part of my face to do so. "I always thought I was selfish, Harry. Up until today, I thought I could keep a hold of her no matter what because when the rest of the world is shut out and it's just the two of us in my room, we feel fucking invincible together."

"Why is it different out here?"

"Because if she loses me any other way, it will kill her."

"Any other way?"

I reached up to my eyes, rubbing across the swellings on either side as I sighed heavily. "She hates me right now because I haven't followed her into the bedroom. She hates me for going out to Gun Barrel City today with Slater and almost getting killed. She hates me because I wasn't, in her words, man enough to deal with my anger without using my fists, and she's only gonna hate me more when she sees Kenny. I'm halfway there already. I may as well push her off the fucking cliff and send her away to someone who can look after her."

"Son…"

"No, Harry. Let me finish." My hands dropped in front of his, clasping together to mirror his pose. Licking my lip that had started to bleed again, I looked down at my fingers and shrugged. "Do you know why I was so mad when I saw her with Kenny today? It wasn't because he was touching her, or the fact that I'd warned him off this morning already. It wasn't even the fact that I saw how much he enjoyed having her ass in his hands."

Harry's eyes widened, his smile falling flat as he waited for me to finish.

"It was the fact that when I saw her so happy, I knew I was going to be the one to end that. In that moment, no matter what I said or did, I was going to strip that away from her. Don't you see? I will always be that guy—the bearer of bad news. She would have to do her usual preachy shit about me riding out with Slater and get pissed, and when I saw that Kenny was the one bringing all the smiles while all I could dump at her feet was more bad news, I flipped. I saw red. I wanted to kill him and, irrationally, I felt angry at her. I don't even know why. I think that's when I knew I wanted her to hate me. I just couldn't see it until the mist had cleared and the dust had settled after the fight."

He sucked in a breath, holding the weight of it high in his chest as he thought about what I'd just told him. I watched and waited, my eyes flickering over every one of his features, expecting the slap up the side of the head any time. When he exhaled slowly and I saw the sadness in his eyes, I felt that sick, twisted knot grow even bigger and tighter in my stomach.

Harry thought I was doing the right thing by letting her go.

"It's not an easy life we lead here," he said quietly.

"My body agrees with you." I swallowed harshly, the pain of my thoughts becoming too much to bear.

"She won't go quietly."

"I love her too much to let her stay just so I can break her. Or worse, make her hard. We're already fighting too much as it is."

Pushing up on his feet as far as his stubby legs would

allow him, he leaned in the final distance so he was sure only I could hear him. "That's because she's a woman who needs to hear the man she loves say he loves her back. Even when she says it's not necessary. That's what women do. They take the loads, carry the burden. Before you make any decisions to do what you're thinking about doing, you should at least try and tell her how you feel. Maybe it could be something for her to take away from all this."

"I can't tell her I love her, Harry." I shook my head violently, my jaw setting almost as tightly as my heart did. If there was one thing I knew for certain, it was that I couldn't say those words to Ayda.

"Why not?"

Locking eyes with his, I swallowed again, my face scrunching up as I bared my fucking soul.

"Because if I start saying it now, I'll never stop, and she won't ever have the life she deserves."

CHAPTER TWENTY-SEVEN
AYDA

Happiness.

It was a word I thought I understood before my parents died, but it slipped through my fingers after their murder; an emotion I thought I'd experienced often, and a state of mind that I wasn't always sure I would return to. These were areas Drew clarified for me on a daily basis. With him, I understood the full extent of the word and everything it had to offer. It was an emotion I felt every time I was in his company, every time he touched me or smiled at me. It was like a thousand fireflies tickling the lining of my stomach, waiting to be set free. When I looked at him, when I thought ahead to our future together, it was something I knew was waiting for me as long as I was with him.

He was wrong about my wanting to change him. I wasn't sure where he'd come up with the notion, and in all honesty, I didn't care. I knew myself, and I knew my daydreams. In every future I'd made for us, he was the man he'd always been—formidable, strong, scary as hell and loyal to a fault. We fought because we were passionate people; we argued because we were both hardheaded and convicted in our beliefs and opinions. Even with our differences, I knew we were right for one another. He was the dark to my light. We worked because we were so different.

Drew and I were tinder and flame. All I had to do was look his way and he consumed my thoughts, and every memory of our nights together would drag me under the surface until I was drowning in need. I'd never felt that with anyone before him, and part of me knew I never would again. I didn't care how many times we fought or disagreed—I knew that would never change.

I took a shower and stripped the mud-caked blankets and pillows from the bed before remaking it hastily. Collapsing on top of it with my earphones in, I closed my eyes and shut out the world as I tried to find some center of balance again. The dulcet tones of some of my favorite singers wrapped around me and I let my mind wander into the maybes of the future. We'd had another fight. Yes, another, but this one was different. He'd never slammed walls down on me before.

I must have searched for answers for hours before the realization slapped me so hard it had me gripping my chest.

That son of a bitch.

How the hell could I have been so blind?

Was it really that simple?

I flopped on the bed until I was on my stomach and crawled to the edge, hopping off as my mind formulated the plan I had to finally get his full attention. It was risky and probably cruel, but I had to prove a point. He needed to open his eyes for a change rather than acting as though he knew what was best for me and us. I needed him to listen to what I was saying. I was an adult. I knew my own mind, and I wasn't going to have it made up for me. I just had to figure out whether or not I was going to get burned in the process.

I paced in front of the dresser several times, gnawing on

my cuticles before I finally found the guts to so much as open the drawer where I'd hidden it. I bought the damn thing after the fire, when we went to the city to replace some things and get us some clothes. I didn't know what I was thinking at the time, and pulling it out, I still wasn't sure. As much as I trusted him, we hadn't ever needed something like this. We still didn't, but there were quite a few men in that room.

My hand moved to my stomach as the nerves ate me alive. It was either going to work like a dream or make matters worse. I wasn't entirely sure which, but Mom had always said some risks were worth taking when it was something worth fighting for. She probably didn't have this in mind, but I figured it was open to interpretation.

It didn't take me long to get ready. The lace lining the satin barely brushed my thighs, and as I stood looking in the mirror of my private bathroom, I realized the top was almost entirely made up of lace. I looked like an expensive whore.

Sucking in a deep breath, I rushed to the door and unlocked it as I rolled my shoulders back and held my head high.

If I could have pushed myself out, I would have. It took everything I had to walk from that room and down the hall to the main room of The Hut. For a while, I thought I'd managed to get away unnoticed, but the din of the conversation died like a blanket being pulled over them and all eyes turned to me.

I was an absolute idiot.

My eyes scanned the room frantically and found Drew exactly where I'd left him. Harry was behind the bar, both hands flat on the surface, his arms rigid as he gave me a once over, blinking like he'd just been stung by a bee. Then he leaned in and said something to Drew, and I held my breath.

Drew's frown was immediate, and I saw him mouth something to Harry before he eventually turned his attention on me. When he had to do a double take, narrowing his eyes as they held mine before he let them trail all the way to my feet and back up again, I thought he was going to at least say something. But then he glanced back at Harry, dropped his hand to his face and started scrubbing wildly, and I was left standing there, alone.

I'd known it wasn't going to be easy. Drew was Drew after all. The thing he didn't count on was me being more stubborn than he ever could be. Moving with slow confidence, I started toward the bar, my steps deliberate, even as my heart was ready to beat from my chest. When I finally reached Drew, I flashed Harry the most confident smile I could manage, doing the best I could not to look at Drew.

"Hey, Harry, you have a bottle of Tequila back there I can have? I'll replace it tomorrow."

Harry pushed off the bar, but stayed put, his eyes fixed on Drew out of respect, waiting for a response. I was pretty sure I was making every guy in the place uncomfortable, but I had my sights set on only one of them.

Drew held his pose. His hand never moved as it covered his temple, but I felt and saw every bit of tension in his forearms. The skin across his knuckles was still bleeding and the bruising across his face already looked worse. Lifting his free hand, he flicked it in the air at Harry, obviously some silent communication I wasn't allowed to understand taking place.

Whatever it was, Harry moved back to reach for the bottle of Tequila, turning back around and keeping hold of it as he looked between the two of us like we were two ticking time bombs.

"Am I going to have to climb over the bar for that, Harry?" I put one knee on the stool, my body rocking forward, the cool air making me more than aware of how much of my ass was on display. I was hoping I could play this off as being drunk already. Harry and Drew would know the truth, but maybe no one else would have to.

Hoisting myself up and swinging my ass around, I sat on the edge of the bar and fought the urge to tug the skirt of the slip down to cover myself. It went against every instinct I had, but Drew was giving me a run for my money in the stubborn department.

His hand slid down to cover his eyes, his finger and thumb squeezing to pinch the bridge of his nose. Considering the amount of marks on his face, I knew it must have been hurting him to touch his cuts that way, but as he muttered quietly under his breath, something that sounded very much like *she's trying to get me killed today,* I couldn't stop the small smile that crept onto my face.

"What the fuck are you doing, Ayda?" he growled quietly.

"I'm making a spectacle of myself, Drew," I said, crossing my legs and aiming them in his direction. "Would you like to know why?"

"I would like you to put some motherfucking clothes on. That's what I would like."

"If you keep walking down the path you're building for us, it'll be out of your hands. You're pushing me away and I really don't fucking appreciate it. So, before you ruin everything we have together, I'm giving you a glimpse of your future. If you keep pushing, I will end up resenting you, and I won't wait forever for you to wise up. You don't get to choose how I dress, or who sees me that way." With my hands on the polished surface, I lifted my ass and slid closer to him, no one else in the room really mattering to me at all. "I don't know about you, but that thought makes me miserable. So, I'm dressed this way for you, and I'm going to apologize if you thought I was trying to change you in any way. I never wanted that. I've only ever wanted you. You, Drew motherfucking Tucker, president of the Hounds, the mean, angry and sexy man I love."

I sucked in a breath, finally taking a break to stare at my thighs and find some of the confidence that was slowly leaking from every pore on my body.

His hand slowly fell down his face to stroke the outline of his beard before he let out a heavy sigh. When he allowed himself to look up, I wasn't sure how to read what I saw staring back. Resting his cheek against two fingers, he stared at me in a way he never had before. There was no emotion that I could pick out and cling on to, just an empty face filled with nothing but war wounds.

"Harry?" he whispered. "Give her the liquor."

Harry held his arm out and I took it with an imperceptible nod of thanks. The humiliation was almost immediate as I felt every eye in the place on me. I could tell the whores were enjoying every second. Even without looking, I could feel their smirks thickening the air until it was cloying enough to choke on.

I was a proud person, and walking into the room the way I had was a huge risk to my pride and it had severely backfired. I slipped from the bar and walked toward the hall, forcing myself to keep my head up and shoulders back. The moment I was free and clear, I was running like Hell was at my heels. At least I knew how little I meant to him. He'd already made up his mind, which meant my old friend Tequila and I could have a party of our own and I could deal with everything else in the light of day.

My hands were trembling almost uncontrollably as I closed the door to my room and turned the lock.

My sanctuary didn't feel very safe anymore. Nothing did.

Stripping the slip off with one hand, and unscrewing the top off the bottle with my teeth, I wandered toward the dresser to dig out my yoga pants and hoodie. I would drink myself to sleep and start a whole new day by going to the diner and getting some of my old shifts back.

I was still in my underwear and a hoodie when an almighty smash made me swing in a circle. My heart made its way to my throat, and my hand, swiping the bottle from the dresser, trembled violently. The wood of the door seemed to cower just knowing what was on the other side and the brutality it was about to be subjected to, but all I was scared of was more pain. I was terrified of the rejection I knew was coming.

The second impact on the door made it jump out of Drew's path. His palm slapped it to the side as it hit the wall and swung back toward him and the frame. The sound was deafening and his face was like thunder. He was pissed, and this was going to be the mother of all fights. I had a feeling that, for the second time in a year, I was about to find myself homeless.

CHAPTER TWENTY-EIGHT
Drew

I stood there in front of her, my legs shoulder width apart as I dragged air into my chest and stared her down. The shock and fear that shone back from her eyes should have made me feel something other than rage, but I couldn't get the fucking image of her parading herself around out of my head. I wasn't even grateful that she was now a little more covered up.

"What the fuck was that?" I growled, my voice straining to get out and stay under control as my eyes trailed the length of her body again.

"That was me getting your attention," she said, waving the bottle of Tequila at me, the fear receding enough that her own anger started to shine through.

"That was you acting like a child—a spoiled child who couldn't wait to stick the knife in just that little bit more. Had I not been through enough today already? Did you want to kick me a little harder than everyone else had managed to? For fuck's sake, Ayda!"

I took a step closer, then another, my body moving closer to the edge of the bed, only stopping from getting too close to her for fear of what I might say, or worse, do. The anger was making my blood boil and I was absolutely fucking exhausted already.

She backed away, her hand brushing through her hair as she looked around the room and down at her bare legs. She was looking anywhere but at me. "I'm sorry you had a shitty day, but you are having a lot of them lately, Drew, and I gotta say, I'm sick to death of you coming home and pushing me a little further away from you. Do you have any idea what it's like to watch you leave day after day and wonder if you're going to come back and pull me closer or keep me at arm's length? I've never wanted you to be anything but who you are, but I ask for just a sliver of respect and I'm changing you."

She took a mouthful of Tequila, her eyes narrowing as she wiped the residue away with the back of her hand.

"You don't ask. You demand. You tell me when you want me to talk, and fuck, if I don't do it in that moment, in front of *all* my goddamn men I might add, I'm the asshole. I'm immature and full of macho bullshit. You see what you want to see. You hear what you want to hear. It's all about that moment, the one you continue to walk or run away from when I don't act or respond the exact way you want me to." My hands flew in the air, both of them shaking violently as I leaned forward and widened my eyes. "Newsflash, Ayda: I have no clue how to do anything but be who I am and do what I do. I'm trying every day, I really fucking am, but I can't put the shit that runs through my veins off. If I want to slam Kenny up against a wall, that's what I'm gonna do. My men won't respect me and I wouldn't respect myself if I was to hold up a hand and say *hang on a minute, bro. I just gotta explain to the old lady why I want to knock all your front teeth out and show your face what your asshole looks like.* Do *you* have any idea what it's like to be *me*? I get that this isn't easy for you, but easy is something I never promised you in this life. Ever. What you just did out there wasn't you. That's not who you are."

Ayda spun away from me, her free hand balled into a fist at her side. I could see the tremble as she pushed it against her thigh, her shoulders rising and falling with her breaths. "Once. One fucking time and it's all I'm capable of doing, right? I couldn't give a fuck about you and Kenny, Drew. It's club business—nothing to do with me, right? Thing is, you're not even fucking getting the point here. You're too fucking invested in making up bullshit reasons to make me the bad guy."

She reached the wall and turned, pressing her back to it.

"I've never demanded a thing from you. I never *once* asked you to change who you are or what you represent in front of your men. I always keep questions and opinions to myself until we're in *your* room. So don't stand there and preach your bullshit to me. Be fucking straight with me. You're tired of being tied down. I'm cramping your style… No, wait! This life is too dangerous for me? God forbid I make up my own damn mind."

I pointed back to the bar and kept my eyes trained on her. "I'm fucking sorry… Was that you keeping your opinion to yourself out there while you were flashing your ass to the entire club? Was that you keeping your opinion to yourself in the yard when you told me what you thought of me and my macho bullshit?" Tilting my head to the side, I frowned and leaned a little closer, lowering my voice. "And you know more than anyone that if I was tired of being tied down, I'd be the first to let you know. Don't taint who I am now with who I used to be when it comes to women. I wasn't the one out there, half naked, making an exhibition of myself. You're right, this life is too fucking dangerous for you, because out there, I wanted to kill every man in that room the moment they laid eyes on what was mine. Fucking mine! I wanted to kill my own family… for you! I would never do that to you. Never. No matter how much I thought you'd fucked up."

I stood up straight, closing my eyes and pulling in a deep breath as my hands found my face before sliding all the way down it. Letting them fall to the edge of my mouth, I sighed and looked back up at her, unable to ignore the absolute agony of the pounding in my chest as all the external cuts and injuries ceased to exist.

"You're basing this whole fucking argument on *one day*, Drew. One. I'm not perfect. In fact, I'm so fucking far from it I don't even feel the rays of it on my face. What that *was* out there was a desperate attempt to keep you in my life. You think I can't feel when you're pushing me away? You think I don't know when you've made your mind up? I'm not stupid, and I'm not as naïve as you seem to think I am." She swung the bottle in my direction, one foot rising to press against the wall behind her as she dropped her chin to her chest. "Loving you terrifies me. You alone have the power to break me. I'm the one that handed that to you, and you wanna know the crazy thing about it? I would do it again and again, because you're worth it. We're worth it, even when I don't like you very much."

"I never promised you an easy ride," I said quietly, my head shaking from side to side. "And I've never once pushed you away before today. All I needed was a little bit of time. I'm a big boy, Ayda. I can take a lot, but I'm one man. One. Man. Sometimes, I can't just be yours, just like you can't be mine and only mine. There are too many other people in our lives for us to always be selfish."

Placing the bottle on the window ledge, Ayda pushed away from the wall with her foot, her hand rubbing under her nose as she walked toward me. Stretching an arm out cautiously, she stepped closer, pressing her palm flat against my chest as she breathed in. "I never expected an easy life. I'm not even sure I wanted one. The fact is, whether you were conscious of it or not, you've been pushing me away in one way or another since the week after the fire. All of this you're throwing at me, you and I both know it's not the *real* issue here. I love you, Drew Tucker, and that scares both of us. It makes everything uncertain. So I'm going to give you an easy out. It's a yes or no question. I rescind any responsibility you think you have for me. I take culpability for my own safety. You have nothing left to keep me here but you. Do you want me to leave?"

I grabbed her wrist quickly, the frown on my face taking over all my features as I held her tightly and pulled her away from my chest. "An easy out? You think anything would be an *easy* out for me at this point? Is it that black and white for you?"

"For me? Never," she said, looking down at my hand wrapped around her wrist, before bringing her eyes to meet mine. "I just need to know *something*, Drew. All these walls you put up... I realize you're protecting yourself, and in some respect, your club, but call me crazy, I need to know if you're going to keep pushing to get that end result. If I'm going to survive losing you, it can't be dragged out."

I was certain I'd been stabbed in the chest with a jagged piece of glass when I stared into her eyes and saw all her pain and confusion. My top lip curled in disgust at this whole sorry, fucked up situation. How could I tell her that I felt what I felt and have any hope of saving her? If she knew I loved her, she would never do what was right for her future. If I told her I didn't love her, I'd never be able to forgive myself for denying my own life the one thing that it now needed more than anything else on this fucking earth. Her.

Letting our arms fall slowly, I kept a hold of her, my chin dropping down as I sighed and attempted to find something right to say.

"None of this has ever been about protecting myself." I looked up, my jaw twitching as I searched her eyes. "I'm fucked whichever way this goes. I can't protect you from pain if you stay, but I can't protect you from pain if you go. You hurt, I hurt. You die inside, I get dragged through Hell for the rest of my life."

"What do *you* want, Drew?"

"What do I want?"

"Yes," she said, squeezing my hand. "*You*."

"I want this day to end," I whispered.

"Tell me."

"Ayda, stop it."

One of the tears slipped free, her lips pushed together in a thin line as it rolled over them, and yet her gaze never left mine. "Drew, please."

My jaw worked back and forth, the muscles flexing harder than ever before as I stared at her, unable to say anything or do anything other than flare my nostrils and curl my fingers tighter around hers.

Ayda swallowed compulsively, the tears beginning to run freely, but she seemed unaware that they were there at all.

She was so focused on me that her words came as a choked whisper. "Please. Please tell me what you want."

The sight of her crying made my blood boil over. It was a slow eruption, starting in my toes and working its way up my body until my head began to shake in protest, but it was too late to stop anything. I chewed on the words, tasting them before closing my eyes and shouting them out.

"You! I want you." I stepped back, letting her go as I threw my hands up to the back of my head and sucked in a breath. "Jesus, Ayda, don't you get it? I want you. I want you safe. I want you happy. I want you to have what you deserve. I want you in a life where shit isn't always so heavy. I want someone to treat you with the patience and the respect you deserve, but the thought of anyone else touching you makes me want to rip the throats of a hundred men out—men I don't even know—just for the sake of being the brutal bastard that I am. I want you to not always give me that look that's begging me to do the right thing when the wrong thing comes so easily to me. I want to never have to disappoint you. I want to give you the world. I want to not want all of these things because wanting them and wanting *you* means that no matter how much I try and stop myself from admitting that I love you…" My eyes flew open to meet hers. "I can't, because I love you. I really fucking love you, Ayda."

The air came out of my nose fast and heavy as I stared at her, my chest rising and falling so hard I could barely create any volume when I spoke again.

"I love you."

Stepping forward, she brought up her trembling hands and cupped my cheeks. They were cool to the touch, a complete contradiction to the warmth in her eyes. "Ask me what I want,

Drew."

I looked in pain. "What do you want?" I whispered.

"You. It's all I've ever wanted. The rest of the shit doesn't matter as long as I have you." She closed the distance between us, her body pushing against mine as her forehead dropped to my shoulder. "I knew what I was accepting when I fell in love with you. I knew what it involved and I don't want anything but you, as you are. I love you. Nothing but you throwing me away could change that."

There were no words forming as she rested against me. My hands found the back of her neck before pushing up into her hair so I could hold her. In trying to do the right thing, I'd ended up saying the one thing I never thought I would. It felt like a weight had fallen from my shoulders, only to be replaced by something twice as heavy. My nose found its way to her hair, the smell of her shampoo taking over my senses as I closed my eyes and breathed her in.

She was the talker in our relationship.

The reason.

The one who cut through the crap and wore us both down until we admitted certain truths.

I could grant her that. It was the least I could do.

My job going forward was to be something else—something she couldn't be. The protector. The man who would keep her safe no matter what the personal cost. The only thing I couldn't save her from was me.

She was on her own with that.

"I'm sorry," I breathed against her.

"So am I. I didn't mean to embarrass you or myself. I was just desperate. I saw the track you were on and panicked." She lifted her head and looked up at me, chewing her bottom lip.

Pushing my forehead to hers, I held her gaze.

"We'll be the death of each other, Hanagan. Mark my words. The two of us will go up in flames."

CHAPTER TWENTY-NINE
AYDA

He loved me.

All of the other bullshit seemed to melt away as the words bounced around in my head and resonated from my skull. I repeated it, sang it and bellowed it, all in the sanctuary of my own mind as I forced myself to stay calm in front of him. I don't think even I had realized quite how much I wanted to hear those words until he said them. Of course, he said them in true Drew Tucker fashion, gruff, pissed off, but with an honesty I'd come to expect from him. Even his last sentence failed to leave any real imprint on my inner joy. I was insulated in that giddy place where Santa used to live, mainly by the simple sentiment of love he'd given me.

I was an adult, and I knew that the revelation of how he felt wouldn't simplify the situation any more than my confession of love had after the fire. I knew there was still a large part of him that almost wished I would take his words to heart and walk away. He would sacrifice what we had in order to save us both, and as admirable as that was, I wasn't buying what he was selling. We were stronger together. I just had to learn to walk away when he was with the other guys, and he had to learn to trust I wouldn't run or push him in a different direction when there was trouble. We had to establish a deeper level of trust and leave the honeymoon period behind.

Staring up at him with every ounce of the love I felt, I ran my hands up his back to his shoulders, following the thick muscle of his arms as they looped around my neck, and entwined my fingers with his. There were so many things I wanted and needed to say. There were questions I needed to ask and answers I had to give, but as the silence wrapped itself around us, I just wanted to lay in his arms and forget the world existed.

Unfortunately, the air between us still crackled and I knew we needed to get a few things out in the open before I could let myself revel in those three little words and the man that had uttered them to me.

"Can I ask you something?"

"No," he said through an obvious smirk.

Dropping my head back against his arm, I sucked in a deep breath and closed my eyes, trying my hardest to hide the answering smile that made my lips tingle. "What happened today? With Kenny? I don't want to get into another screaming match, but if you could help me understand…"

"Understand what?"

"The need to fight," I said quietly.

He inhaled sharply, bringing our hands down my face and holding me in place. "This morning I told him to stay away from you and he didn't. Kenny has been… difficult, lately. I figured out the reason why and I didn't like it. I gave him his warning, and he didn't listen."

Leaning into the touch of his hand, I tried to turn over the implications of that statement in my head. I knew how I would have reacted to anyone else saying something along those lines. There was an unspoken morality there, but this wasn't anyone else, and as I was becoming more and more aware, this world was run by a different set of rules. I just needed to learn them before I put my foot in it again.

"I didn't know that."

"He was going to push me until I let it happen. Kenny wanted the fight; he just didn't know it. After what happened at the Emps' place, I was all out of patience. Seeing him with his hands on you…" He stopped himself from going any further, the usual tightening of his mouth speaking volumes as he searched my face over and over again. "Today hasn't been a good day."

"I didn't know that, either," I admitted, searching his eyes. I couldn't defend Kenny, mainly because I didn't know what his problem was, but I did need to make something perfectly clear to him. "I'm not sure why he feels the need to push buttons, Drew, but you have to know that I wouldn't ever let anything happen. Not ever. I certainly never would have…"

I trailed off and looked at my bare legs. I'd made a complete fuck up of the situation and made matters worse.

"I'm an idiot."

"He's in love with you, Ayda. Can't say I blame him." He lifted my chin carefully. "I never thought you'd do anything. It was about respect. There was only one way he was ever going to listen to me, which is why I did what I did. I didn't enjoy it any more than you liked the idea of it, but this is the life we lead. Blood is shed like water. What we can't say in words, we say through the power of our fists."

I was so naïve. I never once thought about Kenny in that capacity. Sure, he used to flirt with me when I started cleaning The Hut to repay the debt, but I thought that had long since passed. He spent so much time with Tate, I'd started to think of him like another annoying brother to contend with, but with Drew's words, that suddenly felt awkward and wrong.

"I really am sorry. I had no idea, about any of it. If I'd known, I would never have invited myself into the game," I said, dropping my hand and flinging it to the side. "Or insulted him to instigate that chase. I need to know these things, Drew. I treated him like I treat Tate."

"I really hope you don't put your ass in Tate's face like that." He grinned, finding way too much humor in the fact that I was suddenly squirming.

I shuddered and scrunched up my nose. "Yeah, well that was unintentional. New subject, what happened to your ear? And what did you find out?"

"Christ, were you an interrogator in your previous life?"

"No, I'm just bad at segueing to different topics," I said, grinning up at him. "I just want to help any way I can. You've got so much on your plate right now. Maybe a fresh set of eyes can help?"

"Sleep would help," he muttered, looking completely exhausted. "And some TLC from the first woman I've ever said those three words to would definitely help me get over the fact that I lost a part of my ear today."

Tender loving care was certainly something I was more than happy to give him in abundance. Dropping my hands from his, I buried them under the cut he'd pulled back on at some point and worked them up and over his shoulders, slowly guiding the supple leather back and coaxing his hands from my cheeks so I could remove it.

"I thought you'd never ask." I grinned, my hands tugging it from his arms and tossing it carefully to the closest chair.

Taking a step back, my fingers moved to the hem of his T-shirt, dusting the skin just above the waist of his jeans, the heat of him and subtle flinch telling me that it was more than just his ear that was making him weary. "Was there any sign of them, other than the trap, I mean?"

Drew paused and I didn't have to ask to know he was unsure about talking to me about this, but when his body relaxed even more against my touch, I could feel another battle being won.

"They set up cameras to see who came in. By the time Slater had made sure I wasn't about to fall over from taking a bullet to somewhere vital, we'd wasted too much time. They'd seen us. I shot out the cameras and we made tracks. Other than that, the place was empty. This is... These people... It's a war that had no beginning and won't ever have an end. They hit, we hit. It's all about moves now."

His brows came together as he watched me intently, waiting for something he'd said to freak me out or make me assure him that there must be another way.

"So, it's like chess—all strategy and hitting where it hurts?" I asked, my fingers continuing until my palms were resting against his abs. My hands retraced their path up over his shoulders and head then down his arms until gravity took control and the material fell to the floor. I tried to avoid the darkening spots all over his body as I worked.

"Chess. Life. What's the difference?" he said, his voice filled with intensity.

"Nothing, I suppose," I whispered, my body rocking forward, my lips brushing one of the bruises that mottled the tattoo on his chest. "But if it's strategy, they're going to want to take credit for whatever it is they're doing, so there must have been something other than the cameras."

"Yep. Definitely an interrogator." He smirked that Drew Tucker smirk of his. "Our humiliation is their credit, but you're right, it isn't over. Not by a long shot. We just gotta hope that the strategies we have in place are enough. But, Ayda?"

My fingers were tracing a path over his hips when my name pulled my glance to his. "Yeah?"

"Please don't ask me what our strategies are. Trust me to tell you what you need to know. There's a reason that I keep you in the dark sometimes. That reason could save your life."

"Some things I just don't want to know," I said, liberating the leather of his belt and loosening the buckle so I could reach the button. "I trust you to tell me what you think I need to know. Just be honest with me."

I turned us slowly, my body pressing against his as I popped the button and slid the zipper down, forcing him to step back toward the bed, stopping only when the backs of his legs hit the mattress.

He sank down almost immediately, his ass meeting the comforter, his hands reaching up to grab my thighs as he looked up at me. I wasn't sure what that look in his eyes was trying to tell me, but the moment he dropped his chin and glanced down at his body, I saw exactly what he was staring at. The very thing I'd been trying to avoid looking at for too long.

"I'm wearing a few new shades of purple and pink since I left you this morning."

I dropped to my knees in front of him, my fingers exploring the angry spots that covered his skin. I hated seeing him that way. I hated that it was one of his own men that had done it, but more than anything, I hated that I was somehow a part of him being hurt.

"How bad is it?"

"I've had worse," he said through a smile, glancing back up at me with his brows knitted together. "A hell of a lot worse."

I met his smile with one of my own, my hands dropping to the bottom of the hoodie before I pulled it over my head and dropped it beside me. "I guess that just means I'm on top tonight."

Pushing up from the floor, my lips met his, my hands pushing the material of my panties down over my hips and letting them fall to the floor before straddling him. I nudged his shoulders, even as his hands rose and ran along my jaw, the heels of them holding me against him as he dropped back against the mattress with a grunt I probably should have felt guilty about.

Reaching between us, I gave him a slow stroke and bit down on his lip, the growl from his chest just making my need for him flare from the inside out. With a steady hand, I held him in place, sinking down until he consumed me once again.

CHAPTER THIRTY
DREW

There had been a shift in power.

I sat at the head of the table for my men. I sat there for her, too. But before the night before, I'd been coasting on a memory of what was, even when I thought I hadn't. Playing it safe had never been a trait of mine, but since Ayda came into my life, I'd tried to think of other people but myself. There'd been many days to change that way of thinking, yesterday being one of them. It had brought me to my knees again and cracked me wide open.

I loved her and I'd admitted it. That only left one option open for every other problem that lay at my feet. I had to deal with this shit myself. Head on. Take full responsibility, no matter who the enemy.

Including Sutton.

I had a clean shirt upon my back for the slimy fucker. My hair wasn't its usual mess, and as I waited outside on the police station steps, I tried to look at least a little bit civilized. The usual stares and odd looks from the locals didn't go unnoticed. The only difference was that when they smiled their fake smiles, I grinned right back, flashing them a wink and a nod of acknowledgement before they dipped their heads and scurried on past.

My hand coasted up and down the railing as the out of place warmth shone upon my face. Even though everyone else thought it was growing cold, I welcomed whatever sun I could get. There'd been too many days without that inside.

"Tucker," the voice behind me snapped.

I didn't move, instead smirking to myself as I imagined the way he rolled the end of his tash before he thumbed the inside of his belt with one hand while reaching for his gun with his other.

Dickhead.

"Chief," I acknowledged him, poking my tongue into my back teeth as I stayed looking out onto the streets of Babylon.

"I have six other officers on duty today. Any particular reason why you're standing out here demanding *my* presence?"

Howard's voice shook, even though he was trying to hide it. Spinning around on the spot, I raised a foot onto the step above before me I gave him my full attention.

"It's all about respect. You like to keep reminding me that this is your town, so as the good citizen and ex-convict that I am, I'm trying to respect y'all by keeping you informed of what I know. Call it my duty." I grinned at him, unable to miss the look of contempt he was flashing me as he stood there looking down, probably imagining all the ways I'd taken his two dollar whore of a wife before he came along.

"And what is it, exactly, that you think you know?"

"Oh, I know a lot."

"I don't have time for games, dipshit. You're standing on my steps, using my time. Lose the smirk and give me something or get gone."

"Is this the way you speak to all the people in Babylon?"

"Only you."

"I feel special." I took a step up, pulling myself higher on the railing as I drew closer to him. Sutton flinched but tried to hide it, moving to take a step back before he corrected himself and spread his legs even wider apart. He'd watched too many westerns and starred in few too many imaginary gun fights growing up. The chief was too easy to mess with.

Dropping my eyes, I took a moment to focus before I looked back up at him and tried not to appear *too* smug.

"These kids that have been causing problems around town?"

"What about it?" he said with not even a hint of genuine curiosity in his voice.

"What are you doing about them?"

"Tucker, I have bigger fish to fry than a bunch of delinquents who seem to have come off the back of y'all, so if this is all you and your big MC are here to discuss today, I'd not so kindly ask you to vacate my premises and spend more time focusing on your own faults than everybody else's."

"Off the back of us?" I smirked harder, taking another step closer.

"We've all seen their patches." Sutton raised his chin and puffed his chest out like a kindergarten kid facing a high-schooler.

Landing on the same level as him, I walked closer, the leather of my cut creaking and the soles of my boots sounding like an atomic bomb going off in the silence. Shoving my hands in my jeans pockets, I rocked forward, dipping my head to his for no other purpose than to patronize the little fucker.

"You and I both know they have nothing to do with me and my men, so you listen to me and you listen up real good.

This town you claim as yours, well you better start respecting it. You better start paying attention and looking out for it because those kids—those kids that you seem to think serve no purpose—let me tell you, they could cost you your badge. Now, I ain't here to save your ass because I think it's pretty. I'm not even here to do your job for you because I feel it's my duty, and believe it or not, this isn't even about the shit you project on me for having done what I've done to the woman you fall asleep with every night."

Sutton's eyes became frantic, the confusion on his face taking over as he took a step back and curled his fingers around his gun even harder.

"This is about two things," I went on, leaning over him. "One, keeping Babylon safe from gas station fires and the loss of innocent lives. I'd hate to see your record for peace darkened even more than it already is. I'm sure your superiors would start questioning your competence if that happened again."

"You're talking to me about innocent lives?"

Ignoring him, I went on, not accepting the invitation to that particular fight. "And two, maybe I'm just a good guy in bad guy's clothing."

"Forgive me if I don't believe a word of the bullcrap you just fed me."

"You'll listen, Chief, and you'll believe it. Unfortunately for you, you don't live on the edge of society like I do. Protocol: it's your law. You gotta follow it, even when it's the scum that's feeding you the evidence. Can't leave no stone unturned, right?" I grinned harder, the skin tightening around my smile as I looked down on him. These kids were going to be off our back once and for all, and Sutton had no choice but to listen to every little word I was about to feed him.

His balls were now in my hands.

Jedd sat on his bike, not hiding the fact that he looked bored as he focused on the road ahead of us, his head moving slowly from right to left with every car or truck that drove past. His long black beard was reaching epic lengths, the edges of it tickling the handles of his bike as he rested over them like the lazy bastard he was.

Seeing the patch I'd known since birth on the back of one of my brothers always sent me into some kind of nostalgic head spin. The sun caressed each curve of the reaper and it's guard dogs and called to me like it was my home… because it was my home. Those three figures, those three sets of eyes and teeth, they represented who I was and who I stood for, and as job two for the day loomed ahead, I felt a new surge of urgency take over.

I swung my leg over my *Harley*, coughing loudly as I picked up my helmet and gave Jedd a satisfied glare.

When his attention turned to mine, his eyes lingered on me for too long before he shook his head and smiled. "Your life goes from good, to fucked up, to smug, to death, to cocky little shit way too quickly these days, pres."

"Pres?" I scoffed, placing my helmet on my head as I worked the strap beneath my chin. "The fuck do you want?"

"You're my pres, ain't ya?"

"I guess so." Rubbing my lips together, I squinted against the light before reaching into the pocket of my cut and pulling out my shades.

"So what's so shocking about it?"

I looked out onto the streets of Babylon, not able to answer him right away. There was no doubt in my mind that I was a brother. There was not even a doubt that I was their leader, even after spending so much time away.

Casting him a sideways glance, I dropped my hands to the handles and knocked back the kickstand. "It's just rare from you." I grinned bigger. "VP."

"Yeah, well, lotta unusual shit going down in the world today, pres." He smirked, following my lead as he started up his bike and the chugging roar of his *Harley* filled the air right alongside mine. For a moment, we were just two men sitting on machines—no more than two brothers with a love for wheels and speed. The gentle winds blew around us, the cold biting at the exposed skin of our bodies as the road invited us to take a ride out east or west. It didn't matter to them. The asphalt would be waiting for us whichever route we chose.

But our patches soon clutched at our hearts, reminding us that that kind of freedom really didn't exist for the likes of us, and that the only thing we had to look forward to was our own kind of protocol. Our own kind of rules to follow. Our own kind of family, hierarchy and a never ending list of jobs to complete.

The small shit had been passed on to someone else.

The real problems hadn't even been touched.

I looked at Jedd again and sighed heavily.

"I love you, brother."

He turned back to me instantly, his head snapping around quick enough to give him whiplash.

"You feeling okay, Tucker?"

My short burst of laughter was quickly drowned out by

the roar of the engines beneath us. I shook my head at him, both brows rising as I shouted a little louder, "Just got a case of the I love yous, apparently. Suck it up, dickhead and enjoy the taste of my dust."

I took off as fast as I could, tearing out in front of him, wondering what Ayda had been doing since I left her. Memories of the night before floated through my mind and soon brought another shit eating smile to my face that only the sun and sky could see.

From then on, some things would always stay private.

CHAPTER THIRTY-ONE
AYDA

I'd been hiding for most of the morning. When I woke up, my limbs tangled with Drew's, I was so sublimely happy and content I hadn't thought much about my behavior the night before. It could have been denial or ignorance, but for those moments we had together, the world beyond the door didn't exist. It hadn't so much as occurred to me that we were in my little retreat or that the door had been broken and cracked open.

No. All of that only occurred to me *after* Drew got up and wandered toward it, scratching his ass and rubbing his head in that adorable way he had. It was when he tried to pull the door closed that it really hit home. When I finally pulled the comforter back after hiding in embarrassment, I got up and stumbled over the dainty slip I'd been wearing in front of the whole hut and wanted to scream.

I took a shower in Drew's room after a stealthy dash down the hall, and pulled on his sweats and hoodie so I was covered from head to toe in the baggiest clothes I could find. I just wanted to blend in with the walls and not be seen, but the moment I convinced myself to step out of the room, I'd been faced with the whores and their whispering.

I'd been in the laundry room since, even with nothing

to do. I found a game on my phone and killed hours just swapping colored bubbles around. It was a vortex of uselessness, but it was killing time until I could go back to the room without it looking like I was hiding in shame, which is exactly what I *was* doing, just in a more central location, which was less likely to have visitors.

"There you are."

Unless they were actually looking for me...

I almost dropped my phone when Deeks came bursting through the door, his smile firmly in place and lacking the condescending vibe I'd been getting from some of the whores I'd had the displeasure of bumping into.

"I'm not going anywhere, Deeks. You don't have to worry about babysitting me."

"Oh, come on now. It wasn't that bad. Most of the boys out there now just think Drew is a lucky son-of-a-bitch. You think those girls haven't done much worse?"

"Is that supposed to make me feel better?"

Deeks' hearty laugh was comforting. He wandered into the room, stopping in front of me and patting the knee of the leg I had tucked under me. He wasn't laughing at me. I knew him well enough to realize he had a deeper understanding of me than most of the people in the building. Drew and Tate were a tie in first, Deeks a very close second.

"Promise me something, Deeks."

"What's that, kid?"

"If I ever have a really bad idea like that again, remind me of how I feel right now."

"You don't have anything to be embarrassed or ashamed of, woman. You threw yourself at your man. There ain't anything wrong with that. From what I heard, it ended well enough."

This time he was laughing with me. He could see the hidden humor in my eyes as I glared at him and felt my cheeks turn scarlet. He was probably one of the few people in the world that could have pulled it off, too.

"Okay, wise one, what the hell do I do about Kenny? Do I just avoid my brother's best friend like he doesn't exist? Do I talk to him about this shit and hope he moves on? Do I treat him like shit and hope he hates me?"

"You do the only thing you can do."

"Talk to Drew about it?"

"See, you get it, darlin'."

I let both my legs fall down the front of the dryer and swing as I watched him, my hand pushing my phone into the pocket of the sweats I was wearing. I needed some air. I needed to escape The Hut, even if it was just for an hour.

"Will you take me for a ride or a coffee or something? My car has been marked as scrap and I don't have a replacement yet."

"You don't have to ask twice, but I ain't taking you looking like a hobo. Go put something human on."

I hopped off the machine and sped to the door. The best it was going to get was a pair of jeans. I was keeping the hoodie. It smelled like Drew and I found it comforting being buried inside of it.

I met Deeks by his bike after letting Slater know we were going. I knew it was only a matter of time until Drew got back, and I didn't want him to worry if he came looking for me. I'd learned more than one lesson the night before. Respect was a two way street and I needed to start showing it.

The moment he pulled out of the yard, I spread my arms

and threw my head back, ignoring the weight of the helmet as I looked at the sky with longing. I loved the feel of the breeze kissing my skin and the warm embrace of the sun heating my clothes. It was only when Deeks merged onto the interstate that I dropped my hands to my knees and leaned forward.

I knew where he was taking me. Rusty's held salvation for the both of us. He was let off the hook from being a shoulder to cry on, and I was given the only mother figure I had to talk to about my stupid mistakes. He was on the exit when I saw the bikes fly by, continuing down the interstate. They weren't wearing patches, but they were riding together, weaving in and out of traffic with an ease that reminded me of the guys in the Hounds. I honestly didn't think much about it until one of them looked back at us.

"Did you see that?" I shouted, tearing my helmet off as Deeks pulled into his usual spot at Rusty's.

"The riders?" Deeks asked, removing his own helmet and resting it against the gas tank. "I saw them. They followed us for two miles, but I think it was just a coincidence."

I twisted in my seat, my leg swinging over the back as my eyes followed the bikes that were much farther down the interstate. Maybe he was right; maybe it was nothing, but it was one of those moments where all the hair stands up on the back of your neck, inexplicably leaving the cold fingers of suspicion to drip ice water down your spine. A lot of people rode bikes, especially in Texas, and it didn't mean they were in an MC, but it was rare to see people like that around Babylon. I just hoped they were passing through. The last thing any of us needed was more trouble.

"Don't worry about it, Ayda. I'll call Drew or Harry while you're with Janette. It'll be fine."

I nodded in agreement and let my helmet drop to the seat of the bike. If anyone knew what to do about the riders, it was Drew. Looking over at Deeks, I had a feeling this was another one of those *need to know basis* kind of deals that had been laid out, so I headed for the door to the diner and shook off the shadow of doubt that was following me, replacing it with the biggest smile I could manage.

"You're late!" Rusty shouted from beyond the window. I could barely see him, but his voice was like God's as it rang through the place, and was actually filled with mirth for once. I stopped in my tracks and leaned back to get a menu.

"Okay, this *is* Rusty's, but who the hell are you? We all know Rusty doesn't..." I feigned a gasp, "...smile."

"He's just happy to see you, honey, and don't you listen to her, Rusty. You keep on smiling, baby."

I walked straight into Janette's open arms as I skipped behind the counter. The place always gave me the feel of going to Grandma's. It was familiar and homely and filled with people I loved. Not working there for a while was weird for me, and I missed them, but as Drew had reminded me, it was all about my safety as well as theirs.

"You want coffee and a muffin?"

"Two please."

"Deeks with you?"

"Yes, ma'am. He's just making a call. How's things been?"

Janette worked as she talked, her feet carrying her around the place with ease. It wasn't long until I was on the other side of the counter, helping her out, chatting away as I filled up the salt and pepper shakers, combined the half bottles of ketchup and filled the napkins. It was busy work and it felt natural to be doing it as we gossiped like we did.

As it turned out, I wasn't the only one noticing strange people on bikes, or the small gang of kids with fake patches. It was the talk of the town. It hadn't occurred to me that Deeks had been outside for almost an hour until I refilled my coffee and started nibbling at his double chocolate chip muffin. I excused myself and headed to the door, sticking my head out and finding Deeks sitting on his bike talking to three other older gentlemen on their bikes.

"Ayda! Come meet, Michael, Rich and Don. They were the folk on the bikes."

I was pretty sure that in Deeks speak that was the all clear. The small group looked friendly enough, and one of the men stood up and smiled behind his silver beard and offered me a hand in greeting. "Nice to meet you, Ayda. We were just telling Deeks about the Lone Star Rally in Galveston. You ever been?"

"No, sir, but isn't that in the beginning of November?"

"It sure is, but we rented a place and had thanksgiving down there. It's real pretty to ride down the coast, especially around sunset. You should give it a try next year."

"Isn't it cold?"

The guy leaned against his bike and gave me a warm smile before launching into a long story about the days and the weather. I was beginning to understand why Deeks was still outside with them. I just hoped he'd managed to give Drew the all clear, too. These were obviously just riders, no affiliation or club, just good people on good bikes, enjoying what they could of the fair weather.

That was enough to give me pause, but it still had me wondering about the people Janette had mentioned passing through a few days earlier.

CHAPTER THIRTY-TWO
DREW

My finger drifted across the screen, the dorky smile creeping along my face again as it pinged to life.

"You've definitely put her number in?" I asked Jedd, swinging my legs up onto my desk as I leaned back in my chair, leather squeaking against leather.

"Were the first fifty answers to that question not enough?"

"I find myself trusting you fuckers less and less," I said quietly, my attention falling back down to the shiny new phone in my hand. "You'll have stored her under Ayda and next thing I know, I'll have agreed to suck the tits of some Chinese mafia head and have an angry mob on my doorstep."

Jedd laughed roughly. "We have enough enemies for now, Tucker."

"No shit." I smirked.

Crossing my legs at the ankle, I let out a small grunt and began to press on the little square picture things in front of me. Everyone knew I was crap with that kind of technology, and the last thing anyone would be expecting was for me to join them in the modern day and finally admit defeat.

"As if you weren't distracted enough before. This new toy of yours is going to get us all killed."

"It was either this or fix the bat signal." I grinned, keeping my eyes on the screen as I tried to work out where the fuck her name was hidden.

"I thought you had yourself down as more of a villain than a hero."

"Don't you start fucking psychoanalyzing me, Jedd. I'm all therapied out. Now shut the fuck up while I play."

Jedd fell back in his chair, both hands rising to cradle his head as he watched me like I was his kid and this was our first Christmas morning together.

"Shit," I muttered under my breath, reaching up to scratch the side of my beard as I tried to remember what he told me to do.

"Need help?"

"Nope," I lied.

Once I navigated my way through the entire fucking phone, disregarding the maps, the big blue button with an F on it and some other shit, I found her. I'd specifically told Jedd not to store her under Ayda, for reasons that I didn't want to think about for too long. The thought of anyone finding her and hurting her instantly made my blood boil. Instead, she was hidden away under Mol, and Jedd had only given me a small look of congratulations when I'd said it before he looked back down and typed it in. Whether she approved of the term or not, Ayda was my old lady. She always would be, no matter what messed up roads we happened to take along the way.

Pushing my fat as fuck thumb against each letter, it seemed to take me seven hours to type out one single sentence to her.

I'm looking for a Miss Ayda Jane Hanagan. Can you help me?

Who is this?

I'm afraid I can't disclose that information until I know who it is I'm talking to.

Well, you're shit out of luck. I can't disclose any information until I know who I'M talking to!

I asked first.

What are you? Twelve?

Are you talking years or inches?

Do I know you?

What are you? A detective?

Maybe. Wanna play 20 Questions?

Is that something you usually play with strangers?

Not generally, but I'm curious as to who the fuck you are. First question… are you older than 20?

Curiosity is a very dangerous thing to have. Can get you killed… Or you could end up like George and wasn't he the hairy fucker?

Older than 20. Now my go.

Is this the phone of Ayda Jane Hanagan?

Maybe… ;) Q2: Are you under 40?

Are you flirting with me?

NO! I'm actually kinda annoyed. Q3: What do you want?

Don't be angry. It gives you wrinkles. I want a lot of things. Things I can't discuss until I know if you are her or not.

Next question. Did you just stamp your foot?

No! I'm drinking coffee and I don't waste coffee over childish antics. Q4: If I was Ayda, and I'm not saying I am, would I know you?

Most definitely.

Okay. I'm Ayda. Who are you? I'll even say please…

PLEASE!

You'd be shit under interrogation.

Haha... butthead. Was I at question 5 or 6? Q6: Do you like me? And to clarify, I mean as in like and dislike, not like in the other respect.

Thanks for clearing that up. What would it matter if I liked you in the other respect? You got a man in your life already or something?

Well, you said you know me. You must have been lying. Everyone knows who my heart belongs to, which makes the other kind of like irrelevant. Now ANSWER... Are you a HW?

A what?

That's a no then. Question... oh who cares: Who ARE YOU?

My smile must have made me look like an idiot as I stared down at my phone and imagined the face she would be pulling. Jedd left halfway through our game of going back and forth. Apparently I was too slow at replying and it was boring the fuck out of him. I swung my legs off the desk and stood to stretch my muscles before making my way out through the bar and heading outside.

Who do you want me to be?

I'm not playing anymore. Have a nice life, stranger. I hope you've had fun. I'm going to block your number now.

No, you're not. You're way too curious for that.

How do you know I'm curious?

Because you just replied. George.

Give me one more chance. Don't waste your coffee. Order another one.

The user you have tried to reach is currently

unavailable... Asshole!

Shame. I was about to deliver something to her that could change her life forever. I'll find someone else a little less... volatile.

Now I'm insulted. You think I'm materialistic.

I do?

Obviously. I had a cheerleader friend in High School. She had money, so she'd bribe people to do things after they'd said no by suddenly pulling gifts out of the hat to make them change their minds. I hate to break it to you, bud, but I'm on the last of my nine lives... I'm not THAT curious!

I never said I had anything of worth to pass on. I just said it could change your life. Curses do that as well as gifts. Depends how much you like to live life on the edge, I guess. Your choice, Ayda Jane Hanagan. I can walk away now, or...

It was implied that it was something I would covet. *Sigh* If you kill me, my boyfriend will bring me back just to kill me all over again... How do I know this offering is worth the risk? How do I know you're not baiting me into a trap?

You don't. But what is your gut telling you to do?

I'm torn... Walk away and live to hunt you down and strangle you for being so fucking annoying OR risk getting murdered to stop a sleepless night of trying to figure out who you are and what the hell you want!

Want to know why I'm being so annoying?

Yes please! <~ See, I said please and everything!

Because one of my favorite things in life is seeing the way you turn your nose up and curl your top lip when you're angry.

I don't do that. You have the wrong Ayda… :-/

Really? Looks like you're doing it right now. You really should at least acknowledge the other people around you, too. You've been staring at your cell for quite some time now. I think the old, hairy, fat guy is getting worried you're having an affair. Wait. Is he the boyfriend?

Okay… You made me look. Where are you hiding?

Hiding? I'm not hiding. You just got to lift your head up a little higher and pay attention. You know, maybe check out the hot guy in the hat who happens to be behind the cash register ;)

You absolute BASTARD! GET OVER HERE!!!!!

She didn't have to tell me twice, and as I flashed Janette a wink and tossed her Rusty's hat, she caught it against her chest and smiled like a proud mother. Ayda thought she didn't have a home of her own, and she thought she didn't have any family apart from Tate and the men I'd introduced her to, but she was wrong on so many levels. More people loved her than she realized, and as I turned to give her my full attention, the sight of her baby blues lighting up the room as usual, I took a second to pat myself on the back for being one hell of a lucky bastard.

"Hey, darlin'," I said quietly, slipping in beside her.

Her half laugh and lean into my shoulder were followed abruptly by a light slap on my chest. "That was the weirdest thing ever. I had no idea how to handle that situation. When the hell did you get a cell?"

"About two hours ago." I wrapped my arm around her shoulder, my other hand digging into my pocket before I pulled the phone out and tossed it on the top of the table. "I am officially a modern day man. Just don't ask me to do anything quickly."

She picked it up and turned it in her hands before setting it back on the table. "Look at you. Was it Jedd or Slater? I know they were both pissed off at seeing my number when I was trying to reach you."

"Me. I don't follow orders. You know that." I winked and tapped the badge across my chest, raising a brow as she gave me one of those looks of hers.

"I find that kinda sexy, Mr. Tucker."

"I know you do." My smirk was growing as I reached over for my phone and slid it across the surface. Leaning over it so she couldn't see what I was doing, I typed out another message to her then sat back and waited.

Her face lit up, her eyes flickering between the screen and me before they wandered to Janette. "Take me home? I believe we had a date on your bike planned at some point?"

I pulled my face back quickly, realizing something I hadn't given any thought to before this very moment right here. "I've never taken you on a date," I blurted out quietly. "Shit."

"Slacker," she said, grinning playfully. "But you should know by now that that doesn't matter."

"I've never taken *anyone* on a date, Ayda."

Curling into my side almost shyly, she looked up at me with a grin. "Do you want to?"

"I kinda do," I answered, leaning a little closer to her to close the distance. "Something else that's new. You free tomorrow night? If I haven't managed to piss you off or annoy you again by then, I mean."

"I would absolutely love to. I may even buy new clothes and all that good stuff." She smiled up at me, her fingers playing with the ends of her hair. "Maybe we can see how flexible I am over your bike at the end of it. Just to show how classy I am."

"Now I'm wishing we'd said tonight. Good job I'm learning to be patient." I reached up to her face, brushing away an invisible piece of hair just so I had a reason to touch her. "Tomorrow night. Eight o'clock. Clothes optional. Most of Babylon has seen your ass now anyway."

For someone so small, she could hit hard, and the slap to my shoulder had me sliding away with a bark of a laugh as she buried her face in her hands and turned a perfect shade of red. There were few things in life I enjoyed more than Ayda's blush. After the way I'd behaved the last few days, I was determined to see that right alongside an unfading smile tomorrow night. As well as a few more of my favorite things of hers.

CHAPTER THIRTY-THREE
AYDA

I pulled up to the one parking spot left outside The Hut in the huge *Dodge Ram* Drew had loaned me and turned to look at the only woman in the place who seemed to have moved on from all the drama of my initial appearance. Libby and I had become friends of sorts in the last couple of days, especially after the revelation of her and Tate's budding romance.

After Drew and I arrived back from the diner the night before, I bumped into her and, taking a chance, asked her for some help.

I hadn't been on a date in years. Even though Drew was mine, it didn't mean that there wasn't any pressure. I wanted to look nice for him. I wanted to make him smile the way he always managed to make me do. More than anything, I wanted to do him proud, which meant the absolute opposite of the crap I'd tried only days earlier.

Sitting in the truck with cut and fluffed hair, bags full of clothes and makeup, it almost felt superfluous. All those years I'd spent struggling and there I was being frivolous.

"Stop. I can see the buyer's remorse written all over your face," Libby said, unbuckling herself and turning in her seat. She'd been bored waiting for me to get my hair done and had a styling done by one of the people in the salon. Her hair was huge.

"He's worth every penny," I said confidently, putting both hands on the steering wheel. "It's just habit. All those years worrying about where every cent went, it's weird to not have to worry as much. I'm also really nervous."

"You are? Why? You're Drew's old lady. You've got nothing to be worried about."

Leaning farther forward, I dropped my elbows onto the leather and pushed my hands into my hair, before freezing and dropping them under my chin as I stared at the door of The Hut. It was so hard to put my nerves into words. Those women had more confidence in their baby fingers than I had in my entire being, and explaining that there were times I felt like I was playing house with a man that was completely out of my league was difficult. It wasn't that I was buying into the shit that those other women were feeding me. I mostly ignored their comments, but my self-esteem could only take so much before the dents started to appear. It was just a little sooner than I'd expected. I'd always thought of myself as stronger than all that.

"What aren't you saying?" Libby asked softly, grabbing the soda we both got at the drive thru. "Scrap that. Let me tell you a little secret the others would hate me for disclosing."

"Don't get yourself exiled on my behalf," I said just as quietly, tilting my head to look at her as she waved her hand in dismissal.

"I don't care, Ayda. They'd throw me under the bus in a heartbeat if it meant they would be upgraded to one of these guys' old ladies. That's exactly why they hate you. They're so jealous they're ready to spit their teeth out. In their eyes, you didn't have to work at getting Drew's attention. You had it the minute he laid eyes on you."

"And that's my fault?"

"Jealousy doesn't make people rational. You waltzed into The Hut and you not only bagged the most valuable asset, but you were accepted and every one of those men in there respected you. You just gotta lift your head up and ignore the shit that they throw your way. It's all because they want to be you."

As much as I appreciated her candor and her attempt to make me feel better, I wasn't sure it was helping. Not with the bigger picture, anyway. It did make me feel better about the clothes Libby and I had picked out, though. One night of allowing myself to be a girly kind of girl wasn't going to kill me.

"Thanks, Lib."

"Anytime. Now let's go get your war paint on before you change your mind again."

"I didn't change my mind."

"No? What was that then?" she asked, waving her hand around the cabin as she pulled her bag strap over her shoulder.

"A bump in the road."

"Big ass bump."

"I'm not that easily swayed, honey. I would fight tooth and nail for that man. I'm just not confident I deserve him."

Libby mumbled something I didn't quite catch and flashed me a smile as she pulled on the handle and hopped out of the door. If it had been any of the other whores, I would have assumed they were agreeing with me, but there was a mischief in her eyes that told me it was the last thing she thought. In fact, I was pretty sure the wiggle of her eyebrows was saying the exact opposite.

"What's that?"

"What's what, sugar?" she asked, spinning in a circle and trying her hardest to hide the amusement.

"That look, *sugar*," I said in the same tone. "What did you just say?"

"I said I'm pretty sure he'd disagree considering that smile he was wearing this morning."

"You," I said, pointing at her, "are just like Deeks. You're too intuitive and you see too much."

"That man gossips like those old hens in the salon, Ayda. A girl picks a few things up listening to old men who don't realize they're there."

"You're a dangerous woman."

Libby shrugged and pushed the door closed, tipping her head in the direction of The Hut, kick-starting me into grabbing the bags and following her lead. We both got stares as we walked through the bar area. Drew was nowhere in sight, but there was an abundance of whores lounging around with some of the guys, their eyes like lasers on the two of us. I could feel every one of their gazes following us until we were out of sight in the corridor, which was exactly when Libby started singing *Renegade* and walking with a renewed bounce to her step.

"Seems like you're persona non grata." I sighed with amusement, opening the door to my room so she could go inside.

"Damn. Who the hell is gonna run around after them now?"

I couldn't help my small laugh as I pushed my freshly fixed door closed. She was eighteen, but she was smart and she was fierce. I couldn't imagine having that mindset when I was her age, and I actually admired her for it. For the first time since I'd caught them in Tate's room together, I was really starting to understand what he saw in her. If she kept him on his toes and in school then I would never so much as complain about them sharing a room.

I'd never really had many female friends growing up. I had my best friend, but other than that, high school had pretty much been exactly like The Hut. It was an order of hierarchy. I had acquaintances, of course. The girls in the drill team and I got along because we had to. There was a level of sisterhood there, but it wasn't as though we spent much time together outside of school or practice hours. There were the rest of the girls in my grade, who I would exchange pleasantries with, but a true, honest to God friend? I only had one of them that was a girl.

That made Libby something of an anomaly, but to my surprise, she was more knowledgeable than any of my friends had ever been about fashion. Most of them had been happy to go to the nearest store and grab a pair of *Rockies*. I think I spent half of my teenage years laid flat on my back trying to zip them up. Libby, however, went a step further.

As I stood staring at myself in the mirror, tipping my head from side to side in wonder, I realized exactly what I'd been missing out on.

The jeans I was wearing could have been a second skin. They hugged every curve I owned and made them more voluptuous in a way that was complimentary. The sweater she'd picked out for me was much the same, the v-neck revealing the lacy, push-up secret under it when I leaned forward just so, the bottom of it clinging to my hips and ass. Then there were the heels. I'd never really been one for wearing heels in the past. Jacob's idea of a date night was pulling me out into an old field or hayloft so he could get to third base. I was older and wiser, it was true, but I was still fully prepared to make Drew work for dessert. Being a little closer to his height was just one of those added bonuses I hadn't put much thought into before.

"Damn. You should do this more often, Ayda."

"Yeah?" I asked, spinning on the balls of the heels and squeaking at my ass prominently on display, accentuated by the nude pumps I was wearing. I was suddenly feeling nervous for a whole different reason. The last thing I needed was Drew to pull some guy's arms off and beat him with them.

"You're missing something."

"Oh, I don't need jewelry," I said, tugging on the hem of the sweater when she turned her back on me, only to pull it back up when I saw lace peeking out over the top of it.

"It's not jewelry," she said, grabbing the one bag she'd come home with. "I bought this as a peace offering between us, and a thank you of sorts for being so understanding about Tate and me."

She thrust the ball of leather at me and pulled her hands behind her back, her hips swinging from side to side, making her look her age for once. Shaking the thing out, I almost squealed in excitement. It was the vintage 80's leather jacket I'd been admiring in the thrift shop next to the salon. I hadn't thought anything of it when I'd finally been called by the stylist, but it had been gone when we headed back to the car, and now I knew why.

"Remind me to never cross you." I laughed, pulling her into a hug. "You're smart and stealthy. I didn't even see you leave the salon."

"I didn't really have to pee. They have a back door," she replied, her voice muffled from my hair.

"I can't thank you enough." I pushed my arm in one side and swung it around my back, tugging down on the front and spinning back to the mirror. "How does it look?"

"Gorgeous."

All of the self-consciousness I'd been feeling suddenly bled away as I looked at myself. It wasn't like I dressed like that every day, and as long as it had been since I'd gone out on a date, Libby was right about one thing: this was Drew. He loved me, and no matter where we went or what we did, it was with him. That was what I had to focus on. The rest I could deal with in the morning.

"What time is it?"

"Seven fifty—" She put up one finger, her breath firmly held. "Nine."

I gave her a grin and checked the door in the mirror, realizing I had no idea where I was supposed to meet him. With one last hug to Libby, I sucked in as much oxygen as I could manage and headed to the door. It took everything in me to step out and head down to the bar, the heels marking every step I took with a small clip. When I finally made it out there, I found almost every guy in the place congregated at the bar, most of them hiding behind their beers as their eyes widened and followed my progress across the room. The looks they were giving me only succeeded in making me more nervous.

I was practically hyperventilating by the time I reached the door. All the eyes of the MC were burning holes into my back as I forced myself to focus on balancing with the heels, my hands tugging the bottom of the leather like a nervous twitch.

All of that was forgotten as soon as I walked outside. The chatter and gossiping started the moment the door slipped back into the frame, but my eyes were on the man standing at the base of the porch steps, his handsome face angled up at me, his eyes bright as they drank me in.

He looked amazing. The white shirt he had on under his cut was made for him. Where my sweater hugged my curves, his shirt clung to his muscles. Not that I could blame it. I would have been clinging to him if I was that close, too.

As my eyes met his, his smile grew to the one that made my stomach tighten in want while his fingers twisted the most perfect long-stemmed rose I'd ever seen in my life. There were a thousand thoughts running through my mind as I memorized the image, but only one stuck out.

I was in so much trouble that night.

CHAPTER THIRTY-FOUR
DREW

All the thoughts of the rose in my hand being a little too much fell away the moment she stepped out onto the porch. I couldn't tear my eyes away and I couldn't stop them inspecting every single inch of her curves. The backlight that the bar provided made her look like some kind of fucking angel, and as I let my attention finally rise to meet her... no, *my* baby blues again, I was grinning about as subtly as a kid in a candy store.

Damn, she looked fucking good.

I stalked up the steps slowly, the sound of the wood creaking beneath my heavy, black boots. Ayda's eyes never left mine, not even when she hitched in a breath and held it tight in her chest. Her chest which looked slightly bigger than my memory and my hands remembered it looking before.

There I was in a crisp, white shirt and there she was looking finer than I'd ever imagined she could. I thought I'd seen all Ayda's looks already. I'd checked her out in lingerie, dresses, sweats, the whole lot... everything except that version before me.

When I finally reached her, I stayed one step below and placed the rose between my teeth. The small smile that started to creep onto her face spurred me on as I held out my hand for hers and slowly began to guide her down the steps. The second her feet landed on the gravel path, I saw the look of horror flash across her face. I was no chick, but it didn't take a genius to figure out that Ayda, plus heels, plus uneven surfaces could result in more bad than good.

Not giving her time to argue, one arm wrapped around the small of her back while my knees bent and I hooked my other arm under her legs, pulling her up tight against my chest with a smirk plastered on my face.

"'Ha'ose," I tried to get out, encouraging her to take the thing that was now tasting a little too green out of my mouth for me.

With a small giggle, she plucked it away and replaced it with her lips, her eyes meeting mine as she relaxed back into my arms and kicked her legs out. "Drew Tucker, a romantic. I'm kind of digging it."

Smiling down on her before I set her on steady feet, I unhooked the helmet from the front and held it out for her to take.

"I'm full of surprises, darlin'. I promised you a date, so you're getting the full works. I'm pretty sure I must have a little bit of gentleman in me somewhere."

Ayda's cheeks flushed as she stared into the helmet, her lips moving, but the words barely audible. Whatever she said was complimentary. I could tell by the look in her eyes as she glanced up at me again.

All I could do was raise my brow in question and take a step closer.

Pulling the helmet over her head and straddling the bike, she watched me with her lips curled into a smile.

"So, where are you taking me, Mr. Tucker?"

Slipping in front of her, I grabbed her arms and pulled them tight around my waist, turning to look over my shoulder when I spoke. "I'm taking you to the bright lights of Babylon to show you off, the way any other boyfriend would do. Then…"

Shuffling closer, she rested her chin on my shoulder, her hands clasping tightly against my abs. "Then…?"

It was my turn to torment her. Facing forward, I started up the bike and began to back out of my space. The small sound that escaped the back of her throat only made my smile grow wider, and soon enough, we were riding out of the gates and heading to the one place I never thought I'd see myself go, to do the one thing I was pretty fucking certain I would never do.

It was impossible not to stare at her as she shook her hair out after removing the helmet. Being the gentleman I'd promised her I could be, I held out a hand to help her off the bike, my eyes completely focused on hers. As she looked behind us both, the small frown of confusion and surprise finally broke free, along with that perfect little smile of hers.

I was turning into a pussy—the kind that noticed every little thing about the woman they were with, and the truth was, I didn't care one bit. I guess that's why I was there doing what I was doing. The Drew Tucker that had stayed hidden away in the shadows and the cells now had something to flaunt, and I wasn't going to put off that show for a second longer.

Catching her carefully, I turned her around to face the one restaurant in Babylon that I knew wouldn't have a problem serving me while I wore my cut.

Antonio's.

The place my old man used to bring me when I was just a kid, forcing fucking meatballs down my throat at every given opportunity because he was good friends with the even older guy who ran it and gave us everything for nothing.

It wasn't the freshest place around. From the outside, it looked a little on the run down side with half the awning leaning too far to the left. But inside was something different, and even though I hadn't been inside for years, this restaurant meant something to me and I wanted Ayda to be a part of that history, too.

"It's not exactly five star, but I hear they give good spaghetti."

Her smile was beaming as she stepped closer to me. One hand was in mine while the other was wrapped around my arm. "I think it looks perfect. Quiet, intimate and charming."

"You describing me or the restaurant?"

"Since when have you been quiet?"

"I'm quieter than I used to be. Can't think why." I smirked, taking a step forward to guide us across the road.

"Are you saying I talk too much? Because if you are, you're about to lose the charming title, also."

"Talk, scream, cry out in ecstasy, what's the difference?" I laughed, not giving her time to hit me before I pulled her close and pressed my lips against her hair. "I don't think I've ever held any of those titles, anyway. I've got nothing to lose."

"You don't see yourself clearly at all," she said, releasing my arm to tuck some hair behind her ear. "You have no idea how effective *I'm horny* really is. Makes me wild with lust."

I leaned in even closer, half whispering and half growling in her ear. "I'm horny."

Ayda's tongue darted over her bottom lip before her flush forced her to dip her head and giggle. "You owe me food first. Then you can have me any way you want me. Think of it as charging my battery."

She stopped in front of the door, looked up at me boldly and winked.

There were so many things I could have said, that I wanted to say, but I strapped my gentlemanly balls on and stepped to the side to push the door open for her. Waving her through, I watched her every move as she walked past me. There had been such a shift in the way she carried herself since the first time I met her, and while she was gorgeous to me then, this new Ayda was something else. She managed to do what no other woman had ever done before. She'd held my attention far beyond the morning after the night before, and no matter what I did to fuck things up or what she did to send me off-the-wall crazy, I couldn't get enough of us. I didn't think I ever would.

CHAPTER THIRTY-FIVE
AYDA

There were times I couldn't believe how much my life had changed, and in a smaller amount of time than I ever could have imagined. Then again, that's the thing when you love someone. Time ceases to matter because the only indication that it's passing at all is those moments you find yourself coveting more and more.

My date with Drew was like that. I was oblivious to the ticking of the clock, the darkness stealing the last of the light beyond the dust clogged windows and every eye in the place that seemed to be trained on us. I was blind to it all because *he* had my full attention. My heart, mind and body were attuned to him and him alone.

I was aware of how cliché that sounded. Even as I sat there watching him work on his food, all I could do was steal glances and smile at my plate. I knew how lucky I was to have him, and I didn't take the love he offered for granted.

Leaning forward with my chin resting on my hand, I gave him my most content smile. "How are the meatballs?"

Drew glanced across the room at the older man he seemed to know, before he looked back at me and pushed more food into his mouth. "S'good."

I took a sip of my wine, savoring the taste. The old man

that suggested it was right about it being a bold flavor, but I was certain that it had been fermenting for a while before he'd offered it to us. The stuff was potent as hell. Widening my eyes, I sat the glass back on the table and cut into the lasagne I'd ordered. The outside had been an illusion; the slow decaying building had been hiding quite a gem inside the walls.

"So, how did you know about this place if you've never done this before?"

He swallowed carefully, his eyes falling to his plate as he cleared his throat. "I used to come here with my old man when I was younger." Drew shrugged, obviously trying to play it down to me before he looked back up through cautious eyes. "It was kind of our thing. I haven't been here in years, though. That's probably why Mr. Ferrara is trying to poison us with the wine."

Drew didn't talk about his dad much, if at all. Most of the time, he tended to change the subject when it came to his childhood. I never pushed, especially after my short discussion with Deeks. He'd been as hesitant to talk about Eric Tucker, but Drew actively avoided it if he could. I wasn't exactly loquacious when it came to talking about my parents, either. As much as I lived in the happier memories of my childhood, living them out loud hurt sometimes. Acknowledging that they were really gone made it more real. If that was the case for Drew, I certainly didn't want to bring it up on our date.

"I'm not sure about poisoning us, but I would say for sure he's trying to get me drunk. Maybe he thinks you'll get lucky," I said, grinning across the table at him before ripping off a piece of bread and popping it in my mouth. I was actually hoping it would soak up some of the alcohol. "You should probably let him know I'm a sure thing."

"A sure thing, huh?"

"You said the magic words, remember?"

"I remember. I'm just learning to take one second at a time with the two of us. Lot of things I could do or say wrong between now and when I bend you over my bike." He reached over for his glass, pausing before he took a sip, his eyes focusing on mine.

I felt the flush rise to my cheeks at the image that came to mind. We'd brought up sex on the bike several times in the past. It seemed as though it was a rite of passage with him, being who he was and all. Unfortunately, he was right about one thing; something had always come up in the past. Whether it was him or me, or even the club, there was always some kind of distraction getting in the way.

"Maybe we should eat faster then," I suggested, raising my eyebrows in question. Then I leaned forward and lowered my voice, my smile making my cheeks ache. "Or keep your mouth full."

The challenge in his eyes was immediate. He barely moved his lips, but I heard the small growl before he spoke. "Eat your food, Ayda, or my old friend over there and a room full of strangers are going to see parts of us no one else has ever seen before."

It was almost embarrassing how easily he could affect me when he did things like that. I felt the immediate tightening in my stomach as a rash of goose bumps made the hair on my arms stand to attention. With the growl, it was only a matter of time before I began to fidget in my seat. He knew what he was doing to me. It was burning in his eyes as he watched me, his jaw rigid with every chew.

There were times when I questioned whether it was natural to want someone as much as I wanted him.

"Is that a threat or a promise, Mr. Tucker?"

"Both," he answered quietly. His feet slid out on the floor, hooking around mine before pulling my ankle forward. When it came to doing what he wanted in public, there was little that seemed to scare Drew.

I looked down at my plate. I'd managed to eat half of the food on there, but the serving size was huge. There was no way I could fit more in.

"That was so good, but I'm stuffed. I think I may need some bending and stretching to work some of these carbs off." I took his lead, my foot pushing against his jeans and around the bend of his knee to his thigh. I loved being with him like that, no pressure to entertain those around us, not locked away from the world in our room, but openly spending time together, laughing and flirting in a way we never had. Our foreplay had literally been cynicism and snide remarks.

Reaching under the table, Drew's hand found my foot, pulling it farther into him instead of pushing it away. Casting a quick glance around the restaurant, he slid his other hand under to remove my shoe, discreetly leaning to the side to drop it to the floor as quietly as he could. There was a change in the look he was wearing and I knew him well enough to see that the only thing he had on his mind now was me.

Slouching farther down in his seat, Drew relaxed his shoulders and began to massage my bare foot, working his thumbs into the sensitive arches while he wore that signature smirk of his and waited.

"Did you say something?"

My body reacted immediately, the tightness in my

abdomen fluttering up my spine until I was forced to keep my body in place and not arch from the chair with a quiet moan. There was something about being in a position with him where I couldn't react on instinct, knowing I couldn't just head to our room and hope to God he would follow.

My hands fell from the table and gripped the seat of the chair as I narrowed my eyes at him and tried to come up with something witty, while all I wanted to do was lock him in a room so we could fuck like animals.

Words weren't an option. I knew if I said anything, it would come out in a moan. So I mouthed it to him. My lips forming the words in an exaggerated movement. "*I want you.*"

He was unable to hide his smug smile of victory. Tilting his head to the side, he continued to study me as he pressed and trailed his thumbs up and down the length of my foot. His grip only got tighter the more uncomfortable I got. "I think I may have dropped my gentleman gene somewhere next to your shoe."

My laugh was breathless and shaky, mainly because my fingers were digging into the wood of the chair, and my ass was hovering an inch above it. My eyes closed of their own volition, forcing me to pry them open and stare into his.

"How about you take me for a ride on that bike of yours?" I asked, my voice so husky I barely recognized it. There was a part of me that was well aware that if this had been *anyone* else in the world, I would be completely horrified by my own behavior. This wasn't anyone though. It was Drew, my Drew, and I knew he understood that it came from a place of love, allowing me to let myself go. Not to mention the victory he wore like a badge of honor was my reward. I just hoped he wasn't going to wind me up to the point where I dragged him somewhere a little more conspicuous than I'd intended.

"But I just got comfy," he said quietly.

I worked my foot loose from his hand and pressed it against his very obvious erection. "You sure about that?"

It was his turn to close his eyes this time, but his smile only got bigger as he pressed me harder to him and held me there. "Mmmhmm. More sure than ever."

I watched him with rapt fascination, my foot working the length of him as my eyes inhaled every little flex of muscle and twitch of his jaw. I knew what I would be facing the moment he opened his eyes. I'd seen it so often that I twisted my ass to one cheek as my nails bit into the wood below me.

Then I pulled my foot away.

Drew's eyes flew open quickly, but he held on to the amusement in his face.

"I was right about you all that time ago, Hanagan."

I found my shoe with my toes and pulled it closer to me, slipping my foot inside as I bent forward, knowing full well the view he was getting down my sweater.

"I'm going to regret asking, but right about what?"

Clearing his throat as he tried to discreetly adjust himself, he dropped his gaze to my chest and leaned over the table to meet me halfway. "You *are* a cock tease."

"Nice try, but a tease doesn't finish what she started, and I fully intend to." I grinned, biting the tip of my tongue and tipping my head to the side with what I hoped was a seductive smile.

He seemed to take a moment to let the silence thicken around us, his face studying mine with an intensity I was slowly becoming used to seeing from him. The way he looked at me sometimes, I could see the disbelief he held within himself. I knew how hard he found it to accept us as the real deal, because I struggled to believe something so good could be true, too.

"As far as dates go," he started, running his tongue along his bottom lip for effect. "How has this rated so far?"

"Honestly?" I asked, smiling across the table at him.

"Always."

"Off the scale good. The best I've ever had. Good food. Good company. Epic flirting. What's not to love?" I gave him a smile and reached across the table, both of my hands palm up. "And all with the man I'm completely and utterly in love with. You can't beat that."

He reached out, curling his fingers around both my hands before he carefully guided them up to his lips and spoke against them. "There's always room to improve on perfect."

I tugged on his beard playfully before brushing my index finger over his lips. "The only way you could improve this was if you were—"

I was cut off by the arrival of the waiter, my cheeks flaming with the embarrassment of the words he almost heard, not that Drew didn't know where I was going with that train of thought. I'd been practically begging since I'd finished eating.

"Is there anything else I can get for you?" the waiter asked politely.

God, I hoped Drew said the check. I wasn't sure how much longer I could rub my thighs together and have it go unnoticed by the other patrons and the staff.

Not pulling away from my hands, he glanced up at the waiter and gave him a sly grin.

"Just the check, thank you."

I almost sagged in relief. It wasn't as though I wasn't

having fun. I was, more than I'd ever had on a date before, but I meant what I said. I needed him. The ache I had was like an itch I couldn't reach and he was the only man that could scratch it.

CHAPTER THIRTY-SIX
DREW

Ayda was busy shrugging into her tight leather jacket as I threw down a bunch of bills onto the table, not caring if it was too much. I couldn't take my eyes off her, and as I made my way to stand by her side, I felt like the luckiest bastard in the whole of Texas.

"Leather is most definitely my favorite thing on you... besides me," I said, wrapping my arm around her to pull her closer.

Ayda's head met my shoulder easily. "I guess I'll have to get more of it then. I wanna keep my man happy and all."

"You're about to make your man very happy."

As soon as the cool night wrapped itself around the two of us, Ayda curled even farther into me, and I acted on instinct, holding her as close as I could simply because I couldn't seem to get enough of her. Maybe it was because of the fact that I'd almost convinced myself to try and walk away from us, or maybe it was because we'd had such a shitty time of it lately that finding some light in a world so heavy felt like something worth clinging onto. I didn't know. All I knew was that for that night, no matter what happened, I was going to make sure Ayda knew how much I fucking loved her.

"Well, I sure hope so. Don't want my ass getting chilly for

nothing." She grinned up at me, wriggling her ass from side to side.

"Let me worry about your charm." I laughed, reaching down to swat her cheek to show her just how I intended on keeping her warm.

"Who said I was worried? This is you. I don't think I've been cold a day since I met you." She turned, her chest coming against mine, her arms wrapping around my waist as she walked backwards, her head tipped back so she could see me. "And I think you owe me a kiss for teasing me in there. I assume PDA is part of the package this evening?"

"A PD what now?"

Pulling one arm from around my waist, she reached up with the same mischief in her eyes as she'd had through dinner. She was taller than usual with the heels on, but it didn't keep her from pushing to her toes, her thumb pulling down on my chin until her lips met mine. It was a short kiss, her teeth nipping my bottom lip before she fell back and smiled at me again.

"That's PDA. Public display of affection. I'm letting all these bitches know how lucky I am."

"A public display of affection," I breathed out as my hands found the top of her ass. "You want to make the bitches really jealous?"

"I think that's called PDI. Public display of indecency."

"And your point is?" I growled, bending at the knee to pick her up in the middle of the street, hitching her legs around my waist. The moment they tightened around me, I half spun her around and threw my head back to shout out to the whole damn world, "I'm gonna stop traffic for my girl, right here, right now!"

"Well, damn... Any argument I had is now completely invalid." She rocked against me to get closer, her lips brushing along my jaw to my ear where she whispered exactly what she wanted me to do to her.

I had to stop myself from unzipping my jeans in the middle of the street as her words drifted through my mind, her promises of what she was about to do turning me on more than I'd ever been turned on in my life. I was harder than hell as I barked out a small laugh and dropped my head into the curve of her neck. That didn't help, either. She smelled out of this world, and mixing that with the images of her ass in the air while I fucked her was making me way too lightheaded.

"We should go. We need to go. Now. Immediately. Right this second. Go. We should..."

Ayda started to laugh, her head falling back between her shoulders, her hands tightening around mine. Her laugh faded a little as something caught her attention over my shoulder, but the happiness was still shining from her face. "We should definitely go. I don't think the chief would appreciate the PDI you have in mind."

My eyes closed in a heartbeat, and even the mention of the chief made a spark of that fire in my dick float away. Groaning quietly, I spun us both around to see if she was messing with me or not. As soon as I saw that man standing only a few steps away from my bike, I let her slide down my body until she was on her feet again and pressed my forehead to hers.

"He's such a cockblocker."

"Not really. I'm still going to be bent over your bike," she whispered, stepping away and to the side of me, her polite smile directed at Sutton as we approached hand in hand. "Just not on Main Street."

"Please, let's not taint my fantasy with my own personal Sutton nightmare," I mumbled from the corner of my mouth before I copied her exact expression and aimed it directly at the man in charge of Babylon's safety. Apparently.

"Chief," I said with a small nod as he stood there in his usual western pose. For a second, I imagined what it would feel like to smack him square in the jaw, but that quickly faded to nothing as Ayda's quiet giggle slipped free beside me, and her hand curled tighter around mine.

"Tucker. Hanagan." His tone was flat as he watched us move closer, and something about the way he looked Ayda up and down made my spine stiffen until she pulled me back to her with just the smallest of touches on my arm.

"Good evening, Chief. Beautiful night," Ayda said without a hint of animosity in her voice.

"Beautiful," I sang beside her, unable to keep the smile off my face.

"Hmm," Sutton drew out, widening his stance as we came to a stop in front of him. All he needed was a matchstick in his mouth and tumbleweed to roll past and he was fucking set. "If you say so. Unusual for us to be graced with your presence, I must say. Any special occasion?"

I glanced at Ayda briefly before returning my attention to him. "Nope. Just enjoying the delights of our hometown, doing the romance thing with my girl."

He made no effort to hide his snort of derision or the roll of his eyes, and where once it would have made me want to fight back, tonight it just seemed to make the laughter bubble in my chest.

Ayda's hand squeezed mine—no warning or hesitation,

just appreciation at being called my girl, I figured. She ran her fingers along the seat of the bike, unable to wipe the smile from her lips. "It's date night, Chief."

"Date night," I repeated, like I was some kind of fucking moron.

"Date night. *Riiiiight*." Sutton made no attempt to hide his hatred towards me. "Didn't I warn you to stay away from my town, Tucker?"

"Aw, c'mon. I'm not here to make any trouble. I thought we'd made friends the other day."

"Chief, look around. We're not doing any harm. No one's even staring in our direction. We just wanted to eat out and have a good night. I know you can appreciate that." Ayda stepped closer to my side, her hand on my abs as she looked up at me with a grin. I could hardly believe the innuendo she was throwing at me.

My eyes widened and I quickly coughed to clear my throat before schooling my face. "Just… eating. Now if you don't mind, I'm going to take my date home and finish what we haven't even really started yet."

"Hold it right there, Tucker."

"Not tonight, Sutton." I sighed quietly, glancing up at Ayda. "I have somewhere I really, *really* need to be."

"*We* need to be," Ayda added sweetly, the hand on my abs patting gently.

Looking back over my shoulder at him, my smirk said it all. I had nothing left to say to him unless he wanted me to spell out word for word that I was planning on taking Ayda to the nearest secluded spot and fucking her until she couldn't walk.

When his face set to stone and his eyes looked like they

were about to pop out of their sockets, I turned away from him and straddled my bike. Without any instruction needed, Ayda followed me, placing the helmet I made her wear on her head before she wrapped her arms around my waist tightly.

Howard's mouth moved to say something, but he thought better of it. Just as I was about to ride away, the sound of his phone ringing made me pause to look up at him.

He slapped it to his ear, answering with a frustrated sigh as he threw up one hand to worry his forehead. I couldn't put my finger on what was going down with him then, but he was acting weirder than usual, and considering what a mousy little freak he was on a good day, that was saying something.

Ayda leaned impossibly closer, resting her chin on my shoulder again as we both watched him begin to pace. Her fingers curled against my stomach and her ass shuffled behind me, but I couldn't turn away from him.

Then he began to shout.

"The graveyard? Fuck. Again? Okay. How many?"

The mention of the graveyard demanded my attention even more, but my hands curled slowly around the grips of the handles as I looked down at the ground and tried to ignore whatever it was he had going on.

"These fucking kids," Sutton roared, forcing me to look back up at him again. My frown was deeper than ever, even as Ayda whispered quietly in my ear that we should go.

"We're going," I whispered back, and I had every intention of doing exactly that until the chief came charging over to stand in front of my bike, kicking the sidewalk like a frustrated kid.

"Jesus Christ," he yelled out.

"Whoa, easy," I said calmly, pulling my chin back as we

both watched him storming around.

"Drew," Ayda whispered quietly. "If you want to check it out first, we can ride by. Let's just go."

"I'm not doing his job for him, Ayda. I handed that shit over the other day. If he needs my help, he better get down on his knees and beg for it. We're leaving, don't worry." I spoke so only she could hear me, backing us out onto the road as carefully as I could.

Sutton was still on his call, more animated than I'd ever seen him in my life. I wanted to ride away, and I knew it was the right thing to do, but something about his behavior was confusing me, and that weird feeling of trouble ran down my spine like a long lost foe.

Before I managed to turn away, he stepped down onto the road and began walking towards us. There was desperation to the way he was moving. Panic, too, and when he threw his arm up in the air and pointed his finger straight in my face, I struggled not to swing my leg off the bike and bend that fucking finger backwards.

"You. Stay away from my town. One sign of you and those kids are running around wielding their goddamn knives again."

"What?" I choked out, unable to hide the sarcasm on my face.

"You heard me. Stay away. Stay away from Babylon, stay away from the graveyard and stay away from anything that doesn't involve you. This is all your fault."

"What exactly is my fault?"

"The fact that I have two boy scouts on the loose, threatening the whole of my town, wearing your patch on their backs."

"Ain't my fault if you can't keep the ankle biters away from the big boys' toys, Sutton. Like you said, it's your town, not mine. Not my responsibility."

"If people end up hurt, I'll make sure it's your responsibility. You hear me?"

That was all he had to say for me to shake my head, sigh heavily and be done with the fucking conversation. Date night was going to be perfect, no matter how much he or anyone else tried to stop that.

"Whatever you say, Chief. Despite what you think of me, I only want what's best for this town, and by this town, I mean every single person in it. That includes you. If pinning this on me is what gets you off, go for it. I'm not playing. I have a date to finish and a woman to look after tonight, so how about you stop forcing me to be an asshole and just let me ride away. You go do your job, I'll do mine, and hopefully sometime in the future, the two of us will grow up enough to work together instead of tearing each other apart."

Howard stood back quickly, stumbling over himself as he struggled to find his footing. The shock on his face was more obvious than I think he realized, and as Ayda tightened her arms around my waist once again in some kind of approval, there was only one thing left for me to do.

Smile and ride away.

CHAPTER THIRTY-SEVEN
AYDA

I was so proud of Drew. It wasn't something I would ever have said out loud to him, mainly because I didn't think he would understand the idiom that I intended. Drew had always had a reputation as a hardass, a force to be reckoned with, and he'd just walked away from Sutton's provocation as though it meant absolutely nothing. I wasn't sure whether that was something that sat right with him or not. It was hard not seeing his face for the last half of the conversation between them, but as we rode away from the chief, I was comforted by Drew's hand covering both of mine as they rested against his stomach, his thumb circling with silent reassurances. I would have been proud of him no matter how he'd chosen to deal with it; Sutton had been laying it on pretty thick. It was like watching a child prod a sleeping bear with a stick, but Drew had taken the moral high ground and left Sutton looking like the asshole.

After the evening we'd had, existing in the perfection of our own little bubble, Sutton's uncharacteristic insistence in trying to lure Drew into a fight seemed completely out of place, and it was lingering like a bad smell.

It was only when we straightened out from a corner that I let myself slide closer to his body and absorb his warmth while my mind branched out in a million different directions. This little band of wannabes was not a club problem and they never really had been. Sure, they were wearing Hound patches, but anyone who took a good look would see the differences. They were bored kids with too much time on their hands and the money to fix the old cuts they'd found, but that didn't mean that they had a thing to do with us. Sutton was pointing the misguided finger of accusation at Drew and the club, and they'd done nothing but try to help him find a solution. Even Tate had tried to help, but it seemed Sutton was blinded by his hatred of Drew and the club as a whole.

I despised how inquisitive I was sometimes. I disliked that my curiosity made me wonder whose property those brats were destroying, or why they'd suddenly found the need to carry weapons. They were just kids playing adult games that could very well get them killed if they didn't stop.

We'd barely made it over the train tracks that divided the town when I started seeing the signs of the fake Hounds pack a little too clearly.

Some of the older buildings had been defaced by a crude dog baying at the moon. As we took a corner, there was the bad copy of the Hounds' patch I'd seen on the boys, only this time with a cracked skull, and the sentinel hounds now had daggers thrust into their brains. The farther we went, the more they made a mockery of the pack and everything they stood for. Someone was pissing on their pride and I could feel the subtle change in Drew's posture the farther we rode. The man, who only moments earlier had been warm and supple, was now as cold and rigid as a granite statue beneath my touch.

It was another mile or so down the road that everything went to absolute shit. It was there, in an old dirt patch that had once upon a time been a field of crops, that I saw an effigy on a post. The figure was propped on a bicycle surrounded by straw, and flames were already licking at the tires of the thing as a kid stood to the side, squirting lighter fluid all over it. It was eerie how maniacal his smile was. Even from a distance, I could see the intensity of his stare and the joy he was getting out of the destruction.

The closer we got, the more I recognized what I'd missed only moments earlier. The figure of straw straddling the bike was wearing a hoodie with the Hounds' patch emblazoned across its chest. This patch was not a cheap knock off, but one they'd curiously managed to get from the club.

I knew Drew wasn't going to be able to let that go, and I would never have asked him to. The club was an extension of him, and those punks had taken it beyond the point where he could simply ignore it. Whatever battle he had been warring with himself at the signs of disrespect, he couldn't ignore that blatant contempt towards the pack and everyone in it. Especially not when the culprit was standing spraying liquid over the straw figure so it, and the cotton of the sweater, suddenly roared to life with the twisting angry flames of the inferno.

I felt the back wheel lock up under me as Drew's fingers closed around the brakes. It was only seconds later that the wobble took over the back end of the bike and had me burying my face in the patch of Drew's cut as the tail slid out to the right. The rubber screamed as gravity took control, and by all rights, we should have been laid down on the asphalt after a move like that, but Drew was an experienced rider and had been from the time he could walk. There was no way in hell he would do that to his bike or, I realized a little too late, me.

With this newfound confidence, I looked up just in time to realize we were already facing the opposite direction, still on two wheels, and now staring at the back of the kid running away from us with everything he possessed.

At least he had some brains.

I didn't need the pat on my hands to warn me what was about to happen, or the reach of Drew's arm around my back as he pulled me closer. My thighs were already locked in around him, and my hands were gripping the wrist of the opposite arm as he found the gear he needed and almost lifted the front wheel from the gravel as he took off. The yip I let off wasn't in good fun, it was in panic.

As much as I trusted Drew on his bike, he was angry enough for me to sense it through our bodies. I could feel it in his posture, in the way he twisted the grip on the handlebars and kicked up the dirt as we chased the kid toward the rows of broken and forgotten warehouses in the distance.

I wasn't honestly sure how much I could take as the bike hurtled over the field. My body bounced painfully, my back screaming as we caught air and landed hard, but there wasn't much I could do other than cling onto him for dear life. Scrunching my eyes closed and burying my face in Drew's back, once again, all I could do was wait it out and wish for the ride to be over.

Even if I could understand the need for this kind of speed and the desperate urge to catch these little bastards and show them what fear truly was, I couldn't physically stop the roll of the hot damp tear down my cheek. This was something big, something unpredictable, and I suddenly wanted nothing more than to get to the boy and find some back up. Drew needed to teach those kids a lesson. I just wished it hadn't been that night, or off-road with speed that the devil himself couldn't keep up with.

For the second time in a matter of minutes, Drew slid the bike to a stop. This time the ping of stones against the fenders and the click of the hot engine expanding made my ears ring as he killed the engine. The kid was still in sight, hoofing it to the closest rolling door on the right. I couldn't see anyone or anything in the dim light. Even the moon seemed to be hiding.

"Drew, we need to call someone," I said a little too calmly as he dismounted the bike with ease.

Snapping his head from side to side, he frantically looked around and tried to calm his breathing. "I don't know what the hell is happening," he wheezed out. "But this is ending now. No fucker disrespects my club or my brotherhood that way. No one."

"I get that, but maybe we should call Slater or Jedd?"

He paused, moving to reach into the pocket of his jeans before his face creased in anger and he growled. "Fuck. My cell's in The Hut."

"So is mine," I whispered in disbelief. I'd wanted this night to be perfect without any distractions. Just one night alone with the man I love. "Maybe we can go find help."

"We don't have time. This kid is here *now*."

He stopped and turned to face me again, his hands gripping both my cheeks as he leaned in closer.

"I need to end this tonight, Ayda. He's just a kid. Just... a kid."

I blew out all the air in my cheeks and searched his eyes with mine. If there was anything I was confident of, it was that he could handle it. I just didn't like the sudden unease as we sat surrounded by dilapidated buildings in the dark. The chill of the night air was bad enough, but there was something more making all my hair stand on end.

"What do you need me to do?" I asked, my last surge of bravado clawing from my gut and giving me the strength I needed.

"Stay here. If you see anyone or anything, run and don't stop until you get somewhere safe. But I should be back here within minutes. This kid has nowhere to go. Stay in the shadows, okay? Promise me you won't do anything stupid."

I slid forward and onto the warmth of the seat he'd been occupying only moments before. I wasn't sure whether he knew he was asking the impossible of me or not, but I found myself nodding anyway. My first instinct would be to run to him, not away, but I was in the process of convincing myself I would run for help when his hand cupped the back of my head and pulled me close, his lips meeting my forehead.

I didn't like what was happening one little bit, but I could do as he asked and stay in the shadows.

"I promise, nothing stupid."

"Nothing stupid," he whispered against me before tearing himself away and looking up through hooded eyes. I knew him well enough to know that he was trying to curb his anger in front of me, but even as skilled as he was at doing exactly that, I could see right through him. His club was his heart, and someone had just dared to insult it. "I love you."

Drew's hand slipped down onto my knee and he held my gaze for as long as he could. When he turned to walk away and I saw the tension in his biceps and shoulders, I knew he meant business.

The farther he got from me, the more my eyes seemed to focus on his figure. He walked with confidence, his shoulders rolled back and his head held high. Each step he took had his hands balling at his sides with the rage that filled him. There wasn't much I truly believed Drew feared in life, and I envied him that, but thinking about his strength made me all too aware of my own weaknesses. When it came to loyalty and conviction, he had it in bucketfuls for his men and his club. That part of him eclipsed any doubts he had about walking into that place and teaching that kid a lesson.

When he finally neared the warehouse, I felt the distance between us. Every foot seemed like ten. I folded my arms around my body and narrowed my eyes to keep him in my line of sight, needing that lasting connection between us.

Drew needed to do this, and as his old lady, I realized I had no choice but to let it happen.

CHAPTER THIRTY-EIGHT
DREW

There were three things that were certain to make me react. One: seeing Ayda hurt. Two: my brothers being in danger. And three…

People disrespecting my club.

My hand pushed against the steel door, my shoulder soon replacing it when it offered more resistance than I'd expected. The smell that came from the other side had my face scrunching up and my eyes narrowing. Whatever the place was or had been, it fucking stank.

I couldn't let myself think about Ayda out there all alone. I wanted the heat taking off us and all this crap laid to rest for good, and the more time I wasted leaving it to the likes of Sutton to deal with, the more those pack of wannabes trod all over everything my men and I stood for.

Pete was at the forefront of my mind again, and as I pushed through and took my first step into the darkness, I asked him to watch over her while I couldn't.

Yeah, I was fucking praying.

I finally had something to pray for.

My feet skimmed across the surface, kicking against the loose stones, pieces of rubble and whatever else was laid out there I couldn't quite see. The only thing that could be heard were my movements, so once I was in, I stood completely still and let my eyes adjust to the diluted light. I tried to find something to focus on. My neck rolled back as I looked up at the few narrow, wired window panels that lined the top of the bare brick walls. They weren't letting much light in, but in that environment, I was grateful for what I could get.

It didn't take long for the rookie to make his first mistake. The sound of an iron bar rattling against the floor from not too far away had me moving forward carefully. Whoever had entered the place was as blind as I was, and the thought of finding him and dealing with him the way I should have all those nights ago had me rolling my shoulders in my cut.

The old me would have been taunting him into playing a game of cat and mouse like a true man, coaxing him out of the corners he was cowering in, but no matter how self-assured I felt that I could handle whatever I was about to come face to face with, I didn't provoke. Mainly because I promised Ayda I would be in and out in a heartbeat.

I was all about keeping my promises those days.

I sucked in a small breath as my foot nudged something on the floor before sliding it out the way so I could try and create a clear path without falling on my ass.

"Shit," came a quiet voice—a voice that was so close, it felt like I could reach out and touch it, and when the shadow to my right turned into a body, my predatory smile broke free.

"Well, well, we—"

I didn't get time to finish.

The blood-curdling scream from behind me grabbed my attention from the moment my name clawed its way out of Ayda's throat, and before I could even think to reach out for the fucker in front of me, I was moving on auto, turning on my heels to run in the opposite direction. Her name was barely a whisper from my lips when something grabbed the back of my cut, the force of it yanking me back in its grip before I could lash out and attempt to free myself. My whole body turned to shit the moment I heard her piercing scream for a second time. The only thing I could feel with any clarity at all was the blood within my veins turning cold.

I barely had time to blink or breathe when I was struck on the head with a force so strong it felt like it held the power of an army behind it. The world slipped away from beneath my feet, and as the concrete came hurtling closer at a terrifying speed, the pain erupted all over, leaving me paralyzed, until everything around me began to fade away.

Then all I was left with was darkness.

CHAPTER THIRTY-NINE
AYDA

My body hurt everywhere, but my mind was a fuzzy, foggy mess that was stuck in a perpetual state of confusion. I'd known I was in trouble the moment I saw the patch on the back of the man who currently had me draped over his shoulder. The sugar skull smiling out of the regal fur lined cape was a dead giveaway. I'd only seen it twice in my life, but it was one of those things that stuck with me. Then again, anyone who made an attempt on my life would imprint themselves in my head. The swirling mess of panic in my stomach made the bile rise in my throat violently as I realized I had no idea what had happened, where I was, or how I managed to get there.

The last thing I remembered with any lucidity was feeling Drew's warmth through the leather and against my thighs as I'd pressed up to his body, that lingering musk that belonged solely to him making me lightheaded with lust. I'd been on the bike, watching him walk into the warehouse…

That was the exact moment the real panic started to flow like acid through my veins. Drew was in the warehouse.

My eyes darted around the place, trying to pick up as much as I could to figure out how much time had passed, what damage had been done, or ways to escape, but there was nothing distinguishable. It wasn't like I had anywhere to go. I was over someone's shoulder, and my hands had been bound by a zip tie. The unforgiving plastic had been digging into my skin from the moment my coherence found its way back to me. It was then the most relevant thing in my world.

Until I saw Drew—then everything else simply became background noise as the horror of our situation shifted from nightmare to a shocking reality. Not even the stench of the place distracted me from what I was witnessing.

There wasn't much light, but there was enough power to rig one nude bulb that they'd dangled directly above Drew. Rusty chains were looped too tightly around his wrists, both of them hooked to the outer walls of the warehouse, holding him captive in the middle of the open space. Stretched out like he was, the only thing taking the pressure from his arms was the weight he had on the balls of his feet. His muscles trembled under a sheen of sweat through the torn material, even though he was clearly unconscious. His feet and legs were limp and slumped forward along with his head, which hung heavy and listlessly to one side. There was a trickle of crimson blood riding down the side of his face, the thick viscose liquid weaving a slow path down his tanned skin and disappearing into his dark beard where it dripped onto the ripped and torn white shirt he'd been wearing.

I tried to be strong, even if this was a scene that could have been plucked from my worst nightmare. It wasn't like I had much of a choice, and it was the only thing he would have asked of me if he could have. I understood that I had to try and keep my reactions to myself. I couldn't give them more ammunition than they already had, but even I was realistic enough to admit it was useless. I was only human, and the man

I loved, one of the few genuine strengths I had in my life, was unconscious in the hands of his rivals.

There was no comparison to the fear I felt. It was dirty, gritty and more real than anything within my reach as it took control of my body in small waves of trembling. My blood felt frozen in my veins as my heart fought to push it, which made the world quake around me. My panic and fear had incapacitated everything in my body, except, apparently, my vocal chords.

The whimper didn't go unnoticed by my captor. The man carrying me may not have said anything in response, but I felt the tightening of his arms around my legs as he walked us into the shadows, and the shake of his shoulder as he found amusement in my predicament.

We were in the corner of the warehouse, as far from Drew as they could get me. The only thing in my line of sight, however, was Drew and those damn chains. The scene held my full attention until it was seared into my brain, the logical part of my mind kicking in and dampening the fear, giving me something to focus on. To think I could have any kind of escape whatsoever was a ridiculous notion, but giving up hope was almost as bad taking my own life.

The man carrying me stopped abruptly, the scuffing of his boots echoing from the corner before he dropped me to the floor, eliciting another cry of pain from me as I landed on one shoulder, forcing the plastic that circled my wrists to bite deeper into the flesh.

"Don't think about running. We'll kill the motherfucker." The point was reiterated with a kick to my stomach, which sent my body curling inward to protect itself. I gasped for breath, my forehead pressing against the dirt and broken glass littering the concrete as my body slid towards a full-blown panic attack.

Lifting my head without thinking, my body twisted, even as the fire in my wrists and shoulder argued back. There was a voice deep in the shadowy recesses of my soul that screamed I would be okay as long as I could see Drew, that if he was in my line of sight, there was a chance I could breathe and maybe even survive what was happening.

I barely glanced his way when a booted foot came down heavily on the side of my head and pushed it into the broken shards of glass and concrete dust below me. It was done with so much pressure, flashes of light started to invade my vision, and the ringing in my ears deafened me in the same rhythm as my galloping heartbeat. My tears came fast and hard as the reprieve of darkness closed in around me and began blotting out the pain.

"Enough. We need her, asshole."

The pressure was gone, and all too soon my thoughts cleared enough to trigger some kind of familiarity to the sound—a sound that only made the fear wrap itself around me and squeeze until my teeth rattled together like bones in a bag.

Then Chester Cortez stepped out of the shadows.

Something in his hand caught the light as he twisted his wrist. It had my sole focus as the shape identified itself and made the bile rise in my throat. Once again, my reaction was audible to everyone else but me. Cortez's maniacal laughter echoed around the empty space and reverberated from everything it touched. I wanted to close my eyes and hide, to pretend it wasn't happening, but the fear of what he would do if I did made me keep them on him and every step he took toward me.

"Hey, little maid," Cortez purred. He tugged on the legs of his jeans before crouching down in front of me, the chains on his belt dragging along the concrete floor, making the scene even more malevolent than it already was. "You ready to see how a real man fights his battles?"

"Fuck you," I whispered, negating the insult altogether.

"All in good time. First," he said, digging his fingers into my hair and scraping them along my scalp. He tugged roughly, forcing my body to follow until I was on my knees, panting from the pain. "I need you to watch this, and when the time comes..." He leaned in. "You're gonna be my leverage."

"I'm not going to do shit for you."

He bent my head to the side, using my hair to position me before he licked up my cheek and pressed his mouth against my ear. "You're already doing it. Every breath you take means that bitch Hound is in my pocket."

"I could always change that," I growled back, the fear inside me making my voice less than convincing. I was a rat in a maze and he knew it. The bastard could smell my terror and he was taking delight in rolling around in it.

"I'm going to enjoy watching you both bleed." Cortez laughed, slapping my cheek before gripping my chin painfully tight. "But right now, me and your boy gotta talk."

He pushed up to his feet and started laughing that twisted sound again as he released my hair, his hand slapping the chest of the guy standing by me as he strutted back toward Drew. He stepped into his limp body brutally, his fist clenched before it buried itself in Drew's ribs. "Wake up, motherfucker. Nap time's over."

Drew didn't move of his own volition. His body swung with the chains, the rattle of them echoing as his head flopped to the other side and hung limply. He barely rocked from side to side as the blood dripped from his chin and down to the patches of white shirt left on his body. I wanted to scream *stop*. I wanted to get to my feet and plant myself between Drew and Cortez, but I knew the moment I tried, I would be thrown around by the jailer that had been forced to stand over me.

"Come on, Tucker," Cortez growled, the tip of his knife pressing against Drew's outstretched shoulder. The small welling of red had one of my legs pulling up under me, but I was forced back down, the shards of glass slicing the skin on my knees as the guy pressed down with his body weight. "I ain't got all night for this shit."

Rage and fear created a ball in the thick of my gut as I watched Cortez slice Drew's skin and slap him in a bid to rouse him from unconsciousness. I shifted under the weight of the guard dog, my body attempting escape, only to be forced into a spine aching hold that made sure my eyes were on the scene playing out. Cortez wasn't playing games with us. He was out for blood and he was taking it in every small way he could. It was only when Drew finally started showing signs of life that I felt the first real breath fill my lungs.

He was alive.

For how long, I wasn't sure.

His head swung slowly from side to side like it weighed too much for his neck, and his chest expanded with the air he dragged into his lungs. Cortez lost whatever patience he seemed to have. In the same way as he'd done with me, he fisted his hand in Drew's hair and pulled it back, his other hand gripping Drew's jaw and squeezing violently.

"You're not gonna want to miss this, Tucker. Wake the

fuck up." He slapped him across the face hard, and though he wasn't completely coherent, Drew cracked one eye open and curled his lip in disgust before dropping out again.

Releasing Drew's hair and keeping his head upright with the grip on his jaw, Cortez used his index and thumb to pry Drew's eye open. "Have it your way, asshole. I'll go kill your girl right now…"

With a twitch of his head, the man next to me moved his hand to the back of my neck and pressed me forward, his knee planting itself in my back to hold me still. I'd had no idea what he was planning on doing, but I put up a fight anyway, struggling against his grip as Cortez slapped Drew's cheeks.

"Wakey, wakey, Drew. We're gonna make your girl sing."

Then time felt like it stopped altogether.

For a single breath there was nothing but the smell of earth and grease—the only sound was the crunch of glass under foot of the man who had complete control of my body. I could almost count the seconds… until it was all stripped away.

The pain was immediate, raw, and very real. The crack of bone as the man above me snapped my finger was drowned out by a scream I couldn't have held in if I'd tried. It was piercing as the white hot flames of pain ran from the break, all the way up my arm, exploding in my chest until a sob cut everything off and I fell face down toward the concrete.

CHAPTER FORTY
Drew

"**D**rew," he shouted. "Drew!"

My body was floating. I was weightless, traveling on a road I had never been down before. The sound of his voice made me want to smile, but it was too much like hard work for my sleepy muscles. So I smiled in my mind instead, hoping he could see it somehow.

"Drew!" Pete's voice grew louder, more desperate for my attention.

Not even my lips would part.

"You need to wake up. You need to fucking wake up and deal with your shit. You've never quit before now, so don't fucking quit on her or I swear to God, I will come back there and I will kill you myself."

The anger in his voice hit me the same time a hand curled around my jaw. For a moment, I thought I saw a flash of light, but the twist of my mouth caused so much pain, I sunk back onto the road again, choosing to enjoy the lack of gravity over the agony that I somehow knew was waiting for me on the other side.

Then it all happened quickly. She screamed. Pete roared. I gasped for air in a world that suddenly felt like it held no *oxygen.*

"Ay—"

It wasn't even a word, a croak, or a grumble. I tried to push past the grit and the agony that lined my throat. The points of pain didn't register all at once. That would have been too fucking easy. Instead, they started to poke at me in different places. Lightly at first, teasing me into thinking I had enough strength to even attempt to lift my head. They were soon followed by a jolt of electricity down my spine, before the flames that were burning one side of my face seemed to multiply. Random pinpricks of torture started to spread across my skin like some flesh-eating disease that just grew and grew and fucking grew until all that was left was misery.

I almost gave into it. I almost let my eyes close and my chin drop to my chest again, but when her painful whimper floated across to me one more time, I forced my eyes open and tried to find a way to see through the crippling, blinding light.

Ayda. Ayda. My Ayda. Where is she?

I was blinking and squinting forever into nothing but white and yellow. Each flash of color that tried to disturb it had my head rolling from side to side in an attempt to escape the intensity.

"Drew," she tried to say through an obvious sob.

Fire burned up my arms and metal chains cut into my wrists as I leaned farther forward in some feeble fucking attempt to get closer to the sound of her.

My feet slid as the low roar of hatred began to bubble away in the pit of my stomach. As I stretched my mouth to try and speak, a wave of water was thrown over my face, followed by a heavy-handed slap across my burning cheek, sending my head snapping back to the side.

Blood pooled in one corner of my mouth and I hung there limply until I could gather it up and spit it out, the effort proving too much as it dripped from my lips. One small cough made my body tense, and the damage to my ribs soon became obvious as I curled in on myself and winced.

"There he is," a voice sang out beside me. "Our little fighter has returned to the ring once more."

As soon as Cortez spoke, my eyes closed again.

I was fucked.

He walked full circle around me, the noise his boots created against the floor sounding like a small atomic bomb going off in my mind with every slow, calculated step he took.

"Look at me, Mr. Tucker," Cortez said calmly.

I kept my pose, eyes down, body hanging, letting all the pain fall forward as small droplets of my own blood fell at his feet.

"I said *look at me!*"

Fuck you. I would have spat if I could have. I would have said it if I had known she wasn't close by. But instead, I glanced up to the side through narrowed eyes and met his smug little face.

He reached out to grab me, pulling me up in his grip and forcing my body to fall back as the weight of the chains swayed me to and fro in his hands. I was like a fucking puppet to him and this was his finest show.

"So, she *is* your weakness," he said in a whisper, pulling my face impossibly closer to his. "I thought you weren't human enough to ever fall into that trap, Tucker. All those fights you won, all those games you played, all those people you killed without thought or feeling or fear, yet here we are, the two of us surrounded by this weird energy again. Just like the good old days when we stepped into the ring and only one man could survive—the man who was willing to lose the most."

I tried to register what he was saying, but the side of my head that had taken the hit was drowning him out as the buzz of the aftershocks started to ring around in my mind, causing me to blink slowly. As if the world wasn't spinning enough.

Cortez's fingers squeezed me tighter until the small smirk on his face turned into a toothy grin, and the gold trophy in his mouth shone out like some kind of sick, twisted joke. One day, I was going to hang that on my wall, along with the fucker's balls, whether that was in this life or the next.

He stepped back, releasing me from his grip with a shove, forcing my body into a back and forth swinging motion again. As I hunched over, it gave me time to pull some much needed oxygen into my lungs. No matter how much pain slashed through all my organs, I sucked that shit in as carefully as I could while my eyes roamed the floor.

"Where—?" I choked on my own word, swallowing as bile rose in my throat. I cleared it as quickly and as roughly as I could before trying again. "Where... is... she?"

"I'm fine," Ayda said from somewhere in the room, followed by the sound of a slap and a grunted whimper that she was obviously trying, and failing, to hide.

Fine. I remembered that word. I knew what it meant and I was grateful for it in that moment. It meant she was anything but fine and it forced me to dig deep and pull some magic from somewhere dark inside.

Stretching until my feet found some kind of half-assed balance on the tips of their toes, my face set to stone as I used all my strength to ignore the torture going on throughout my body. I glanced up enough to see the other people in the room, and when their blurred outlines came into view, I knew where she was, and I hated it with every fiber of my fucking soul.

"Cortez," I ground out.

His boots skimmed over the rubble as he pushed both hands into his pockets and came to me again.

"Did I give you permission to speak?"

"What..." I inhaled sharply, my head rolling forward as I tensed my jaw and glared at him. "What do you want?"

"What do I want? You're asking me what *I* want?" Cortez rocked back on his heels, the heavy shrug of his shoulders only serving to remind me of the weight his punches could carry. "What do I want? Hmm. Let me think. I want a lot of things, Drew. I want a life filled with motorcycles and women. I want a life filled with riches and gold. I want good fucking sex, served up from the finest pussy around. I want peace in my home and I want safety for my children." He stopped to take a step closer, the tone of his voice becoming as serious as the new look on his face. "I want safety for my club. I want revenge for the ones who have fallen. I want my enemies dead, the same way you do. I want enough of their blood to spill so that I can bathe in it for weeks. I want to rip those apart who have tried to rip me apart. I want to watch them cry out in pain and beg for mercy. I want them to see I hold no mercy in my heart at all. I want them to realize that they played with the devil and the devil fought back, and he took no prisoners. He showed nothing but rage when he ripped out the hearts of those that even dared to breathe in his direction."

The muscles in my face twitched as my body swayed back and forth, but I never looked away from him. I never broke his stare.

"I want to win, and I will win," he whispered. "But first..." Stepping to the side, Cortez swept an arm out and shouted to his men. "First, I want to play. Isn't that right, boys?"

The cheers of The Emps filled the room, and it was only when I heard the different tones and the different accents that I began to realize just how fucked we were. There was no hope of getting out alive. They were never going to set me free as long as they had me as their torture toy.

I allowed myself to look over his shoulder and down at the figure behind him. When Ayda's face came into focus and the fear cried out to me, I became numb. For a second, it was just the two of us, each one kept away from the other in their captor's grip, but we were together and we were there, and we were going to look at each other until we were forced to look away, because right then, we both knew what was happening, and neither one of us could be certain we would ever have that chance to be us again.

"Bring out the girl," Cortez commanded.

Just like that, our connection was broken and I was forced to look into the shadows, until another female figure stepped out into the dim, murky light.

The swollen eyes of the woman from the forest glared back at me with both fear and anger shining outwards. She looked at me with uncertainty, the memories of that night washing over her face and the images of her dead boyfriend forcing her to shake her head as she tried to stay calm.

She was present in body, but not in mind. The girl was back on the battlefield again.

Only she was the one with the tools in her hand and the wolves at her back, while all I was left to do was stare at her like she was a ghost.

A ghost I should have killed when I'd had the chance.

As we stood there staring at each other, the real war began. It was time to play the game. Ghosts versus demons. Savages versus the weak and the woeful. Two wrongs fighting to be right while death hovered over us with a smirk on his face and a one-way ticket to Hell in his hand. He was watching and waiting with baited breath as each one of us stood silently and prepared ourselves for that inevitable, eternal fire.

Our souls were damned. Now it was only a question of time.

CHAPTER FORTY-ONE
Ayda

I didn't look at the new addition in the room. I couldn't. It was my only opportunity to take Drew in and memorize every pained line on his face. The look in his eyes told me he'd accepted our fate and even though, to a certain extent, I had, too, there was still some fight left in me. I wasn't going to give up that easily, but the outcome was bleak.

As I knelt watching Drew, there was no doubt in my mind that I would do anything it took to get him out of there alive. If only one of us could survive, it had to be him. He had so many people depending on him, and I knew in the deepest parts of my heart that he would look after Tate if I asked him to.

It was only when the frown marred his face that I followed his line of sight to the woman that stepped out of the shadows. She was pissed off, that much was obvious in the balling of her hands, but she was scared, too. I could see the fear as her eyes met Drew's. Not even him being bound and her having the whole MC at her back seemed to take that away. There was a frailty in the way she held herself. For a moment, I even entertained the thought that I could, at the very least, take *her* down.

While all eyes in the room were on the mousy woman,

I tested the plastic holding my wrists together. There wasn't a lot I could do in a warehouse full of the enemy, but I had to believe I could cause enough of a stir to give us a fighting chance.

"Is this the guy, Sofia?" Cortez asked, lifting the hand with the knife and pointing it at Drew.

The girl's head darted around the room, her eyes bouncing off the few men that were hiding in the shadows. I wasn't sure how many of them were out there, and I didn't want to know. My ignorance meant I had the opportunity to cling to hope, and for now, that was the only thing keeping me going. That, and Drew.

"I… I don't know. I didn't see them clearly, Chester. I just heard their voices."

Cortez scratched the back of his head with agitation. Even with his back to me, I could sense the eye roll directed at her. Even though, from what I could tell, she was a part of his club in some way, he didn't have a lot of respect for her.

"It's like working with those bastard kids all over again. Tucker, enlighten her."

All attention turned to Drew, including mine. I was so desperate to see those eyes of his, I knew he could feel my stare boring into the side of his head, but he was all about business. Just as he should have been.

Drew tore his attention away from the woman as he looked back at Cortez. His eyes flickered wildly around his rival's face until a small, broken, and ever so weak smirk tugged at his lips. With his arms strapped up in chains, it was difficult for him to move in any direction, but he attempted to shrug anyway.

All eyes seemed to be on the interaction between the

two men, while mine stayed firmly on Drew, my shoulders relaxing slightly as I realized he wasn't going to give them what they wanted. Not completely and not without a fight.

Cortez wasn't playing, though. He strutted forward with the same casual stride and spun the tip of the knife on his index finger. Drew wasn't intimidated. He didn't so much as lean away. He just tipped his head to the side in question, inviting the torture to begin.

"You're an arrogant fuck, Tucker. Hardheaded. I know you don't fear death, and pain is a drug to you," he said, balancing the knife on his finger and knocking on his own temple. "But you're not the only one I can hurt."

With another nod of his head, my hair was almost ripped from the roots before I was thrown forward. I tried to catch myself on my shoulder, my face turning to the side to protect my nose and chin from the brunt of the force. The shift in my body had the right effect, but it sent me sprawling on my back, enticing my cry of pain to come almost immediately as the jolt of my body sent the throb in my finger escalating into something more apocalyptic. My feet hit the floor quickly, my ass and hips rising to relieve the pressure on my bound hands and broken finger.

Chester started laughing, his boot coming down on my stomach and pushing my body toward the ground again. "Your whore likes her ass in the air, Drew. I can see why you like her so much."

There was no sound coming from Drew, but that didn't mean he didn't have a lot to say.

"Oh, and what an ass it is." Cortez slammed his foot down so hard on my stomach it crushed my finger between my body and concrete yet again. I swallowed the scream of pain that sat in my throat like a baseball. It felt like a red hot poker was being pushed into the joint while it was being slammed in a car door over and over again, but the only sound I gave him was a grunt. I wouldn't be the reason Drew was forced to talk. Whether he'd done what he was accused of or not, I didn't care. It was club business and I wasn't going to be used in that particular game against him.

The moment Cortez's foot was gone, I forced myself to roll onto my stomach without a sound, and buried my face against the concrete in an attempt to gather my strength. My breath forced waves of dust to scatter across the surface, giving me something other than the pain to focus on. I couldn't let Drew see my agony, but it meant I left myself open in other respects.

When I felt the hand on my ass, the only thing I could do was scrunch my eyes closed and pray for it to be over soon.

"These pants are like a second skin, man." I felt the cold blade of the knife through the denim and remained still. Nothing good would come from fighting him on what he was doing, no matter how much I wanted to protect Drew from the inevitable.

The chains rattled furiously until the sound of them snapping into a sharp line caught Cortez's attention, as well as the small growl of frustration that Drew just couldn't keep in.

"Close, but not close enough," Chester said through a smile, fixing his eyes on Drew as he began to move the knife.

Drew didn't say anything for the longest time, not until he inhaled loudly, the intake of breath obviously causing him pain, before he blew out again. His head rose slowly as he looked across at the girl and let his eyes linger.

Then he began to speak.

"You're going to watch as I tear your world apart in front of you…"

Sofia's gasp was instant, her hand flying up to her mouth to catch her sobs.

"Every limb, every tooth, every single hair on his head will fall at your feet. Then, and only then, will you get to leave," Drew said slowly in a raspy, dark, malevolent tone I'd never heard him use before, but one that immediately sent chills down my spine.

I'd always known there was a side to him that I wasn't acquainted with, and there was a time I wasn't even sure I wanted to know it. This was the business face of the man I loved—one that belonged to the Hounds, and the side that his enemies got to see and experience. Whatever I felt in hearing his voice that way, the shout of redemption inside of me made it possible to separate the two, which in turn helped me to ignore the violent undertones and just see the man I loved. The only problem now was the threat being used against me. It had more than exposed his participation in whatever it was Cortez was pissed about.

Lifting my head defiantly, I silently pleaded with Drew to stop talking. I understood that he wanted to protect me, and that was admirable and I loved him for it, but as Cortez had pointed out, it was becoming glaringly obvious that I was his one weakness.

"Don't do this," I choked out, my voice hoarse from the last scream I'd given. I could have said so much more, but my head was once again forced down with a boot until all I could hear was the metallic ringing that drowned out everything. Unfortunately, Drew didn't look at me. Instead, he kept his eyes narrowed at the girl as another smile played on his lips.

Before he could react, she was throwing herself at him, her balled up fists hitting at his chest and face over and over again as her sobs echoed around the derelict building.

"You bastard," she cried. "It *was* you. It was you, you evil bastard."

Drew stood rigid between the chains, accepting her blows against his sliced and bruised skin for all that they were worth, his face tilting to one side as he tried to lean away and hold his balance.

"That's enough," Cortez commanded, but the girl kept on hitting Drew over and over again, and all I could think about was finding a way to get to her so I could scratch her eyes out. "I said that's *enough!*"

Wrapping an arm around her waist, Cortez dragged her aside and tossed her away as though she was worthless, her body making a dull thud reverberate off the walls. My eyes had only one target. They were locked on Drew, who was coughing up more blood and avoiding my stares as much as he possibly could.

My head slowly started to swim, flashes of white light peppering the edges of my vision. With the pressure of the boot still there, the buzzing was making me nauseous, and with the dull red from the blood that seemed to come from even more spots on Drew's body, I was becoming lightheaded. It was only sheer will and the fear of what would happen if I blacked out that had my breaths coming in long, even pulls. When the guy standing over me put more of his weight on my head, I forced my finger to bend and focused on the pain there instead, refusing to give into their games. My eyes, however, were now trained on the girl who had curled into the fetal position the moment she'd hit the concrete, her sobs drowning out the shuffle of boots from the shadows.

This wasn't a situation where you could anticipate anybody's next move, but when Drew began to laugh sadistically, spitting out as much of the blood as he could in between his sharp and shallow breaths, I truly believed I was seeing things.

"I would say I was sorry, but..." Drew sighed.

Cortez didn't waste time in stepping up to him, his fist smacking him square across the jaw sending him swinging as much as his body would allow him to as he was held within the restrictions of the chains. The sound was one of those things you can't put words to—flesh on flesh, blunt trauma that comes so hard and fast, the sickening echo of it lingers.

"That one was just a warning. The next one goes across your woman's face, not yours." Chester began to walk in a slow circle, making sure every inch of the sole of his shoe connected with the floor with each step he took. "I wonder what the Navs would say if they knew you were imitating them to gain higher standing in the MC world."

Drew glanced up, both brows rising as far as they could considering how swollen his face was becoming.

"You're talking to me about imitating, Chester?" He coughed again, shaking his head slowly. "The Widow Makers were all you had? I can't *believe*... I didn't see it."

Cortez threw his arms out to the side, showcasing himself to Drew. "You went big, I went small, and still, I am not the one who ended up in chains."

"Not yet," Drew added quietly, and I didn't know if he was bluffing or if his confidence really was growing, but I knew I couldn't tear my eyes away from him.

"Not ever."

"I guess I should congratulate you on your chess move. Well played. I didn't see you being behind those pissant kids."

Cortez feigned a bow, sweeping his arm down and back up again. "I have more surprises where they came from."

"So do I." Drew coughed up even more, almost choking as he sucked in his stomach to try and combat whatever pain he was in. I felt helpless, but I was being caged by a man almost twice my size who seemed more than happy to prove how much stronger he was.

Stepping forward, Chester closed the gap between them, once again, tilting his head to the side. "I think I know all your surprises by now, Mr. Tucker. I know more about you than you think. I knew your arrogance wouldn't allow you to see what I was doing with those bastard boys. I know now that the smirk you wear on your face is for nobody else's benefit but mine. I know your mind is racing with ways to save your bitch, even if that means sacrificing your own life. I know pain doesn't bother you, but shame does. I know all about the way you tore my man apart in front of Sofia without so much as a thought for the family he was leaving behind."

Drew's smile faded as he began to work the strong muscles along his jawline and the sound of the chains tightening rang out again.

"I also know you killed four of my men at the house fire."

"Men who tried to burn two innocent people alive," Drew hit back through gritted teeth.

"Ah, innocent lives. Let's talk about those, shall we?" Cortez widened his stance, bringing both his hands behind his back as he leaned in closer to Drew. "Where is Hernandez?"

"He's dead," Drew answered matter-of-factly. "Buried in a shallow grave somewhere on the outskirts of town."

The blow to his stomach was immediate, forcing all the air out of his body as he curled in on himself again and grunted in agony, unable to catch his feet beneath him as he rocked forward. I didn't know what I was thinking I could do to help, but my legs moved under me, only to receive a kick from the man standing watch. He had to remove his foot from my head to do it, but he was reminding me of his constant presence.

"I'll ask you again," Cortez said, pulling Drew up to a more stable stand and resting his hand on his shoulder. "Where. Is. Hernandez?"

"I don't know the location." He sucked in a breath before rushing out to speak again. "But there's a man in this room who does."

Cortez paused in his next assault, the confusion across his face evident as he pulled back and leaned farther towards Drew. "Excuse me?"

"I said," Drew forced his head back up to meet his stare head on. "One of your men was with me the night we buried him. He also helped lure Sofia and her boy to the forest." The slow smile on his face appeared again as he glanced over Chester's shoulder and pushed out a humorless laugh. "Y'all have got a rat up in here who's played us both."

"No," Cortez breathed out, uncertainty tainting his voice.

"Denial is to be expected." Drew smirked.

"You're lying."

"I wish I was. I paid that bastard ten big ones of my club's money to dish your shit out, and here I am strung up like fucking Jesus. I've got no reason to lie to you anymore. I'm dead anyway."

Cortez spun on his heels quickly, glancing around at all

the men he had with him in the shadows before he turned back to Drew and growled quietly. "Name. Now."

"I'm no rat."

"Name," Cortez persisted.

"Look every one of your men in the eyes and you'll see for yourself which one betrayed you."

"Tell me who, *now!*"

Drew didn't answer for such a long time, I felt like the walls were closing in on all of us, sure someone was going to pull a trigger at any given moment that would end his life and mine. The tension was thick and just one wrong move from anyone and the whole place would erupt.

When he eventually glanced up again, he found some strength in his arms and pulled his body back, only to laugh that sadistic laugh of his right in Cortez's face. "Doesn't matter who it was who helped me bury him. I killed him—these two hands of mine. They beat the last breath out of his body, just like Ramirez did with Pete. I enjoyed every second of his pain. I watched him bleed and cry out for me to stop. I got high off the stench of his blood. The more he cried like the pussy he was, the more I—"

The shriek from the shadows was so piercing it cut through the pain in my mind like a red-hot poker. Before anyone had time to question what the hell was going on, the sharp click of heels came from one of the darkest corners of the place. It seemed to take a lifetime for her to make it into the dim pool of light that was bathing Drew, but in reality, it was seconds. It was the shock of what I was seeing that stopped time from having any meaning whatsoever.

Maisey Sutton appeared like a banshee, her lithe body ducking under the chains as she used Drew's arm for leverage to swing her own body around to face him. Her scream was still bouncing from the walls when her hand met his face. It was slow at first, and everyone in the place seemed frozen in surprise as she clawed at his chest, half weeping and screaming at him.

I couldn't stand to see her touch him. I pulled my legs under me and was halfway to standing when the asshole watching over me kicked the back of my knee, sending me sprawling on the floor yet again.

"You son of a bitch. I hate you. I fucking hate you, Drew," Maisey screamed.

I pushed to my side, completely helpless, even though I could feel the rage pooling in my stomach.

"Maisey?" Drew asked with as much confusion as I felt right in the depths of my soul. "What the fuck are you doing here?"

"Hernandez was innocent, you asshole. He didn't deserve to die. He was mine. Fucking *mine*!"

Drew looked as stunned as I did, his eyes flickering over Maisey's face for a trace of a lie. I knew she hated me. It was pretty fucking obvious that she did, but I'd always thought it was because Drew wanted me. Maybe to some extent it was. I just wasn't sure how long she'd been fucking an Emp.

"How long?" I demanded, shrinking away from the eyes that seemed to turn to me.

"Fuck you, Ayda," she hissed back.

Cortez stepped away for a moment, his thumb tracing a path from his chin to his bottom lip again and again. He didn't seem inclined to stop the line of questioning. In fact, he seemed to be enjoying it.

"It was never about you *wanting* Drew, was it? You just

needed to get to him for Hernandez and his club," I spat out.

Drew's head fell back between his shoulders instantly, hanging limp as he stared up at the ceiling and let his disbelief fall free in a huff of laughter. "Well, fuck me."

"Oh, I did," Maisey snapped, turning her full attention to me. "Over and over and over again I fucked you, Drew. I did what I had to do. I stroked your ego and everything that went with it because I *had* to."

"Of course you had to." He sighed through a disbelieving smile, dropping his chin to his chest. In any other circumstance, he would have almost looked relieved. "You had to be the rat in the short skirt for the Emps, and we just let you walk right on fucking in like the welcoming fuckers we are, right?"

She turned to look at him, pushing her chest out as if to show him what he was now missing. The surge of anger in my body went from wild to off the scale as I watched her taunting him.

"Your ego always let me in, just never quite as much as we needed you to."

Drew raised a brow over his swollen eye and snarled. "There was a reason for that, Maisey."

She moved closer to him. "I don't give a fuck, Drew. You were a means to an end. I did what I had to do. I put up with Rosie's constant crying, all your mens' shit, your insatiable demands and then you went and got yourself locked up inside. I had to find some other dumb fuck to screw info out of."

I couldn't take much more. I pushed up to my knees again, shrugging off the asshole's hand that clamped down on my shoulder. "Who?"

"None of your business, bitch. You ain't nothing but a

trick anyway." She waved me off, her head rolling back to Drew, her body gravitating closer so she could bait us both.

"You're calling *me* a hooker? You're the one fucking people with an agenda. Why go after Sutton? If you were all about this Hernandez guy, why marry the chief?"

Maisey rolled her eyes, but she never looked at me. She kept her hooded eyes on Drew, working them down his chest like a rabid dog in heat. "You're an idiot if you can't figure it out."

I was trying, but my slow, aching brain was also trying to put a round peg in a square hole and was coming up with triangles.

"You were counting on my rivalry with him." Drew snorted with disgust.

"You surprise me sometimes, Drew. You're too pretty to be intelligent," she purred, slapping his cheek and turning to look at me. "Unfortunately, you showed up."

People always say that the cock of a gun is one of the single most distinct sounds around. It was in that moment I finally understood what that meant. It cut through the silence that had settled after Maisey's accusation.

"Well don't I feel like a fool?" Sutton said, his service weapon pointed at Cortez's chest as he stepped out of the shadows from what looked like an old, abandoned office in the corner of the building. It was so dark it was hard to make anything out. There was a mumble of surprise that was followed by four more guns repeating the same sound Sutton's had. It was clear no one had known he was there, and as he stepped to the side to get a better aim at Cortez, I could see the dim light from where the door behind him had been left open. He'd only just arrived.

I looked from the shadows to Drew in the middle. Another flash of fear ran down my spine, because by all accounts, he was in the crossfire of every single one of them.

"It's not—" Maisey started, but Sutton cut her off, shaking his head.

"You used me?" he asked painfully. "It was all a lie?"

"No…"

"We had *children* together."

"Howard, wait."

"You're never gonna see our kids again, Maise." He reached for the radio on his shoulder and pressed the button. "This is Chief Sutton requesting back u—"

He never got to finish the sentence. The deafening roar of a gun going off triggered a domino effect, and all I could do was drop to the floor, keep my eyes on Drew and pray for a miracle.

CHAPTER FORTY-TWO
DREW

The second I saw Sutton, I knew what would happen. The sound of the first shot going off sent my eyes darting straight to Ayda's, and when she looked back at me through the roar of the noise around us, I was unblinking.

If I was going to die, she was the last thing I wanted to see.

It didn't last long, and by the time the guns had been put down, it was Maisey's screams that were making more noise than anything else. She was hunched over in front of me, her hands clasped to her ears as she cried out at the horror of what she had planted herself slap bang in the middle of.

Cortez reacted immediately, gripping the back of her top and yanking her to his side to tell her to shut the fuck up.

Then it fell quiet again, and all that could be heard was the low, painful groan coming from the other side of the room from Chief Sutton. He'd been shot, but he wasn't dead. Not yet, anyway. Something told me that it wouldn't be long before he was silenced for good.

"Howard," Maisey whimpered quietly, her hands moving to her mouth.

I was still focused on Ayda, staring into those baby blues

as she tried not to show the horror she was so obviously feeling.

"I didn't mean for you—"

"Didn't I just tell you to shut the fuck up?" Cortez shouted in her ear, yanking her around like she was nothing more than a rag doll.

"Put her down," Sutton groaned as he rolled around. My eyes darted up in his direction as his movements caught my attention. His hand was gripping his arm, but I couldn't see blood pouring from anywhere else as he tried to scramble across the floor for his radio.

Before he could get there, an Emp kicked it way out of reach and Cortez suddenly flipped gears beside me.

"Put her down?" he shouted, pushing Maisey to the floor as her sobs turned to screams once again. She shrieked in surprise as she landed beside Ayda in a heap, the force with which he'd thrown her causing her to skid across the rough surface before she finally came to a stop. "Put her down, he says."

Cortez wasted no time giving his signal. With a swift snap of his fingers, he'd pointed to the guy next to him and given his order. There wasn't time for anyone to do or say anything before the gun was pulled out from his cut and aimed directly at Maisey's head.

"The law wants her put down. It shall be so."

The eruption of the bullet felt sharper than the others had, the sound of it hitting her square in the head like a dull thud as it met its target swiftly and sent blood spraying out all around her.

The moment the sound stopped bouncing from the walls around the empty space, Ayda seemed to realize exactly what had just happened. Her eyes widened in horror as she tried to scramble away using only her feet. She made no other sound than a horrified whimper, even as the asshole behind her twisted her hair around his hand and pulled her back into place and onto her knees so she was facing Maisey's lifeless body.

I could take anything they had to serve to me. I'd been through it all before. I'd seen men die. My body carried more war scars than that of a soldier's. I was a patchwork of horrors. Anything that could ever have happened to a man had happened to me, but as soon as I saw Ayda's face as she was forced to stare at Maisey, I knew that not a single one of those wounds had ever hurt me as much as the look she was wearing right then.

Ayda was there because of me, and in living the dream with her the way I had been doing, I'd brought her to her worst nightmare. She was staring death in the face and neither one of us could do anything to ever take that away from her. From that moment on, she'd be changed forever.

"Someone shut him up," Cortez snapped, pointing over to Sutton who was trying to hold back the sobs of grief for the wife he'd loved, hated, and lost in a mere matter of minutes. I couldn't see what they did to him, but the sound of flesh meeting flesh silenced him enough for the beating to end quickly.

Chester sighed, scratching the back of his neck as he surveyed everything around him.

"If it ain't bitches, it's kids. If it ain't kids, it's cops. This is already getting too sloppy."

Someone beside him started talking, a man I didn't know with a voice so rich and thick that it sounded almost comical in this fucked up situation. "Want me to clean up the mess?"

"Not yet. I came here for revenge and that's exactly what I'm going to get."

I blinked slowly, turning my attention back to him as I tried to focus through the haze of my left eye that was quickly swelling to the point of rendering me blind. As if having the same thoughts as I was having, Cortez stared at me for the longest time before making his final decision.

Turning to face his men, he tossed his knife on the floor and clasped his hands together. "Get him down from there. It's time for the real shit to start before any more uninvited guests from unexpected love triangles show up."

There should have been some feeling of relief flooding through me at the mention of getting me down, but I knew that in this world it only meant something even worse was about to happen. I took a moment to close my eyes and gather some strength, regulate my breathing and try to do a full body analysis of what muscles were still of use to me and which were shot to absolute shit.

Ayda barely made a noise as they moved her around, only a small whimper escaping her followed by a sniff as she tried to keep her emotions in check. With my eyes closed, it was like I could sense her more. I could feel what she was feeling. I was aware of something that I hadn't felt before that night—our unexplainable connection.

When the chains around me were loosened, the fire started to roll through my arms. As my muscles slowly fell and the chains allowed me to drop down, someone came to grab me around my thighs to catch me. It was only when I opened my eyes slowly that I realized they weren't there to catch me at all. They were there to restrain me before I could regain any power in my arms to use against them.

They didn't have to worry about that. My body was fucked. My chest ached, having been stretched out. The burn in my biceps was raw, like a million tiny needles were being forced in and out of my skin repeatedly as the blood tried desperately to feed its way through all the veins that it had been starving for so long. My vision blurred for a few seconds before I was dumped to my feet, my legs immediately giving way and forcing me straight down to the concrete.

With the ends of the chains still wrapped around my wrists, I brought them crashing down around me, each steel link clapping together in a thunderous roar.

I couldn't help the groan that forced its way out of my throat as I rolled over, but it wasn't long before my hands were pulled together in front of me by some fucking beast of a man. His palms were so big, I was starting to believe I was hallucinating and King fucking Kong was the one manhandling me.

"Fuck," I whispered.

Then I was dragged over into the middle of the warehouse like some kind of animal, and all I could do was wait and wait and wait until my body started waking up again. For now, I was useless. Lifeless. Like a limp dick in a brothel. I couldn't do shit.

When I was eventually dumped on my ass and forced to sit up, I saw her.

They were treating her the same way they were treating me. A push here, a shove there, a sly kick to get into place until we were both made to sit directly in front of one another, my legs around her waist and hers around mine. It was like some sick, twisted, perverted show, two bodies being made to press up against one another, chest to chest, blood to blood, when, even though I couldn't think of anything better than holding her, I didn't want her close to me like this. I didn't want my blood on her skin.

Forcing myself to look up into her eyes, her fear and pain stared straight back and I swallowed instantly.

"Foreheads together," Cortez ordered quietly.

Ayda's mouth moved, but no sound came out. I didn't need to hear it to know she was saying my name.

Flaring my nostrils, I pulled in a breath and tightened my legs around her. I couldn't show her any other way, not with all those men around, but I wanted her to feel me, to understand that I was there and that if I could find a miracle in any of this shit, I would.

"I'm sorry," I said in a rush of breath.

Her newly liberated hands fell to my legs. One of her fingers was sitting wrong, but her eyes weren't on her hands, they were on my face. I could feel the shake of her head as she catalogued the injuries she could see. When she finally did open her mouth to speak, her voice was a hoarse whisper of the one I recognized. "I love you, Drew."

Whoever was behind me started to unwind the chains from around my wrist, and something else that should have felt like a blessing left me feeling like I was having knives pulled out of my tender skin. I winced in front of her, unable to stop myself from gritting my teeth before I pulled my arms free so they were in between us and let my hands carefully fall to her waist.

Just touching her felt like some kind of medicine.

"I love you," I whispered back. My lips could barely move and my eyes were now scanning her face as much as they could, taking in every tear track, every fleck of dirt, every freckle that I'd ever had the pleasure of waking up next to. "And I'm sorry. I promise you, you're going to make it out of this."

Cortez faked a cough beside us, his knees cracking loudly as he bent down to our level. "Do you two want a minute alone?" he said through a pout. "Maybe say your vows, a prayer, recite a poem to her from your new, mushy, warm heart, Tucker?"

I tried to pull her closer and run calming circles over her waist with my thumbs. It hurt to do anything, to use any muscle I had, but I didn't care as long as I had her in my grip.

"I love you," I repeated, ignoring Cortez. "No matter what happens, remember that. You were the one who made a man out of me."

There was a flash of determination behind her eyes that seemed to disappear just as quickly, the resolution immediate. "I tried to run, just like you told me, but it was useless. I love you, too, and nothing will ever change that."

I couldn't help the small, sad smile that tugged at one side of my mouth. Digging my fingers into her tighter and pressing my forehead harder to hers, I sighed softly. "You're a fighter. My fighter. Don't give up, not even if…"

There was no need for me to say the rest.

"Okay, time's up," Cortez said, and you could practically fucking hear the roll of his eyes. "Gentlemen, bring in the guns."

The frown on my face was immediate. When one of his goons dropped a box full of weapons at the side of either of us, I felt like someone had just handed me the winning lottery ticket. I could reach one of those fuckers quickly and it would be all over.

Only that trail of thought went nowhere as the two of us became surrounded by more men again. As I looked back up into Ayda's eyes and felt our faces suddenly being forced even closer together than they already were, that small glimmer of hope quickly drifted away.

We each had two guns pressed against the back of our heads.

One wrong move, one attempt to do anything that wasn't an instruction and we'd both be wearing each other's blood.

All I could do was close my eyes and wait.

I finally understood it all.

"I like to call this game, *he loves me, he loves me not.*"

"You sick fuck," I growled.

"Thank you," he said through an obvious fucking grin. "As I was saying, here we have twelve guns. Six loaded, six not. You each have three turns to pick up a weapon of your choice, point it at your Romeo *or* Juliet's head and pull… the… trigger."

Ayda's tremble ran through every connection of our bodies. Her breathing picked up as her eyes darted to the side to look at the box next to her. I thought she was going to protest, but then I saw her head rolling to where Maisey was lying dead, and she forced her eyes closed instead, an almost inaudible *oh God* coming from somewhere deep inside of her.

"That gives you a fifty-fifty chance of survival, my little lovebirds, which, considering how much I'd really like to see you both at the bottom of the ocean, I think is incredibly fair. And all *is* fair in love and war, no? Here we have both love and war. I wonder which one proves to be more powerful?"

My jaw rolled back and forth in some kind of rhythm that made no sense to me, but had the adrenaline slowly rising through my broken body again.

"I guess what the two of you need to ask yourselves today is this…" He paused, leaning closer towards us until his stale breath washed over the sides of our faces and clung to all the open wounds on our skin. "Who will be on your side tonight? Will it be God? Or will it be the reaper you so proudly wear on your chests every day?"

I shook my head slowly against Ayda's as the trembling of her body started to take on a more violent form.

"Breathe," I whispered softly. "It's going to be okay. You can do this. We can do this," I lied to her. "We're not dying today."

Ayda's eyes moved between the boxes and me again. She balled and released her good hand several times before letting it rest on my leg, squeezing with more strength than I expected from her. She seemed to have accepted that, even if we made it out of this particular torture, there was a chance this wouldn't be the end of it.

Dragging in a deep breath, she released it and nodded, her lips forming words that were never spoken out loud.

"Do what they ask," I said so only she could hear. "I need you to stay alive, Ayda."

"Let's get to it!" Cortez jumped up, kicking the guns closer to us until they crashed into our legs. "Ladies first."

I'd never been one to tremble at the reality of death, but before Ayda came along, I'd never really had such a significant reason to live. Nodding slowly against her head, I inhaled her as much as I could and held onto her waist tightly. My body seemed to protest and I swear to all that was fucking holy, all the wounds that were already slashed across my body opened up even more just to protest and make themselves heard. They cried for me to stop this. They begged for me to save her. My biceps suddenly felt wet and warm again. A small trickle of blood fell down past my eye and over my cheek, but I was ready. I was ready to die for her if that's what I had to do.

Letting off a shaky breath, Ayda's hand reached for the box. The moment her fingers glided over the cool steel, her eyes slid closed and another tear made a track through the dirt on her face. The gun rattled slightly in her grip as a sob broke and her eyes opened again.

"I can't do this, Drew," she whispered, her gaze flickering to the gun in her hand. "I'd rather turn it on myself."

Staring into her eyes with determination, I reached out to her arm, guiding the gun up to my head and positioning it where it needed to be. My chest was heaving, every breath I took not doing enough, not giving me what I needed.

"If you don't, they'll shoot me anyway. This could be empty," I whispered, curling my fingers around her wrist to try and soothe her in any way I could. "It *will* be empty. We were meant to be together, Ayda. We were meant to cross paths. Not even God is cruel enough to take me away from you now. It will be empty. It *will* be *empty.* And if it's not, you win."

I attempted to smile, but all that came out was a paralyzed smirk that held no other emotion behind it but grief.

"I love you. Pull the trigger, darlin'."

CHAPTER FORTY-THREE
AYDA

Even with Drew's hand wrapped around mine, holding the gun to his head, I wasn't sure I could do it. There was conviction and confidence behind his eyes as his hand squeezed mine, but all I could do was cry. The unbroken sobs that were thick in my throat and chest made every bone in my body ache, but my heart...

My heart was in my eyes, begging Drew not to ask me to do this.

I couldn't live with myself if he died at my hand. I couldn't live knowing that his blood was spilled because of something I'd done, even if I'd been forced into it. The truth was, I couldn't survive this without him. I needed him more than I could ever have admitted, even to myself.

As I met his eyes, I realized that the moniker Cortez had given the two of us, was absolutely fitting.

Romeo and Juliet.

She'd sacrificed herself when she realized he was gone. The thought of living without him had been too much to bear.

For the first time in my twenty-five years of life, I *finally* understood. I knew in that moment that if mine was the gun that killed Drew, I would go through every single one of them at my own head until I found the next loaded chamber, because death was surely better than living without him.

Swallowing almost compulsively, I pushed my forehead against Drew's with the last ounce of strength I possessed. It was a silent promise that I would be strong for him if I had to be.

Then I squeezed the trigger.

The empty click had my breath leaving me in one swift stream, the sob I'd been clinging to breaking free as I threw the gun away and brought my hand to his cheek.

"I'm sorry. I'm so, so sorry."

Drew's palm covered mine quickly, his cheek leaning into our touch as he closed his eyes and exhaled. "That's my girl. You did good. You always do good." When he looked back up at me, his breathing became more erratic.

The hand still left around my waist tried to pull me closer, but there wasn't anywhere for us to go. We were a tangled mess of arms and legs, dirt and blood, heavy breaths and falling tears.

"I love you," he whispered again.

Cortez's boot hit the side of Drew's body, forcing us both to flinch in surprise. "Get on with it, doggy. Play your part properly. Kiss her dirty tears away before you kill her."

I could feel the tension in Drew's jaw under my hand. Cortez was pressing every button he had and he knew it. I was a mess. My face was sore from being pushed into the dirt and glass on the floor, and my skull ached from being knocked out, dragged around by my hair, and the crushing weight of the fat bastard who had been made my warden. Drew wasn't faring much better. The cut on his head was still bleeding. I could feel the thick liquid pooling against my hand. His eye was swelling and his lips were cut up and split. That should probably have been the single kiss we'd had that would be less than passionate due to the circumstances... and yet, it wasn't.

I was the one who instigated it, knowing he would never want to put me in a position like that, and the moment our lips touched, I had sanctuary. For one blissful moment in time, it was just the two of us again. Not even the pain bothered me. I clung to him with everything I had, the familiarity of his lips giving me the last push of strength I needed.

Pulling away, my eyes met his, and though my voice was shaky, it was filled with just as much conviction as his had been. "Do it."

Cortez leaned closer in to us again, his eyes switching from me to Drew and back again over and over, but Drew refused to look away or let me go.

"You heard her, Tucker. You're up."

Drew's hands tightened around me before he unwound them from my wrist and reached blindly into the box. His fingers drifted through the weapons, shifting them along the base until he found the one he wanted. When he eventually pulled it out, he readjusted it in his grip, catching it into a tighter hold and feeling the weight of it in his hand.

"Cortez?" he said quietly.

"I don't do requests," Cortez answered sharply. "Put the gun to her head and pull the trigger."

"I'll pull the trigger when that dirty rat of yours pulls his dick away from my fucking back."

Just like that, Cortez's attention snapped away from us to look at the two men behind Drew, and the second his focus was on trying to figure out who the rat in their club was, Drew raised his elbow up high and smashed the end of the gun square into Cortez's jaw.

All hell broke loose. Cortez didn't take kindly to being hit, and neither did his minions. I felt the grip on my hair almost instantly and the cold barrel of the very obviously loaded weapon at my temple as Drew was punched and kicked mere feet away.

It probably wasn't my smartest move, but I couldn't sit there and do nothing. The moment one of the men stepped around to get in a better punch, I kicked out my leg, the heel of my shoe digging into the back of his knee forcing him to fall. My hair was almost yanked from my skull in a fistful, but everything came to a screaming halt when I felt the cold, biting edge of Cortez's knife against my throat.

"Enough," he shouted in a growl, while all I could feel was the pressure on my skin.

"Let's just fucking end him. This is going on too long. Let's blow this place like we planned," one of the Emps shouted, the frustrations in his voice clear as his head snapped from side to side and he began to breathe like a bull.

Cortez looked up, raising both his brows high. "In a rush to leave, Bones?"

"Bones," Drew coughed and spluttered out as he tried to ingest air into his broken body. "There you are. Long time no see."

Pressing the blade and twisting it onto its edge even more, Cortez's train of thought practically bounced off the walls as he tried to figure out the same things I was. Was all this a bluff or not? Did the Emps really have a rat in their midst?

"Get Tucker back over here," Cortez demanded quietly. "Remove his shirt. Let us see the patch on his skin."

The scraps of Drew's shirt were ripped almost violently from him as three men dragged him back to the position he'd been in before he fucked up Cortez's nose. He was in worse shape. There were more blossoming bruises, more cuts on his face, one particularly nasty one that was oozing blood just under his eye socket.

"Before we go on, why don't we remind Tucker exactly what's at stake when he pisses me off." Cortez removed the knife from my throat, but I wasn't comforted by its new placement. He'd pushed it below my sweater, the blade pointing out. He seemed more fascinated by Drew's reaction than mine, and with one snap of his wrist had cut through the top of my sweater.

His rank breath washed over me as he got closer, the nauseating odor making my own breath stick as he grabbed the two sides of the sweater and ripped them apart.

"Much better," he purred, dragging the scraps of material down my arms and leaving me in my bra. My eyes met Drew's and for just a second, I regretted the decision to wear a push up. It had been for his eyes only, and now all I felt was dirty and tainted.

I'd thought I'd seen all his faces before then, but not even murderous could describe the look in Drew's eyes as he looked up at Cortez and violently pushed three words out through his teeth.

"Get. Off. Her."

Sliding the flat surface of the knife over the exposed parts of my breasts, Cortez leaned over my shoulder and began to moan in appreciation.

"I can see why you chose her. I wonder..." He kept his hand moving in a slow pattern, and I knew he felt me flinch whenever the heel of his palm made contact with my naked skin. "Did you worship these enough the last time you touched them? Did you always caress them like it was the first and last time? Or do you need another memory to take with you when you die?"

The touch of his hand made me shudder in disgust, but my concern was more for Drew than for myself. Whatever this man was doing to me, it didn't matter. I could burn my flesh later if we got out of this alive. The only problem was, if Drew followed through with whatever was rolling around in his mind, we wouldn't survive at all. A living hell was rising behind his eyes as he watched Cortez's hands. It wasn't jealousy. It was protection.

"Drew." It was one word, but I hoped he could hear everything I couldn't say planted in the syllables.

He'd turned from man to beast as he watched his enemy like he was his prey, but the moment his name passed my lips, I saw that flicker of reality come back to him. His eyes were frantic as he looked between the two of us and the knife.

Then something changed.

"I want another memory," he said quietly.

"Did you forget something?"

Drew swallowed. "Please."

Cortez grinned beside me, that golden tooth of his shining like a target that needed to be knocked out. "And so it is love."

He pushed me forward violently, and whoever was behind Drew did the same to him until the two of us were sitting pressed against one another again, only this time we were skin on skin. The second Drew could pull me closer, he did, our legs scissoring again as he guided me into his arms and held me by the waist.

We were damp with sweat, tears and everything else we'd been thrown around in all mixed together, but when he pressed his cheek to mine and buried his nose in my hair to breathe me in, I let myself do the same with him.

"Do you trust me?" he whispered so only I could hear.

"Always," I breathed back, my head pressing against his and my eyes closing.

"Do as he says, and when the chance arrives, please… run . Run as fast as you can. You'll know when it's here. Don't ask questions, Ayda. Don't wait for me. Don't look ba—"

"Get to it, Tucker." Cortez's voice oozed with the perversity of the moment as he pressed the flat of the knife against my neck.

Dragging his forehead back to mine, Drew's hands found the bare skin on my shoulders, and I didn't have to look at him to know that his eyes were now closed, too.

The pads of his fingers were warm against my rapidly cooling skin, and even though the situation didn't call for it, my skin flared into goose pimples, following the line as he traced the faint veins in my shoulder and down my bra strap. My breath stuttered as I dragged it in, and despite every eye in the place burning into the two of us, all I saw was Drew.

Leaning forward, he ran his nose down mine, his warm breath bathing me until his lips met mine. It was so hard to stay focused with him so close, when he was touching me that way, but his whispered words and the eyes of every asshole in the building kept me focused. The gentle tug on the lace made me shiver in horror at the thought of anyone seeing more of me than they already had, but he rolled the material down, exposing more of my skin and brushing his thumbs where he wanted them to go.

It was like the air had been taken from the building. It was a collective inhale from the simple shift of the material, and

Drew seemed to feel it the same way I did.

He was focused—focused on me, and with every touch he made, I started to believe that he was losing himself the way he did when it was just the two of us in the privacy of our bedroom. He hitched in a breath, sliding one hand up to my neck while the other stayed over my breast, and when he began to kiss along my jaw and I could practically hear the hammering of his heart, I felt his tension.

All eyes were on Drew's touch, sickeningly encapsulated by their perverted natures and the curiosity of how far he was willing to go with his last wish. They were too engrossed, wondering if Drew would use his last moments alive to fuck me in front of them all. Their minds had gone to such a depraved place, they didn't even seem to register how close Drew's hand was to the blade of Cortez's knife.

Neither did I. Whether it was love, hope or the simplicity of wishful thinking, my body had fallen under his spell. Every brush of his lips and fingers had me sinking deeper into the security net he had fabricated for me.

It was then that it happened.

"Run," he whispered, his lips still against my skin.

My mouth parted to ask how, but before I even had time to form the thought, Drew's arm had tensed and snapped for Cortez's blade, the sudden movement of his attack catching the Emp off guard as he ripped it from his grip, twisting it around in a half circle to slash it through the air and stab it directly in the waist of the man behind him.

The warehouse filled with primal growls and gasps of disbelief as Drew pulled the knife out of his victim's flesh, spun it in his grip, only to launch it through the air straight in Cortez's direction.

I didn't look behind me. The only reason I knew it had hit was the loud groan of pain that was distinctly Chester Cortez. I barely had time to shift my shaking limbs when Drew had a gun shoved into my hand and was grabbing one in each of his, swinging them around on the men closest to him. One fired, one didn't, and as much as I wanted to stick around and make sure he was safe, there was a louder part of me—one I'm pretty sure he'd conditioned—that knew if I stopped now, I would get us both killed. We had the element of surprise but that wasn't going to last forever.

I couldn't fuck up his plans now. I had to run.

I dodged every hand that seemed to reach for me as I moved, my head finding solace from my predicament by throwing football plays in my mind, keeping me occupied away from the horrific reality I was slap bang in the middle of.

My eyes darted around the place, looking for the best means of escape. I couldn't double back on myself, which meant the only way I had to go was forward, toward the only door I could see in the darkness.

I burst through it like hell was on my heels, and barely stopped to glance around. All I knew was that it wasn't the exit I'd been praying for. Instead, it was an even darker room than the one I'd been in before. There were no lights, not even a bared, dull bulb that had been the only illumination in the torture room. It was just dirty, grimy windows that barely allowed a diffused glow through them.

I didn't stop running. I couldn't, and as I passed all the old machinery, I heard boots slapping the concrete behind me.

I was being followed, which was only confirmed all the more when I heard the metallic slam of the door being thrown closed and locked behind us. I darted between the machines as fast as I could and looped around on myself in the maze, effectively losing him and forcing myself into a crouch behind a corner. In order to stay alive, I had to be silent, and I had to keep moving.

I just hoped it was enough.

CHAPTER FORTY-FOUR
DREW

I didn't breathe until I saw her run away. My face was tense, each cheek blown out as I held all the air in my body and kept my focus on the men in front of me. Cortez was stumbling around to my side, one man dead on my left next to Maisey Sutton. The gun with the blank had done shit except stun the Emp it was aimed at as he froze and closed his eyes, waiting for his own impending death.

Every fucking part of my body creaked under the weight of the pressure I put on it as I rolled back onto my front and reached into the box. Pulling another two guns out, I spun them around as fast as my beat up bones would allow me, falling back on my ass again as another Emp came towards me. His gun was most definitely loaded and when he moved to stand over me, his arms locked in a hold with the barrel aimed directly at my forehead.

The look in his eyes said it all. He had no time for the fun and games of Cortez. This fucker wanted me dead hours ago. He wanted revenge for his fallen brothers.

As he moved to stand over me, there was no small smile of satisfaction, no smartass words to tell me that today was a good day to die, no arrogance or confidence oozing out of him.

Just absolute pure fucking hatred for the Hound at his

feet.

He sniffed quietly, landing his foot on one of my arms to crush it down, forcing the guns away from his direction before he shook his head and sucked in a giant breath.

That's when I lost sight of him. All I saw was the small black tunnel in front of me that would eventually deliver my own death.

Then the gun went off and the blood splashed all across my face like a warm fucking shower of red.

But I was still breathing. I was still breathing, and as I opened my eyes to see what had happened, the man above me began to fall forward, gravity making him sway one way, then another before it took over and he came crashing down beside me with a bullet hole straight through his head.

I grunted loudly as the weight of him pressed against all my existing injuries and the ear piercing scream of the girl, Sofia, sang out around the warehouse. I didn't have time to wait around. I didn't know how many Emps were even in there, but Cortez was wounded and two were now dead. As I pushed the guy away and rolled him to the side, I slid back, pushing my feet against the concrete to find some movement.

Picking up the guns and swiveling on the floor, I spun to a shaky stand and pointed both guns straight ahead of me at eye level.

Sutton was standing there limply, his shoulder hanging to one side and half of his face covered in more blood than I bet he'd seen in his life. He was a fucked up painting of black and red, but he'd just saved my motherfucking life by putting a bullet through an Emp's head.

Every breath I took in was heavy as I stared at him in disbelief, but then the real shit hit the fan and I was lost again.

Charging at his waist, a heavy-set guy in leather threw Sutton down like he weighed nothing. The sound of his head cracking against the concrete was almost as loud as the gun going off, sending a bullet whizzing straight past my ear. I ducked out of the way, acting on instinct rather than knowledge, and it was impossible to ignore the heavy wave of noise and the banging inside my head as the injuries I'd sustained throbbed at the sudden movement.

My vision was blurred in one eye, making it seem like there were two of everyone no matter which way I turned, so I did all I could do with all that I had. Aiming the two guns left and right, I fired, my shoulders flinching hard as two bullets went flying out of either end. Cortez cried out again from one side of me, but the other side, the side where my head was the most fucked up... that was quiet.

Too quiet.

I was deaf there.

Just like Sutton, I was attacked from a lower angle, the arms of a thick bruiser wrapping himself around me and knocking my weapons out of my hands. That's when it became the street fight it was always meant to be.

As I crashed hard on my ass, the wind poured out of my lungs and the fire began to spread through every muscle in my body. Roaring out at the head that was currently pressed against my chest, I swung and drove a fist into his kidneys as hard as I could, not stopping as I kicked up and tried to force him off me.

His own swing landed just short of my jaw, skimming the end of my chin and only managing to catch my shoulder. It gave me the leverage I needed as his body stumbled forward, having not connected where it was supposed to. As soon as he was over me, I gritted my teeth together, grabbed the back of his head and smashed his face down onto all the rubble and glass.

It hurt. It really fucking hurt. I was too broken for it not to, but his wince of pain was addictive, and as soon as I'd heard it the first time, I needed to hear it again. Pulling his hair back and turning on my side to move from beneath him, I groaned and kept on smashing his face down as hard as I could. With each slam, I gained more power, more adrenaline, and more fucking desire to kill. The pain in my own body began to fade, being replaced by the need to survive and to rip the limbs off anyone who tried to change the ending to my story.

It happened so fast but so hard, it wasn't long before his body went limp in my grip and I pushed him away from me.

I'd barely managed to turn my back on my enemies long enough to scramble to a stand when another threw himself onto my back, wrapping his arms around my neck so tight the pressure in my head became unbearable. Luckily for me, that one was young and scared. I could feel it. Even broken and out of fuel, I was still strong enough to snap his body in two if I had to, so that's what I did. Reaching up desperately, I tugged on his grip in a jerky movement, throwing him over my shoulder before stamping on his chest and pulling his arms in a direction they were never designed to go. The cry of pain was almost as loud as the sound of the bones breaking, but I didn't wait to give him any sympathy.

I was gone—in another headspace. There was that dangerous black around me again.

The bulb hung limply over where I'd been chained up, allowing just enough light to show the shadows in the darkness. It wasn't that easy for me, though. My eyes were tripling in size with every minute that passed by, and my body kept falling to the side no matter how much I tried to keep control.

I couldn't see Sutton. I couldn't hear Ayda. All I could see was Cortez and another man beside him.

I knew then more than ever that not all enemies could be seen.

Cortez was standing there with a knife hanging out of his shoulder, doubled over as he clutched at his ribs. The fact that the gunshot had caused some sort of damage made the small war smile creep up on my face again.

"I guess this wasn't part of the plan, Chester?" I wheezed out.

He didn't say anything at first, instead choosing to look at the man beside him as if he had a plan of escape written on his forehead for him to take advantage of.

"You may not have died the way I wanted you to, Tucker, but you will die today," he growled back in my direction.

"I don't doubt it," I said, taking a step forward as I tried to hide the fact that one of my legs was now dragging more than the other. "I guess I was just expecting a little more from you. The show was impressive for a while. You gave good game. Now…" I stopped, holding my arms out to my sides and gesturing all around us. "Not so much."

Cortez looked back at his brother, nodding his head in my direction for him to finish it. I knew the instruction he was giving without him having to say a word. My toe hit the head of the Emp who Sutton had shot with a dull thud, and I glanced down as discreetly as I could, watching as a pool of dirty blood framed the whole of my boot.

That's when I saw it.

It was like we were in the middle of a western after all, and a small thought of Sutton flashed through my mind, and how much he would have probably enjoyed that moment more than anyone, no matter who walked out of there alive.

"Do it," Cortez ordered quietly. The man next to him stepped forward, pulling his gun out of his cut and aiming it straight at me. I tried to move fast enough, but by the time I'd bent to grab the loaded gun by my foot, it was too late. A bullet was flying through the air in my direction and the pain as it pierced through the skin of my shoulder rendered me silent. I fell quickly, slipping in the mess of the dead and injured that I'd created.

I was all out of chances.

I could feel death getting ready to throw me over his shoulder and take me away.

The air around me became thick, like the walls were closing in on my life. I glanced around for the gun but I couldn't see anything, and all my thoughts went to Ayda. I tried. I fucking tried... and I hoped that by some miracle she'd gotten free, 'cause no matter how indestructible I thought I was, I knew a miracle was exactly what she needed. But we'd already had all our luck. By some grace of that fucked up guy everyone calls God, we'd already been handed too many miracles since we arrived there.

I just wasn't expecting the final one to show up when it did, and when the sound of aggressive gunfire filled the air and the doors burst open like a stampede of wild animals had entered, I held my breath and waited.

The moment I heard Jedd's commanding voice shout for Cortez's man to drop his gun, I knew it was time to start praying more often.

"I won't repeat it. Drop the fucking gu—"

Bang.

His body fell hard and with no grace at all.

"Oops," Slater growled. "Finger slipped."

"Don't you hate it when that happens?" Jedd muttered through gritted teeth.

"Nope."

"Me either. Good work."

I rolled to my side, unable to believe they were actually there. The sound of their boots charging closer to me almost made me sick with relief, but I was convinced that I was hallucinating. My head fell sloppily from side to side as I tried to widen my eyes and focus on them to see if they were real.

"Cortez, you dirty, rotten bastard," Slater roared, charging towards him. "You're dead."

"No," I croaked out weakly, raising a hand in the air. "No."

"Fuck," Jedd said, obviously registering the state of me for the first time as I lay there rolling around in shit. "Jesus Christ, Slater, we need to get him out of here."

Slater was too busy smashing his gun around Cortez's head, knocking him sideways before catching the back of his cut in his grip and forcing the fat bastard to stay standing.

Jedd was by my side in a flash, crouching over me but keeping his gun aimed high in case anyone else jumped out from the dark.

"Let me kill him." I blinked slowly, my voice hoarse and weak. "Find Ayda. She ran somewhere. I told her to get out of here, so you better find her alive or so help me God…"

Jedd nodded, not questioning me for a single moment

before he jumped back and grabbed whoever was beside him. I couldn't bring myself to look as I pushed myself up and growled out at the absolute agony I felt everywhere. I was unfixable, but I wasn't through yet.

I had two more things to do before I gave up and let my body fall to the floor in a crumpled heap.

I had to kill Chester Cortez without any mercy what-so-fucking-ever.

Then I had to pray again for Ayda. I had to find my girl; otherwise I'd be picking up the nearest gun and ending my own life in a heartbeat.

CHAPTER FORTY-FIVE
AYDA

"Dogs like the chase, but you should know the Emps crave the kill. I can smell your fear, bitch."

I pushed my hand over my mouth to hide the whimper of terror. The guy was huge. Even if I hadn't known it from being under his boot, I could hear it in every measured step he took as he chased me through the room.

We'd been playing cat and mouse for what felt like hours. Every time he got close to where I was hiding, I moved as quickly and quietly as I could into the heart of the warehouse and hid anywhere I could find. It was like one of those horror movies Tate was always watching. The taunting going on only served to create more fear the longer it was drawn out. There was only so long I could run until I started to believe I was the proverbial mouse. What was worse, there was no exit other than the door I'd come through; the one fire exit was locked shut.

All I had was what I was doing, running and hiding for my life as I prayed and wished with everything I had that Drew was holding his own in the other room. I had no chance against this monster if he caught me, and even as I scurried around the place like a rat in a maze, I had no idea how to tell whether the gun I had was loaded or not.

Running. It was all I had, and something I'd taken for granted when Tate had asked me to go with him almost every day for the past year. It reminded me of something Deeks had said once, when I complained about being a slow runner as an excuse not to run with Tate.

"You don't have to be fast, Ayda. Just faster than the ones around you."

I tried to ignore the ache in my chest at the thought of not seeing him, Tate, or any of the guys again. My fate right then was a pair of combat boots zigzagging through the dirt and broken glass of a dilapidated warehouse. My salvation was a gun that may or may not have been loaded in my hand, but I had to at least believe I was faster than him. Smarter.

I listened to him move around the place, stopping and starting as he searched for me. The footfalls grew more distant and closer in little waves of sound. I followed him around the place, dashing off in the opposite direction for as long as I could until I was faced with a wall and forced to turn back around to the side. I was trying to stay lost and it worked for a while… Then there was nothing but silence.

My only source of reference had stopped. The only reason I could imagine to explain why was that he'd figured it out. With no idea where he was, my heart was racing in my chest with a ferocity I hadn't thought it capable of. I was crouched on my bent legs, my head swiveling and my eyes squinting to try and see the exit in the darkness, but the walls were closing in on me, making the blindness so oppressive I was struggling to breathe.

One wrong move and I was hopeless against him.

I sat panting as quietly as I could, the air burning as I

inhaled and exhaled. I had been running around on the balls of my feet to avoid the heels of my pumps hitting the floor and giving away my position. As much as I wanted to rip them off, I knew that the glass would tear my feet to shreds and leave a path of blood that led him right to me. So I dealt with the cramps that were settling in my toes and the arches of my feet in exchange for another breath pulled into my lungs.

The sudden scraping of glass behind me was so close, I instantly panicked. Standing and spinning forced my legs to twist under me, which wasn't a good idea. I felt the instability of bad weight distribution as I swung the gun around and aimed directly at his chest. It all happened so fast, but I wasn't fast enough. I hadn't thought it through whatsoever. One swipe of the asshole's arm and the gun was falling to the floor and sliding under a huge piece of machinery that looked as intimidating as he was.

"Now you're fucked." He growled with humor, his hand grabbing at my throat and forcing me against an exposed mechanism that seemed more fit for torture than creating something of use. If Cortez's breath had been rank, it had nothing on that guy's. All I could smell was stale cigarette smoke, stale beer and tuna. It made my stomach turn more than it already was until the bile rose with urgency.

Unaware, and probably not caring about my predicament, he slammed me against the metal machine violently with the hand around my neck while the other gripped my breast with brute force. It had been hard enough to breathe without the sudden thought of where this could be going flashing in my mind, and for a whole minute, I was certain I'd given up all hope.

It was only when I allowed the darkness in that I heard

my subconscious screaming in protest. Giving up wasn't who I was, and it never had been. Before my parents died and even after, I fought tooth and nail, never once losing sight of that. Not just for me but for Tate and the people around me who I loved. I couldn't give up now. No matter what horrors laid ahead, I had to fight the good fight and survive.

"Fuck. You," I spat out, sounding much braver than I felt. The insult pissed him off, forcing him to release my breast so he could drag my body forward and slam it back against the machine until every ounce of oxygen I had in my lungs was brutally forced out. I couldn't breathe, and my spine felt as though it was in a vise, but at least I could focus on something other than the position of his hands against my skin.

"Oh, I plan on it, little hound whore. So does every other fucker in this place."

I cringed, and he must have seen the disgust on my face. It took only one shove and I was on my hands and knees under him. I wheezed in a breath now that the obstruction around my neck was gone and tried to crawl away as the sound of his buckle loosening sent my head spiraling into another vortex of fear and panic. The word *no* played deafeningly loud over and over in my head as I tried to find my balance to crawl and run, but my fingers found purchase in nothing as they grazed the concrete, forcing the nails to bend back painfully as I dug deep for the fight I knew I had.

No matter what I tried, the push of my knees, the awkward twist of my feet, nothing seemed to work. I was in such a panic that I hadn't realized the asshole was holding me back by the belt loop on my jeans. The moment I did, I slowed, giving him the opportunity to flip me over like I weighed nothing at all, forcing my shoe to slip from my foot and drop to the floor.

I didn't know why it hadn't occurred to me earlier. Maybe it was the threat of what was to come or the absolute blinding need to escape, but I suddenly realized that without a gun, I still had a weapon I could use.

I just had to get to it.

My feet slid over the dust and tiny shards, making my legs scissor under me. I was annoying him with my squirming, but he seemed oblivious to my intent. Whether it was a good thing or not, I managed to move at least a foot in the right direction before his fist found my gut and my body froze in agony. My aching fingers didn't give up the fight even when he straddled my hips and pinned me down while I coughed and flopped under his weight. Stretching out my arm, I tried to get close enough, my body struggling against the renewed grip of his hand against my throat and the winding of his weight over mine. I knew the shoes couldn't be far. I just had to believe my luck wasn't that bad.

I was twisting and writhing in his grip when I finally found one. My fingers slid over the thin heel first, and if I could have, I would have cried out in relief. The bear of a man was already squeezing my neck in an attempt to gain my submission, forcing me to pat around in the dirt so I could get a decent grip. The hand that had found the shoe was, unfortunately, the one that was housing the broken finger. By some divine intervention—or rush of adrenaline—I was able to ignore the pain as I got a good grip on the thing, which was exactly when I struck.

My arm launched and swung up through the air as though it was spring loaded. My finger was screaming in protest, but it only steeled my determination all the more. This was life and death and my fear was being caged by my urgency to survive. When I made contact, the jolt of it sent white hot embers of pain through my finger and down my arm to my chest. I knew I'd hit something, but it was impossible to tell what until the grip on my neck released, oxygen burned a path down my neck, and the grunt of pain had the bastard rolling away from me.

I hadn't won, not by a long shot, but as I rolled to try and escape, I barely managed to put a few feet between us when his hand clamped on my ankle and pulled me back.

It was there, in my twisting, writhing struggle, that I saw the gun that was, with a little work, within my reach.

Kicking out with my free leg, I caught the soft flesh of his gut, which gave me enough leverage to shoot forward and half crawl and squeeze under the mechanics to reach the gun. I felt the rips in my flesh as the sharp corners ate into the bare skin of my shoulders and back. The space was much smaller than I originally thought, but hooking my arm around an anchored support in the center of the machine finally gave me something to work with.

The pounding of the guy's fists came in flurries along my legs, his arms circling my calves as he pulled and attempted to drag me free. I wasn't going easily, though. I could see my freedom less than three inches from the tips of my fingers, and as I kicked and wriggled for my life, I finally touched the butt of it.

I was just about to wrap my fingers around it. I'd loosened my grip on the anchor piece to make it, my body stretching to its limits, when I felt everything suddenly move around me.

His thick hands clamped down with everything he had and gave one last, almighty pull with every ounce of his strength. Unfortunately, I was pliable now that I wasn't holding on, and the sharp edges and corners tore and shredded my skin as he dragged me out. The mess of glass and discarded machine parts on the floor made the skin on my stomach burn almost as intensely as my back. When I was out from under the damn thing, he twisted me to my back yet again, his body moving in to lock down my kicking legs.

There was just one thing he hadn't counted on…

I had the gun in my hand, and in one tiny adjustment, had my finger on the trigger.

He saw it the same time I did and dived forward, his body almost crushing mine. His knee pulled up, the scrape of his boot louder than the grunts of our struggle. I fought as well as I could, but his knee landed on my chest as his hands closed around mine, twisting the gun and my fingers painfully. We fought for control for a while, my adrenaline giving me the extra burst of strength I needed as I pulled the trigger.

My ears rang, my breath caught, and the warmth of blood against my skin was immediate. So was the deafening scream that fell from my lips and wouldn't stop.

CHAPTER FORTY-SIX
DREW

Nothing else mattered the moment I heard her scream.

My brothers had gotten me to my feet, but I'd barely been able to recognize one from the other as I hung over their shoulders, limp and trying to regulate my breathing. Slater was busy wrapping the chains around Cortez's hands when the sound of her agony brought me back to life.

Quickly looking between all my men, I watched as their faces set to stone as firmly as mine did. Before I even realized what I was doing, I was pushing forward, not needing to tell Slater to hold on to Cortez.

"Drew, easy!" Jedd called out.

"I'm right behind you, brother," Moose shouted.

"Fuck," Kenny cried. Kenny. I hadn't even seen him, but just knowing he was there somehow made everything seem a little clearer to me. We were still brothers. We were still on the same team.

I limped as hard as I could long after her screams died down, and all that was left was the echo of her suffering bouncing off every wall.

"Ayda!" I called out, but my voice was broken and weak. There wasn't any real power behind it. Coughing up and clearing my throat to remove the razor blades, I tried again, knowing full well that no matter how much the men around me shouted her name, it would only be mine that would register.

"Over here," Moose yelled.

I turned towards him without thought, even though he was on my left and all that side of my vision was screwed. I had to use the full rotation of my neck to find him properly and when I did, I saw him pushing against a thick, steel door. It didn't budge, so he tried using his shoulder, barging into it once, twice, three times before eventually giving up and stepping back. Moose didn't even wait to ask what he should do. He was a silent type, a man of war. He acted first and thought later. He rarely spoke. Aiming his gun right at the three different joining points, he fired over and over again and I watched as small sparks flew off against the metal.

He charged at it, barging it with his shoulder another four times before it eventually broke and creaked open.

"It's too dark. Can't see nothin'," he groaned, but I didn't give a shit about that. I pushed past him as fast as I could. I only prayed I found her screaming because of her actions rather than her fate.

"Ayda? Ayda, where are you?"

There was nothing for a while, only the sounds of my panicked breaths. The place was full of old machinery. Shit I wouldn't be able to figure out even if this place was lit up like a Christmas tree. Every turn I took, I stumbled into something, until I heard the one sound that had me releasing the breath I hadn't even realized I was holding.

Her whimper was small, but it was enough. It gave me the direction I needed to move in, and when I turned a corner and found her backed up against the wall with her knees pulled against her chest, the rest faded away.

She was alive.

Moving carefully, I came to a stop beside her, unable to ignore the dead body that lay at her feet surrounded by blood and other parts that needed no description. The light in there was dim. It reminded me of the night in the forest with the girl and her dead boyfriend. The moon barely shone through any of the old, grimy windows. All there was were shadows and outlines. I guess nobody wanted to witness the first time an innocent girl killed a guilty man that night.

Bending down, I swallowed the massive lump of pain and regret that had formed in my throat and gently placed a hand on her knee.

"It's me. I'm here."

Ayda pulled her knees tighter to her chest. The only acknowledgement that I was there at all was her hands covering mine, clawing at my skin until she was practically folded around it, a small sob breaking quietly from her.

The first kill was always the hardest.

Seeing her that way had me wanting to close my eyes to wash the image away, but instead, I did what she needed me to do. I turned my palm in her grip, curling my hands even tighter around hers until we were both left squeezing life back into one another, even though it sent a searing pain into my shot shoulder.

The back of my other hand found the edge of her jaw, moving slowly along to show her I was there and I was on her side. I wasn't going to hurt her. I wasn't going to be rough. I wasn't an enemy. I was the other half of her. I was *her* man. The one who should have been here doing the killing on her behalf while she remained ignorant to this world I lived in. When my fingers grazed the edge of her hair, I tucked it behind her ear and waited, holding her head in my palm for as long as she needed me to be still this way.

"Come back to me, darlin'."

Her head lifted from her knees, her blank eyes finding mine as she tried to blink some coherence back into herself. Her mouth opened and closed a few times before she gave up and shook her head.

"I had to," she finally whispered. "I had to. He was going to kill me."

"I know," I whispered back. "You did the right thing. You did what I told you to do. You kept yourself alive for me. We're together now. We're together because of you."

My face creased up as the pain of seeing her this way eclipsed anything that was going on on the surface of my body. I would never forget that moment for as long as I lived. There was no going back for her now.

She didn't so much lean as fall forward, landing on her knees as her arms moved slowly and gently around my shoulders until she buried her face in the crook of my neck and her body began to tremble like a tuning fork.

I didn't think to avoid touching her back, but the moment I reached around to bring her closer, I felt the wet and warmth of blood across the obvious tears in her flesh and my body stiffened. My hand froze, all my fingers lifting themselves away, even though she didn't cry out in pain. Between my little finger and my thumb, a small dance was performed, inspecting the edges of the ripped flesh before realizing it was everywhere.

She was a mess.

Moving my hand to the back of her hair, I pulled her to my lips and kissed her head as gently but as passionately as I could.

"I love you," I said quietly, needing her to feel those words. "I love you and you're safe now. You're with me, but I need to get you out of here."

She didn't say much. She didn't have to. Her rapid, panicked breaths spoke volumes to everyone standing around us.

"Take me home," she whispered in my ear, her voice pleading.

I wished I could. I wished it was that simple, that I could just sweep her off her feet, lift her out of her worst nightmare and take her home. But that wasn't the reality. The truth was that her safety was no longer in question, but in order for us to live together after what had just happened, the heroics and romantics would have to wait until a debt had been paid. There was no way I was going back to a world where neither one of us slept at night.

It all ended then.

Calling Moose over, I held her against me before asking him to do what my beat up body couldn't. I somehow managed to get her to stand, ignoring the way my skin tore even further every time she pressed against it or I had to stretch to hold her in my arms. When Moose eventually swept her up like a newborn child and cradled her to him, I swallowed and limped on pathetically behind them.

For as long as I lived, I knew I wouldn't get the image of her and that night out of my mind. There was only one thing that was going to make the bitterness slightly less offensive.

Moose guided her like the giant he was, holding her in

his grip while I somehow weaved my fingers through her hair as we walked. When we fell back into the main part of the warehouse with the dirty, diluted light, I saw the whole of my pack standing around our enemy. Every single one of them was there, their faces pointed in our direction with their chins held high, their hands down by their sides as they waited for their next instruction.

Pulling her closer to his chest, Moose kept Ayda's face buried away from the world, but the flash of light that wandered over her ripped back had the eyes of all my brothers narrowing. The low growl that each one gave out turned into a war cry from a pack of animals that were baring their teeth to their attackers, ready to strike.

Cortez was fucked.

Deeks was the only man to rush over, the lapels of his cut flapping back as he charged forward and ran his hands over her bare arms.

"Sweet Jesus," he muttered.

Lifting my hand to his shoulder, I tried to ignore the layer of moisture that had covered my eyes. To see her that way was one thing. For all my men to see her this way was another. We were a family and the truth was, whether she'd been there for ten years or ten minutes, Ayda had become the heart of it.

"Take care of her for me while I do this, Deeks. You're the only one she will let touch her after what she's just been through."

Deeks turned to me, his palms still resting on her as he spoke. "Kill him quick. Don't waste time. That stuff is more precious now than ever before."

"I don't have the restraint to take it slow," I said as my jaw tensed.

"But make him pay. Make it fucking hurt."

The fact that it wasn't like Deeks to speak that way didn't go unnoticed. He was feeling what I was, only he didn't have the black blood running through him the way I did. He had more compassion. I had more hatred.

"It's done." I gave him a nod before lifting both my hands to Ayda's head and stroking her hair. When my lips met the side of her face, I pressed against her much harder than I intended, closing my eyes as I poured out every ounce of life I had left in me and aimed it all into making her better.

God, I loved her. I loved her so fucking much.

There was no sign of life coming from her, just a small roll of her head as though she was acknowledging I was there before she lost herself in Moose again.

I had to look away. The pain she was in was making the anger rise, which was perfect for what I was about to do, but I also needed to wait until just a few more things had been cleared up.

Turning to my men, I glanced up through my better eye and pressed my hands together in front of me. I was a body of blood. Their faces failed to hide their horror, which coming from a group of men that had done what they'd done in their lives, pretty much said it all. I took a moment to glance down at my feet before I managed to collect my thoughts, swallow my emotion, and roll my jaw. When I pushed my shoulders back and tried to focus through the haze, I made sure every word I spoke counted.

"Get Sutton out of here and treat him well. I'd have been dead before you got here if he hadn't done what he did. He saved my life. Take him back to The Hut. Someone else make sure his kids are safe. All of them. If they're scared or hurt, take them back to The Hut, too." I stopped to swallow, ignoring the way each word sliced my throat. "Deeks and Moose will take Ayda home. The rest of you, I need you here. As you can see, I'm pretty fucked up, but I'm still here, hanging on by a thread. I need your strength. I need your vision. I need your help. I need my brothers at my back."

My head rolled in the direction of Cortez and the disgust on my face was immediate. I wasn't going to take a single step closer until Ayda was out of there. She'd seen enough death and destruction for one night.

Cortez looked up at me through narrowed eyes, curling his lip as he tried not to show his own agony at having his limbs twisted around behind him with a knife wound in his shoulder and a bullet in his gut.

I intended on showing him that what he was feeling then was barely an itch on the agony scale.

"Chain him up high. Feet off the ground. No mercy."

Then my men all howled around me. Our war cry had gone out.

CHAPTER FORTY-SEVEN
Ayda

The pain was everywhere. It seemed to attack in waves the farther I got from Drew. My only source of comfort seemed to come from the quiet mumblings of Deeks as Moose cradled me against him as carefully as he could. There were no arms I wanted more than Drew's, but these guys were my family and there was a comfort in that I hadn't expected.

I was aware of a couple more guys around us, and that Sutton was being dragged between two of them as they headed toward the van. Other than Moose and Deeks, I was completely oblivious as to whom. I was so tired, I actually blinked the small twinge of guilt away and forced myself to focus on pain management while not thinking about the fact that I was in a bra and heavily shredded jeans. Modesty seemed a pointless and painful exercise that I shouldn't waste time on.

I heard the slide of the van's door open, the squeak of suspension and the thunder of boots loud, even against the faint chirp of the insects that inhabited the surrounding fields. I didn't bother looking at anything but the stars above our heads, the million points of light suddenly a thousand times more profound than they'd ever been before.

I was alive.

I wasn't sure how, but I was, and so was Drew.

Rolling my head and pushing my temple into the leather covering Moose's chest, I tried to find my breath. Yet again, the sobs were rising in my chest, but they weren't out of fear or pain; they were in gratitude.

"It's alright, Ayda," Deeks whispered, his cheek pressing against the top of my head. "We got you, kiddo. We got you."

There was a flurry of activity around us, a slump of someone being dropped in the back of the van, the grinding of dirt and rocks in the asphalt under us, whispered voices and then Moose moving carefully.

"Hey, chica, I'm putting you in the van with Deeks. I gotta drive."

I nodded in agreement and sucked in a hiss through my teeth as Moose set me gently in the van next to Deeks, who sat on the floor with a blanket and open arms. The material was harsh against my skin as he folded it around me, but I settled in against him quickly, my cheek against his shoulder as my trembles progressed into full body shakes.

"Get us the hell out of here, man."

"I'm on it, Deeks."

The door had barely started sliding against the rails when I heard the first scream coming from the warehouse. I'd never heard a man make a sound like that in my life. It was the manifestation of pain in a corporeal form, twisting into the night and stealing my breath from my lungs.

Blood for blood was the last thought I had as Deeks hissed out another command to get us out of there and then the darkness invaded everything.

"Easy, Sutton, you're not in any danger here, man."

I was pretty sure the voice was Deeks', but I couldn't be certain. The response and the rocking of the van sent wave after wave of pain and nausea through me. Arms tightened around my shivering body and held me closer. A gentle stroke of my arm was lulling me into a state of sleep yet again, even as another voice mumbled from somewhere close by. I couldn't hold onto it long enough to give it my full attention. Sleep called and promised a reprieve from the pain, although I wasn't entirely convinced it wasn't all just a dream.

I woke up on my stomach in a dark room. Someone was sitting close, their fingers moving gently through my hair. My hand felt heavy and cumbersome, my skull felt as though it was in a vise, and the skin on my back as though I had been flayed alive. I could feel other cuts and bruises littering the surface of my skin, but those seemed to be the big ones. I closed my eyes again, a slave to the gentle rhythmic stroke of the fingers through my hair.

I must have been dozing in and out, because with every intermittent stream of consciousness, I was more than aware of the sudden change in situation.

I heard Tate arguing with someone.

I heard a bike starting, followed by the growl of acceleration as the gate rattled open.

I heard shouting from somewhere.

I heard Deeks whispering above me and a gentle dip in

the bed as Autumn let out a little gasp of shock.

There was nothing connecting each event, just breaths, darkness and overwhelming pain that felt as though it was drowning me. Those thoughts weren't all selfish. After every miserable thought for myself, my mind immediately moved to Drew. I didn't know where he was or what he was doing. I wasn't even sure whether he'd made it back or not. Whenever I tried to move, the hands around me pushed me down with soothing coos and reassuring hums of encouragement, while all I could manage was *his* name.

I knew the moment lucidity had its hooks in me. Whatever they'd given me to ease the pain had well and truly worn off and left me with nothing but a waking nightmare and an inner turmoil that made my stomach roll brutally.

"Easy, Ayda, you're okay," Autumn whispered, her warm hand folding around mine while the other brushed my hair from my forehead. Her reaction alerted me to the fact that I'd made a noise I hadn't meant to.

"Is he okay…? Drew?" His name came out hoarse and gravely. It was all I could manage. The comfort of her voice and touch weren't fitting with what my conscience was telling me. I knew what I'd done. I understood what my hands were capable of, and all I needed to breathe was the one person in my life that understood what had happened in that warehouse.

"He's home. The doc is with him. So are Harry and Deeks. He's a fighter, darlin'. Right now, I need you to relax, sweet girl. I'm going to change the bandages on your back. You need to take a deep breath for me. It's not going to feel good."

I nodded into the pillow, my one good hand sweeping up over the cool sheets and pushing it against my face as she worked at peeling the tape from my back. The dull, throbbing ache quickly gave way to the stinging pain as the cool air met with the wounds, pulling a hiss from my lungs that was eaten by the pillow I was holding against me. I could feel the tears stinging my eyes as I sucked in as much oxygen as I could through the side of my mouth. It was possible that crying was a perfectly natural response to the pain and the unrelenting imagery that fluttered behind my closed eyes. Anyone else and I would have been holding them and comforting them, but I wasn't capable of being objective. In my mind, I had no right to cry. I deserved the pain. I'd taken a life. I'd taken their ability to heal while I wept into a pillow.

"Ayda," Autumn said quietly, her fingers as gentle as air on my back. She worked diligently, the scent of herbs and ointments filling the room and permeating the pillow I was using as a barrier to hide me from the world. "I know what you're thinking. I know how you must be feeling, but you did everything you could to survive. Nothing will take what you're feeling away, but I need you to understand that it was self-defense. It was kill or be brutally abused and killed yourself. Don't beat yourself up over this, sweetheart. You're still who you've always been, even if it doesn't feel like it right now."

I'd always known Autumn was intuitive, and even if I hadn't picked it out myself, Deeks would have pointed it out to me, but this—the fact that she knew the exact thoughts running through my mind—spoke volumes. It was just unfortunate that I couldn't allow myself to process them. My mind seemed more inclined to think of other ways out of the situation I'd been in. The need to put the blame on myself was like the necessity to breathe. I relived every soul-crushing second through to the end, backing up and changing choices I'd made in the process, but no matter how many times I hit a wall and backed up to find another, the result was always the same.

He was going to kill me. It had always been his end game.

"Why?" I croaked out, turning my head slowly to stop the waves of shooting pain and nausea from taking hold.

"Why what, sweetheart?" she asked, taping a new set of bandages to my back as carefully as she'd removed them.

"Why does love have to be a weakness, Autumn?" I didn't know why all the answers suddenly hit me in that one moment, but so much became clear to me as I puzzled a way out of the situation.

The room was so quiet, I heard her sigh as she shuffled to lay next to me, her hand curling around my good one while her head rested on my pillow facing me.

"It's not a weakness, Ayda. To love, you have to be strong. You have to have faith, trust and belief in one person and give them the ability to hurt you when you hand your heart and soul to them." She swept a tear away with her thumb and cupped my cheek. "It does make you more human and more vulnerable, though. You just have to remember that no matter how many people expose that, it's that vulnerability that sets you apart. It makes you human and makes you stronger. When you have so much to lose, it makes you fight harder to keep it."

"But you didn't see—"

"I didn't need to. You are both fighters and you fought

for one another. You would have given up much sooner if you hadn't been aware of him so close by, and he wouldn't have been able to wait for the boys to show up if he hadn't had to fight for you."

She was right. No matter what angle I tried to approach it from, it was partly knowing that Drew was in that room fighting for his life that had given me the strength to go against my natural inclination to ball up and wait for the storm to pass. He was the reason I had defied death and taken the hits. He would always be the reason I fought. I would never give up on him or us, and even though I had been certain before, I knew he wouldn't, either.

As the words settled, I pushed my cheek into her hand and used my elbows to push up from the mattress. I needed to be with him. I needed to see him with my own two eyes and touch him. Being apart from him was more painful than every wound I'd sustained balled together. The last interaction we'd had was so vague, and I needed him to know I was alright and strong enough to face another day by his side. I also needed him to understand how essential he was in my life—how, in a few short months, he'd become one of the reasons I woke up every morning and smiled, and why I took every breath.

I also needed him to understand that no matter how many people tested the bonds of our relationship and our family, I would be by his side, my hand in his, giving my strength and support in any way he needed it.

As it turned out, I didn't have to do much moving. I'd barely pushed to my aching knees when I heard his deep, gruff voice throwing orders out and yelling at the doctor to leave him the hell alone. The sound of it brought a smile to my lips regardless of the throbbing that gripped me from head to toe. I knew beyond reasonable doubt that if he could be that pissy, he would be fine in time. Even as frustrated as he was, the familiar sound of his voice wrapped around me like a warm, comforting blanket, sending the wings of a thousand butterflies to fill my stomach as I waited to see those beautiful and unusual eyes of his. Even with the shit life had thrown at us in the last however many hours, we'd lived through Hell. I knew the moment I met those eyes and saw the love there it wouldn't matter anymore. We'd survived it and what hadn't broken us entirely could only make us stronger.

The rattle of the door handle had me dropping to my hip, my legs a tangle at my side as Autumn leaped forward to stop me from falling face first off the bed, quickly settling me as the door practically stepped out of the way.

Whatever I'd been expecting was mild in comparison to his reality. The man I knew was hidden behind swollen, mottled skin that was still in the process of changing color. Dark, dried blood clung to freshly tended wounds, and even as the determination shone through his one half-open eye, I could see how much effort it had taken to walk down that hall. He was limping with one arm wrapped around his ribs. Yes, he was alive, but from the looks of him, it had been a close call—something I didn't want to think about too much as we held each other's gaze.

CHAPTER FORTY-EIGHT
DREW

I didn't hang around to spend time analyzing what I saw. The moment she came into view, there was only one thing that held my attention, and it was the same thing that always had: the blue of her eyes. They were staring back at me with a look I couldn't read properly, but I'm pretty sure it must have mirrored the shit on my own face. Relief. Disbelief. Anger. Sadness. But more than anything, the heavy stuff—the stuff that got me through the last however many hours of absolute torture. The love stuff.

Doc didn't speak once I'd opened the door to her room. I wasn't even aware of where he was anymore as I pushed the wood into the frame behind me and made my way over to her, trying my hardest not to show the agony that stormed its way through my entire body with every step I took.

As soon as I saw the epic fuck up of her back, I crouched down beside the bed and reached out for her one good hand as carefully as I could. There wasn't anything I wanted to do other than pick her up in my arms and hold her to me, just so I could feel her and know she was still alive and still real. But neither one of us were capable of doing what we really wanted to do.

I eventually looked up and stared into her eyes.

Curling my fingers around hers and ignoring the splintering pain through every knuckle, I found myself swallowing as the emotion and relief threatened to take over. Leaning forward, I pressed my lips to her hand over and over again and pulled in a breath through my nostrils.

"Look at you," I whispered, closing my eyes to compose myself before staring up at her again. "No words will ever be able to tell you how sorry I am, Ayda. Please, don't…"

I stopped, not wanting to beg her not to leave me after all this, but needing her to know how fucking sorry I was.

The palm of her hand was so close to my lips, she trailed her fingers over them and down through my beard as she took in every cut and bruise that was there. "You didn't do anything you need to apologize for."

The tear tracks on her cheeks looked like a permanent tattoo of the torture she'd been put through, yet there she was comforting me.

Breathing out, I tore one hand away from hers and lifted it to her face. I wanted to trace every mark on her skin just to remind myself that what I'd just done to Cortez was the only option I'd had. I wanted her wounds to burn me, just to remind myself that letting her go from that warehouse in the arms of someone other than myself was the only thing I could have done, because I had to be the one to make sure he paid the highest price.

I had to be the one to spill his blood, own his last breath.

The marks her body wore were my validation.

Letting my bust up hand fall to the side of her face, I pushed my fingers through her hair and brushed my thumb over the apple of her cheek.

"I have so many things to apologize for. The main one

being that for the last few weeks, all I've done is break all my promises to you over and over again. I vowed to keep you safe and I didn't. Tonight—last night—whatever day we're on now, I don't know and I don't care, but it was the worst night in the club's history beside—" I cut myself off, knowing his name was on the tip of my tongue. "Besides the night Pete died. I'm sorry you were a part of that because of me, just like he was."

Ayda looked up, the shuffling of someone slipping from the room the only indication that Deeks' woman had been there at all. The moment the door clicked closed, she shifted slowly, trying to hide the wince as she slid her bruised legs to either side of me and shuffled to the edge of the mattress. "You haven't broken a promise to me, Drew. Okay, I'm a little beat up, but I'm alive, and so are you. That is all that's important right now. That's the only thing either of us needs to focus on. This isn't your fault. Up until we saw that kid, it was one of the best nights of my life."

I stayed down, my hands on her as much as they could be without causing her pain.

"Don't do that," I said softly.

"Do what?" she whispered, meeting my eyes.

"Panic," I answered, rising up until my face was level with hers so she could see the absolute certainty of what I was about to say. "I'm not going to push you away again, Ayda. This isn't me telling you your life would be better off without me. I realized a lot of things in that room, and one of them was the irony of that stupid fucking quote that tells everyone that if you truly love someone you should set them free. I don't believe that anymore. I don't even know if I believed it in the first place. I'm not going anywhere and neither are you. We belong together and I know that now more than ever before. I won't lose you. Not now, not ever. Where you go, I go."

When her lips began to tremble, I was sure she was about to cry, but she surprised me as they formed into a smile.

"Good, because you're stuck with me whether you like it or not. You're not the only one who realized a few things in that place." Her tongue darted out to run over her dried and cracked lips. "Like I realized I can't and won't live without you in my life."

"Damn right you won't."

I tried to offer her a smile of some sort, but I had no idea if it looked as bad as it felt. I was all blood and torn up skin. Everything was three times the size it was yesterday and a hell of a lot more painful. Dropping my hand to her chin, I let my thumb hover over her bottom lip before gently tugging it down.

"This is it now. You and me. I mean it. No more half assing it on my part. You and me."

"Took you long enough, asshole," she said with a laugh as the tears formed. She tried to blink them back, but one of them escaped, forcing her bad hand up so she could brush it away on her wrist, her eyes rolling.

I reacted without thought, pulling her focus back to me as gently as I could, my face falling serious as I reached for and held both her wrists in my grip. "Don't do that, either."

"Do what?"

"Refuse to believe that what I'm saying isn't just more bullshit words that I'm whispering in your ear to comfort you," My voice was smaller than a whisper as I let my forehead brush against hers. "I mean it, Ayda. I'm not going anywhere. Not tomorrow. Not next week. Not in a year, a decade, or any amount of time you can come up with. I'm never going to leave you or ask you to leave me. I want every single bit of you I can get... *forever*."

She continued to search my face, the tears now flowing easily and cutting through the marks on her cheeks. Her voice was choked as her tears fell from her chin. She sniffed quietly, a small cough coming as she tried to clear her throat with no luck. "Drew Tucker, I love you."

"Took you long enough, asshole." I smirked.

She stifled a giggle, groaning in pain a little as her good hand moved from mine so she could cup my cheek with a feather-light touch. "Do you think you could do me a favor?"

"That depends…"

"On?"

"If it involves heavy lifting, physical exertion or me applying broken lips to any of your body parts that deserve way more attention than I am capable of giving right now."

Tipping her head forward, she looked up at me from under her lashes. "Does that include just holding me in a bed with the lights out?"

"I thought you'd never ask."

Moving sounded easier than it was, and it took me way too fucking long to hold all my body parts in place and rise to a stand.

Shuffling on the bed slowly, Ayda looked up at me and with a small, humorless snort, covered her face with both hands.

"Jesus, would you look at the two of us, moving around like ninety year-olds." She reached out slowly and thought better of it. "Just how bad are you?"

I didn't answer right away, instead reaching out for her offered hand and lowering myself down beside her. All I was wearing was my sweat pants. The doc had been trying to clean me up before I stormed in here, unable to listen to any more of my injuries because all I could focus on was finding the one medicine I needed.

My shoulder was strapped up to cover the bullet wound that would be a new addition to the ever expanding war artwork that was splashed across my body, but that didn't stop me from creasing my face together and holding it up high for Ayda to fall under. It might not have made sense to her or anyone else out there, but I just needed to feel her against my chest. I needed her to breathe life back into me again.

"I've had worse."

"Liar," she whispered, settling in against me as gently as she could, her breaths coming in small puffs as her fingers traced the packing slowly. "But I promise, you've got yourself the best little nurse around."

"You're not nursing anyone." I smiled, resting my hand on the top of her ass. "For once, you're going to let me look after you. No arguing."

Ayda went quiet for a while before she released a quiet yawn. "You always look after me."

"There's always room for improvement. You might want to prepare yourself for me dressing you up in bubble wrap from now on. Three guard dogs everywhere you go. No venturing out after dark. Maybe a collar…" The smile on my lips hurt as I teased her, waiting for her to bite the way she always had.

"You don't think one's enough?" she asked thoughtfully. "I mean, technically, with…" She lifted her head an inch from my chest and sucked in a breath. "Wait. What happened to the girl? Sofia?"

I frowned quickly, my body tensing slightly beneath hers. "What?"

"The girl that identified you?" she asked, tipping her head back slowly so she was looking up at me. "What happened to her?"

"I..." There was no way to say what she wanted to hear, and while I never wanted to shut her out of anything anymore, I also knew that then wasn't the time to relive more pain. Sagging into the mattress, I closed my eyes and nudged her closer. My body was working hard to pump blood to all the places that needed it the most. It was a feeling that left me floating but grounded me at the same time. I was anchored by agony, yet lost in a headspace that made everything seem unreal. Especially what we'd just done. Pushing my lips to the top of her head, I held them there as I spoke through the haze of the memories and the pain.

"Ayda, you don't need more answers that will haunt you. Not today."

"I understand," she whispered with conviction, her palm landing flat against my skin as her head tipped back down. "So what now? Are we safe?"

Safe. Wouldn't that be a peaceful thought?

There would be a time for me to tell her what we were and where we stood. There would be moments of quiet in the future where the boredom and silence would leave her with little option but to think and wonder what had happened when she left that warehouse. I made another vow as I lay beside her, holding her in my arms—a vow to always answer as honestly as I could when she asked what was going down with the club. She'd earned that right in the last twenty-four hours. She'd earned it the first night I met her when she stood up to me the way no other woman ever had.

It just wasn't the time to go into it all. She didn't need to know how I'd made Cortez take his last breath. She didn't need to know about the explosion Kenny had rigged at the warehouse, or the scene that Jedd and Slater had pieced together to make it look like some kind of Emps fucked up ritual gone wrong. She didn't even need to know about the conversation we'd had with Sutton to fill him in and officially get him on our side for the first time in the club's history. This wasn't just a schoolyard plan we'd hatched that could be told in a few simple sentences.

It was a complicated MC web of lies, deceit and murder.

It was about our survival and their destruction.

What happened beyond that was anyone's guess, but all I cared about as I held her *was* her. Everything I did was for her. Without Ayda to live for, I'd have died several times over already.

As the dusty morning sunlight tried to peer through the cracks of the heavy curtains in the room, I curled my free hand around hers that lay against my chest, sighing into her hair before pressing a painful kiss to her head.

"We're safe."

For now.

CHAPTER FORTY-NINE
Ayda

I'm not usually the kind of person who remembers their dreams. The moment I open my eyes, reality seeps in and anything that lingers is eaten with the appearance of the sun. That morning, curled into Drew, I woke up sweating with my hair plastered to my damp cheek and the lingering nightmares of what we'd been through making my head feel gritty and dirty. I was so confused. It took a moment for me to realize that the heat wasn't from my body at all. It was radiating from the chest below my cheek. Drew's body. I wasn't sure what to make of the situation at first. For a full minute I was convinced that it was just the heat of the day and our bare skin generating too much warmth, which for us wasn't that unusual.

Eventually, it was the shivers and the twitches that finally alerted me to the fact that something wasn't right.

"Drew, baby?" I asked quietly, pushing up and away from him. One look at his body in the fading light and I knew it wasn't a good situation. His skin was pale and damp, his dark hair plastered to his forehead, and his eyes were darting around behind the membrane of his eyelids. Reaching out with a tentative and shaky hand, I brushed the sweat from his face and pushed myself onto my aching knees, ignoring the scream of pain in my body as my palms moved from his clammy cheeks to his forehead.

He was burning up.

"Drew? Wake up!" I pleaded as my hands moved to the sweat covering his chest only to find the angry looking wounds on his body.

He groaned, the sound throaty like he was struggling to breathe, while his body curled in on itself with no obvious instruction from him when my hand barely brushed his abs. As I watched him struggle, I could feel the panic clutching at the walls of my sanity again, but I shoved it back to the deepest recesses of my mind. Drew needed *me* this time, and there was only one thing I could do for him, but he could be damn sure I wouldn't let him down.

Without further thought, I launched my aching body from the bed, limping and stumbling toward the door, grabbing a stray shirt to cover myself with on the way out. It took everything in me to stretch my back to pull it down over my head, but I managed before tugging on the door with both hands, forcing it out of the way so I could stumble into the corridor.

There were about five people lingering outside at first glance, but I was in no place to put names to faces even if I knew them well. There was only one person that could help me and I wasn't even sure I knew what he looked like.

All of them were startled as I appeared, panting in pain and completely frantic about Drew's condition. Even the walls heaved in a breath as though waiting for me to finally spit the right order of words out.

"Where's Doc?" I shouted, my volume and tone completely out of my control. The faster my fear and adrenaline pumped through my body, the more limber I became, my own agony pushed aside at the thought of Drew's pained groans.

"Drew?" Slater asked, pushing past men and bearing down on me. Any other situation and I would have shrunk back, but this was Drew's health and not even the Reaper himself was going to get past me.

"Where the fuck is the doctor?"

"Here."

The voice was unfamiliar, but the face was one I recognized as he appeared behind Slater and searched for a way past the human wall of muscle blocking his path. For the first and, I hoped, the last time in my life, I pushed my shoulder into Slater's gut to move him aside and let the doctor through. I, more than anyone, appreciated who and what Drew represented to him, but if he thought for a second he meant any less to me, he needed a reality check. I'd always loved Drew, but the thought of losing him had done something to me. It was a trigger to a stronger and more aggressive woman inside of me. Kneeling in that warehouse, I'd come to the realization that I would die for Drew. If it meant he got to live, I would die a thousand deaths.

That was the only reason I was able to get Slater away from the door and stop him from entering with one look. It was the strength and conviction that I'd always had when it came to Tate. Drew was just as much my family as my brother was, and no one was getting past me until he was ready to see them.

The moment the doctor was inside, I backed up with hobbled steps. My legs weren't matching my determination, but I managed to shut the door without so much as an argument, even as the doctor flicked on the lights and rushed to Drew's side.

"God dammit. I told him to stay where he was, but the man is as stubborn as a mule."

"It was me, wasn't it?" I asked, dropping my ass to the foot of the bed and resting my hand on his ankle as the doctor threw his jacket into the chair behind him and started rolling up his shirt sleeves. "He wanted to check on me."

"Don't blame yourself. No one tells Drew what to do but Drew." He flashed me a smile as he pressed the stethoscope to his ears and leaned forward. "But it is kinda nice to see him happy."

"Happy?" I snorted, gripping Drew's ankle as he kicked out at the cold end of the diaphragm against his chest.

The doctor listened for a while, pushing gently on Drew's shoulder so he could hear properly. The moment he was finished, he pulled the equipment from his ears and slung it around his neck, peering up at me with a small, reassuring smile.

"Yes, happy. I don't tend to put words in people's mouths, but I know what I saw when he got back, and I saw the concern he had for you. These boys worry about one another, it's true, but worrying about you? That's big, darlin'."

"I love him, too," I said without hesitation, meeting the doctor's eyes. "Which is exactly why I need you to do your damn best and get him better."

"Yes ma'am."

Time had stopped—at least it sure as hell felt like it. The

doctor worked diligently. His nimble hands checked every part of Drew's body and pushed through the agonizing sounds of his pain without so much as breaking a sweat. I knew I was probably doing more harm than good, sitting there asking question after question about what he was doing and why, but it was the only way I could get through the torture he seemed to be performing. Drew was strong, but there was no anaesthetic involved, and he was human.

Eventually, the doctor called Harry in to help him, but he spent most of his time trying to stop my reactions to Drew's pain. His arms became bars around my waist as I struggled and held me up when I'd exhausted myself physically and emotionally.

Drew's injuries were worse than anyone had anticipated. He'd lost a lot of blood, but like Harry told me repetitively, "He has heart, Ayda. He's a fighter. There ain't no way that kid's ready to give up yet."

The doctor stayed for a while, just like Harry did, but he left sometime in the early hours of the morning when he said Drew's heart rate and blood pressure were stable and he was on the mend. Harry was brave enough to try and convince me to go to another room and sleep but realized, probably too late, that it would have been easier to try and move a mountain. So he finally left to get some sleep, leaving me alone with Drew again.

"You stubborn ass," I whispered, slipping into the chair next to the bed that the doctor had been using.

I picked up Drew's hand and brought it to my forehead. I shouldn't have been okay with his healthcare being performed in my little private room, but the privacy was something I was embracing. My room, my rules, and I suspected that was the only reason people like Slater and Jedd were pacing the floor outside to splinters.

"When are you going to realize that I need you?" I asked quietly, the moisture filling my eyes slowly. "You bring me into this amazing world of yours, tell me that you love me, and you make me happier than I've ever been before, and then you don't take care of yourself? That's not acceptable, Drew. I'm selfish enough to admit that I need you. Just remember this: the next time you try and take care of me first when you're this fucking hurt, I am going to kick your ass. Broken ribs or not."

Blowing all the air from my lungs, I could feel the energy start to seep from my body, the adrenaline finally giving way to pain and exhaustion. Unfortunately, there was no sleeping— not when he was unconscious and in as much pain as he was. So the only option I had was to rest my head on his hand and hope that he came to soon.

I woke with a start, the tickle on my hair making me sit up quickly, which was immediately followed by a groan of regret as pain shot through my body in places I wasn't entirely sure belonged to me. It took a while to process anything, but the moment my mind went to Drew, my eyes followed the train of thought and landed on those beautiful blue-green eyes of his.

I'm not sure where I managed to find the restraint to not jump on him with a scream of happiness, but I pulled it off, only for the emotions to cumulate instead. Bowing my head to hide the tears, I placed my lips on the back of his hand and pressed my eyes together in a silent thank you to any deity that was willing to listen. I had so much to say to him, but none of it would come to my lips. The only thing I could even begin to form were those three little words over and over again. They started as a whisper and played on repeat until I felt his hand twitch against mine.

"I love you."

He stared down at me, neither one of us aware of the passage of time as he slowly blinked over and over again and tried to find some strength to make a sound. The moment his lips twitched up into a slow, lazy smirk, I knew he was back in that room with me the way I needed him to be. "*I love you,*" he mouthed, closing his eyes again.

There was nothing I wanted more in the world than to climb into that bed beside him and just hold him against me and never let go. I needed to feel his body against mine, and not in a sexual sense, but just to know he was there, that his body temperature was safe and that he was breathing normally.

"You ever walk away from a doctor when you're that hurt again, I swear to God, Drew Tucker, I'll have them castrate you while you're out," I whispered against the back of his hand. "And if you scare me like that again, I'll be the fucker with the scissors."

Drew let his head roll to the side, his half smile never leaving his lips until he attempted to open his eyes to look up at me again. He struggled to take in a big breath, holding it high in his chest until a small groan came unstuck from the back of his throat.

"I thought you might need a little more drama in your life. It's been quiet around here lately."

"Not funny." I sniffled with a half laugh. Using the back of my free hand, I swept the tears away from under my eyes and gave him a watery smile. "You scared me, Drew, and you know I hate to cry."

"I hate to see you cry," he whispered.

There was no restraint anymore. I was on my feet in a grunt of pain and had my lips pressed as gently against his as I could manage. I could feel the swelling on his mouth, along his jaw where I cupped his face, as well as the split as I swept my tongue against his lips, but trying to stop was like asking me not to breathe.

It was only when he hissed that I eased back, pressing my lips against his a couple of times before our foreheads came together. "Please don't do that again. I'm not sure my heart can take it."

"I don't know what happened. I feel like I've been hit by a train." Drew tried to lift his hand, the effort clearly too much for him as his arm fell against me, only allowing his fingers to graze the side of my thigh. "Tell me you're okay."

"I'm fine—a couple of aches and pains, some scratches on my back, which will heal, and this," I said, holding up my finger. "It will heal fine, though. Deeks set it while I was out and I didn't feel a thing. You, on the other hand? Your body went into shock because you neglected your injuries."

"You sound like Doc."

"I just spent hours with him while he tried to keep you with me."

"I wasn't going anywhere." He paused, trying again to lift his hand and this time succeeding. When he wrapped his fingers limply around my forearm and tried to pull me even closer, I gravitated towards him without thought. "I promise. I meant what I said to you."

The pull on my arm was even more demanding as I looked up at him, and with a small smile and a roll of my eyes,

I climbed up on the bed next to him, careful to avoid the areas that the doctor said would be most tender.

"Tell me again," I whispered, my body settling next to his, my breath washing over his naked shoulder. I was being needy, but it was just the two of us, and I didn't mind him knowing how much I needed him, because as long as he was fighting, I would be, too.

CHAPTER FIFTY
DREW

I wasn't aware of much throughout the next few hours of my life. Three could have passed the same as seventy. Light came and went from the room and the darkness took over. The only time I ever felt truly conscious was when Doc had filled me with enough drugs to ease the pain in my shoulder, and when Ayda was by my side. We were two broken bodies, but for the first time since we'd become a couple, we felt like one whole.

I'd known I loved her for weeks. I'd known she'd been the one to turn my head in a way the hundreds of women before her hadn't been able to, but now things felt different. Things felt stronger even though physically, we were both weaker.

She didn't have to speak whenever she entered a room. I could feel her, and every time I heard the slide of her bare feet along the floor, that small smile of mine crept upon my face. Even if it did sting like a motherfucker.

The cuts to my body were everywhere, in all the most strategic places. Places that weren't designed to heal easily, like the creases of my skin that would always tear if I stretched, and over old scars that had already taken too many years to heal. It was what made it feel like a slow process and a long time before I could lift my ass out of the bed without having someone else pull me up.

After what must have been a few days, possibly even a week, I'd had enough. I needed out of the room and I needed to go deal with the shit I knew was out there waiting for me in The Hut. The nights were about to become heavy with nightmares and worries if I didn't act quickly, and to be perfectly honest, I was really fucking tired of being tired.

There was a fresh start waiting out there for all of us. If I raised my hand up to the sky and stretched enough, I felt like I was only an inch or two away from touching it. All I had to do was reach and push myself that little bit harder.

The first time my feet hit the floor of The Hut and I pushed up from the bed to stand on shaky legs, I had to close my eyes and dig deep to find my center. Ayda was in the bathroom, and there was no doubt about the fact that had I tried to move when she'd been around, she'd have been planting my ass back down. But I needed to do this now.

What I wasn't expecting was for her to walk back in the moment I had taken my first few steps forward. The door swung open slowly and we both froze in place as we eyed each other's expressions.

When all I saw staring back at me was a small shake of her head and a smirk that I was sure was starting to resemble my own, I grinned at her.

"Don't challenge me to a race. I'm not a good loser."

Crossing her arms and resting her hip against one of the dressers, she tipped her head to the side, her smile growing even bigger. "At the risk of pissing you off, what would make this easier for you? You're too stubborn to go back to bed, aren't you?"

I shuffled forward, keeping my eyes on hers until I was towering over her. It felt like forever since I'd looked down on her. She'd been the one peering down at me since we got out of that warehouse, and it was only then that I was realizing just how strong she'd been for the both of us.

Lifting my hand to her chin, I pinched it between my finger and thumb before planting a kiss on the end of her nose.

"Shush, woman. I'm good. Never felt better. I'm a lion, remember?" My attempt at a fake roar sounded more like a dying cat.

"My lion get an antelope stuck in his throat?" she asked with a quiet giggle. Uncrossing her arms, she slid them around my waist, mindful of the injuries there. "I won't say another word about your invalid status, as long as you don't push yourself too hard. We got a deal?"

"Deal," I said through a smile, wishing I could tell her how good it felt to be held that way again. I eyed the door over her shoulder before looking back down at her. "You can keep your eyes fixed firmly on my broken ass if it will put your mind at ease. I have a feeling it's gonna get rowdy out there once they see me up on my feet. Care to be my guard dog, Hanagan?"

Pushing up on her toes, she kissed the edge of my jaw. "I thought you'd never ask."

I clung to her way more than it felt natural to, but I was discovering a little something about myself with every new hour that passed us by. It was okay for me to lean on Ayda. I fucking needed her.

The guys saw me before I registered any of them. The slow murmur rose into a loud boom of throaty howls, laughter, hand clapping, foot stamping, with a few insults thrown my way as a way of showing their affection. Despite the pounding in my head, I creased my face together, let my brows rise up awkwardly and gave them all a smile. Ayda's fingers curled into me that little bit more every time one of the men got too close, and I made sure to look down to reassure her I was okay whenever I felt her tense. She loved the men as much as I did, but right then, I was her only concern. That much was obvious.

"Nice to see you back on your feet, brother," Slater said as he stood beside me, taking small steps forward while I tried to keep up with the pace and the excitement in the room. I wasn't wearing anything but my sweat pants again, and it was pretty obvious from the way the men's eyes fell to my exposed skin that all my injuries were being added up, noted and stored away in their revenge banks. They'd seen me messed up before, but never like this.

I glanced up at him, smiling flatly and giving him a small nod. "Is that polite conversation from you, Slate? No asshole, fucker or stupid bastard? I'm touched."

"Don't be a stupid bastard, you stupid bastard." He smirked.

Jedd was up next, never touching me or greeting me with a slap on the shoulder the way he usually would, but his face said enough. He was glad to have me back.

"Don't cry, Jedd," I coughed out, straightening up and trying to stand taller as I pulled Ayda closer to me.

"If you weren't fucking ugly before, you are now, bro." He smiled brightly, the movement of his beard making the whole thing change shape as he stared on like some weird cross breed of dog.

"Stitches are in fashion, apparently." I flipped him off

over Ayda's shoulder, unable to stop the small fit of laughter from breaking free.

"And swollen eyes, fat lips, bruised skin..."

"All adds to my charm."

"You need all the help you can get." He laughed.

"I love it when we flirt."

The insults carried on back and forth until I found my way to the corner of The Hut. Ayda tried to get me to sit down in one of the chairs, but after pulling her in front of me and resting my ass on the arm of one of the sofas, I looked up and swore that I would let her know if anything hurt. There was a twinkle in her eye that hadn't lived there before the incident at the warehouse, and as soon as I was healthier and strong again, I was going to tie her down and find out exactly what that was. I was too broken to be turned on, and she would pay for making me think about things I shouldn't have been thinking about. And shit, even that thought made everything twitch and wake up again.

Watching her back away, I narrowed my eyes on her and failed to hide my grin. It was only when Harry came up beside me and pulled my attention away that I coughed and shuffled my ass back where I was sitting, praying to all the drugs in my body to keep me numb that little bit longer so I didn't get *uncomfortable* in front of my men.

"Harry, please tell me you're here to give me a whiskey."

"That's not my department. Your doc and your woman are in charge of what goes on with your body."

"My woman." I groaned, lifting my hand to rub it across my forehead as I tried again to think about anything other than how much I missed Ayda being in charge of my body, and me being in charge of hers.

"That bad?" Harry laughed.

"Fuck off," I pushed out through slightly gritted teeth before dropping my hand to my leg and looking back up at him. My smile was fake and sarcastic as I waited for the usual shit to happen. Since becoming one half of a whole, I wasn't immune to the constant ridiculing that went hand in hand with having a regular piece of ass on your arm. "Please," I added.

"Sorry, son, no can do. Looks like you came out from hiding just in time."

"In time for what?"

"Sutton's surfaced, too."

Despite how much of my life I'd spent hating that man and that name, I found my eyes falling behind Harry and an unexpected *good* falling from my lips. "Just the man I was looking for."

Harry gently tapped my good shoulder on a part that wasn't fucked up. "Be gentle with him. I think you'll be as surprised as I was when he—"

I didn't give him time to finish, instead quickly holding my hand up and shaking my head as carefully as I could. "No need for the lecture. Believe me. I know more than anyone that I owe my life to the man I always thought wanted to end it."

"Right."

"Before you go, just tell me one thing." I looked back up at him again, holding his gaze as I spoke. "Does he blame me?"

Harry studied me for a moment, his eyes searching mine as though he was looking for something or seeing something he'd never seen before. When he slowly began to shake his head and failed miserably to hide his smug smile, my body relaxed and I readjusted my position on the chair.

It didn't take long for Sutton to appear, and I'll admit to blinking once or twice when I saw a shadow of the man he used to be walking forward. Wearing sweats that obviously didn't belong to him, given that every item that hung from his body had our patch on it, he shuffled as slowly as I had moved through the club. The men around me parted like the sea, falling into two lines as he made his way through.

Sutton was a mess. Every hair on his head was standing up instead of smoothed back the way it used to be. His eyes were surrounded by shadows of both shock and grief, and I swear he was trying to mask the slight quiver of his top lip beneath his tash as he worried it between his teeth.

Poor fucker.

"Chief," I said, acknowledging him quietly. "Welcome to my home."

Howard's eyes met mine and where he would once have stood taller at the sound of my voice, he simply ran a hand through his hair and gave a few small nods.

"Sorry it's taken me so long to get back out here." I sighed, signaling for him to sit down on the chair beside me. I guess he hadn't fully disappeared. He shook his head and declined my invitation, instead choosing to stand. "I trust my brothers have looked after you since they brought you back here."

"They have," he answered, clearing his throat. "Quite the little motorcycle hotel you have here, Tucker."

"We respect those that respect us. It's always been our way."

"I see that now."

My smile was more sympathetic than anything as I

watched him fidget and look around.

"I'm glad to hear it," I said softly. "How are the war wounds?"

Sutton sighed, the tiredness pouring out of him as he scratched the back of his neck and shrugged awkwardly. "Nothing on the surface that won't heal in time." It was then he swallowed and the light caught the moisture that coated his eyes. Not wanting me to notice, he moved his hands to rub at them.

Giving my men one single look, they began to move around the room, distancing themselves from the private conversation that needed to take place. Once I was sure the chief had the personal space he needed, I leaned forward and ignored the pain that shot down my arm from my shoulder.

"I know you and I haven't always seen eye to eye, and I know that me even speaking her name is something that's always got your back up, but I need you to know that I am sorry about Maisey."

Sutton swallowed again, not hiding the way he struggled to regain control of his voice before he spoke. "Are you?"

"Yes," I answered firmly.

"Why?"

"Sutton, she was your wife."

"Only on paper."

"I doubt she ever intended to hurt you."

"You sound so sure."

"I only ever try to be honest."

"I'm not sure how I feel."

"That I can believe." I nodded my head in understanding, not looking away from him as he dropped his arms down by his sides before shoving them in the pockets of the oversized sweats he was wearing.

"I want to mourn her more than I do, but all I can see is her face when she spoke to you. All I can hear is the way she said that other man's name. That kind of betrayal runs deep no matter how much you thought you loved a person."

"She was in over her head, Howard. Doesn't mean everything was false."

"No?" he asked, lifting his head again.

"You've got your daughters. She can't ever take them away from you." As soon as I said it, my head spun around to the side and I looked for them. In the haze of everything that had happened, I hadn't a clue where they were, but I distinctly remembered giving an instruction for them to be taken care of and kept safe.

"They're in one of your rooms, Tucker," he said, obviously sensing my question before I even had the time to formulate it in my mouth. "Another thing I've got to thank you for."

My eyes closed briefly before I turned back to look at him and shook my head. "No need. You saved my life. I'd be dead if it wasn't for you."

"Likewise."

"Then I guess we're even."

He sucked in a small breath, the weight of what I'd just said showing in the way he creased his brows together and took a moment to stare his old enemy in the eye—an enemy who he would probably now have to call a friend.

"I know it ain't easy," I began to offer. "It's never easy to change the way you've seen something or someone your whole life. I get that. But in order for us all to stay safe, for you to keep being the father to your girls you want to be, for me to be able to keep being the father to my club that I need to be, we have to work together now, Howard."

"Together," he repeated in a whisper.

"Together. All of us. My men will have your back and your girls' backs for as long as you need us."

"And what will I have to do in return, Drew? Be your bitch cop who gets paid a nice fee for letting you run things through my town that used to turn my blood cold?"

I didn't snap at his attack. It was expected and it was understood. We were the devil's sons in his eyes. We wore the reaper on our chests and had black in our hearts, or so he thought. His confusion was going to throw a million questions out before any kind of comfortable friendship was truly formed.

"We're not that club anymore. At least, we're trying not to be. Do we attract trouble?" I looked down at my bust up body before swaying my head from side to side. "Evidently. Do we like it? Somedays. Do we want it as a permanent feature in our futures? No. And if you struggle to understand why I've had such a change of heart, you just need to look at that woman over there and see for yourself."

I didn't have to look up to see where she was. I could feel her, my hand rising and pointing in her direction as I kept my eyes on Sutton. He took one glance over his shoulder, spotted Ayda and turned back to me.

"You expect me to believe that one girl has changed a whole history of corrupt morals for you?

"No," I said, lowering my voice and peeking up through hooded eyes. "I expect you to believe that *that* girl has changed a whole history of corrupt and fucked up morals for me. For all of us. Shit happens, Chief. Sometimes it's good;

sometimes it's bad. Sometimes it's the most unexpected shit you can imagine. She's my good and my unexpected, and right now, she's all that matters. If she matters to me, she matters to my men. Everything she loves matters to all of us. I don't expect you to understand, but you better fucking believe it, because I've never been more serious about anything in my entire, miserable-before-she-came-along existence."

His eyes went wider the more I spoke, forcing him to swallow down again as he took one more look over his shoulder and stared at her for a length of time that would have made me feel uncomfortable had we been in any other situation. But I needed him to see what I saw.

When he eventually turned back to face me, his nod was a silent communication to let me know he understood.

"Good," I said through a sigh, straightening up and pushing my hands carefully into the tops of my thighs. "So we're friends? Two people working together for once instead of trying to tear each other apart?"

"I'd like that." He ran his hand down over his mouth, resting it on the edge of his chin before shaking his head at the weird situation we were in and locking eyes with mine. "I'd like that."

"Then it's already done."

"Thank you."

"No, thank you. Without you doing what you did, I wouldn't be here. That's the kind of stuff that never gets forgotten in this club. It's a mutual respect. We'll help you keep your involvement covered from the rest of the law, we'll deal with Maisey's…" I trailed off, not wanting or needing to say the word funeral. We both knew where I was going. "The girls will be safe and they'll get to keep their father at home."

Sutton's nostrils flared as he pulled in another deep breath and held it high in his chest. When he spoke, it came out through the exhale, followed by a weird, misplaced smile I hadn't expected to see.

"Seems like a few knocks to the head has made you a better man, Tucker."

My responding grin was immediate, my eyes widening as I straightened up and took a quick glance at Ayda before meeting his gaze again. "Or maybe I was just a good guy all along, Chief?"

CHAPTER FIFTY-ONE
Ayda

My eyes were drawn to him. No matter who I was talking to or the topic of conversation, my gaze consistently moved back to Drew. It seemed ridiculous considering how much time we'd spent with one another over the last few days, and in close proximity. Yet, I couldn't seem to stop. I needed to know he was still taking those breaths. I wanted to study the lines of his face and those intense eyes as he tried to read the situation going on around him. More than all of that, I had to remind myself how lucky we both were to be alive and still have one another.

"How's that back of yours?" Deeks asked, pushing a beer in my hand with an awkward shuffle of his shoulders as he bounced on the balls of his feet a couple times. I'd known he'd taken the whole thing hard. In the few conversations I'd had with Autumn when she brought Drew and me food, she'd mentioned his concern. That was exactly the reason I threw my arms around him the moment I had the beer in my good hand. I was still aching, but the sentiment was to tell him to stop worrying and that I would be fine. It worked, too. His thick arms folded around me and tightened only briefly before he let me go and stepped out of my embrace.

"I'll be good as new in no time," I said quietly, taking a mouthful of beer before tipping the neck of it in his direction and encouraging him to do the same. "Just a couple of scratches, and my finger is setting well."

Deeks paled, his bottle tipping higher as he took half of it in one go. The small gasp for breath was muted by the swipe of his arm across his mouth, and the reprimanding glare he shot me hadn't gone unnoticed.

"I hate wishing people dead when they're already there," he growled, polishing off his bottle. It was my turn to pale. As much as I was aware of the deaths that had to take place, I'd been conveniently avoiding any thoughts regarding them, or the blood of the man I'd killed that still felt as though it was on my hands most days.

Deeks released another breath as he took me in and shook his head.

"I'm sorry, kid. I didn't mean to bring that up, but if anything worse had happened to you…"

"It didn't."

"But it could have."

"Has anyone ever told you you'd have made a pretty amazing dad?" I asked. I was being serious, but I kept my tone light and paired it with a smile.

"Oh, Jesus, you must be high on pain pills," he grumbled, lifting the beer bottle to study and avoid meeting my eyes. He was hiding his reaction and we both knew it, but there was no way I'd ever call him on it. It was another thing I stored away to ask Autumn later. "On that sick and twisted note, I'm going to grab another beer and let the girl talk to you seeing as she's been sitting there bouncing around impatiently."

I glanced over my shoulder and found Libby with

her arms over her chest, pretending to be enamored in the conversation that was going on between two of the HW's. There was no Tate in sight, which was becoming increasingly concerning seeing as I'd only seen him once since we'd made it back from the warehouse in one piece.

"Deeks," I said, turning to find him already slipping away.

"Yeah?"

"Thank you."

He waved a hand at me and huffed indignantly as he disappeared in the direction of the bar. He had no idea what I was thanking him for. He had no clue how deep it ran or how many limbs it had grown since the day I met him in the bathroom I'd been cleaning. He'd become a pivotal part of my life, and he'd given me something I thought I'd never have again: a paternal guidance that was invaluable.

All of the people in the pack had a place in my heart, some more than others, but all of them had my love, respect and, more importantly, loyalty. Over the days I'd been laid in the bed next to Drew, I'd had more than enough time to think about shit that hadn't occurred to me in the past. A little too much time, but it had put things into perspective.

"Ayda?" Libby asked, stepping around me and offering a small, polite smile that never reached her eyes. Something was bothering her, and if I had to bet what little money I had to my name on it, I would have said it was about Tate.

"Hey, Libby."

"You're looking much better. How do you feel?" she asked shyly, tucking her loose hair behind her ear as she avoided my gaze. I knew she cared in her own way, but her concern was lying elsewhere in that moment, and as awkward as it was, I appreciated it. Knowing Tate had picked a girl that cared enough about him to approach me actually made me like her more, even if I was aware I was to blame for her squirming. I wasn't being hostile, but I hadn't exactly made her welcome, either.

That just made me feel guilty, so I offered her a smile and took a mouthful of beer, letting my eyes dart to where Drew was. The moment our eyes met, I felt better and turned my attention back to Libby. "I feel much better. Some aches and pains but nothing that won't go away with time. How's Tate?"

I knew what I was doing when I ended with a question about my brother, and the look Libby gave me told me she was grateful for the opportunity to segue into the conversation she *wanted* to be having. As much as she respected, and maybe even liked me, her main concern was somewhere else, and I approved. She cared about Tate and for me, that was all that mattered.

"Not good. He was there when Deeks carried you in." She looked up at me with a quiet apology. "He hasn't been right since, and he won't talk to me about it."

"How bad?" I asked, putting down my bottle and tugging her to a quiet corner, making sure I was still in Drew's line of sight. I could see the sadness in Libby's eyes even though I could tell she was torn about the situation.

"Growing up surrounded by the MC isn't easy, Ayda. You see things you never wanted to see, things that you will always have imprinted into the back of your eyelids, scenes that come back to you in your darkest moments. I have plenty of them. My mom was in love with a Hound after my dad died. She went through hell and back on a daily basis. What happened to you will always be one of Tate's darkest memories if he doesn't start talking about it soon. I've tried to get him to open up, but he won't budge. He won't even talk to Kenny about it."

"I'll talk to him," I said, reaching forward and squeezing her hand. She may have been older than Tate, but she was falling hard. She was wearing her heart on her sleeve and I could see that this was costing her. As much as she didn't want Tate to hurt, she knew that there could be a resolution to this that wouldn't end well for her.

"Thanks, Ayda. I hate seeing him like this. He hasn't even been to practice since it happened and Kenny's been trying to keep the coach away from here. I just…" She trailed off and looked down at her hands briefly. "I should get back to the bar. The beers won't open themselves."

"Don't give up on him, Lib. He's stronger than he looks."

"He's younger than he looks, too," she sighed with a sad smile.

"That's never mattered to you before. Just don't count those chickens before they've hatched. No matter what he's going through right now, no matter what plans he's making, I'm pretty sure you're a big part of them."

"Well, I guess we'll see about that. If you go looking for him, he's with the chief's daughter."

With that, she was gone, her tiny figure disappearing into the sea of people loitering around the room while all I could do was blow the air from my body. I wasn't sure what Tate was thinking, but I couldn't imagine it was anything good with Sloane. Libby was a relaxed kind of girl, but I wasn't sure their young relationship could survive my kid brother's idiocy.

I'd barely made a decision to go and find him when I felt the involuntary smile curl my lips as Drew approached. I didn't have to look to see if he was there. As cliché as it sounded, my skin tingled every time he was near, just like my eyes constantly gravitated toward him when he was on the other side of the room. When I finally turned in his direction, I could see how slowly he was moving, but the satisfaction of moving of his own volition was evident in his grin.

I returned it tenfold, my heart swelling as he slung an arm around my shoulder and pulled me close, his lips meeting my head as he held his own weight like the stubborn ass he was.

"You'd better be keeping your promise to me," I whispered, burying my face in his neck and breathing him in. I needed to go and talk to Tate, but that didn't mean I couldn't look after my man at the same time.

"Have I ever told you I find you irresistible when you're bossy?" He pressed the unbroken part of his mouth against my hair, his fingers grazing through the ends of it over and over again.

"Don't be charming like that when I can't take full advantage of your good mood," I whispered, my lips curling, even though I knew he couldn't see my smile. "I think I need to have a discussion with Tate, who, by the way, is with Sloane."

"Who?"

"Sloane Sutton."

"Of course he is. Go easy on the kid, Ayda. He's younger than we seem to think he is."

My hand flattened on his shoulder, careful to avoid the part I knew still hurt. "I know he is, and I think it's completely innocent. He's got a big heart and he knows how close Sloane got to her step mom in that last couple of months. I also know he'd never do anything to hurt Libby, even if she can't see it right now."

"I can't imagine where he got his big heart from."

"Will you come with me? I think this whole thing really scared him, and maybe…" I sighed and pulled back to meet his eyes. "Maybe you could let him know that if he does go to college, it doesn't mean he's not welcome here. I think he's so torn about what he wants because this is his family now. Two years can change a lot of things, but knowing he has options could help him."

Drew raised his hand to brush away a stray hair from my cheek before he looked back at me through his swollen eyes and sighed. "I'll do whatever you want or need me to do. He'll always be welcome here. This is his home for however long he wants it. I just gotta warn you, when it comes to pep talks, I usually end up saying the wrong thing at the worse time."

"Why do I always have more faith in you than you do?"

"Because you see me differently to everyone else." He pulled me closer, being careful to avoid the injuries on my back versus the injuries on his chest. It was like an awkward game of body *Jenga*, trying to pull at the pieces that wouldn't send us tumbling down. "And stop turning this around on me. Take me where you need me to be," he whispered with a grin.

Pushing up on my toes, I pressed my lips to the part of his that weren't swollen or split. When I landed back on my feet, I slipped casually under his arm, ignoring his growl of protest as I headed toward our room. I would bring Tate to us. It was easier than explaining to Sutton why we were all in his daughter's temporary living quarters.

"There's several answers to that, which could possibly get me in trouble with your doctor." I grinned back at him.

"Definitely trying to kill me."

"I'm the one torturing myself here." I laughed, pushing

the door out of the way and guiding him toward the bed. Helping him to sit on the edge of it, I looked down at him with a smile and backed away to leave again. "I'm going to get Tate. Try and stay out of trouble, Mr. Tucker."

"Sure thing, darlin'."

Swinging around the doorframe with one last grin back at him, I made my way through the corridors of The Hut to find my kid brother and the ex-girlfriend he was alone with. I knew him better than anyone, and the fact that he'd stood up to me about Libby and his relationship told me everything I needed to know. Sloane was his friend now, nothing more, nothing less, and if he proved me wrong, I was going to kick his ass.

When I could finally move without groaning.

The one thing that truly sucks about having injuries is that everything becomes a gargantuan effort. The corridors I'd navigated so easily in the past now felt a mile long, and the floors might as well have been at awkward angles for all of my nimbleness. The fact that I was huffing out breaths when I arrived at the right door was just humiliating. It didn't stop me from knocking, though.

Sloane answered in a pair of ratty sweats with her hair in a messy bun, one of the twins asleep with her head on her shoulder. Her eyes were red and swollen and her skin was pale, which told me she'd been crying a lot over the last couple of days, and that my intuition about my brother had been right the first time.

"I'm so sorry, Sloane."

"Thanks, Ayda." She looked at me like she wanted to say more, but decided against it, rearranging the toddler in her arms. "You looking for Tate?"

I nodded, reaching out to take the little girl's miniature

hand that was balled up into a fist as she let off a sigh, while Sloane simply stepped to the side and revealed my brother sitting on the bed, cradling the carbon copy of the kid she was holding against his chest. He looked entirely too comfortable with a child in his arms.

"Hey, you."

"Ayda." He and Sloane traded a look that said a hundred things before he got up and laid the sleeping toddler on the bed. The moment he stood straight, he curled his shoulders in and pushed his hands into his pockets as he walked toward me.

Smiling at Sloane, I stepped back and out the way, not at all surprised when the door behind him closed.

"I know what you're gonna say."

"Do you?" I asked, heading down the corridor with a slow limp. "Because if I'm being honest, I don't have a clue what I'm going to say."

"You're not pissed about Sloane?"

"Unless you slept with her, no," I said, looking up at him. "I know who you are, Tate. Libby's hurt, but trust takes time, and I'm pretty sure what she has is invested in you anyway. You just have to be honest and open with her about your friendship."

"Sloane's messed up. I'm just listening."

"How bad?"

"She feels guilty because she's upset with Maisey for dying, pissed at her dad for assuming she would take responsibility for the twins, and scared that she won't get to go to college now."

"And you?" I asked, veering into his body and bouncing off. Tate and I had never been awkward around one another and I was diffusing the situation before it got to that place and

433

stayed there.

"I'm pissed at you for getting yourself into that situation, Ayda." He didn't bother looking at me and he wasn't pulling his punches, which was fine with me. I understood he was upset, but the longer he let it gather inside of himself, the more it would be blown out of proportion.

"Okay, but you have to know I didn't willingly walk into that situation." He opened his mouth to speak and I put a hand up in his direction, knowing exactly where he was going with it. "And neither did Drew. You think for a second that he wanted me there?"

"No, but—"

"There are no buts, Tate. Put yourself in his shoes for just one minute. I already know you've figured that out, but you need a few people to aim your pain at, right? I'm here. Aim it at me, kid, but know that shit happens and understand that Drew is the one of the only reasons I'm still alive."

"Then it all comes down to me," he said, stopping outside of the room I shared with Drew. "I broke in here, I tried to steal their shit, and I'm the reason you met him at all."

"Then you're the reason I'm happy."

"Ayda!"

"No, hear me out, Tate," I said, placing my hand on his over the door handle. "I know this new world we live in is terrifying. I understand how much the thought of losing more people makes your insides shrivel up. Believe me, I get it, but these risks, these moments of gut wrenching fear, they're worth it for me. That doesn't mean I expect you to do the same. You know if you want to go live somewhere else, all you have to do is say the word. I love Drew, I love these boys, and I love The Hut, but you're my brother, and you will be for every day of forever."

"I could never ask you to give this up... I couldn't—"

"You couldn't give it up either, huh?" I asked gently. "Then it's probably best we sit down and have us a good, old-fashioned heart to heart about it, and it's about time you were honest with yourself about what you want out of life, Tate. The Hut, the pack, they're always going to be here."

It was at that point the door opened, and Drew, in all of his broken and bruised glory, leaned against the door frame, looking between us.

His eyes landed on Tate's as he folded his arms across his chest. "Not that I was eavesdropping or anything, but your sister's right. We're always here for you, brother." The way he said the word brother had Tate's eyes flickering nervously between the two of us. It wasn't said as just a term of endearment, but as a mark of respect. It was Drew's way of telling him he was one of the pack now, and that they loved him like he had always been their own.

I smiled, gravitating toward Drew as I always did when he was nearby, but my eyes were on Tate. "You have the world in the palm of your hand. You have choices that not many do, and you have the support of everyone around you, because believe it or not, we just want you to succeed. You still have a few years to explore your options, to be a kid and enjoy it. All I've ever wanted for you was to follow your dreams, Tate, because I found mine."

I grinned up at Drew. I'd always had big dreams for myself growing up. I had a career planned out, I knew what city I wanted to live in, and I'd always known that I would have a big family one day. The one thing I hadn't counted on was circumstances changing, but life had put me on a path, and no matter how much I hated some of the things that had happened along the way, I would never regret where I ended up.

The smirk he gifted me with that time wasn't filled with certainty or arrogance. It held nothing more to it than a happiness he was getting braver at showing, day by day. He eventually tore his gaze away to focus his attention back on my brother.

"No one expects you to find this easy, T. Truth be told, I'm still learning about all this myself. I'm walking blind, but if I've learned one thing this last week, it's that I can't control what I feel for your sister. Not every kind of love is gonna be easy, but all I know now is that I'd rather spend my life on the edge with her than doing or being with anything or anyone else out there and playing it safe. I've got something important to protect, and you're included in that. The stuff on the outside heals, but I can't fix myself if I lose Ayda. I'll do whatever it takes to make the two of you happy. I'll fund any college you want to go to. You have options. You just need to talk to us."

I smiled up at Drew. The man I saw behind closed doors wasn't always the man everyone else got to see. I knew that Tate rarely got to see anything other than Drew Tucker, president of the Hounds. This time, he was witnessing the man I loved with every part of my body, heart and soul.

"See, Tate? There are no rules, no right and wrong. You can have the whole world. You just have to go after it."

Drew leaned down to whisper something in my ear, leaving me no time to protest, even if I'd wanted to before he stood up straight again.

"Why don't the two of us step away from your sister for a second, Tate. Let's have a man to man chat about what options you have. You can ask me anything. Shoot any shit my way, I can take it. I'll be honest with you about the club, the lifestyle, your sister, anything you want."

I hadn't expected the comment to come, but when Tate's eyes lit up and moved between us, all I could do was nod and smile, my hand reaching out and squeezing his before I backed away and winked at them both. "I'll leave you to it then."

I'd only taken two steps back when Drew grabbed a hold of the door frame, twisted his head back over his shoulder and gave me a look. "Don't you go too far. A favor for a favor." Then he shut the door carefully, leaving me standing bewildered and amused. There were no words for how much I loved that man.

CHAPTER FIFTY-TWO
DREW

When I finally walked back out into the bar, I didn't head straight for her the way I should have. I meant what I said to her about needing her to return my favor. I just had to hope that what I was about to ask her to do wouldn't be too much.

After pulling Harry to one side and having a quiet word in his ear, I got the nod from him and headed back to my room to get dressed, passing Deeks in the corridor before I slid inside.

"Hey, Deeks," I said, clearing my throat and crooking my finger at him. "I never thought I'd see the day when you moved faster on your feet than I did, but is there any chance you could find Ayda for me and bring her back here? If she asks questions, just plead ignorance."

Deeks threw up both hands and shook his head. "I don't have to pretend to be ignorant around here. I learned a long time ago that if I asked no questions, I'd have no lies to tell. Consider it done." He laughed and took off, rolling his shoulders in his old cut while I turned away and went inside my room. It hurt to try and dress too quickly, so I threw on a baggy zip up hoodie and stood there, waiting in front of the door with my hands hidden deep inside the pockets of my sweat pants.

When she pushed through, I held my breath and smiled flatly at the woman that had finally given me a reason to live.

Her eyes widened briefly at my appearance before meeting my gaze, her tongue sweeping her lips before she smiled brightly. "You look nervous, Mr. Tucker."

"That's because I am, Hanagan."

She walked toward me slowly, her smile fading a little as she reached out and wrapped one of her hands around my wrist lightly. "What's going on?"

"Remember that returning favor I mentioned before?"

"Anything. What do you need?"

I studied the blue of her eyes the way I always did. No matter how often I looked into them, I always seemed to find myself getting a little lost inside the magic. My voice cracked when I spoke, and I began to wonder if this was a good idea at all.

"Tate's going to be fine. It's a long road ahead, but we can talk about that later. Right now…" I paused, pushing out another breath. "Right now, I'd like to take you somewhere. There's someone I need you to meet."

"Who?"

"You'll see."

"On one condition."

"That figures," I whispered back, trying not to smirk.

"Well, you can't really drive like that, but I know you're gonna try. So I'm taking the option away."

"Always so bossy," I said through a smile. "Sweetheart, I know I can be an idiot, but just trust me sometimes, okay?"

I pulled my hand out of my pocket and wrapped it around hers, making sure the fingers of her good hand were intertwined with mine. Keeping her close to me as I took the lead, I didn't acknowledge her mutterings behind my back, but I could imagine her frown as I struggled to keep my pace faster than was probably sensible of me.

When we walked back into the bar, I headed for the door where Harry was standing with the keys to the van swinging around his finger.

Ayda came to a stop beside me, and I cast a sideways glance her way, raising a brow.

"Our carriage awaits, milady."

"You're such a gentleman." She laughed with a small curtsey. "Whisk me away, Prince Charming."

"I might struggle with the whisking, but I'm sure Harry will be happy to carry you down the steps if you need it." I held up my hand for her to take, acting like the big bad biker prince she expected me to be as I grinned and waited. "No questions until we get there, okay?"

"I promise."

As soon as she reached out and accepted my hold, I walked her out into the daylight and soaked up the clean air. It felt like a lifetime since I'd been out there, breathing in the world around me rather than the smell of medicines, whiskey, cigarette smoke and leather. I was already feeling cleansed with every breath I inhaled.

Ayda stayed true to her word the whole journey, never asking a question, even though she made no attempt to hide the fact that she wanted to. Her constant fidgeting, chewing of nails and jigging of her legs gave her away, but every time I looked her way and smiled, she straightened up and smiled right back. We were both nervous about what we were about to do—her because she didn't know what that was, and me because I knew exactly where we were heading.

This was something that had the ability to make me sweat without having to lift a single muscle in my body.

The closer we got to our destination, the more I found myself sucking in breaths and blowing them out a little too loudly. I kept glancing from left to right, inspecting the town around us as we drove down street after street after street. Harry didn't say much, either. He was fucking good like that. He knew when to talk and he knew when to stay silent. He also knew just how big this was for me, and I was convinced he was expecting me to yell for him to stop and turn around at any moment.

But that wasn't going to happen. Even though I was nervous, I was ready. I was more ready than I'd ever been.

When the van eventually slowed and reached its destination, my heart dropped into the very depths of my stomach. I leaned forward in the front of the van, rubbing my palms over the tops of my thighs, making an 'O' shape with my mouth as I tried to find a steady rhythm to my breathing.

"We're here," I whispered, slowly turning to see her face. Ayda's eyes glanced all around us as she took it all in. There was nothing for miles around, just empty fields with a few trees scattered here and there. Her eyes were wide as she tried to work out what was going on, until she turned to face me and stared deep into mine again. "We're here," I repeated quietly.

"Where's here?" she asked almost shyly as she reached out for me.

I glanced at Harry over her shoulder, but he was facing forward, his eyes closed as he took in this moment for what it was. I had no doubt he was praying.

Looking back at Ayda again, I took her hand and held it gently. "Here is where Pete is."

"But—" Her eyes flickered to the window and back before dropping to her lap. "I thought he was in the cemetery, where my parents are."

"That's where his body is." I looked back out at the overgrown land that meant more to me than I'd ever admitted out loud before. The feelings of longing and loss hit me at just the merest glimpse of it, and I began to wonder if I could do this, until I spotted the place I wanted to take her, and all the determination I felt earlier came flooding back. "But this is where my brother Pete is. This is where he rests."

I found the door handle and pulled it back before I began to push the thing open. The smell of my childhood wrapped itself around me and I took a second to do what Harry was doing before I turned back to Ayda and looked up at her through cautious eyes.

"Will you come with me? I'll explain everything out there."

She didn't hesitate. Her nod was immediate as her body carried her forward. "There's nowhere I'd rather be than with you."

When we were both standing on solid ground, I pulled her closer and pressed my lips to her forehead. It was purely selfish. It was all for me. I needed to find some strength to go through with it, and I found it the second my lips touched her skin.

There wasn't anything else to say or do so I turned and held her hand, making the journey through the overgrown blades of grass I used to hide in when we were kids. Every shaky step I took seemed to hold a memory. To the left were the trees that Pete had made me climb to try and conquer my fear of heights. He'd brought me there for weeks on end and told me to scale those things, one after the other, until I reached the top and shouted down to him that I wasn't scared no more.

I was always scared. I just didn't let him see.

To the right, a short jog away, was a small stream that ran the length of the entire field and disappeared into a dense cluster of trees that Pete had told me held the ghosts of all the most infamous buried bikers, just to scare me.

He was such a bastard sometimes, always playing the older brother he should have been to me, and always pushing me to be the best I could be. He wanted me to be fearless, to be formidable, to be unbeatable. He spent so long trying to turn *me* into something unforgettable, he forgot to take care of himself.

With every memory that flashed through my mind, my jaw set tighter and my frown grew more painful. I hadn't been there since he died. I hadn't been for years.

All those years were now slamming into me hard, and if it was at all possible, causing more pain than anything my body was feeling on the surface. I was tired, aching and broken, but as I squeezed Ayda's hand in mine and looked up ahead, I saw the huge pecan tree that had been a part of Texas far longer than any one of us Hounds had been.

"You okay?" I asked as I turned to face her, curling my fingers around hers again.

Ayda was still looking around with curiosity until her face finally swung around and her eyes landed on mine. She reached up with her bad hand, her thumb running over my frown. "This place is beautiful, Drew, and I'm good. Just worried about you. Talk to me."

"I'm good, darlin'. Don't worry. It's why Harry is here."

I smiled at her and stepped a little closer, taking the few final strides until we were just to the left of the tree that stood at the top of the small incline.

I did the same thing I'd always done as a kid. I stood beneath it and looked up, allowing my lips to part and my eyes to widen as I tried to commit every detail of it to memory. It was a relatively cool day, but I felt warm being there. I felt like the boy who'd run in the sun and raced his idol through the blades of grass for hours on end. I felt free.

"We used to come here as kids," I said quietly, still looking up as I pulled her closer to me. "The two of us, we used to escape the club life for hours on end and just be who we wanted to be. There were no rules out here, no code to follow, no unspoken laws that could be broken. We couldn't smell anything to do with bikes, leather or smoke." I huffed, shaking my head as a small smile tugged at my lips. "We were just Pete and Drew—two boys running instead of riding."

Leaning in, she rested her cheek on my shoulder and followed my gaze up into the tree. "You got to be a kid out here."

"I did. At first I thought he brought me here for my benefit, but looking back, I think it was for his, too. I was such a burden on him, even though he loved me." I dropped my head and let it fall to the side, looking down at her from the corners of my eyes. "I saw the responsibility he carried because of me. Tate sees it on you, too. I know how he feels, wanting to save you from saving him all the time."

Ayda just stared at the tree, her free hand tapping against her thigh until she stepped forward and faced me. "I think that's a lesson for us both to learn here, Drew. You don't have to protect me all the time, and those men of yours, they see it, too."

She brought our joined hands up to her face, pressing the back of my hand against her cheek before lifting her head to look up at the tree again.

I kept my focus on her the whole time, wondering how the fuck I'd survived before her.

"I miss him," I admitted quietly. "I miss him so much, some days I feel like I can't breathe."

Bringing our hands to her lips, she straightened her head again to look at me. "I know what you're going through, Drew. I know that pain, the hollow ache in the center of your chest that feels like it has glass edges to cut when your mind so much as heads in the direction of thinking about him. This right here, though—this is your chance to talk to him. This is where you feel him, where you're closest to him. He may not answer, but he can hear you, and if you need me to step away, all you have to do is ask."

"Don't go anywhere," I whispered through a smile, moving my hand away before I lowered my mouth to hers to taste her on my lips. "I know what I have to do. I've spent so long trying to bypass the grief stage, beating myself up, putting myself behind bars, taking any punishment anyone has to offer... I can't survive that way anymore. I need to say goodbye."

My jaw set tight, even though I felt no anger at all. The reality of the situation was sinking in, and I was about to face the one demon I never thought I'd be man enough to face.

Breaking away from her, I turned to face the tree, holding onto the very end of her fingertips until distance tore us apart and forced both our arms to fall down by our sides. Knowing she was close was enough, and as I hitched up the knees of my sweat pants and struggled down into a crouch at the base of the trunk, I let my eyes fall to the ground. With one arm resting over my thigh, the other reached out to touch the grass my brother and I had sat upon a hundred times before. There wasn't an inch of this tree we hadn't touched. It was such a part of our history, I felt like I was embracing an old friend as my fingers reached out to trace the ridges in the bark.

The words didn't waste time in finding their escape. They'd been held prisoner for half a decade. They were tired and defeated. They needed to breathe as much as my suppressed grief did.

"How do I even begin to say what I need to say to you, brother? Where do I start? With apologies? Regrets? With all the things I did wrong that you would have done right? How do I find an order to my thoughts?" I swallowed the painful lump in my throat, bringing the tips of my fingers back down to run over the blades of grass. "I have so many things to say sorry for, but I know how you always got about me making excuses for my fuck ups. I'm not stupid enough to think you don't hear the shit that goes on in my head in the middle of the night, either. I may not have been here before, but I know you've been to me a million times over."

My face scrunched together, every muscle in my jaw flexing as I tried to fight off the pain in my chest.

"I thank you for that," I whispered. "I thank you for all those moments you've come to me when I've needed you. You never let me down when you had breath in your lungs, and for so long, I thought that once your body stopped working, it meant you were gone for good. Call me stupid, thickheaded, or just an idiot, I don't know, but I realize how wrong I was about that now. Those ghost stories you used to tell me, I believed them all so easily, but I refused to believe that you could be one yourself. I guess that's what this fucked up world of the MC does to us. It makes us cynical, non-believers. If we can't feel the flesh beneath our fingers or see the blood drip from our knuckles, it can't exist, right? I hadn't realized what a non-believer I'd become. Not until recently."

Darting my tongue out to the swollen part of my lip, I pressed it against the wound in an attempt to make the pain there worse than it was anywhere else, but it didn't do anything. Lifting my hand to the bridge of my nose, I pinched it tight and closed my eyes, dipping my chin to my chest as uninvited tears started to form behind my eyelids.

"Don't make me cry, you fucker," I croaked, flaring my nostrils as wide as I could. "If I start crying over you now, I'll never stop, and Ayda didn't sign up for that."

I could almost see the look on his face as he towered over me and watched as I fell apart, the small smirk, the shake of his head, the roll of his eyes and the flick of his thumb across his nose. I could hear the words, *who knew I'd be the first person to break your heart, Tucks,* before he barked out a rough laugh and dropped down to tap me on the chin with his fist.

The thought of that image was so powerful, I opened my eyes and looked to the side to see if he was there, but when all I saw was the open field and the endless memories running past me, I let my shoulders sag forward.

"I thought I'd figured a lot of shit out when I was in prison, Pete. I thought I had all the answers and every problem could be solved with violence again. All I wanted was revenge, to earn my respect back and to kill who had taken you away from us. I kinda got that in the end, only it took something, or should I say some*one* else to get me there. I know you know all about her, and I swear to God, if you spy on her in the shower, I will find you in the afterlife and we will go ten rounds like the old days," I whispered, my smile breaking free as I narrowed my eyes and looked up to the clear blue sky. "There's a part of me that can't wait to see you, to get to that place where we can be free again. No shackles, no history or bad blood. If it hadn't been for her, I would probably have given up in the warehouse and let them kill me, I needed to see you that badly. I love my brothers and my club, Pete, but only you and Ayda have ever known me better than I know myself. You left me. You left me like the bastard you are. I swore for so long you did it as some kind of test again. But that test was too much. Watching you take your last breath was *too* much. I didn't have a reason to live before I went to prison, I didn't have a reason to live while inside, and I didn't have a reason to live for the first few hours after I came out. I had reasons to survive, sure I did. I had responsibilities. I had people I loved who were relying on me. I had things to finish. But reasons to live, really *live*…"

I shook my head and looked back down to the base of the pecan tree. Plucking a few blades of grass from the earth, I held them up in front of my face and twirled them between my index finger and thumb.

"I wanna live now, brother. I wanna fill all the gaps, even the dark, fucked-up, never before touched upon parts of my soul. I wanna face all my fears, be softer, laugh more, avoid death, blood and digging ditches for men who died too young at my hands. I want to be better, just like you always wanted me to be, but to do that, I've got to find a way to believe that you're resting in peace and move on. I've got to find a way to shake off this cloud of anger that hangs over me, Pete. I fucking love you. A part of me thought I hated you for so long for putting yourself in that ring. I couldn't understand it when our other men could have taken the hits and lived. But I get it now. I understand. I know what I would do to save the ones I love, the ones I need to survive. I know every slash to the skin and to the heart would be a blessing so long as they had a chance to breathe. You... You took the fall for me because you loved me. Now I've got to rise from the ashes because I love *you*. I've got to make your skinny ass proud."

My voice trailed off as I dropped the grass back down against the ground and somehow shuffled that little bit closer to the tree. "It's not goodbye, brother. It'll never be goodbye. This is just a catch you later and keep a beer cold for when I get there. This isn't an apology for all the things I should have done. This is a thank you for getting me this far. You can hand the baton over to the woman behind me now. Just... don't forget me and I promise to never forget you. Not even for a minute."

My eyes flickered all the way up to the very top of the tree, taking in every branch that veered off and created a shelter above that had always managed to make me feel safe. As one last mark of respect, I closed my eyes and smiled, mouthing a silent howl up to the sky before I play-punched the trunk one final time.

That was my last mark of respect to him before I let my chin fall back down to my chest, opened my eyes and took several slow, heavy breaths. It felt like the weight of the world was falling from my shoulders, down my arms, dripping from the ends of my fingers like some thick, heavy tar that had been living there without me knowing. There was a weird sense of peace settling over me. As a smile crept onto my face and a layer of unshed tears coated my eyes, I spun on my feet and turned back to look at the woman that had somehow gotten me to where I was.

Where one door closes, another one opens, and as I watched the small breeze blow her sun-colored hair over her shoulders and the light catch the twinkle of sadness in her eyes, I couldn't help but smile.

She had no idea what she did to me. She had no idea of the light she'd brought into my dark.

She had no idea how I intended to spend my every waking breath showing her just how much I loved her, and she had no idea how I was going to make sure that every single second she spent with me would be the ride of her life, no matter what the future tried to throw in our paths.

I was finally ready to live again and I was in love with the idea that she would be riding by my side...

The whole

Fucking

Way.

Without Mercy Playlist

Before I Ever Met You ~ Banks

R U Mine ~ Arctic Monkeys

Love Was Blind ~ We Are Twin

Human ~ Aquilo

Then Came The Morning ~ The Lone Bellow

Gold ~ Imagine Dragons

Wild And Wasted Waters ~ Kill It Kid

Undivided ~ Adelitas Way

Need It ~ Half Moon Run

In Dreams ~ Ben Howard

Southern Boy ~ John The Conqueror

Beautiful War ~ Kings Of Leon

Capital T ~ Walking Papers

Ink ~ Indiana

Blood Hands ~ Royal Blood

Morning ~ Rhodes

Shining ~ X Ambassadors

Bottom Of The Bottle ~ The Heavy Heavy Hearts

The Wicked ~ Blues Saraceno

Elysium ~ Bear's Den

THANK YOU FOR READING

Other books available by these authors:

Without Consequence

Izzy Moffit's Road to Wonderland

Ethan Walker's Road to Wonderland

Made in the USA
Lexington, KY
15 July 2018